Past Tense

(Schooled in Magic X)

Christopher G. Nuttall

Twilight Times Books
Kingsport Tennessee

Past Tense

This is a work of fiction. All concepts, characters and events portrayed in this book are used fictitiously and any resemblance to real people or events is purely coincidental.

Copyright © 2016 Christopher G. Nuttall

All rights reserved. No part of this book may be reproduced, stored in a retrieval system or transmitted in any form by any means electronic, mechanical, photocopying, recording or otherwise, except brief extracts for the purpose of review, without the permission of the publisher and copyright owner.

Paladin Timeless Books, an imprint of
Twilight Times Books
P O Box 3340
Kingsport TN 37664
http://twilighttimesbooks.com/

First Printing, June 2017

ISBN: 978-1-60619-316-7

Library of Congress Control Number: 2017942679

Cover art by Brad Fraunfelter

Printed in the United States of America.

Prologue

T HEY WERE DOOMED.

Lord Whitehall knew it, knew it with a sick certainty that could not be denied. The magic swirling around the small gathering of magicians would overwhelm their defenses soon enough, no matter how hard they struggled. The brilliant—and sickly—light burned into their minds, making it hard to think clearly. Their wards were cracking, on the verge of breaking, yet abandoning the work would spell instant death as the tidal wave of magic from the nexus point overwhelmed their defenses and crushed them like bugs. It would have been safer to stand in the path of a rushing river and demand it bow to their collective will.

Coming here had been a dreadful mistake, he knew now. The castle had seemed their only hope—it was far from civilization, far from anyone who might want to hunt their commune—but the nexus point beneath the castle was a wild thing. It could not be tamed; the merest touch had unleashed a surge of magic so strong that all of the masters, working together, had barely saved themselves from instant death. And yet they could not even break free to warn the rest of the commune to evacuate the castle. They—the masters and a handful of their most trusted apprentices—would only be the first to die.

His head started to pound as he thrust more and more magic into the wards, knowing it was futile. All he could hope to do was keep his people alive for a few more seconds, before the wild magic slammed into them. Those who lived would envy the dead, if the whispered rumors were true. The monsters they'd encountered as they hacked their way through the forest, towards the castle, might have been human once, before the wild magic transformed them. Now? They were just beasts.

I'm sorry, he thought.

He wasn't sure who he was apologizing to. His teacher, the man whose secrets would now be lost; his fellow masters, who would die beside him; his apprentice, who would never become a master in his own right; his daughter, who would never have a husband or children of her own...? He'd failed them all. They were all going to die in the next few minutes, no matter what he did...

The demon tricked us.

It was a bitter thought. He'd known for years—his *master* had hammered it into his skull, when he'd been a young man barely starting out as a magician—that demons were untrustworthy, but they'd been desperate. They'd *known* they were desperate. And so Lord and Master Alfred had summoned a demon and put the question to the entity, asking where they could go that was *safe*. The demon told them about the nexus point...

...And sent them straight to their doom.

Power surged around him as the nexus point grew larger, wild magic spilling into the air and pressing against the wards. They couldn't hold for more than a few seconds...he heard someone screaming, but he couldn't tell who it was. Perhaps it was himself, in the final seconds of his life, all dignity torn from him by the grim awareness that he'd led his people into a trap.

And then there was a flash of light and...*someone*...was kneeling in the middle of the circle, just in front of the nexus point.

There was no time to stare. The wave of magic—the final wave of magic—built up, slowly sliding forward as if it were guided by a mind that *wanted* the magicians to watch helplessly as their doom approached them. He pushed the last dregs of his power into the wards, knowing it would be futile...

...And then the newcomer added his strength to the wards.

The wards *changed*, snapping into a new and complex configuration that was bizarre, yet perfect. Whitehall would've been astonished if he hadn't been concentrating on holding the outer wards in place. It was working! Whatever the newcomer had done, it was working!

The wild magic flashed and flared inside the wards, but it couldn't escape. A final shudder ran through the entire building, then the wild magic was gone. The blinding light vanished at the same moment, plunging the room into near-darkness. And the nexus point hung in the middle of the room, tiny and yet immensely large at the same time, tamed.

They'd tamed a nexus point!

He found it hard to keep from giggling inanely as he collapsed to the stone floor. For a long moment, all he could do was lie there and fight to keep himself awake. Everything around him blurred as fatigue threatened to overcome him. And then, drawing on his last strength, he pulled himself to his feet, grabbed a torch and stumbled towards the newcomer, heedless of the risk of stepping too close to the nexus. He...

...No, *she*.

Whitehall stared. He'd traveled widely, first with his master and then with a string of apprentices, but he'd only heard wild rumors about witches. He'd certainly never *met* a real witch, just a handful of women who knew a couple of spells. And yet, the girl before him was clearly a full-fledged magician. Her power was faint, perhaps as drained as his own, but he perceived it as it surrounding her, infusing her body and giving her a strength she would not otherwise possess.

She blinked up at him, clearly half-blinded by the light. Her face was perfect, almost too perfect; there were no scars or blemishes, none of the marks carried by the girls and women waiting in the castle above. Her arms were muscular, but it was clear that she was not used to the backbreaking labor of a farmwife. And she was *clean*, as if someone had scrubbed away all the torments of womanhood and left behind nothing but purity. She was tall, almost as tall as he was; she was easily the tallest woman he'd seen outside royalty. Her long brown hair hung down to the small of her back, contrasting oddly with the shapeless grey garment she wore. He'd never seen anything like it...

And he couldn't even *begin* to guess at her age. But she looked young...perhaps too young.

He held up a hand, motioning for the others to stay back as the girl looked at him. He couldn't help noticing that her eyes were soft, with none of the hardness that he was used to seeing in women. His own wife had lived a harsh life, even after she'd married a magician; she'd never dared reveal such...*vulnerability* to anyone, not even him. The women upstairs, waiting to hear what the magicians had done, were hardly less harsh. Whitehall knew the world was an unkind place, but it was harder on women. And yet, the girl before him was different.

And she was a magician.

The girl seemed to steady herself. "Who...who are you?"

Whitehall contemplated her for a long moment. Her words were understandable, but they were oddly accented. The common tongue was clearly not her *first* language, he decided; boys were normally taught the common tongue in childhood, while girls were rarely taught anything other than their mother tongue unless they were destined to marry a merchant or a magician. *His* wife had spoken three languages and considered herself accomplished, for the youngest daughter of a magician. She'd been a remarkable woman. And yet, she'd died in childbirth...

"I am Lord and Master Whitehall," Whitehall said, gravely. He didn't miss the expression of shock that passed across the girl's face. This was not someone, he reasoned, who was used to concealing her feelings or minding what she said. Had she an indulgent father and no husband? Or perhaps she was powerful enough not to care about her words. "Who are you?"

He held out a hand to help the girl to her feet. It was dangerous, but his instincts insisted that the girl wasn't a threat. She seemed oddly hesitant to take his hand—that, at least, was a normal reaction—but she eventually allowed him to help her up. Her legs were concealed within her garment, but Whitehall could tell she was tired and drained. Doing what she'd done—doing the *impossible* thing she'd done—had to have cost her dearly.

"I...I am Emily," the girl managed. "I shouldn't be here."

Whitehall surprised himself by laughing. "Nor should we," he said. "Nor should we."

He snorted, then pushed his humor aside as he heard the others whisper behind him. Solving the mystery of just how the girl—*Emily*—had arrived in the castle was important, but he would be damned if he was going to rip her mind open to find out. They owed her their lives—and those of the men, women and children who had followed them to the castle.

"We are in your debt," he added, grandly. "And you are welcome here."

Chapter One

"I AM LORD AND MASTER WHITEHALL," THE MAN SAID, GRAVELY. FOR A MOMENT, EMILY honestly thought the translation spell had glitched. "Who are you?"

Emily stared up at the speaker in absolute disbelief. She couldn't have gone back in time, could she? It was impossible! Going forward in time was easy enough—she'd adjusted the flow of time within pocket dimensions to skip forward nearly an entire day—but going backwards in time was impossible. Or so she'd been told. Five years ago, she would have believed that turning someone into a frog was impossible, too!

Her head spun. "I...I am Emily," she said. She could feel the nexus point behind her, twisting in and out of her awareness as though both infinitely large and impossibly tiny. "I shouldn't be here."

She tried hard to think clearly as Whitehall helped her to her feet and welcomed her to the castle. Her head hurt as she considered the implications. If she was lost in time, she didn't dare say or do anything that might alter the timeline for fear of accidentally altering the series of events that led up to her departure from Earth. But, at the same time, she'd *already* interfered—and, in doing so, *protected* the timeline. Everyone knew Lord Whitehall was the first man to tame a nexus point. No one had ever suggested that he might have had help from the future.

And if I'm meant to be here, she thought numbly, *what else am I meant to do?*

She looked at Whitehall, feeling oddly intimidated. She was in the presence of a *legend*, the man who would found Whitehall School and lay the groundwork for educating hundreds of thousands of young magicians. The men behind him, watching her with wary eyes, had to be part of the Whitehall Commune. She wondered, absently, if she knew their names, and if recorded history had been remotely accurate. There were so many gaps in the records that it was hard to know just who was truly significant and who had merely been shoehorned into reconstructions of past events because his writings had survived.

Whitehall himself looked nothing like his portraits. They'd depicted a grand old wizard, Emily recalled, but the man before her was clearly in his late forties rather than pushing into a second century. His face was a dark olive, his beard slowly shading to white as he grew older. His hair was cropped close to his skull; his eyes, darker than hers, seemed to bore into her very soul. She couldn't help thinking of owls as she let go of his hand, trusting her legs to hold her upright. There was something about the way he moved that reminded her of an owl.

He wore no robes, she saw, as he turned to face his companions. Instead, he wore heavy trousers and a dark shirt, making him look more like a laborer than a magician. Runes and sigils were sewn into his shirt, almost all of them unknown to her. And yet, she recalled seeing a handful of them in the tunnels below Whitehall...below *old* Whitehall. If she was truly back in the early days of the school, perhaps even *before* the school, the tunnel network might not have been constructed yet. She reached out to the familiar wards, but sensed no response. They didn't exist either, not yet. The only thing she could sense was the constant presence of the nexus point.

She rubbed the snake-bracelet on her wrist, silently grateful that she'd kept it on when she prepared for bed. She wouldn't be completely friendless...

"Master Baju-Merah is dead," a voice said. "The strain killed him."

Emily sucked in her breath as she saw the body. The man—the old man—had died badly, his face twisted in pain. A heart attack, perhaps, judging from the lack of physical wounds on his corpse. There was no way to *know*. Perhaps a strand of wild magic had escaped...she shook her head, dismissing the thought. If the wards had cracked, even slightly, everyone in the chamber would be dead...or wishing they were.

She looked at the other magicians as they clustered around the body, glancing at her as they talked in low voices. There was no point in trying to match names to faces, not when the portraits were so wildly inaccurate. They looked...odd, at least compared to the magicians *she* knew. A number looked surprisingly old, surprisingly *dirty*, for magicians; others looked physically young, but mentally old. She found herself staring at a young man who was looking at her, unable to be sure just how old he actually was. But then, she'd never been very good at guessing ages on the Nameless World. People without magic aged at terrifying speeds.

They're all men, she thought, numbly. *There isn't a single woman amongst them.*

The realization struck her with terrifying force. *My God*, she thought. *I'm the Dark Lady.*

Her legs buckled, threatening to send her crashing to the stone floor. The Dark Lady was a legend, a person who was only mentioned in a couple of sources...a person who half the historians in the Nameless World believed to be nothing more than a myth. Her story had either been wildly exaggerated or written out altogether...there was no way Emily and *she* could be the same person. And yet, it was impossible to convince herself that she *wasn't*. It didn't look as though there was any other role to play.

She closed her eyes for a long moment, trying to decide what to say when Whitehall finally demanded answers. He *would* demand answers too, she knew...and she doubted the Sorcerer's Rule held sway a thousand years ago. Or was it only seven hundred? The thought made her smile, despite the shock and growing fear for the future. She might be able to learn answers to questions that had vexed historians for the last thousand years.

I have to get back, she told herself. The past was fascinating, but she wanted to get back to *her* Whitehall—and Caleb. And everyone else she knew and loved. *I can't stay here forever.*

"Emily," Whitehall said. She opened her eyes. He'd dismissed most of the magicians, leaving only himself and the young man in the chamber. "I need to ask you some questions."

Emily nodded, sensing Whitehall's exhaustion under his words. Up close, it was surprisingly easy to sense his magic. He didn't seem to be masking his power at all. *That* was—would be—considered incredibly rude in the future, a bare-faced attempt to intimidate her, but his body language didn't *suggest* anything of the sort.

He certainly wasn't trying to lean into her personal space. Perhaps he was just too tired to keep his magic under control. There was certainly something...*discordant*... about it. Behind him, it was impossible to sense the young man's magic at all.

"This is quite a hard place to reach," Whitehall said. "How did you get here?"

The young man leaned forward. "And how did you appear in the chamber?"

"Bernard," Whitehall said, reprovingly. "One question at a time."

Emily felt her mouth drop open. The young man before her was Bernard De Born? The man who would be the first *true* Grandmaster? The man who would write a history of Whitehall and dozens of other books that had been lost over the years? It was impossible to reconcile the image of the older man with the younger one in front of her.

She forced herself to focus on choosing her words. There was no way she could tell Whitehall the truth, even if she swore him—both of them—to silence. And yet, the more lies she told, the greater the chance of being caught out. Whitehall wouldn't trust her—at all—if he caught her in a lie. She would be surprised if he *wasn't* already concerned—and suspicious—about her appearance. She'd arrived right at the moment of their greatest need.

"My tutor and I made our way here," she said, finally. "He had a theory about..."

"He?" Whitehall repeated. "*He?*"

Emily cursed under her breath. She had the nasty feeling she'd just put her foot in it. But there was no going back now.

"He had a theory about taking control of a nexus point," she said. "He'd worked out a complex set of spells he believed would be sufficient to take control. But it wasn't enough to save his life. There was a flash of light and I saw him die, a moment before you arrived."

Bernard's eyes narrowed. "There was no one in the chamber when we arrived."

"She might have been trapped in the nexus point," Whitehall pointed out. "And our attempt to tame the wild magic freed her."

"Then I thank you," Emily said. "But I don't recall anything between his death and your arrival."

Whitehall frowned. "Who taught you?"

A dozen answers ran through Emily's head. She could claim to have been taught by Dumbledore, or Gandalf, or Yoda...it wasn't as if Whitehall could disprove her words. But she needed to keep it as simple as possible. She knew enough about telling lies to know just how easy it was to say too much and give the listener the key they needed to untangle the entire web of deceit.

"I swore an oath to keep the details of my training to myself," she said, finally. If Whitehall and his commune were anything like the magicians she knew, they'd respect an oath. "Even though he's dead, he never saw fit to release me from it."

Whitehall nodded. "It is...*uncommon* for a girl to be schooled in magic," he said. "Your father, perhaps? Teaching you because he had no son?"

Emily kept her face blank with an effort. Whitehall—*her* Whitehall—taught girls and boys equally, assuming they had magic. But the history books had made it clear that girls were *not* originally taught magic. It had been Bernard—Grandmaster Bernard—who'd first permitted girls to study at Whitehall, assuming that wasn't something else the history books had managed to get wrong. There was no point, not any longer, in pretending to be an untrained magician. They'd seen what she'd done to the nexus point.

"I swore an oath," she said, again.

Whitehall nodded. "I understand," he said. "He must have been a very smart man."

"He taught a girl," Bernard said. "How is that *smart*? The curse..."

Emily frowned. "What curse?"

"He didn't even tell you that?"

Bernard turned to his master. "She's lying," he said. "I sense no magic from her."

"I sense no magic from you either," Emily snapped back.

Whitehall gave her an odd look. "My apprentice has more than enough magic," he said, coldly. "But yours is well hidden."

Bernard stepped forward. "This is a joke, master," he said. "I don't know how she got here, but she is no magician."

Emily scowled at him, feeling oddly disappointed. *This* was the Grandmaster who would invite girls to study alongside the boys? She reached out with her senses and frowned as she sensed magic surrounding Bernard for the first time. He wasn't trying to mask his power at all; indeed, the only reason she hadn't sensed it earlier was because Whitehall's magic had obscured his apprentice's power. Professor Lombardi would have summarily failed any student who failed to mask his power within his personal wards, she knew. Allowing one's power to roam free was...sloppy.

"You sensed what she did to the nexus point," Whitehall said. He sounded puzzled, but calm and composed. There was no anger in his tone. "She showed us how to patch the wards in place to tame the wild magic."

"She's a girl," Bernard protested.

Emily felt her temper snap. "Then fight me," she said. "I challenge you to a duel, if you dare."

Bernard glared at her, then turned to his master. "Master..."

"She challenged you," Whitehall said. He smiled, rather dryly. "Are you going to take up the challenge?"

"It wouldn't be a fight," Bernard objected.

Emily resisted—barely—the urge to stick out her tongue. "Then you don't have anything to fear," she said, instead. "You'll beat me with ease."

"Fine," Bernard snapped. He turned and paced across the chamber, then turned to face her, his hands clenching into fists. "Master, will you set up the warding circle?"

"I doubt one will be necessary," Whitehall said. He stepped to one side, nodding shortly to Emily. "Try not to kill each other."

Emily kept her expression blank as she tensed, testing her protections carefully. Challenging Bernard was a risk. She could lose. And yet, his casual dismissal of her abilities *hurt*. She was damned if she would allow him to talk down to her, let alone treat her as a silly girl who needed a man to make all the decisions for her. It wasn't as if *she* was one of the stupid noblewomen who'd made Alassa's wedding preparations such a trial. And Bernard was a disappointment anyway.

"Begin," Whitehall said.

Bernard didn't hesitate. His hand snapped down as he unleashed a spell she didn't recognize, a spell that bled *mana* in all directions. It was sloppy work—Professor Lombardi would probably have broken Bernard's hand if he'd cast *that* in class—but it was powerful. The spell slammed into her protections, shaking them roughly, yet it was really nothing more than brute force. Part of her mind analyzed the spell quickly, noting how it made no attempt to seek out weaknesses in her protections and break through the cracks. Bernard had a great deal of raw power, although it was so sloppy she couldn't tell *just* how much power, but very little actual skill.

"Impressive," Whitehall commented.

Emily kept her eyes on Bernard as she deflected or drained the last remnants of his spell. He looked stunned, as if he'd expected her to be knocked out...or killed...by his magic. Emily wasn't *quite* sure what the spell had actually been intended to do. It had just been thrown together so poorly that merely striking her defenses had been enough to disrupt the spellware beyond repair. She gathered her own magic, readying a retaliatory blow, but waited to see what he would do. And then he tossed a second spell at her. This one was tighter and sharper...and felt *unpleasant* as it crawled across her wards. She felt a flicker of horror as she realized what *that* spell was meant to do.

"Careful," Whitehall said. His smile was gone. "Using *that* in a duel could get you in real trouble."

I suppose it could, Emily thought. *Trying to take control of your opponent...*

She summoned a fireball and threw it at him, watching dispassionately as it crashed into his magic and exploded into nothingness. His protections were nothing like hers, she saw; they were crude, utterly unfocused. It looked as though he was using his own magic as a baseball bat, swatting away spells as they approached, rather than embedding wards within his magic and concentrating on offense. Emily hated to think what Sergeant Miles would have said to any of his students stupid enough to try *that*. Splitting their attention between offense and defense meant that they couldn't concentrate on either.

Bernard flung a third spell at her, so powerful that she stepped aside rather than try to catch it on her protections. Bracing herself, she threw back a ward-cracking spell of her own and followed up with a prank spell. Bernard let out a yelp of shock and pain as his wards came apart—Emily realized, too late, that the ward-cracking spell had actually attacked his magic directly—and then shrank, rapidly, as the prank spell took effect. Moments later, a tiny green frog was looking up at her with disturbingly human eyes.

"I think I win," Emily said.

She looked at Whitehall and saw him looking back in shock. "You did it so casually?"

"I had a good teacher," Emily said. She cursed her mistake—if it had been a mistake—under her breath. She had no idea when transfiguration spells had been invented, but it was possible that Whitehall didn't know how to use them—or regarded them as too demanding to be practical. "He taught me everything I know."

Whitehall studied her for a long moment. "I think you win too," he said. "Undo the spell, please."

Emily nodded and cast the counterspell. Bernard looked astonished as he reverted to human form, his face pale and wan. A lingering greenish tone hung over his skin for long seconds after the spell faded back into the ether. He would have been trying to break free, Emily knew. If he had no experience with pranking spells—the spells Emily had learned in her first year of studies—he might assume that his mind was on the verge of sinking into the frog's and being lost forever.

"I am sorry for doubting you," Bernard said. He stood upright, then held out a hand. Emily shook it firmly. "And you are clearly a great magician."

"A useful lesson, young man," Whitehall said. "You are strong, but your training is far from complete."

Emily kept her thoughts to herself as Whitehall turned towards the gaping door. Bernard, at least, didn't seem to bear a grudge. But then, Sergeant Miles had told her she might have to fight to prove herself, if she was dumped in with the men. Beating a man fairly would work far better, he'd said, than whining to his superiors. The former would earn respect, the latter would breed resentment.

She rubbed the side of her head as she followed Whitehall, Bernard falling into step beside her. Her head hurt, a dull ache that was making it hard to think. She'd been awakened in the middle of the night, after all. She needed to sleep, to rest and figure out a way home before she accidentally tore a hole in history and erased her friends from existence.

And hope I can survive here long enough to find a way home, she thought, grimly. *This isn't the Whitehall I know.*

Chapter Two

IF THE HISTORY BOOKS WERE TO BE BELIEVED, EMILY RECALLED, WHITEHALL CASTLE PRE-dated the Whitehall Commune by at least two hundred years, perhaps longer. No one knew who had built the castle or why, let alone what it had been called before Whitehall arrived, but it was clear that the multidimensional interior had come later. Old Whitehall looked like a darker, grimmer version of King Randor's castle: stone walls, no windows, empty rooms or sealed doors. The passageways were hauntingly familiar, yet all the details were gone. There was so much dust and grime on the floor that they left trails as they made their way up to the Great Hall. The only source of light was burning torches, which hung from the walls and added an unpleasant stench to the air.

"Stay on the beaten track," Whitehall called back, without looking around. "We found hundreds of traps scattered throughout the castle. Clearing a path down to the nexus chamber took a week."

Emily nodded, silently grateful he couldn't see her face. She would have been fascinated with the castle if she hadn't been tired and hungry. Her headache was refusing to fade, while her stomach insistently reminded her that she hadn't eaten for hours. She had to concentrate to keep walking, unwilling to show weakness in front of either of the men. Bernard didn't seem to like the idea of women learning magic—at least, he didn't like it now—and Whitehall was a hero. But then, just how much of what she knew about him in the future was false, based on half-remembered stories and outright lies? Professor Locke, for all of his research, had never had a clear idea of just how much his idol had actually done.

He'd love to be here, Emily thought. *She'd love it too, if there was a way home. The chance to actually meet the ancients in person...*

Whitehall tossed questions at her as she walked, asking if she knew the name of any of the local kings or warlords—or magicians. Emily was quietly impressed—if she'd been telling the truth, it would have allowed him to deduce how long she'd been trapped in the nexus point—but she pleaded ignorance on all such matters. She was a peasant girl, after all; a peasant girl would not be expected to know the name of the king, not when she would probably never leave her home. Whitehall seemed to understand her ignorance, although it was hard to know what he thought. She could only hope that he'd accept her story without asking too many more questions.

They stepped through a stone archway and into the Great Hall. Emily stopped and stared in disbelief at the scene before her. This—*this*—was the Whitehall Commune? Dozens of people—men, women and children—sitting on the stone floor, their eyes going wide as they looked up and saw Emily. Their clothes were ragged, their faces were dirty...it looked like a refugee camp, not the start of a brand new era. She couldn't help noticing just how many of the people before her were scarred, a handful nursing broken bones or walking on wooden legs. Healing—true Healing—had come later. The thought made her feel sick.

She sucked in a breath and instantly regretted it. The Great Hall smelled worse than the slums she'd seen outside Swanhaven, a year in her past and nearly a thousand years in their future. Too many people in too close proximity, too little washing...she looked towards a makeshift tent and shuddered, inwardly. Whitehall had been the cleanest place in the Allied Lands, by her reckoning; she was, perhaps, the only student whose living conditions had degenerated after moving to the school. But that, too, was in the future. A handful of children—she thought they were five or six years old—had pockmarked faces, while most of the adults looked almost painfully thin. Disease and deprivation had to be rife.

They're running, she thought, shocked. *And they're on the brink of starvation.*

They stared back at her, their faces torn between hope and fear. The women, in particular, seemed to find it hard to look at her, even though she caught them glancing at her when they thought she wasn't looking. Several mothers even caught their children and pulled them away from Emily, while a number of young men stared at her as if she was a vision from heaven. It struck her, suddenly, that she was the cleanest person in the room, even though her nightdress had picked up a great deal of dust and grime. And if women weren't allowed to study magic, the young men might not know how to relate to her at all.

"Wait here," Whitehall ordered, nodding to a small campsite. Someone had set up a fire for warmth, adding to the smell. Emily hoped they had good ventilation within the castle, although it seemed unlikely. "I'll be back in a moment."

Emily sat, crossing her legs and wishing—desperately—that whoever had pulled her out of bed and lured her down to the nexus chamber had thought to make her get dressed first. The nightdress was surprisingly decent, compared to some of the garments Imaiqah had worn during her time at Whitehall, but she was still underdressed compared to most of the women in the hall. They wore several layers of clothing apiece, judging by the way their garments bulged in odd places. Were they trying to cover themselves, or were they merely trying to stay warm? It had been cold, down in the nexus chamber. It might well be cold in the upper levels too.

And I don't even know the time, she thought, grimly. *It could be the middle of the night for all I know.*

Whitehall had walked over to a handful of men—she recognized four of them from the chamber—and was chatting with them in a low voice, too low for her to hear anything more than a couple of words. She briefly considered trying to cast a spell to make it easier to overhear their conversation, but she knew there was a very good chance she'd get caught trying. The tutors at Whitehall—*her* Whitehall—wouldn't be amused if someone tried to spy on them, and she dared not assume that Whitehall was any different. His commune had no reason to trust her.

I did help them tame the nexus point, Emily reminded herself, as Whitehall beckoned a young woman to join the group. *Surely they'll want to keep me around.*

She settled back—Bernard had headed off to join a couple of other young men—and studied the Great Hall. It seemed to be no smaller than the hall she remembered from the future, but the walls were nothing more than bare stone, save for a handful of runes carved just below the ceiling. She didn't recognize them from her studies, but she did recall seeing a couple just like them in the tunnels below Whitehall. The fireplace was gone—no, it hadn't been built yet. Her head swam as she tried to grapple with the implications. It was hard, so hard, to know just how much she knew about the castle might still be relevant.

A young woman walked towards her, carrying a bowl in one hand and a mug in the other. Emily looked up and frowned as the girl stared at her, her face torn between fear and...and a kind of awe that she'd seen on peasants, back in Cockatrice. The girl was strikingly pretty—she had soft blonde hair and blue eyes that shone, despite the dirt and grime on her face—yet there was a hardness to her that chilled Emily to the bone. This was a girl who had seen terrible things.

"This is all we have," the girl said, as she passed the bowl to Emily. "Father"—she nodded towards Whitehall—"bids you eat."

"Thank you," Emily said. Her mind reeled. Whitehall had a daughter? There was no mention of any *children* in the texts, as far as she could recall. But a daughter might go unrecorded. She smiled at the girl, forcing herself to be friendly. "I am called Emily. What are you called?"

"Julianne," the girl said. She stepped backwards. "I must go."

Emily watched her go, then turned her attention to the bowl. It contained something that resembled stew, although it didn't smell very appetizing. But then, some of the meals Sergeant Harkin had concocted hadn't smelled very appetizing either. He'd insisted that skunks could be eaten, when wandering travelers couldn't catch and butcher rabbits. And yet, she'd been able to eat his food without stomach cramps afterwards.

She used a spell to test the stew, just to make sure it was safe to eat, then started to eat with her fingers. The food tasted little better than it smelled, as if it had been cooked for so long that all the flavors had merged into sludge, but she was too hungry to care. She wolfed it down with her fingers, then checked the water. Her spell warned her that it was far from pure, so she used a third spell to purify it before taking a long gulp. The food made her feel somewhat refreshed as Whitehall finally separated himself from the other magicians and walked back towards her. She started to rise to her feet, but he motioned her back down. He sat, facing her.

"We don't know when you entered the castle," Whitehall said. He sounded tired, as if he'd pushed himself right to the limits of his endurance. "And we have no idea what happened to your family."

"Neither do I," Emily said, truthfully.

Whitehall shrugged. "We are grateful for your help," he added, after a moment. His daughter brought him a mug of water and he sipped it gratefully, without using any magic to cleanse the water. "We would not have survived the day without you."

Emily nodded. She'd had no time to analyze the spells they'd been using, but it was clear that they'd been on the verge of losing control completely. And once they lost control, they wouldn't have had a hope of surviving more than a few seconds.

There were horror stories about what happened to people who lost control. The surge of wild magic would have killed everyone in the castle.

"Still, we don't know what to do with you," Whitehall added. "Some of my...companions are proposing that you should be sent out of the castle. Others...think you should join the women."

That's gratitude for you, Emily thought, darkly.

The thought made her scowl. She couldn't afford to leave the castle, not when the nexus point was probably her only hope of getting home. And yet, it didn't *look* as though the women were treated as equals. She was damned if she was allowing herself to be bossed around like a servant. But what could she do? She could hide—probably—but it wouldn't give her any time to plan a way home.

"I have decided to offer you a provisional apprenticeship, at least for the moment," Whitehall said, after a moment. "You are clearly a trained magician, despite being a young woman."

Emily nodded, relieved. Whitehall would be foolish to simply let her go, after she'd saved their lives and beaten his apprentice in a duel. And yet, she didn't want to swear any oaths to him, certainly not ones that would oblige her to tell him the truth. She didn't dare tell him that she was from the future. It would change history and quite probably erase her from existence.

"I can do that," she said. "But I can't offer you any oaths."

Whitehall eyed her, narrowly. "Your tutor is dead."

Emily cursed under her breath. Telling them that her tutor was dead had been a mistake, clearly. She could have claimed she had no idea what had happened to him and escaped the need for swearing oaths. It wasn't as if she could be oathsworn to two different masters.

"Some of his family may still be alive," she said, reluctantly. "I must keep their secrets as long as I suspect the oath binds me."

"True, I suppose," Whitehall said. He didn't sound pleased. She rather suspected he'd been intending to grill her extensively. "You do understand that refusing to swear an oath means I won't be teaching you some of my *private* spells?"

Professor Locke would give his right arm to see them, Emily thought. She was starting to think the Whitehall Commune was nowhere near as powerful as the legends insisted. The magicians were clearly powerful, but their magic was slopping everywhere and they hadn't shown any of the subtle spells she used on a daily basis. *But would they be worth the risk of damaging the timeline?*

"I understand," she said. "But I am already a trained magician."

Whitehall nodded, curtly. "You'll be learning alongside Bernard, for the moment," he told her. "Treat your fellow apprentices with respect—and if you can't do that, try not to kill each other."

Emily had to smile. Some things never changed, it seemed. Magicians would always be competing, always testing their powers and skills against their fellows. It would be different too, she suspected, when there was one master to one apprentice.

The masters would be pleased to see their apprentices win fights, even though they were supposed to remain above the fray. But judging from some of the arguments she could see on the other side of the hall, they weren't *that* far above the fray.

They're only teaching one student at a time, she reminded herself. *They have far more emotional investment in their apprentices than any of the tutors from Whitehall.*

"I can try," she said, dryly.

She wondered, briefly, what Bernard De Born would think of Whitehall taking on a second apprentice. She'd already beaten him in a duel. Would he accept her presence or would he resent her? And what would Whitehall do if they started fighting?

"It won't be easy," Whitehall warned. "Apprenticeships are never easy."

"I know," Emily said.

Whitehall gave her a sidelong look. "Why did your tutor choose to teach you?"

Emily frowned to herself. Was Whitehall always going to be prying? But then, it was hard to blame him for being curious. Emily had shown him two impossible spells in less than an hour, assuming she was right about prank transfigurations coming later. He had to be wondering just who had taught her and why he hadn't heard of him. And, perhaps, just what other secrets might be locked up in Emily's head.

"I believe I was a good choice," she said, tartly.

It was hard to keep her voice under control, but she had no choice. She didn't want to tell too many lies or she'd have problems keeping them all straight. Whitehall might not be as capable as Void or Lady Barb, but he was far from stupid. If he caught her in a lie, he'd start hacking the rest of her story apart. And who knew what would happen then?

She hesitated, then asked the question that had been bothering her from the moment she'd entered the Great Hall. "Who are you running from?"

Whitehall tensed. "You don't know?"

"No," Emily said. She kept her face under tight control. Was it common knowledge, something she should have learned when she was studying magic? Her ignorance would be suspicious, but what else could she do? "What drove you to the castle?"

His eyes studied her face for a long moment. Emily forced herself to look back, even though she was afraid that he might be able to tell she wasn't being entirely honest. No magician in *her* era would want to mess with a sworn oath, but that might not hold true for Whitehall and his commune. They might not understand Soul Magic—the power that binds oaths—any more than they understood Healing.

"We were attacked," Whitehall said. "We were being *hunted.*"

Emily leaned forward, alarmed. "By who?"

Or what, her mind added.

"We don't know," Whitehall said. "But they seem to hunt magicians."

He rose, slowly. "Bernard will take care of you, for the moment," he added. Emily had the feeling he was going back to consult with his fellow masters. "And then I think you had better bed down with Julianne."

"I need some sleep," Emily agreed. She also needed more food, but she suspected the commune simply didn't have any to spare. It wasn't as if they could walk down to Dragon's Den to purchase food. The town had only been founded three hundred years—give or take a few decades—prior to her arrival. "Which tent is hers?"

"We cleared a room for her," Whitehall said. He made an odd gesture with his hand, casting a spell. "I'll have her take care of you instead, if you don't mind. You can talk to Bernard tomorrow."

Emily nodded, relieved. Bernard might seem to be the typical cocky teenager, but she'd read his writings, his *future* writings. He'd been no fool. And she was too tired to engage in pointless verbal duels. Besides, she'd probably shocked him quite badly. A good night's sleep would do them both a great deal of good.

Julianne walked over to her father, looking as tired as Emily felt. She gave Emily a sharp glance as Whitehall explained what he wanted her to do, then beckoned for Emily to follow her towards the nearest door. The corridor outside was dark, illuminated only by a single burning torch. Emily resisted the urge to cast a light globe as Julianne led the way down to a line of doors and opened one, revealing a tiny bedroom. A handful of blankets lay on the floor.

"This is my room," Julianne said. There was an odd note in her voice—resentment? "I've only got a couple of blankets."

"I don't mind," Emily said. She'd slept in worse places on camping trips. And there were spells she could use to keep warm, if necessary. "Thank you for sharing."

"Father insisted," Julianne said, wryly.

She nodded towards a bucket at the far end of the room. "Make sure you don't tip it over," she added. "You'll have to help me scrub the floor if you do."

Emily shuddered. It wasn't a pleasant thought.

"I will," she said. She took one of the blankets and lay down. "And thanks again."

Chapter Three

S HE COULDN'T SLEEP.
    Her body felt tired, her *mind* felt tired, but she just couldn't fall asleep. The floor
was hard, despite the blanket; no matter how she tossed and turned, she just couldn't
get comfortable enough to relax. And she was too tired to cast any spells that might
have made the makeshift bedding more comfortable. She could hear Julianne snoring
quietly, sleeping peacefully, yet Emily couldn't follow her into dreams. The constant
sense of being out of place, of being in danger, nagged at her mind.

    She sat upright, cursing her body as she rose. It had taken her time to get used
to sharing a room at Whitehall, but it shouldn't be a problem any longer. She'd had
no trouble sharing her bedroom with Cabiria. And yet...now, she just couldn't sleep.
Her mind was too active to let her rest. She tested the privacy ward she'd cast on
the door—Julianne hadn't noticed, somewhat to Emily's surprise—and then stepped
through the door, out into the corridor. It was as dark and cold as the grave. Someone
should be on watch, she thought, down in the Great Hall, but she could hear nothing.
She closed the door behind her and cast a night-vision spell, then started to walk up
the corridor towards the stairs. They, at least, seemed to be where they *should* be.

    No one blocked her way as she reached the stairwell and headed upwards, reach-
ing out with her senses for traps. Whitehall had warned her, after all, but she sensed
nothing until she reached the fifth floor. A nasty little hex lay on the stairwell, ready
to blast anyone stupid enough to step on it. It looked odd, compared to some of
the hexes Sergeant Miles had taught her; she honestly wasn't sure just how it had
endured for so long. It didn't *seem* to be connected to the nexus point.

    And power doesn't run through these wards, she thought, as she dismantled the hex
and walked further upwards. Two more hexes barred her way, but she took them
apart just as easily. *These hexes couldn't have been set that long ago.*

    She reached the top of the stairs and stepped out onto the battlements. Her eyes
widened as she saw the night sky, the stars twinkling down in all their glory. There
was nothing beyond the battlements, save an utterly unbroken darkness. The wind
blew hot and cold, blasts of icy air alternating with gusts of warmth that left sweat
trickling down her back. She was used to the weather surrounding Whitehall being
somewhat unpredictable, but this was odd. There was magic in the air, she realized
slowly, that was far stronger than anything she'd sensed back in *her* day.

    Bracing herself, she inched up to the low barrier and stared out into the darkness
again, trying to see something—anything—that would remind her of the world she'd
left behind. But she saw only darkness. The lights that would have marked Dragon's
Den were gone; the lights that marked the edge of the wards surrounding the castle
hadn't been created yet. It struck her as she turned to peer east that she was actually
back in the era before the necromancers, before the southern continent was overrun
and turned to ash. The Blighted Lands had yet to exist.

    And the reality of where she was crashed down like a physical blow.

    This is not good, she thought, numbly.

She sat down on the hard stone and forced herself to *think*. She'd fallen back in time—and she had no way back to the future. Or did she? If she'd crafted a pocket dimension that had allowed her to skip forward a day, she could create one that would last for much longer...couldn't she? And yet, she wasn't remotely sure just how long she'd need to hide in the pocket dimension before emerging back into her world. Professor Locke had made it clear, more than once, that even the dating system was imprecise. She had no way to be sure how much time had passed between Whitehall and Grandmaster Hasdrubal, let alone timing her emergence to make sure she didn't clash with her past self. And if she went too far into the future, she wouldn't have a hope of getting back.

No, she told herself. *This is definitely not good.*

She frowned, considering her options. Perhaps she should simply leave the castle and step outside recorded history. It was the safest way to ensure she didn't fiddle with the historical record—unless, of course, she was *meant* to be there. She'd seen nothing to disprove her theory that she *was* the Dark Lady. And if she did leave, what would that do to history? She was living proof that different worlds and alternate universes actually existed, but if time changed around her...what would happen? Would there be two timelines, or would she simply blink out of existence? Or would she set off a series of catastrophic changes in history?

A flash of light, in the distance, caught her eye. She was on her feet before her mind had quite registered what she was doing, peering into the darkness in desperate hope of seeing something—anything. A flicker of lightning danced in the air for a long moment, followed by faint glimmering lights near the ground. It looked almost like a forest fire, save for the eerie—almost translucent—lighting. Wild magic hummed on the air as she looked closer, then pulled back before she could accidentally tumble over the battlements and fall to her death. There was more magic in the past, she realized dully, than she'd ever seen in the future.

Rain started to fall seconds later, drenching her. She cast a spell to shield herself from the downpour, then cast a second one to dry her clothes. The magic felt normal, as far as she could tell, but there was a faint resonance in the *mana* that bothered her. And yet, the spells had worked perfectly. She turned to watch as the rain fell harder and harder, water washing over the battlements and draining over the edge; she hoped—prayed—that someone had had the sense to set out barrels to collect the falling water. But would it be safe to drink?

She cursed inwardly as her stomach rumbled, reminding her that she hadn't eaten anywhere near enough. But there was nothing she could do about it...she shook her head, irritated, at just how spoiled she'd become in five years. There had been days on Earth when she'd eaten so little that she'd had trouble concentrating on anything, yet she'd managed to keep going until she'd finally had a bite to eat. But three regular—and large—meals a day at Whitehall had clearly ruined her endurance. Hell, thanks to the sergeants, she could even live off the land, if necessary. She disliked cutting up rabbits or fish, but she could endure it if there was no other choice.

But I have to stay here until I find a way home, she told herself, firmly. *If nothing else, I'll need the nexus point to power my spells.*

She wished, bitterly, that Lady Barb had fallen through time with her. Or Sergeant Miles. Or even Master Tor. Someone—just someone—who would have understood what she was going through, someone whose understanding of modern magic was far in advance of her own. She *thought* she could construct a pocket dimension, with or without the nexus point, but keeping it going for nearly a thousand years would be beyond even *her* magical reserves. And yet, the spellware that had controlled the nexus point in her time didn't exist yet. She'd have to wait until it did before using it to get home.

The downpour stopped, as suddenly as if someone had thrown a switch. She looked up as the skies cleared rapidly, revealing the stars once again. Sergeant Miles had tried to teach his class how to read them, to use them to navigate, but Emily had never mastered the skill. And yet, even if she had, she doubted the skies changed that much in a *mere* thousand years. She couldn't even *begin* to use them to deduce how much time had passed between Lord Whitehall and her arrival on the Nameless World. It should be possible, in theory, but she didn't even know where to begin. Maybe some of the people sleeping below her knew, yet she didn't dare ask. It would be far too revealing.

They wouldn't know what the skies looked like in the future, she told herself, as she peered back into the darkness. *And I couldn't tell them that either.*

She shivered, cursing the nightgown under her breath. It was heavy, but hardly warm enough to serve as an overcoat. Julianne had promised to find her something to wear, in the morning, yet Emily doubted the commune had much to spare. Was someone going to be walking around naked because of her? She *could* transfigure her nightgown into something more useful, she knew, but it wouldn't last forever. A single cancelling spell, cast at the wrong time, would put her right back in the night-gown. She shook her head, dismissing the thought, then resumed her silent vigil. The darkness almost seemed to welcome her.

A chill ran down her back. The strange glimmering lights were still there, flickering out in the darkness. She couldn't escape the feeling that something out there was looking back at her. Whitehall—*this* Whitehall—was no longer safe, had perhaps *never* been safe. Who'd laid the traps? Who'd been so determined to build a castle around a nexus point and then abandon it? All the records agreed that the castle had been empty when the Whitehall Commune arrived...

Maybe they were experimenting with the nexus point, Emily thought, as she forced herself to turn away from the darkness. *And something went wrong, killing them.*

She yawned, tiredly. Gritting her teeth, she walked back through the door and down the stairwell. It was harder to know just how far down she had to go now, she discovered; there was no way she could use the wards for directions. Her footsteps were barely visible in the dirt and grime...she shook her head as she reached what she thought was the right floor and padded towards her bedroom. And then she stopped as she heard voices ahead of her, a faint mumbling that drew her onwards.

She resisted the urge to use magic to spy on the speakers, even though she had a feeling it would be safe enough. Instead, she slipped closer and listened.

"...Not natural," a voice was saying. "She shouldn't have survived for a second in the nexus."

"People have been killed or transformed by wild magic," a second voice said. "Why *can't* they be trapped in a nexus?"

"She's a magician," the first voice said. "The wild magic should have killed her outright."

"Maybe she's a fake," the second voice said. "How many women do you know who can cast spells?"

Emily felt her cheeks heat. They were talking about *her!*

The first voice sounded amused. "You were there when she saved us all," he said. "She is very definitely a magician."

"Then she's cursed," the second voice insisted. "You know it to be true."

Emily blinked. *Cursed?*

"She's dangerous," the second voice continued. "If she could beat Bernard in a duel..."

"Whitehall has chosen to take her as an apprentice," the first voice pointed out.

"An unwise choice," the second voice snapped.

"She's a magician," the first voice reminded him. "Do you want her walking around with incomplete training?"

He spoke on before the second speaker could interrupt. "If she's cursed...well, it's not our problem," he added. "She's already gone too far to step back to safety. It isn't as if she was ever *our* responsibility."

"Whoever taught her was derelict in his duty," the second voice snapped. "Do *you* think her story makes sense?"

"Her tutor is dead, if she is to be believed," the first voice said. "And if you have a problem with her joining the commune, take it up with Whitehall."

Emily heard the man striding along the corridor and pushed herself into an alcove, calling on magic to hide her presence. Sergeant Miles would probably not have been fooled, certainly not if he was *looking* for her, but the first speaker strode past her and into the distance without looking back. She stared after him, then peered back down towards the Great Hall, feeling oddly conflicted. Cursed? She wasn't cursed. What did they *mean?*

I need answers, she thought. Her thoughts churned as she slipped back down the corridor and into the bedroom. *And I don't even know who to ask.*

She glanced at Julianne—still sleeping peacefully on the stone floor—and then settled down herself, closing her eyes as she tried to concentrate on her meditation. Maybe, just maybe, she could go to sleep now. And yet, sleep was elusive...her mind just kept going back to the conversation she'd overheard, wondering just what they'd meant. A curse on female magicians? She'd never heard of such a thing...or had she? There had been that vague note from one of Professor Locke's books, suggesting that female magicians had trouble bearing children. But she could name a dozen magicians she knew who *had* had children.

Whitehall won't believe how ignorant I am, if I start asking questions, she thought. She'd been given a great deal of slack when she'd first come to Whitehall because she wasn't even from the same *world*, but she'd already told Whitehall that she'd had a tutor. *And yet, if I don't know the basics, I will keep making mistakes.*

She sighed. It was clear that not everyone had believed her story. She really shouldn't have been surprised. But it had been the best story she could make up on short notice...if she'd *known* she was going to fall back in time, she'd have taken the time to do her research and compose an airtight cover. And yet, given how inaccurate the history records seemed to be, it was unlikely she *could* have come up with something perfect. Maybe, just maybe, she'd come up with something that would suffice. Maybe...

There was a flicker of magic. Emily jerked awake, shocked. She'd fallen asleep... when had she fallen asleep? Julianne knelt beside her, unable to move. Emily stared at her, blearily. It took her several seconds to realize that Julianne had tried to wake her, only to trigger one of her protective spells and wind up frozen. Surely, that spell had been invented before Whitehall...?

"I'm sorry," Emily said, sitting upright. The spell was normally an easy one to cancel, but she took a moment to catch her breath before casting the counterspell. Julianne unfroze and toppled forward; Emily caught her before she could hit the ground. "That's just one of my protections."

"It must be a very useful protection," Julianne said. She sounded annoyed—and bitter—as she pulled free of Emily and stood. "I wish I could do that."

Emily frowned. "Your father hasn't taught you?"

"Girls are forbidden to learn magic," Julianne said, flatly. "Those who do are cursed."

"Cursed," Emily repeated. "In what way?"

Julianne shook her head. "There's a set of trousers and a shirt for you," she said, tossing Emily a bundle of clothes. "They should fit, but if they don't I'll make the alterations now, before we go to breakfast."

Emily frowned as she unwrapped the bundle. Julianne wore a long dress that wouldn't have been out of place on a peasant farm in Zangaria, but *Emily* had been given male clothes. She had a sneaking suspicion it had something to do with her status as an apprentice, yet she didn't want to ask when Julianne was clearly out of sorts. Did she *want* to learn magic? If she had the talent—and she should have the talent—she shouldn't have any trouble learning...

I could teach her, Emily thought. *But what would her father make of that?*

There were no underclothes, she discovered, as she undressed and started to don the new outfit. The clothes were clean, but itchy against her bare skin; the shirt was loose, while the trousers felt uncomfortably tight. Emily couldn't help thinking that the outfit had been designed to show off male muscles, just like some of the more absurd fashions she'd seen at King Randor's Court. Julianne looked disapproving, then motioned for Emily to step back out of the trousers and let her fiddle with them. Moments later, the trousers were much looser around her thighs.

"You look relatively decent," Julianne said, finally. "But you really should cut your hair."

Emily gave her a sharp look. "Why?"

"You never know what might try to grab hold," Julianne said, evasively. Emily couldn't help noting that *her* hair was long too. "I can cut it for you now, if you like."

"No, thank you," Emily said. She hadn't cut her hair for nearly a year. It was her one true vanity. Besides, Caleb liked playing with her hair. "I like it the way it is."

"As you wish," Julianne said.

Emily sighed, inwardly. There was so much she didn't understand, so much she didn't know...so much she didn't dare ask about, when it would reveal just how much she didn't know. If only someone else had fallen through the nexus and into the past with her!

There was a sharp knock at the door. "Company," Julianne said. "Are you ready?"

Emily glanced down at herself. She looked odd, she thought, in clothes that had definitely been designed for a man, but Julianne was right. She *was* decent.

"Yeah," she said. "Shall we go?"

Chapter Four

"LADY EMILY," BERNARD SAID, AS JULIANNE OPENED THE DOOR. "MY MASTER—OUR Master—bade me escort you down to breakfast."

Emily nodded, slowly. Bernard didn't look as though he bore a grudge, she decided; indeed, there was something about him, now she'd had a good night's sleep, that reminded her of Caleb or Jade. His face had been washed clean—she hoped she could find a place to wash after breakfast—although it remained pockmarked. Either he couldn't remove the marks, or he just didn't care enough to try.

Another boy stood behind him, gazing at Emily. His face was scrubbed clean and very pale; his short dark hair was cropped close to his skull. Emily could sense his magic jumping around him, flickering and flaring in a manner she found rather alarming. The last person she'd sensed with such chaotic magic had been in the Halfway House. He wore a brown shirt and a pair of trousers exactly like the ones Julianne had given to Emily, although there was an odd rune sewn into the garment just below his right shoulder. She didn't recognize the rune at all.

"This is Robin De Bold," Bernard said, introducing the stranger. "Apprentice to Lord and Master Chambers."

"Pleased to meet you," Emily said. She didn't recall a Robin De Bold from any of the books she'd read, although that proved nothing. Master Chambers had only been mentioned once or twice. "I think I saw you in the nexus chamber."

"You did." He had an odd voice. He spoke as though he was trying for dignity, but his voice wasn't deep enough to pull it off. "I thank you for saving my life."

"All of our lives," Bernard corrected. He glanced at Robin. "Perhaps you could escort Lady Emily down the corridor...?"

"Of course," Robin said. He smirked. "Remember to leave the door open."

Bernard wants to be alone with Julianne, Emily realized, as Robin led her through the door and a short distance down the corridor. *He likes her.*

She shook her head at the thought—people never changed, no matter the time or place they were born—and then leaned against the wall, waiting. Julianne was unlikely to be in any real danger, certainly not from her father's apprentice. Bernard didn't have anything like enough power to challenge his master, unless he was far better at masking it than she assumed. She found it hard to believe that Whitehall would allow his apprentice to molest his daughter—and besides, she didn't get those sorts of vibes from Bernard. He might be a jerk—he'd certainly *acted* like a jerk—but he didn't seem the sort to be a rapist.

Her stomach growled, unpleasantly, as they waited. She didn't know what to say and Robin seemed content to keep his mouth closed, although he looked at her with undisguised curiosity. There was something about him that bothered her, something that put her hackles up, something that was oddly familiar. And yet it was impossible to put her finger on it.

"Thank you," Bernard said. He strode down the corridor, Julianne following a pace or two behind. "Shall we go eat?"

Emily glanced at Julianne—she looked red, but otherwise unharmed—and then allowed the two boys to lead the way down to the Great Hall. Sunlight was streaming in from the far wall, something that caught her by surprise—the wall she knew, from her time, was solid, impossible to move. A number of young men—she put them between thirteen and twenty—were sitting on a rug, eating bread and butter. Bernard glanced back at her, then walked over to a smaller rug, waving to a pair of young women. Julianne threw Emily an unreadable look and then strode away. Bernard didn't seem inclined to call her back.

"We don't have much to eat," Bernard said, as he sat down on the rug and motioned for Emily to sit facing him. "But you are welcome to join us."

"Thank you," Emily said, as she sat and looked around. Save for herself, the only women in the hall seemed to be servants. "You don't want to join the others?"

"They're not linked to a *proper* master," Robin said. "They cannot share our food."

Emily frowned as a serving girl brought bread, honey and a jug of water, which she placed in front of them. "They're not apprentices?"

"They're apprentices," Bernard explained. "But they don't have a master."

Emily's confusion must have shown on her face, because he hastened to explain. "There was an attack on another commune, near where we were staying. Their masters were killed, but the apprentices fled to us. Lord and Master Whitehall took them in, even though teaching them more than the basics is impossible."

"This is the largest commune in the world," Robin added, with obvious pride.

"It is," Bernard agreed.

Emily took a piece of bread, spread some honey on it and ate slowly, savoring the taste. It was clear that *someone* had found the kitchens and started to bake fresh bread for breakfast—and, perhaps, located a beehive too. Or maybe they'd just carried it with them as they'd made their way to the castle. It wasn't the breakfast she was used to, in the future, but it would have to do.

"And so you came here," she said. "Why did you come here?"

"My master, Lord and Master Chambers, is one of the greatest DemonMasters of all time," Robin said. "It was his idea to consult a demon to find a safe place for the commune."

"It was Lord Alfred who actually *summoned* the demon," Bernard countered, rudely. "He..."

Emily barely heard him. A demon...she was back in the time of the DemonMasters! Her blood ran cold as she considered the implications. Meddling with demons was considered part of the Black Arts, in the future; but she'd *seen* demons. They lived outside the normal framework of time and space, free from the petty concerns of cause and effect...a single demon could break her cover easily, if anyone thought to ask.

And if one of them urged the commune to head to the castle, she thought numbly, *there's probably a sting in the tail somewhere.*

"Emily," Bernard said. "Are you all right? You've gone pale."

Emily gathered herself. "My tutor forbade me from summoning demons," she said. It was true enough. Aurelius had warned her never to take the risk unless she was desperate. At best, demons were always jerkass genies, taking advantage of each and every loophole to screw around with the fools who summoned them. "I've never dared use them."

"Mine won't allow me to use them either," Bernard said, regretfully.

Robin smirked. "I have seven demons under *my* command," he said. "Master Chambers allows me to use them for *anything* I wish."

Bernard sighed.

"You should summon one secretly," Robin urged. "I could show you how."

Emily stared at him, shocked. His magic had felt oddly familiar...was it because he had used a demon? And then she *saw* the little creature sitting on his shoulder. It looked humanoid, but it was barely larger than a finger...and, the more she stared at it, the more she sensed a limitless malice hidden within the tiny form. The demon stared back at her, its eyes cold and sharp and very cruel. She had no doubt it would tear them apart if Robin ever lost control.

"You shouldn't," she said, unable to tear her eyes from the demon. "It would be very dangerous."

"Life is dangerous," Bernard said. He sounded tempted. "And demons could teach me so much."

"You could never trust them," Emily said. "Ever."

Robin sorted. "And yet a demon led us to you."

"I know," Emily said. She forced herself to look away from the demon. "And what did it have in mind when it did?"

She changed the subject quickly, before Robin could talk Bernard into doing something incredibly stupid. "How many people are in the commune?"

Bernard looked relieved to be able to talk about something else. "There are seven masters and fifty apprentices," he said. "I think..."

"Seven of us are *real* apprentices," Robin injected. "The remainder are just... hangers-on."

"They have some skills," Bernard countered. Emily had the feeling that it was an old argument between the two of them. "And they can learn more."

He cleared his throat. "There're also two hundred others; workers and camp followers..."

"And whores," Robin added.

"And a number of children," Bernard said, ignoring the interruption. "This is very much the largest commune in the world."

"And also the biggest target," Robin pointed out. "If something is hunting magicians, Bernard, this commune makes a pretty big target."

Emily frowned, wondering just how far she dared probe. Magicians were being hunted? By what? And why couldn't they defend themselves? Whitehall was a solidly powerful magician and she assumed the others masters were almost as good. But if they were on the run...she recalled the refugee camp-like atmosphere and shuddered.

The castle might be their last hope of survival against a powerful and deadly foe.

It could be the Faerie, she thought. If the history books were accurate, she could have arrived just before the First Faerie War. *Or mundanes hunting dangerous magicians...*

She leaned back and listened as the two young men bickered. They seemed to be close friends, yet there were discordant flickers in their words that bothered her. Bernard seemed to envy Robin, while Robin seemed too conceited to care. Their magic flickered around them, pushing at their emotions...they didn't seem to know how to mask their powers, even if they cared enough to do it. The more she looked at it, the more it bothered her.

Bernard turned to look at her as she finished the last piece of bread. "Why *were* you trained?"

"My tutor believed I would be a good student," Emily said, stiffly. "Why were *you* trained?"

"Touché," Bernard said. "But still...it's unusual for girls to be trained."

"I might just have noticed," Emily said, dryly.

Robin laughed. "You've certainly done your tutor proud."

"Thank you," Emily said.

She allowed herself a moment of relief as a middle-aged man carrying a staff strode towards them. Bernard and Robin hastily stood and bowed; Emily followed suit, unsure if it was the right thing to do or not. The man gave her a long considering look, then turned his gaze on Robin.

"I want you to assist in clearing the upper levels today," he stated. Emily had to fight to keep her expression under control as she recognized the voice. He was the speaker who'd doubted her, even after she'd saved them all. "I have too much else to do to teach you. Drake will show you what to do."

Robin bowed his head. "Yes, Master."

Master Chambers, Emily thought. Up close, his magic was discordant, wilder than Whitehall's. She thought she could sense the lurking presence of a demon as he peered back at her, although she couldn't see anything. *A DemonMaster...*

She studied him, grimly aware of his eyes scrutinizing every inch of her. Master Chambers was tall and muscular, his brown hair cropped close to his skull. That, at least, explained why Julianne had wanted Emily to cut her hair. Demons had a nasty habit of grabbing hold of exposed hair and tugging, hard. Sometimes, she'd been warned, they yanked hard enough to pull the magician across the circle and into their hands. And no one, not even a Lone Power, could hope to escape.

And he didn't like her. She could see the distrust in his eyes as he gazed back at her.

Of course he doesn't trust me, she thought, as Master Chambers finally looked away. *He knows nothing about me.*

"Bernard, your master will meet you outside in forty minutes," he added. "Take... Lady Emily...with you."

"Of course, My Lord," Bernard said.

Master Chambers gave Emily one final look, then turned and strode away. Robin nodded politely to them both, then hurried off towards the nearest door. Emily felt an odd stab of sympathy. Having Master Chambers for a tutor, she rather suspected, wouldn't be a comfortable experience. But then, anything involving demons was incredibly dangerous.

"Demons," she said. "Is he really the most powerful of the DemonMasters?"

"He claims to have thirty-one demons in his thrall, bound to his power," Bernard said. "I have no reason to doubt his claim."

"I find that hard to believe," Emily said. From what she'd been told, holding even one demon in thrall was hard enough. "Thirty-one?"

"He couldn't fool my master," Bernard said. There was a hint of obvious pride in his voice as Julianne reappeared and started to collect the plates, jug and honey pot. "Julianne's father is not so easily fooled. He never lets me get away with anything."

Emily concealed her relief with an effort. Bernard might *try* to summon a demon, if Robin gave him the instructions, but Lord Whitehall would never let him get away with it. The stink of demonic malice would give him away, long before he could come up with a plausible lie...if, of course, there *was* such a thing. Could anyone hope to conceal a demon? Shadye had concealed a demon within a ring, she recalled, but he'd had the demon's cooperation. She doubted that any demon would see value in assisting Bernard to stay out of trouble...

And if he does get caught, he'll be in deep trouble, she thought. *Whitehall, if the stories are true, never liked demons.*

She watched Julianne leave—and watched Bernard, watching Julianne leave. He was smitten; the tenderness on his face made him look very different. She wondered, absently, just what *Julianne* thought about him. Maybe she should ask. She'd always found it hard to talk about such matters, but...

"Forty minutes," Bernard said. "What do you want to do until then?"

"Get clean," Emily said. "Is there a place I can wash up?"

Bernard looked awkward. "I'll have to ask Julianne," he said. "She's the person to ask if you want anything like that. We just had a basin of warm water."

"That would be enough," Emily said.

She frowned as she spotted one of the other masters entering the hall. "I meant to ask," she said, remembering how they'd bowed to Master Chambers. "How *does* one address a master?"

Bernard considered it for a moment. "You were never taught etiquette?"

"Not enough," Emily said. It was likely to have changed and evolved before she'd arrived at Whitehall. Besides, if nothing else, talking about etiquette would keep Bernard from asking more awkward questions. "I don't know how to introduce myself, let alone ask for help without getting into trouble."

"I imagine your tutor didn't plan to introduce you," Bernard said.

He paused, stroking his chin. "You address your master as *Master* or *My Master*," he said, after a moment. "In conversation, you would call him Master Whitehall. All other masters are addressed as *Lord* or *My Lord*, unless you were friends before he reached his mastery. In that case, you can address him by name. Apprentices can be addressed by name, unless you have a reason to give their rank—in which case, you would address them as Apprentice Whatever."

Emily nodded. "Why is Whitehall..."

Bernard pointed a finger at her. "*Master* Whitehall."

"Why is Master Whitehall called *Lord and Master* Whitehall?"

"He combines both titles," Bernard said. "Address him as *Master* unless you're being strictly formal or begging for mercy."

He shrugged. "If a master approaches you first, make sure you rise and bow to him," he added. "If you approach him, go down on your knees and wait for him to acknowledge you before rising. Should he offer something to you, take it with your casting hand. Do *not* offer your other hand, whatever happens, unless you need both hands..."

Emily held up a hand. "My casting hand?"

"The hand you use to cast spells," Bernard explained. His eyes narrowed. "How do you not know that?"

"I was taught to use both hands," Emily said. She was right-handed, but her tutors had insisted on their students using alternating hands when they cast spells. Only a couple of students in first year had been unable to use both hands—and the problem had cleared up, she recalled, with practice. "Aren't you?"

"That's odd," Bernard said. "I was always taught to use my right hand."

He frowned. "I suggest you hold out both hands, then," he added. "But be careful."

Emily swallowed. Whitehall—*her* Whitehall—had been very different from Earth. But *this* Whitehall was familiar enough to be disconcerting. Something that would have passed unremarked in *her* Whitehall might start a fight here, hundreds of years in the past. She'd have to watch herself, but she wasn't sure how.

"I will," she said.

Bernard rose. "I'll find you a place to wash," he said. "And then my master will..."

He paused, then bowed hastily as an older man hurried over to them. Emily bowed too, realizing that she was looking at yet another master. He looked to be in his nineties, although that proved nothing; he might well be no older than forty. She couldn't help thinking of Albert Einstein as the man studied her. He had the same impression of being nothing more than a kindly old grandfather.

"Lady Emily," he said. "I need to talk to you."

Bernard cleared his throat. "Lord Wolfe, Master Whitehall wishes to talk to her in thirty minutes," he warned. "I..."

"I will have her there for him," Lord Wolfe said.

"Don't worry," Emily said. "I'll be fine."

Bernard nodded. "I'll inform my master," he said. "He may want to give you more time with Lord Wolfe."

"That would be good," Lord Wolfe said. He grinned at Emily. "This way, please."

Chapter Five

THE CAMP FOLLOWERS HAD DONE A REMARKABLE JOB AT CLEANING THE DIRT AND GRIME from the floor, Emily decided as she followed Lord Wolfe through a maze of disconcertingly familiar corridors. It might not be anything like as clean as King Randor's castle—at least, not yet—but the future school was starting to look livable. Small groups of workers swept the corridors, while apprentices—some throwing doubtful glances at her as she passed—prowled the corridors, searching for more traps.

Probably keeping them busy, she thought, as they walked into a small room. *They will have cleared or triggered all the traps in this section, surely?*

"I have no idea what this room was, once upon a time," Wolfe said. He closed the door behind them, but made no move to cast a privacy ward. Was that technique still to be discovered too? "But it will suffice as an office, for the moment."

Emily nodded. Someone had set up a rickety-looking wooden table and a single chair that seemed to be on its last legs, but otherwise the room was bare. The only source of light was a torch, burning merrily against the stone wall. It made her realize, again, just how lucky she'd been to live in a world where electric power was cheap and simple. Castles without magic were dark and gloomy places.

Wolfe motioned with his hands towards the table, which was covered in ancient books and pieces of parchment. One of the rolls of parchment was unrolled, with the four corners held in place by small stones. Emily took a look at the writing; her eyes widened as she realized she was looking at spell notations. Very primitive, compared to what she was used to, but clearly a step in the right direction. She took a step forward, wondering if Wolfe would seek to bar her from studying the parchment, yet he made no move to stop her. His eyes merely watched as she bent over the table, slowly tracing out the notations.

"You've seen something like it," Wolfe said. It wasn't a question. "What do you make of this?"

Emily hesitated, unsure how much she could say. It was hard to be certain—there were plenty of differences between the spell notation in front of her and the techniques she'd been taught by Professor Lombardi—but it looked as though Master Wolfe had been trying to unlock the secret of tapping a nexus point. She couldn't think of any other explanation. The spells he'd detailed required a power source an order of magnitude more powerful than any living sorcerer.

"You're trying to tap the nexus point," she said, carefully. There was no point in pretending to be an idiot. She'd shown too much command of magic. "How long have you known the point was here?"

"There were stories of nexus points," Master Wolfe said, vaguely. "I've always wondered what one could do with a great deal of power."

"Anything," Emily said.

She studied the diagrams for a long moment, slowly working her way through them. They were flawed—she could see a number of serious problems that Wolfe would have to overcome—but she could recognize the bare bones of what would eventually become the control room. The control room they'd discovered under Whitehall. It had a long way to go...

Perhaps too long, she thought. Master Wolfe had done a good job, but his proposed network of spells was far too inflexible to control a nexus point. *And yet, the nexus point was tapped in this time.*

"Your tutor clearly had *some* idea of what to do," Master Wolfe said. He picked up a roll of parchment and unfurled it. "The spells you used to tap the nexus point *worked*."

"Imperfectly," Emily said, as she studied the parchment. Master Wolfe was clearly brilliant, perhaps the smartest man she'd ever met. He'd not only copied the work she'd done, with assistance from the commune, but used it as a starting point to devise his own spellwork to control the nexus point. "It nearly killed me."

"But it worked, once you had help," Master Wolfe said. "Your tutor must have been truly brilliant. Master Stark? Master Joffre? I know that both of them chose to withdraw from society to carry out their own research, rather than taking more apprentices. One of them could have taught you."

Emily shook her head, wordlessly. It was tempting to claim she'd studied under one or both of them, but Master Wolfe had *known* the two men he'd mentioned. He'd catch her in a lie and then she'd be in real trouble. She considered, briefly, telling him the truth, yet she knew she didn't dare take the risk. It would blow a hole in established history. And yet...

She looked back at the parchment. Master Wolfe had done a remarkable job, but he still had a very long way to go before he could hope to tap the nexus point properly. It was unlikely that he would make the breakthrough he needed tomorrow. The more she looked at his work, the clearer it became that he'd crafted a brute-force solution to the problem, rather than something capable of adapting and evolving to changing circumstances. There was no Warden—and there wouldn't be, if he didn't alter his approach.

And if this is a stable time loop, she thought, *I need to help him.*

She leaned on the table, thinking hard. If time *couldn't* be changed, then she was *meant* to be here -- *meant* to be in the past. And if that was true, perhaps she was *meant* to be helping Lord Whitehall and Master Wolfe establish the school. It was what the Dark Lady had *done*, if the remaining stories were to be believed. And no other candidate for the role had shown up, as far as she knew. None of the other women in the castle knew magic.

The possibilities opened up before her. If she was *meant* to help Master Wolfe, she'd have a chance to use the nexus point to get back home. And watching—and helping—as the original spellwork slipped into place would show her how to do it for herself, later. She'd be able to answer all of Professor Locke's questions, even if it didn't look as though there *were* any real secrets of the ancients. Only demons...and the start of something more.

Find out what else needs to be kicked off, she told herself. She'd have to pick Bernard's brains and find out what he knew—and what he didn't know. *And then see how you can start the ball rolling.*

"Lady Emily," Master Wolfe said. "Are you going to answer my question?"

Emily blinked. What question?

"I'm sorry, Master," she said. "I was miles away."

"I could tell," Master Wolfe said, sardonically. "I was asking you what your tutor taught you about controlling a nexus point."

"I didn't learn everything," Emily said, carefully. "He didn't trust me with *all* of his secrets."

"A common problem," Master Wolfe said, disdainfully. He sounded angry, although not with her. "A sorcerer discovers something new, then refuses to share it with his friends and apprentices. The secret is lost when he dies, only to be rediscovered years later by another sorcerer."

"And the whole pattern just keeps repeating itself," Emily said. "Time and time again."

"I've been trying to convince some of the other masters to share their secrets more openly," Master Wolfe told her. "But very few of them are willing to discuss such matters."

He sighed, then looked up at her. "What *did* your tutor tell you?"

Emily took a breath, thinking hard. She didn't know everything. She'd barely had the time to start unlocking the secrets beneath Whitehall before she'd been tossed back into the past. She couldn't help feeling that Professor Lombardi would have done a better job, if *he'd* been sent back in time instead. But what she *did* know would be enough to start Master Wolfe working towards a *proper* control system. And he'd put it together personally, so he'd understand—at a very basic level—how it worked.

"He believed that basic spellware was too...*rigid* to handle the power flow," she said, reaching for a sheet of parchment. She stopped herself a moment later. A piece of parchment would be hideously expensive in *this* time. Paper...there was no way she could introduce paper, not now. "You need something that adapts to changing circumstances."

"Like a living mind," Master Wolfe said. She'd half-expected him to dismiss the concept out of hand, but he sounded thoughtful rather than dismissive. "Did your tutor believe he could take control of the nexus point directly?"

"He might have," Emily hedged. *Shadye* had certainly believed *he* could take direct control of the nexus point, but he'd been halfway to being an eldritch abomination at that point. "I think it wouldn't have worked."

"Trying to channel that much power would have been fatal, surely," Master Wolfe said. "Do you think that was why he died?"

Emily shrugged. She had *no* idea what would have happened if Shadye had tapped the nexus point, but she didn't want to find out the hard way. If necromancy could drive a person mad, she hated to imagine what tapping a nexus point could do.

Perhaps it would simply have shattered his mind beyond repair...or, perhaps, it would have turned him into a dark god. It wasn't a pleasant thought.

"There are supposed to be rituals for transferring power," Master Wolfe mused. "But they don't always work."

He looked down at the parchment for a long moment. "The spellwork would have to be more than merely adaptable," he said. "It would have to *be* a living mind. But how to make it work? How to make it survive?"

"Tell it to survive," Emily said.

Master Wolfe looked up at her. "What do you mean?"

"You'll be setting the conditions when you create the living mind," Emily said. "You can just tell it that it can handle the power. It won't be smart enough to realize it should be dead."

"I shall have to meditate on that," Master Wolfe said, slowly.

He reached for a slate and started to scribble down notes. "Taking control of the nexus point was risky enough," he added. "But if we have so much power at our disposal, making it do anything—without worrying about spell structures—would be quite possible."

Emily watched as he worked, unsure if she'd said too much or too little. There were too many gaps in her knowledge, both of the school's history and of the ancient piece of spellwork, for her to be sure. Master Wolfe seemed to have taken her ideas and run with them, but who knew how far he could go? How much did *they* know?

"I wish your tutor had left you some notes," Master Wolfe said, grimly. "Did he have anything written down?"

"Not as far as I know," Emily said. It was true enough. "All I have is my memory."

Master Wolfe muttered several unpleasant-sounding words under his breath as he returned to scribbling. Emily didn't blame him for being frustrated, not if new tricks and techniques were discovered, lost, and then rediscovered time and time again, rather than allowing later researchers to build on the early discoveries. Even in *her* time, the Sorcerer's Rule had made it harder for research notes and details to propagate through the Nameless World. A sorcerer could not be forced to share his work...

...And even though it had worked in her favor, she knew it was a problem.

It will be worse here, she thought, numbly. If history was to be believed, Lord Whitehall had been the first person to set up an actual magic school. *The unattached apprentices are lacking even the basics of magical education.*

She cleared her throat. "Do *you* share what you know of spellwork?"

"Far too many magicians are not interested in my work," Master Wolfe said, flatly. "I have offered, regularly, to teach them, but they do not care."

Emily blinked in surprise. Spellwork—understanding spellwork—was the key to everything from transfiguration to subtle magic and wardcrafting. She'd thought Master Wolfe's spell notation was primitive...perhaps it *was* primitive. Perhaps she was looking at the very early stages of what would become charms...

"I care," she said. "My tutor cared."

Master Wolfe looked up. "Master Myrddin? Myrddin the Sane? No one knows what happened to him after Lord Whitehall was released from his apprenticeship."

Emily shook her head, surprised. Myrddin...Myrddin was an old name for Merlin, a *very* old name. A coincidence? Or, perhaps, a hint that she wasn't the first person from Earth to walk the Nameless World. She'd often wondered just how humans had managed to evolve in a *mana*-rich environment, but perhaps they hadn't. If *she* could be yanked across the dimensional barriers and dumped into the Nameless World, why not a few hundred thousand others?

"I've never heard of him," she admitted. "Who was he?"

Master Wolfe gave her an odd look. "Only the sorcerer who managed to make magic *work*," he said, softly. "Without his work, none of us would be here. He *shared* his secrets."

Emily met his eyes. "What happened before him?"

"Sorcerers would go mad very quickly," Master Wolfe said. "They would start showing signs of magic as they grew older, then rapidly lose control as their powers grew. No one could reason with them...they did terrible things to everyone unlucky enough to be nearby...men were killed, women were enslaved, children were blinded merely for laughs. Smart villagers killed magicians as soon as they began showing signs of power, which didn't make matters any better. But what choice did they have?"

"None," Emily said, quietly.

"None," Master Wolfe agreed. "You don't know any of this?"

"I had a very sheltered upbringing," Emily said.

Master Wolfe frowned. "Your tutor did you no favors," he said. "But then, teaching women to use magic is frowned upon."

He went on before Emily could ask why. "Master Myrddin was the first to work out how to control and channel magic to prevent accidents," he said. "He devised the first true spells and taught them to others. In his later years, he would walk from village to village, taking magical children and teaching them how to control their powers. Those magicians, in turn, taught others."

Emily considered it for a long moment. She *had* heard of Myrddin, she recalled now, but only as a throwaway line in *Life of Whitehall*. Offhand, she couldn't remember if he'd been mentioned in any of the other history books she'd read. But then, there were so many legends about the time that it was impossible to tell just how much was true and how much had been added later. Lord Whitehall might well have overshadowed his former master.

"I see," she said, finally. *Necromancy* drove its practitioners insane, but she'd never heard of other magicians going mad. And yet, all of the older magicians were a little erratic. Lady Barb had even suggested that *Void* was dangerously unstable. "I didn't know any of this."

"Then I suggest you learn," Master Wolfe said. He gave her a reassuring smile. "You're part of our commune now."

He frowned down at his notes. "The spell structure will have to be built up, piece by piece," he said. "Putting something so...so *big*...together would be impossible, even for us. I'm going to have to give this a great deal of thought. The binding we've placed on the nexus point may not last if we start fiddling with it."

"Channel the power elsewhere," Emily suggested. "Make it work for you."

She closed her eyes in thought. It wouldn't be *hard* to make one of her batteries—she'd practically *have* to make one of her batteries to expend her power, unless Whitehall kept her busy casting spells. They could channel the power from the nexus directly into a pocket dimension, then use it to power...something. But they could only do that if they could tame the nexus.

Master Wolfe scowled as there was a sharp knock at the door. "Enter!"

The door opened. A boy—he looked around twelve, although there were faint hints of stubble on his dirty chin—stepped into the room and knelt before Master Wolfe. He didn't look at Emily. "My Lord," he said, "Lord Whitehall wishes to remind Lady Emily that she is to meet him in the courtyard."

"Then she will go to the courtyard," Master Wolfe said. He looked at Emily. "I'll want to go through this in more detail with you later."

"Of course, My Lord," Emily said. If nothing else, she had a feeling that Master Wolfe was well on his way to understanding how to tap and manipulate the nexus point. How long would it be before he started crafting basic wards? "Just call me when you need me."

She turned and nodded to the messenger, who looked back at her with a mixture of curiosity and bitter resentment. It puzzled her until she realized that she'd taken one of the handful of apprenticeship slots, even though she'd only been with the commune for less than a day. The other apprentices would have to wait longer for formal training, thanks to her. She'd be unpopular through no fault of her own. And it was hard to blame the apprentices for feeling that she'd gained an unfair advantage.

But there was nothing she could do about it. Shaking her head, she motioned for the messenger to lead the way and followed him out of the room.

Chapter Six

EMILY HADN'T REALIZED JUST HOW FOUL THE AIR INSIDE THE CASTLE WAS UNTIL SHE STEPPED into the courtyard and took a breath of fresh air. A sweet scent hung on the air, tantalizing her senses as she walked towards where Whitehall and Bernard stood, at the far end of the courtyard. The sky was a brilliant clear blue; she could hear the sounds of birds singing in the trees, not too far away from the castle. And the courtyard itself didn't look too different, although the carriages and carts she recalled from her time were missing. It made her feel as though she was back home.

"Lady Emily," Whitehall greeted her. His voice was strictly formal. "I trust Master Wolfe didn't give you too much of a headache?"

"It was very interesting," Emily said. She saw Bernard's eyes open wide with astonishment and smiled. "I enjoyed it."

"I enjoyed it, *My Master*," Bernard said, although there was no real rebuke in his tone. "You have to be polite."

Whitehall shot him an amused glance, then looked back at Emily. "Before we begin the task of completing your education," he said, as he turned towards the gates, "we have to know where you are. Did your tutor give you any idea of how long it would be before your apprenticeship was declared concluded?"

"I'm afraid not, My Master," Emily said. She still had a year and a half at Whitehall School, but she had a feeling that her experience and his would be incompatible. "He would never be drawn on such matters."

"Most masters would refuse to answer unless they felt the student was on the verge of being ready," Whitehall said. He didn't seem surprised by her response. "How long were you his student?"

Emily frowned. She had no idea what a convincing answer would be.

"Around three years, My Lord," she hedged. "I was never very good at keeping track of time."

"It does feel much longer," Bernard said.

"Disrespectful young man," Whitehall said. He didn't sound angry. Indeed, he sounded rather amused. "The average apprenticeship lasts around five to ten years, unless something goes very wrong early on and both parties agree that the bonds should be dissolved. Bernard has been with me for five years."

Emily glanced at Bernard as they strode through the gate and into the field. The sculptured gardens she recalled were missing; instead, there was a large grassy field that led towards a forest. A handful of horses—smaller than the ones Alassa had taught her to ride—grazed peacefully near the walls, watched by a pair of young boys. She looked back at the castle, feeling her head spin. Whitehall seemed to be what she remembered, but the Arena and the Zoo were also missing. She wondered, vaguely, when they'd been built.

"Don't worry," Bernard whispered, as Whitehall motioned for them to stop. "He's not going to push you *too* hard."

"I'm glad to hear it," Emily whispered back. She was nervous, despite herself. "What does he want me to do?"

"*He* wants you to copy *his* spells," Whitehall said, sternly. Emily flushed. Whitehall's hearing was evidently better than she'd assumed. "Do what I do."

He held up his right hand and cast a fireball spell, throwing it down the grassy field and straight into a tree. Emily shuddered—the spell leaked badly, by her standards—and watched as the tree shuddered, then tumbled to the ground. Lady Barb had taught her to use similar spells to produce firewood, if one was in a hurry, but she'd never had to use it for real.

"Try it," Whitehall ordered.

"Yes, My Lord," Emily said.

She braced herself, wondering if she should try to mess up the spellwork. Whitehall's fireball had looked odd, wavering backwards and forwards as if it had been permanently on the verge of exploding or simply flickering out of existence. Indeed, there had been something remarkably *oily* about the way the fire had moved. And it had leaked *mana* in all directions...

Bad habit, she reminded herself, as she cast the spell. *Professor Lombardi would rap my hands.*

The fireball lanced across the field and struck a tree, sending it crashing to the ground. It was hard to be sure, but she thought Whitehall looked impressed. *Her* fireball had been a *real* fireball. Whitehall turned slightly, lifted his hand and threw a second fireball of his own. It flew barely twenty yards before it exploded outwards and vanished. The spell simply hadn't held together very long.

"See how far you can throw the fireball," Whitehall ordered.

"Yes, My Lord," Emily said.

She tossed the second fireball and watched, feeling a mixture of pride and sadness, as it covered fifty yards before exploding. Whitehall was powerful—she could sense his power even from five yards away—but he didn't have the skill Professor Lombardi and Lady Barb had hammered into her. How could he? She'd been the beneficiary of hundreds of years of spell research and development in the school he'd founded.

"Not bad," Whitehall said.

Emily heard Bernard gasp behind her. Not bad? She'd thrown a fireball further than his master. She smiled at the thought, then looked at Whitehall. He was studying her with a contemplative expression that bothered her. It was one thing to outdo his apprentice, she realized dully, but what if she outdid *him*? He might not take that very kindly at all.

"Not bad," Whitehall repeated. "Let's see what else you can do."

Emily held back, as much as she could, as he showed her a handful of other spells. There was nothing subtle about his magic, no hint that he understood the spells he used; he was powerful, true, but he was wasting a great deal of his magic. She rather suspected he was far more powerful than she was—he might actually be stronger than Sergeant Miles or Professor Lombardi—yet he was draining his reserves at a terrifying rate. If she had to fight him, she might even be able to lure him into expending power fast enough to allow her to win.

"You don't seem to be able to fly," Whitehall observed, nearly two hours later. "Is there a reason for that?"

"My master never taught me, My Lord," Emily said. "Can *you* fly?"

Whitehall levitated himself into the air and looked down at her. "It's not a hard skill to learn," he said. "But it requires a great deal of concentration."

"And magic," Bernard put in. "I have never been able to master it."

And you could be knocked out of the sky easily, Emily added, silently. *A single spell—or a simple ward—would be enough to send you plummeting to your death.*

"I will teach you," Whitehall assured her, vaguely. He gave her a sharp look. "Let's see what else you can do."

Emily was sweating, hard, by the time he finally stopped showing her spells and inviting her to try them for herself. His spells were simply too crude for her to duplicate easily, not when conserving her power had been beaten into her from the day she'd started. Whitehall seemed to push the limitations of spellware through raw power. He could transfigure something, if he tried, but it took so much power that she suspected he'd prefer to avoid it.

"You're holding back," Whitehall said. He gave her a sardonic look. "Do you know what the penalty is for lying to your master?"

"I'm not lying," Emily protested.

"You're holding back," Whitehall said. "And that *is* a form of lying."

He met her eyes. "You don't have to worry about Bernard," he added. "I assure you his ego will survive meeting someone better than him."

Emily glanced at Bernard, who shrugged. "It does happen," Bernard said. "Robin is better than me at many things."

Whitehall's expression darkened. "And many of those things are forbidden," he said. "How many times do I have to remind you of that, My Apprentice?"

Demons, Emily thought. She shivered, even though it was a warm sunny day. There wasn't a cloud in the sky. *Bernard wants to play with demons.*

"I understand your feelings, My Master," Bernard said.

"But you do not agree," Whitehall stated. "Consider it incentive to learn."

Bernard smiled. "That is what you said about dueling with stronger opponents, My Master," he said. "Learning to *lose* is important."

Emily smiled. Sergeant Miles had said something similar, long ago.

Lord Whitehall looked at her. "Your tutor clearly saw remarkable promise in you," he said, seriously. "Enough, perhaps, to ignore the curse."

"The curse," Emily repeated. "*What* curse?"

Whitehall frowned. "You do not...ah, you *wouldn't* have been told," he said. "Women who use magic are cursed."

"I am not cursed," Emily said, flatly. Her temper flared. "Do you refrain from teaching women magic for fear they will be better than you?"

Bernard started to laugh, but stopped when Whitehall tossed him a sharp look. Emily wondered, suddenly, if she'd crossed a line, then decided it didn't matter. She needed to know what the curse was, if there *was* a curse. *Her* Whitehall was split evenly between male and female students. There was certainly no suggestion that any of the female students were *cursed*. They had the same chances as their male counterparts.

"Women with the gift are needed to bear children," Whitehall said, quietly. "Magic is a rare gift and it does not always breed true."

Emily stared at him. "I don't understand."

"Women who use magic openly cannot have children," Whitehall explained. "They...they lose the ability to have children or care for them."

"That makes no sense," Emily breathed.

"No female magician has ever had children," Whitehall said. "My daughter wants to learn magic, but if I teach her I will deprive her of the chance to have children of her own."

Emily considered the problem for a moment. Whitehall was wrong. She *knew* he was wrong. Fulvia had been a powerful magician and *she'd* had children. And she was hardly the only female magician Emily knew who was also a mother. There was no way so many girls would be invited to study at Whitehall if learning magic cost them the chance to have children. But Whitehall clearly believed it was true.

She looked up at him. "How many female magicians have you met?"

"You're the most powerful witch I've encountered," Whitehall said, flatly.

Emily met his eyes. "How *many* witches have you encountered?"

"I've encountered a few women who were able to do basic spells," Whitehall told her. "None of them had children. And I have never heard, in all my travels, of a woman who was both a witch and a mother."

"It doesn't make sense," Emily protested.

She tossed it over and over in her head, thinking hard. Master Wolfe had told her that the early magicians had rapidly turned into monsters...had they only been men? Or were female magicians killed quicker? She could believe it—as horrible as it seemed, male children were often regarded as more important than female children. And yet, she hadn't learned anything to suggest that magicians had trouble conceiving. Caleb's mother had five children.

Her face fell as she remembered her boyfriend. She'd left him in bed when she'd been summoned...what had happened to him? Would she be back before he realized she was gone? Or would she overshoot the mark by days or weeks?

"Your master should have told you," Whitehall said, gently. "He should have offered you the choice."

It took a moment for Emily to realize that he'd misinterpreted her expression. He thought that she was mourning the loss of her children, the children he thought she could never have...not wondering what had happened to the world she'd left behind. Cold anger flared through her, driven by rage and bitter grief. To deny his daughter the chance to learn...

"You didn't offer your daughter the choice," she snarled. She, of all people, ought to have known better. The past wasn't a long-lost paradise. "If Julianne wants to learn magic, why don't you let her?"

"Because girls with the gift are badly outnumbered by the boys," Whitehall said. "We cannot afford to lose someone who can bear magical children."

That's not a problem back home, Emily thought, sourly. *But if there really are so few magicians here, he might have a point...*

She closed her eyes for a long moment. Julianne wasn't mentioned in any of the books, as far as she could remember. She'd just fallen out of history, like so many others. It didn't matter, she supposed, if Julianne learned to use her magic or not. Whatever happened to her had *already* happened, from Emily's point of view. And yet, she was an individual in her own right, a living breathing person.

Bernard coughed. "*Can* you bear children?"

Emily colored, angrily. "I assume so," she said. She certainly had no reason to assume there was anything wrong with her reproductive system. None of her medical checks at Whitehall had shown any problems. "And Julianne should be able to bear them too."

She scowled. She'd never really *considered* the idea of having children, even after she'd started her first serious relationship. Her mother had soured her on the idea of being a mother herself. And yet, she knew Caleb wanted children. She'd be the mother...

Unless I never get home, she thought, morbidly. A year ago, she wouldn't have believed she could have real feelings for a young man, but now...the thought of losing him was unappealing. *How long will Caleb wait for me before he finds someone else?*

Whitehall cleared his throat. "Perhaps we should discuss something more relevant to your apprenticeship," he said, stiffly. "There is definitely something odd about your techniques."

"I use less power," Emily said. She was silently glad he'd seen fit to change the subject. "I think you use too much."

"Explain," Whitehall ordered.

Emily took a moment to gather her thoughts. "You're a strong man carrying a...a very heavy object to and fro," she said, finally. It was a fairly good analogy, although it did have its weaknesses. "I'm placing the object on a wheelbarrow and pushing it to and fro. We're both accomplishing the same thing, but I'm using less energy to do it."

"Which gives you more power to use for other things," Bernard observed. "Could you teach me?"

"*No*," Whitehall said, sharply.

Bernard looked down. "But Master..."

"No," Whitehall repeated. "Learning magic from two different magicians is likely to complicate your studies."

He had a point, Emily suspected. Given how crude his spells were, there was a good chance that his training wasn't compatible with any of the other masters.

Master Chambers might be able to cast his own fireballs, but they'd be very different from Lord Whitehall's. That wasn't a problem in the future—she'd had no difficulty studying charms in both Whitehall and Mountaintop—yet it was clearly a problem now. If she taught Bernard something—anything—it might make it harder for him to learn from his master.

"Yes, Master," Bernard said, reluctantly.

"You can experiment on your own, after your apprenticeship is complete," Whitehall told him, gently. "Right now, you have to learn from me."

He gave Emily a long look. "There isn't much more I can teach you, without the oaths," he said. "Did you really enjoy spending time with Master Wolfe?"

"It was interesting," Emily said. "He has a number of thoughts and concepts that reminded me of my tutor."

"You will have more time to spend with him," Whitehall said. "He stayed up all night studying the spells you used to bind the nexus point. I couldn't stop him raving about them this morning. Your master must have been a remarkable man."

"He was," Emily said.

"He's dead," Whitehall reminded her. "You are no longer bound by any of the oaths you swore to him."

"I don't know what will happen if I break them," Emily said, quietly.

"If he's dead, nothing will happen to you," Whitehall said. "Even a vow of perpetual secrecy loses its power over time. But you're right. You shouldn't take too many chances."

Emily nodded, relieved. Breaking a magical oath was impossible, as long as one *knew* one was breaking the oath. They could only be abandoned by believing, truly believing, that the oath was no longer valid. That, it seemed, was true in Whitehall's time too.

"I'm sorry," she said.

"Don't worry about it," Whitehall told her. "I swore oaths to my master too."

He paused, staring towards the forest as a handful of young men emerged. "But I do think we should talk about your techniques at some point."

"Yes, Master," Emily said.

She watched the young men hurrying towards the castle, carrying a number of dead animals over their shoulders. One of them was carrying a wild boar and grinning hugely from ear to ear. Emily understood. Wild boars were tasty, she had to admit, but killing one without magic was difficult. They were savage creatures. Sergeant Miles had warned his students not to mess around if they had to hunt for food.

But at least we'll have something more to eat, she thought. *We need food to power our magic.*

"Dinner," Bernard said, cheerfully.

"One would hope so," Whitehall said. He looked at Bernard. "I need to think. Take Emily and get some lunch, then join the teams sweeping the upper floors. I'll restart your lessons tomorrow."

"Yes, My Master," Bernard said. "Do you want me to bring you some food?"

"I have to speak to Alfred," Whitehall said. He shook his head. "We'll come down and get something ourselves, afterwards."

Bernard bowed, then motioned for Emily to follow him.

Chapter Seven

"I THINK YOU IMPRESSED HIM," BERNARD SAID, AS HE LED THE WAY INTO THE DINING HALL. There was still no sign of any tables. "I never saw him quite so much at a loss for words before."

"Thanks," Emily said, dryly.

She saw Julianne on the other side of the room, talking to a pale-faced older man and waved to her. Julianne nodded back as Bernard sat down on the rug and waited, looking impatient. Moments later, a serving girl hurried over with two bowls of soup, bowing deeply as she presented them and withdrawing as soon as she could. Emily watched her go—clearly, the tradition of treating servants well hadn't started yet— and then tested her soup before starting to drink. It tasted faintly oily, a taste that grew stronger with every mouthful. She decided, reluctantly, that she didn't want to know what had gone into the soup.

Probably the remains of an animal, she thought, wryly. Sergeant Miles had insisted that every last part of a slain animal was useful for *something.* Boiling the bones added flavor to stock, if nothing else. *The legs, perhaps, or the bones.*

"Your tutor must have been *very* capable," Bernard said, after he put his bowl aside. "I've never seen spells like yours."

"He was a good teacher," Emily agreed. "I've never seen spells like yours either."

"Master Whitehall says I need to grow older before I can use some of his spells," Bernard said, ruefully. "I just don't have the reserves to make them work."

Because you can't redesign the spells to use less power, Emily thought. Bernard was strong, perhaps stronger than she'd been a year ago, but his spells were as crude as his master's. *The spellwork you dismiss as boring is the key to becoming a more powerful and dangerous magician.*

Bernard nodded over at two of the other apprentices, who didn't look pleased to see either him or Emily. "It could be worse," he said. "We could have to *wait* for our education."

"They might wait too long," Emily mused. She had no idea what would happen if someone's gift wasn't used, but she had a feeling it wouldn't be pleasant. "The old system is doomed."

Bernard looked up at her. "I beg your pardon?"

"You have one apprentice to one master," Emily commented. "And here you have umpteen apprentices per master, some of whom may never get a complete education."

"They *can't* get a complete education without a master," Bernard pointed out. "They *need* one-on-one education."

"You could also teach them in groups," Emily countered. Whitehall School had taught a number of students at the same time. The largest class she recalled had had twenty students, all learning from a single teacher. "But that would be difficult with your magic."

"Yes, it would be," Bernard said. He rubbed his forehead. "Master Whitehall took weeks to show me how to cast spells safely."

"I learned quickly," Emily said. "But I think I started with smaller spells."

She leaned forward. "What can you do?"

Bernard looked back. "What do you mean?"

"I saw you cast a handful of spells," Emily said. "Could you turn me into a frog?"

"Of course not," Bernard said. He shook his head firmly. "That's *advanced* magic, you know. Even Master Whitehall would have problems doing it so casually."

And first-year students at Whitehall can turn their fellows into frogs or mice or small bedside ornaments, Emily thought. *It only took me a week or two to master some really dangerous spells.*

She contemplated the problem for a long moment. "What *can* you do?"

"I can use my magic to fight or defend myself," Bernard said. "Or defend others, if necessary. What *else* do I need to do?"

He frowned. "What else *should* I be able to do?"

Emily leaned forward. "Can you *heal* a wounded man?"

"No," Bernard said. "Lord Gila was once a great healer, but he's now advancing towards utter madness. His poor apprentice will take his place once his mind snaps completely."

"And you can't heal yourself," Emily mused. She'd have to learn what Lord Gila had been able to do and compare it to what she knew from her own time. "Did you ever think to ask him to teach you the skill?"

"Master Whitehall would never have permitted it," Bernard said.

Emily nodded in irritation. None of the tutors in Whitehall School would have been upset if their students had asked other tutors for advice, certainly not when the other tutors were specialists in their fields. But here...Lord Whitehall had made it clear that she wasn't to teach Bernard anything, not as long as he was Lord Whitehall's student. Afterwards...she shook her head. She had no idea if she'd be remaining in the past long enough for Bernard to graduate or not.

"I should talk to Lord Gila," she mused. "See just what he could do."

"He's on the verge of madness," Bernard said. "Talk to his former apprentice, if you must."

"Understood," Emily said. She frowned, trying to remember what other skills she took for granted. "Can you work alchemy?"

Bernard frowned. "What's alchemy?"

"Tapping the magical proprieties of plants and animals," Emily said. "Brewing potions to help people...?"

"No," Bernard said. "I didn't even know it was possible."

Emily frowned. He didn't know...alchemy had been *invented* at Whitehall. Or so history said. Was it something else she was meant to introduce? She had hardly been a stellar student, but she knew enough to get them started. She'd just have to see if she could find the ingredients and then brew a potion or two, just to prove the concept was workable.

And that won't be easy, she thought. She knew where to find *some* ingredients—Professor Thande and Sergeant Miles had taught her a little about harvesting supplies—but Whitehall School had sat at the center of a trade network that had spanned the entire continent. It was quite likely that she'd never be able to find *any* of the rarer ingredients she'd used in her first year. *But I should at least try.*

"It is possible," she said. "I'll have to show you."

Bernard eyed her. "Your tutor taught you this...this *alchemy?*"

"Yes," Emily said, flatly. "He was a man of varied interests."

"So it would seem," Bernard said. He sounded envious. "My master is rarely interested in anything other than his magic."

Emily nodded, then spent the next twenty minutes bouncing questions off him. Bernard knew nothing of teleporting, nor subtle magic; he certainly didn't understand how the runic alphabet worked or how to use it to craft spells. He talked about a couple of ceremonies that sounded like rituals, but they bore so little resemblance to anything Emily knew that she had no idea what to make of them. And his ward-crafting was appallingly weak.

I could punch though his wards by brute force, she thought. *But I could also break them by cracking through the weak points.*

But there were also some oddities in what he knew. He knew how to craft illusions, but they didn't seem to behave like the illusions she knew; he understood how to influence a person's mind, yet not how to avoid doing real damage while tampering. Whitehall had even taught him how to shield his mind without using magic, just in case he was captured and deliberately drained by his captors. Emily had heard of similar techniques, but she'd never had to use them. Void had made sure of that.

"We should talk about something else," Bernard said, finally. "I feel a headache coming on."

Emily nodded, feeling a glimmer of sympathy. She wouldn't have enjoyed the interrogation either. Whatever Whitehall said, she would have been surprised if Bernard hadn't been a little embarrassed—and humiliated—by watching her out-class him so effortlessly. Perhaps, by their standards, she was practically at master-level already. And if Whitehall spent more time with Emily, he'd have less time for his apprentice.

And that would relegate him to join the others, Emily thought. *He'd hate that.*

"I think it's time you answered a different question," she said, sternly. "Why did the commune flee to Whitehall? Who was chasing you?"

"We don't know," Bernard said.

Emily stared at him. "You don't know?"

Bernard took a breath. "It's a long story," he said. "Really."

"Then start at the beginning, go on to the end and then stop," Emily said. Professor Lombardi had said that to her, after she'd messed up badly in her second year. "Who's chasing you, and why?"

For a moment, she thought Bernard wasn't going to answer. And then he started to talk, so quietly that she had to struggle to hear him.

"I was born in a small town," he said, gently. "I started to show signs of magic at twelve, so my parents sent me to the Gathering. Master Whitehall met me and tested me, then offered me an apprenticeship with the commune. We had a small village to ourselves, deep in the forest: masters, apprentices, and servants. Master Whitehall taught me how to control my powers..."

He broke off for a long, chilling moment. "The commune was a lot smaller then," he added, slowly. "There were just four masters and four apprentices. But there were other villages nearby, so we would travel to them or they would come to us...and, of course, there was the yearly Gathering. Did your tutor never take you?"

Emily shook her head. It was possible, quite possible, that Bernard's Gathering was the start of the tradition she'd encountered in the future, but there was no way to know for sure.

"You should have gone," Bernard said. "There were masters and apprentices from all over the kingdom, gathered together to exchange news. But there were rumors too, rumors of...*things*...attacking magicians. Villages being destroyed, masters being killed...apprentices being left to roam free. We didn't want to believe them, but they were spreading too rapidly for our comfort. I recall Lord Alfred summoning demon after demon, trying to glean some hint of what was going on from them."

He paused, his face darkening with remembered horror. "Seven months ago, more or less, we went to a village that had welcomed us before," he continued. "It had been destroyed, houses smashed flat and temples pounded into rubble. There was no sign of any bodies, no sign of who had attacked a magical settlement and destroyed it. We didn't know who to blame."

Emily frowned. "Mundanes? People without magic?"

"The king has banned the hunting of magicians," Bernard said. "As long as we take magical children away from their families, they have as little to do with us as possible."

He shook his head. "It was only the first village to die. Another died a month later, even though the masters had tightened their defenses; two more died afterwards, with no clue as to who was doing the attacking. And then a number of refugees ran into our village, apprentices and camp followers from another nearby village. They claimed that the village had been attacked by monsters."

Emily frowned. "Monsters?"

"Monsters," Bernard repeated. "And then we were attacked ourselves. The defenses were broken with very little effort and so we had to flee. I saw them, but... but I can't remember what they looked like. No one can. They just came and killed and destroyed and hunted..."

His voice trailed off. Emily forced herself to think. If he couldn't remember what the creatures had *looked* like...it suggested subtle magic or a very powerful and unusual glamour. And yet, subtle magic worked best when its victim had no idea he was under attack. Breaking the spell—by hitting the target directly—would ruin the effect.

"We fled," Bernard said. "Masters Poe and Wallace talked about making a stand, but it was useless. They were crushed. We picked up more masters, more apprentices, but we didn't know where to go. In the end, Lord Alfred summoned a demon and put the question to it."

"And the demon pointed you here," Emily mused.

The thought made her smile, humorlessly. She'd heard plenty of stories about Lord Alfred, but most of them had been badly exaggerated. Even *Professor Locke* had believed that Lord Alfred's reputation had grown in the telling, something that was genuinely surprising when Professor Locke had believed that the ancients had possessed all kinds of long-forgotten magics. And if Lord Alfred had been a DemonMaster...

"It did," Bernard said. "We thought we'd gathered enough supplies, but we were on the verge of starvation when we finally reached the castle."

He frowned. "How did you get here?"

"We walked," Emily said, shortly. "Getting here was not easy."

She rubbed her forehead, feeling her temples start to pound. She needed time to think. She'd assumed that the commune had been fleeing mundanes, but it was clear that things were a little more complex than she'd thought. If the creatures were truly inhuman, they might well have some connection to the Faerie. The Faerie War couldn't be *that* far off. And if they were hunting magicians specifically...

But they didn't follow the commune to Whitehall, she thought. *Were they afraid to go too close to the castle?*

Bernard met her eyes. "How many people accompanied you to the castle?"

"Just me and my tutor," Emily lied. She shook her head. "I don't want to talk about it."

"You should," Bernard said, earnestly. "It might help you come to terms with losing him."

Emily sighed. Talking about it was the *last* thing she wanted to do. If she was caught in a lie, she would be in real trouble. But she didn't dare tell the truth.

"Let him rest in peace," she said, instead. "Were those creatures going after mundanes too?"

"I don't believe so," Bernard said. "But we rarely spoke to mundanes."

Emily cocked her head. "You never went back to see your family?"

"They wouldn't want to see me," Bernard said. "Having a magician in the family isn't a good thing, Emily. They see it as a sign of tainted blood. My father...my father wondered if he was truly my father. Magicians...don't have good reputations when it comes to women."

"Lord Wolfe said that magicians had a tendency to go mad," Emily said. And Bernard had said that Lord Gila was on the verge of going mad. "Is that what they meant?"

"Among other things," Bernard said. "If I didn't have my father's nose--" he pushed his finger against the tip of his nose "--I would wonder if someone had seduced my mother nine months before I was born."

"There are paternity tests," Emily commented. "Can't you check...?"

"I have no idea how," Bernard said. He looked down at the rug for a long moment. "And even if I did know, I wouldn't *want* to know. My father discarded me the day my magic first started to reveal itself. Master Whitehall is my father now."

"I'm sorry to hear that," Emily said, seriously.

She rubbed her forehead again. There was something about the whole explanation that didn't make sense, something she was missing, but she was too tired to put her finger on it. It was easy to believe that a mundane family might discard a magician child—Frieda had certainly been discarded and Imaiqah might have gone the same way—yet something was nagging at the back of her mind. What was it?

Bernard looked back at her. "Tell me about your family."

Emily winced, inwardly. She should have seen that question coming.

"Father died when I was very young," she said. She had no idea what had happened to her *real* father, but she'd certainly never seen him again. "Mother remarried. My stepfather didn't like me very much, so...things were a little rough. And then my tutor found me and took me in."

"That was lucky," Bernard said. "You would have died in the cold, if he threw you out."

Emily nodded. Her stepfather had been thoroughly unpleasant, but a stepfather from the Nameless World might well have been worse. No one would have given a damn if he'd kicked an unwanted girl-child out of his house or sold her to a passing merchant or a brothel, particularly if he'd had children of his own. The cold logic of survival, in the Cairngorms, dictated no less. Old folks sometimes walked outside to die—or were thrown out—because their families could no longer afford to feed them. It still horrified her to see just how casually some were sacrificed so that others could live.

"He gave you a good grounding in magic," Bernard added. "I was surprised he didn't show you more."

"He was never interested in socializing," Emily said. "If he hadn't sensed me, I suspect he would have remained alone for the rest of his life."

"I see," Bernard said. "And did he...?"

It took Emily a moment to realize what he meant. "He wasn't that sort of person," she said, flushing. *None* of her tutors had ever shown *that* sort of interest in her. "He was like a father to me."

Bernard looked relieved. "I'm sorry."

He sighed as he rose to his feet. "We should go find Robin and help clear the corridors," he said. "A few hours of clearing away the nastier traps should keep us on our toes."

Emily nodded, happy that he wasn't asking any more questions. Hopefully, he wouldn't pry further into her cover story. She doubted it would survive if he kept poking away at it, looking for discrepancies. She simply knew too little about her new environment to tell convincing lies.

And the more I lie to them, she thought as she rose and followed him, *the harder it will be to keep everything straight.*

Chapter Eight

"BE CAREFUL," ROBIN CALLED, AS THEY WALKED UP THE STAIRS. HE STOOD ABOVE THEM, stroking his chin thoughtfully. "There's something very nasty at the top."

Emily frowned as she sensed the swirling magic. A young apprentice stood at the top of the stairs, trembling like a leaf. He wasn't frozen, she realized; his feet were stuck to the ground. She wondered if he'd had the sense to try to remove his shoes and escape, leaving them trapped, but a closer look told her it would be futile. Bending over to try to undo his shoes would merely trap his hands too.

"Bastards," Bernard said. "Who the hell puts a trap like that at the top of the stairs?"

"Someone who wanted us to be caught," Robin said, dryly. He gave Emily a sardonic smile. "Do you think you can break the spell?"

Emily frowned as she reached the top of the stairs. The spell—the booby trap— was very much like spells she'd seen in martial magic, although it looked as though it shouldn't have endured for very long. And yet, it was more advanced than anything she'd seen from Whitehall and Bernard. She couldn't help wondering if it was actually drawing power from the nexus point. There didn't seem to be any other source of power.

"I think so," she said. She allowed herself a moment to study the spellwork. A simple cancellation spell ought to be enough—indeed, she was surprised Robin and the other apprentice hadn't already tried. Unless they didn't know how to cancel spells...it was possible, she supposed. None of their spells seemed very well crafted. "Let me try?"

Robin shrugged, expansively. "Why not?"

Emily gave him a dark look. She had the feeling she was being tested—and judged—but there was no way she could simply leave the apprentice stuck permanently. If Whitehall and his commune didn't know how to cancel spells, they'd have to use brute force to destroy the trap...which might injure or kill the victim. She cast a basic cancellation spell and watched, holding her breath, as the trap faded back into the ether. The apprentice jerked free a moment later and darted back down the stairs.

"He thought he was going to be trapped permanently," Robin said. He sounded amused, rather than concerned. "I *told* him not to take anything for granted."

"Good advice," Bernard said. He looked at Emily. "How did you *do* that?"

"All spells have a weak point," Emily said, vaguely. "Lord Wolfe would probably be able to explain better than I."

Bernard frowned. "Can you teach me how to do that?"

"Maybe," Emily said. She wasn't sure when such spells had been invented. Lord Wolfe might well be able to duplicate it though, once he heard what she'd done. "We can take a look at it later, if you like."

Robin grinned, showing teeth. "We just broke into this floor," he said. He pulled a wooden stave from his knapsack, pressed it against his torch until it caught light and then passed it to Bernard. "There was a particularly unpleasant trap down at the bottom of the stairs. Master Drake had to untangle it for us."

He must have thrust his magic into direct contact with the trap, Emily reasoned. *She could have done that—she* had *done that, during exams—but why take the risk? Their magic seems to be far more brute-force than ours.*

"And now we have a whole new world to explore," Bernard said. He grinned back at Robin, then motioned down the corridor. "Shall we?"

Emily followed the two men as they inched down the corridor, checking constantly for other booby traps. Whoever had last occupied the castle, she decided, as a series of traps were uncovered and disarmed, had to have been both skillful and paranoid—and, perhaps, a little insane. There were traps scattered everywhere, but there didn't seem to be any rhyme or reason to their placement. One was lurking behind a door, while another was hidden on a window frame or by a fireplace. Some of them were certain to catch a mundane who wandered into the castle; others were all too likely to be nothing more than wasted effort.

Bernard put her thoughts into words. "Who hides a booby trap up a chimney?"

Someone who doesn't want a visit from Santa Claus, Emily thought.

Robin snorted. "Someone could sneak through the chimneys if they wanted to pass unnoticed," he said. He peered up the shaft thoughtfully. "They'd climb up to where this chimney merges with another, then crawl back down into the next room."

"Pretty uncomfortable if there's a fire in the grate," Bernard pointed out.

Emily suspected that Robin was right, but she kept her thoughts to herself. King Randor's castle was *crammed* with secret passageways, some intended to keep the servants hidden from their lords and masters, others designed to allow the royal family to move around unseen. Using a chimney struck her as risky, but the shaft was easily large enough to allow her to scramble up, if there were enough handholds. Dropping back down into the next room wouldn't be too difficult, either.

Unless there was a fire, she thought, wryly. *The smoke would make navigating the chimney difficult.*

It was hard to believe that she was in the castle that would eventually become Whitehall School. The rooms they swept for traps were completely empty, nothing left behind to betray their original function; the corridors were bare stone, without even the omnipresent runes she'd seen on the lower levels. Robin and Bernard chatted as they walked, but they started to speak in hushed tones as their torches began to flicker and die. The atmosphere grew more oppressive the further they moved into the castle.

"We need better lighting," Robin said, as his torch died completely. "I don't know who built this place, but they didn't know anything about lighting a castle."

Emily had her doubts. A mind capable of creating the booby traps they'd disarmed would certainly be capable of crafting a light globe, with or without tapping the nexus point. They shouldn't have had any problems lighting the castle. She was tempted to cast a spell herself, but she held back. Robin might have a different solution in mind.

Bernard looked doubtful as the shadows grew and lengthened. "Are you thinking what I think you're thinking?"

Robin smirked. "I don't know," he said. "Are you thinking what I think you're thinking I'm thinking?"

He reached into his knapsack and produced a small, leather-bound book. Emily recoiled in shock as Robin sat down, unable to hide her reaction to the pervasive aura of *evil* surrounding the book. It rolled off it in waves, a chilling sense that even *touching* it would mean eternal damnation. She'd had bad reactions before, touching books she *knew* to have something to do with the dark arts, but this was terrifying. Merely looking at the tome made her want to wash herself thoroughly.

"Master Whitehall will not approve," Bernard said, as Robin opened the book. "He..."

"He isn't *my* master," Robin said. He held up the book, showing a blood-red rune dominating the first page. "And *my* master approves of demons."

"That's a Book of Pacts," Emily said.

Robin frowned. "You've never seen one before?"

"No," Emily said. Aurelius had made use of demons—he'd even shown Emily books *about* demons—but if he'd had a Book of Pacts, he'd never shown it to her. "I've heard of them, but..."

"Each page is devoted to a single demon," Robin said. He opened the book to a second page, revealing a very different rune. No, Emily recalled; they were *sigils*, not runes. "I summoned each of these demons and bound them to my will, allowing me to call on them whenever I need them to work a particularly complex piece of magic."

"At a price," Bernard said in edged tones. "What do you pay for these spells?"

"A little blood," Robin said. "I have plenty."

Emily blanched. She, of all people, had good reason to know *precisely* what some-one could do with a sample of her blood. Whoever had summoned her down to the nexus chamber and thrust her into the nexus point had worked through all of her protections, even though she'd spent the last four years mustering all the defenses she could. Robin was being careless—hideously careless. She opened her mouth to point out just how many horrible things she could do to him with a drop of his blood, but closed it without speaking. If he didn't know the dangers by now, her words would merely give him ideas.

"And a little of your strength," Bernard said. "Is it worth it?"

"Yes," Robin said. "You spent weeks learning to levitate a single stone into the air, didn't you? I spent an hour learning how to summon a demon and have *it* levitate the stone for me."

He smiled up at Emily. "Lord Whitehall believes that demons are *dangerous*," he said, darkly. "But they are so very useful."

"That's the trap," Bernard said, flatly. But he didn't sound as though he believed his own words. "If the demon is doing everything for you, how will you ever be able to do it for yourself?"

"Demons have shown me how to work spells," Robin said.

Emily frowned. "What spells?"

"A few," Robin said, vaguely. He gave her a challenging look. "I'll show you mine if you show me yours."

Bernard snickered. "Smooth..."

Emily felt her cheeks heat. "It would depend on what spells you have to offer."

"I have a *lot* to offer," Robin said, complacently.

He placed the book on the floor, then drew a small knife from his belt and made a cut on his hand, allowing the blood to drip onto the sigil. Emily felt a sudden surge of magic—*tainted* magic—and stepped backwards sharply until she felt her back pressing against the stone wall. Robin tossed her a mischievous look, then began to chant in a language she didn't recognize. The magic built up rapidly, gathering above the book until it coalesced into a tiny imp. It looked vaguely human—the haze of magic was so strong that it was hard to pick out any details—but the proportions were all wrong. And the sense of *malice* surrounding the creature was terrifyingly strong.

"Well, now," it said. It looked male, insofar as any gender could be assigned to such an odd apparition, but the voice was distinctly female. "I have not seen you in many days."

Emily blanched. *Days?* Not weeks or months or years? Robin called upon this creature regularly? Was he out of his mind?

"I bind you by rod and book, by blood and light," Robin said. Emily looked at him—it was preferable to looking at the demon—and saw a faint sheen of sweat on his forehead. He might act as though it was all a game, but he was clearly nowhere near as confident as he pretended. "I bind you..."

"Come now," the demon said. Its voice became ingratiating. "There's no need for such words between old friends."

"Our way needs to be lit," Robin said. He hunched forward until he was almost squatting in front of the demon. "I require a spell of light."

The demon giggled. "But of course, my son," it said. "And what will you offer in return?"

Robin made another cut on his hand, allowing the blood to rest on his palm. The demon leaned forward and licked the blood. Emily's gorge rose and she turned, hurrying out of the room and down the corridor as the demon's hissing laughter echoed in her ears. The sense of its presence only grew stronger, pervading the atmosphere with something unbearably foul, then it was gone, as if someone had simply flicked a switch. Emily stopped and leaned against the wall, breathing hard. Robin and Master Chambers had to be completely out of their minds. Using anything from that creature would be utterly disastrous.

And a demon led them here, she thought, numbly. She closed her eyes as her body began to shake. *There has to be a nasty sting in the tail somewhere.*

"Emily," Bernard called. "Are you all right?"

Emily forced herself to stand upright, opening her eyes. Bernard was hurrying down the corridor towards her, Robin following at a more sedate pace. The look on his face reminded her of the drug addicts and drunkards she'd seen on the streets, back on Earth. A light globe, flickering and flaring, hung above his head, pulsing brightly enough to make Emily's eyes hurt. It reminded her, all too well, of the light globes she'd tried to create after the duel, when she'd pumped too much power into the spell.

"I've been better," she said, looking at Robin. "How...how can you stand those creatures?"

Robin shrugged. "I was nervous, the first time I summoned a demon," he said. "But I soon got used to calling on them."

He elbowed Bernard. "But *his* master won't let him summon a demon."

"Shut up," Bernard said.

"I could show you how," Robin said. He looked at Emily. "Or you. Do women call on demons?"

"I don't *need* demons," Emily said, tartly. She eyed Robin nervously, unable to comprehend how he could summon and use such creatures. And now...he was acting like someone who'd had far too much to drink. She nodded up at the light globe? "Did it teach you that spell?"

"Yes," Robin said. "It's better than the one my master uses."

Emily eyed the globe doubtfully. It was still brightening and darkening, seemingly at random. She wanted to cast a spell to analyze the spellwork, but she didn't quite dare, not when it would reveal far too much about her to the boys. Robin gave her a wink, then directed the light globe down the next corridor, the pulsing light driving back the shadows.

"I can teach you the spell," he called back. "But it *will* cost you."

Bernard looked sullen as Robin hurried ahead. "It would take me weeks to master such a spell," he said, sourly. Emily would have been surprised if she hadn't seen how clumsy many of Lord Whitehall's spells actually were. "And he gets it in bare *minutes!*"

He strode off down the corridor, leaving Emily staring after him. Bernard wasn't stupid, she knew; how could he envy Robin? But then, she had a feeling that she understood him all too well. Robin appeared to be moving ahead by leaps and bounds, while Bernard was stuck repeating the same spells over and over again until he understood them perfectly. And *her* presence probably didn't help much either, she had to admit. She'd not only distracted Bernard's master from his education, she was both a woman and a superior magician. He would have to be more than human if he didn't resent it, just a little.

But Whitehall is right, Emily thought, as she followed him. *That spell might actually be dangerous. And Robin doesn't even know it!*

Robin was showing off, she realized, as she caught up with the two boys. He was creating a whole string of light globes, one after the other, directing them to hover in the corridors or float into unoccupied rooms. Emily had to resist the temptation to cast her own light globes—better than any Robin could have managed—as she walked into one of the rooms, following the light globes. It was a bare room, like every other chamber in the castle; grimly, she took advantage of being alone to examine the light globe.

Sloppy, she thought, as the spellwork unfolded in front of her. The light globe looked to have been patched together from two different spells, the sort of hodge-podge that would have had Professor Lombardi exploding with rage and demanding expulsions. She doubted that any student at Whitehall would have dared present him with such a poor piece of work. *Sloppy...and dangerous.*

She scowled as she realized just how dangerous it actually was. The spellwork wasn't remotely focused; it worked, she noted, but it was so inefficient that raw magic was spilling in all directions instead of being concentrated on the spell. Robin was wasting his strength and he didn't even *know* it! She dreaded to imagine what it would do to his mind if he kept pumping out so much uncontrolled magic. Void had admitted, to her face, that he'd been ready to kill her if *her* boosted magic had driven her insane. Robin...

He'll become unstable, she thought, angrily. The demon hadn't been particularly subtle, but it hadn't *had* to be subtle. Robin would use the spell gleefully and teach it to others, unaware of the damage it would be doing. *And he'll drive hundreds of others insane.*

"Emily," Bernard called. He sounded...*odd*. "Can you come out here?"

Emily tensed, hastily cancelling her analysis spell. Bernard *definitely* sounded odd. Had something gone wrong already? She readied a couple of defensive spells, then strode through the door, leaving the light globe behind. The spellwork was so mangled that it was impossible to say just how long it would last. Bernard stood outside, looking down the corridor. Julianne Whitehall waited for them at the top of the stairs, looking tired and worn. And yet, the long dress she wore made her look attractive. Emily couldn't help a flicker of envy.

Robin nudged her as Bernard hurried down the corridor. "He needs a chaperone," he said, mischievously. "He can't talk to Julianne alone."

"Oh," Emily said.

"And now you know why he likes you," Robin added. His smile grew wider. "You can watch his master's daughter for him."

Chapter Nine

EMILY FOUND IT HARD TO CONCEAL HER AMUSEMENT AS SHE AND ROBIN FOLLOWED Bernard down the corridor. She doubted that Bernard would try to do anything stupid with Julianne—she was the daughter of one of the most powerful magicians in the world—but she knew just how much could happen by accident. Whitehall had been a young man himself, once upon a time; he wouldn't be too happy at the thought of his apprentice courting his daughter. But what did Julianne herself think about it?

"Julianne," Bernard said. He suddenly sounded very shy. "You're looking good."

Julianne smiled back at him, her eyes flickering from Emily to Robin and back again. Emily knew she wasn't the most observant of people—she'd been the last person to realize that Jade and Alassa had fallen in love—but she thought that Julianne had feelings for Bernard too. It made her wonder just what Bernard thought of Julianne asking her father—begging her father—to be taught magic. Would he approve, if they became husband and wife, or would he refuse to teach his wife himself? He'd want children, wouldn't he?

"We'll just be down the corridor," Emily said. "You can talk in private."

Julianne gave her a look. "You can stay, if you like," she said. "Father..."

Emily nodded, torn between envy and sympathy. To have a father who cared... she'd have given a great deal to have a father who actually cared. But there was a fine line between being caring and being overbearing and most fathers on the Nameless World definitely *were* overbearing. King Randor was a better father to Alassa than Emily's father or stepfather had ever been to her, yet he'd planned to marry his daughter to someone who suited his long-term plans for the kingdom, not someone who suited her.

"Marry me," Bernard said, suddenly. "Julianne..."

A dozen emotions flashed across Julianne's face. Emily found it hard to follow them; Julianne seemed to move from relief to fear, pride to concern. She thought— she still thought—that Julianne had feelings for Bernard, but were they really romantic? Or had she placed him firmly in the friend-zone? She doubted it—friend-zoning wasn't really a thing on the Nameless World—but she had to admit it was possible. Julianne would have a closer relationship with her father's apprentice than she would have with almost anyone else in the commune.

And an apprentice is practically part of the family, Emily thought. *She might not see Bernard in that light at all.*

"I can't," Julianne said, finally. "I've already told you how I feel. My father is not marrying me off without my consent."

Emily frowned. Clearly, she was missing something. Had Whitehall attempted to convince Julianne to marry Bernard? Or was she waiting until Bernard gained his mastery? Or was Emily misreading the situation so badly that she was completely wrong? She wasn't sure how she could ask Julianne, let alone Bernard. Both of them might tell her it was none of her business.

"I can get his consent," Bernard said, earnestly. "He has no reason to disapprove of me."

"But I won't be married off without *my* consent," Julianne said. She turned, slightly. "My father cannot be asked, not yet."

Emily felt Robin nudge her and glanced at him. He beckoned her back down the corridor as Bernard and Julianne talked in low voices, their words rapidly becoming inaudible. Emily wasn't too keen on the idea of being alone with Robin—she couldn't trust anyone who relied on a demon—but she didn't see any polite way to avoid it. As long as Bernard and Julianne were within eyeshot, she would be comfortable enough.

"They've been dancing around one another for the last two years," Robin said. He sounded faintly amused. "He spends half of his time moaning about her."

Emily narrowed her eyes. "And why doesn't she marry him?"

Robin shrugged. "Who can fathom the mind of a woman?"

"Another woman," Emily said, tartly. "Is Bernard as...*inconsiderate*...as you?"

"He keeps promising her the world," Robin said. He shrugged, expressively, ignoring her comment. "Her father should just marry her off to him. She's of good blood, he's a skilled and powerful magician...their children will be great. And we are short on children."

There's more to women than merely producing children, Emily thought, crossly. In her era, male and female wizards were regarded as equals. *But here women aren't permitted to learn magic.*

She leaned against the wall, keeping one eye on Bernard. "What has her father said about it?"

"By custom, he can't say anything until Bernard asks for her hand in marriage," Robin said, bluntly. "And then he can either give his consent or refuse."

Emily frowned. "And what would happen if he refused?"

"I imagine Bernard would be sent away," Robin said. "It would be quite awkward all around."

He looked up at Emily. "Do you have a father?"

"Not among the living," Emily said. Her father wouldn't be born for the next eight hundred years, give or take a few centuries. "Why do you ask?"

Robin smiled. "Who would someone ask if they wanted your hand in marriage?"

"Me," Emily said, flatly.

"A woman as pretty as you should be married already," Robin said. "Do you not have anyone?"

"I don't know," Emily said. Caleb, too, wouldn't be born for another eight hundred years or thereabouts. She felt her cheeks redden as she realized that Robin was trying to flirt with her, poorly. "I..."

"You don't know," Robin repeated. "How can you not know?"

"I had someone," Emily said. It was true enough. "But I haven't seen him for a very long time."

"Then he's probably married off by now," Robin said. "You don't need to worry about him."

Emily shook her head. If there was no chance of getting home, she'd have to admit that she would never see Caleb again. There was no hope of him jumping back in time, not when neither he nor anyone else—save for the person who had shoved her into the nexus—knew what had happened to her. She'd turn to dust long before Caleb was even born. But then, she wasn't about to give up so quickly. She had an idea. And given time and access to the nexus point, she could make it work.

"He won't have been faithful," Robin pointed out. "How long were you trapped in the castle?"

Emily scowled at him. "And what would you suggest?"

"Find someone else," Robin said. He leaned forward, parting his lips as if he were inviting her to kiss him. "I think it would be for the best, don't you?"

"No," Emily snapped.

She found herself unsure of just what she should say, let alone do. Robin was flirting with her, he was flirting clumsily with her...and she had no idea how to handle it. She didn't like him personally—or at least she didn't like the stench of demons that surrounded him—but what should she do, if there was no hope of getting back to the future? Find a husband and get married—or walk into the shadows and stay out of history?

"You have a duty to the community," Robin said, softly. "If you can have children..."

Emily turned and stalked down the corridor to where Bernard and Julianne were standing together, just an inch too close for friends. They *did* like each other, Emily realized, but she thought she understood Julianne's concerns. If her father approved the match, it would become compulsory soon enough. Julianne would lose what little freedom she had to a husband who might not be so tolerant of her wish to learn magic.

"Lady Emily," Julianne said. "There will be a bath for us before supper, if you would like to join me."

"That would be good," Emily said. She *knew* she was grimy. The only reason no one had commented on it, she suspected, was because everyone else stank worse. "Where do we go?"

"It's been set up next to the kitchens," Julianne said. She glanced past Emily and looked at Bernard. "If I go grab some clothes for us, can you show her to the kitchens?"

"Of course," Bernard said.

Emily watched Julianne go, then glanced at Bernard. He had an oddly mournful expression on his face. "She's beautiful, isn't she?"

"And smart, too," Emily said. She wasn't sure *just* how smart Julianne actually was, but her father was *brilliant*. And very well-connected. "Do you *like* her?"

Robin cleared his throat, loudly. "Of course he likes her!"

Bernard scowled. "Go tell Master Whitehall just how much of the corridors we've cleared," he ordered. "I'll show Emily to the kitchens."

Emily looked at him as they hurried down the stairs. "Do you want her to learn magic?"

"I don't know," Bernard admitted. His face heated. "You know about the curse, don't you?"

"You were there when I was told about it," Emily said. "Would you *want* her to learn magic?"

Bernard stopped and turned to face her. "I want her to be happy," he said. "And if she wants to learn magic, I can teach her magic. But we wouldn't be able to have children. And I want children, too."

Emily frowned. Bernard was young, but a forty-year-old man would be considered old on the Nameless World. It wasn't unknown for young commoner women to be grandmothers by thirty, assuming they survived long enough to see their grandchildren. Even for magicians, there was strong social pressure to marry and have children as soon as one graduated. And if that was true of her era, how much worse was it in a time when medical care was weak and female magicians practically non-existent?

"You might have to decide what's more important to you," she said, finally. It wasn't as if *she* had any right to advise someone on their love life. "Having children or allowing her to study magic."

"Her father wouldn't approve of her studying magic," Bernard said. "He could have taught her..."

He shook his head. "I don't know what to do."

"Give it time," Emily advised. "And don't try to push her into anything."

"I won't," Bernard promised. "But she's almost *nineteen*. It won't be long before she's too old to get married."

Emily shook her head in grim amusement. On Earth, nineteen would be considered far too *young* to get married by most civilized people. But it made sense in a world where life expectancies were so much shorter. Julianne would be lucky—very lucky—if she lived to fifty. Emily was mildly surprised she wasn't married already. It suggested that Whitehall was ridiculously progressive, by the standards of the time. She couldn't help wondering just what—if anything—he knew of the relationship between his daughter and his apprentice.

"Give it time," she repeated.

Bernard looked at her. "How did you avoid getting married?"

"There was a young man I was seeing," Emily said. It was true enough. "But we came to the castle and...and I have no idea what happened to him."

"He wouldn't have waited for you," Bernard said. "If he had no idea what happened to you, Emily, no one would blame him for marrying someone else."

Emily shrugged. Bernard was trying to be nice, she realized, but she didn't want to talk about it. It was the same old problem, over and over again. The more lies—or half-truths mixed with lies—that she told, the greater the chance of tripping up badly. And then they'd know she was lying about *something*. And then...

"Your young man," Bernard said. "Didn't he know about the curse?"

"He believed I could have children," Emily said, stiffly. "And I don't want to talk about him anymore."

Bernard gave her an odd look, but said nothing else as they reached the bottom of the stairs and headed down to the kitchens. The smell of roasting meat wafted out towards them as they walked past the open door—Emily glanced in to see a makeshift fire burning merrily in the center of the room—and down towards a larger room. A grim-faced woman was standing in front of a door, her arms crossed under her breasts. She looked to be in her late sixties, although Emily suspected she was much younger. And the look she gave Bernard was far from friendly.

"You can't go past this point," she said, sternly.

"Of course," Bernard said.

Emily glanced at him. "I'll see you at dinner?"

"Probably," Bernard said. He gave Emily a mischievous smile. "I don't know where you're going to sit, of course."

He turned and strode off before Emily could ask what he meant. She watched him go, then shrugged and turned back to the door. The old woman stepped aside without a word, her eyes flickering over Emily's body in a manner that seemed to combine fear and disdain—and an odd sort of yearning that worried Emily more than she cared to admit. She pushed the door open and walked into the room. Inside, a large wooden tub of water sat on the ground, a handful of smaller buckets piled up against the wall. Julianne stood on the far side of the room, placing two small bundles on a single large chair.

"Make sure you lock that door," Julianne advised, as she picked up one of the buckets and carried it to the tub. "We don't want any of the lads walking in on us."

"Definitely not," Emily agreed.

Julianne gave her an odd little smile. "They don't know what to make of you," she said. She poured the water into the tub, then started to undress. "They keep asking if you're *really* a magician."

Emily snorted. "*You* could answer that question," she said.

"Yes, I could," Julianne said. "But I won't."

She stepped out of her dress and started to splash water on her body. Emily blinked in surprise, then reminded herself that a hot tub of water was the height of luxury outside Whitehall, even in her time. Hot and cold running water was a rarity, certainly outside the mansions and castles of the rich and powerful. The servants—the camp followers—would have collected the water from the lake and carried it up to the castle...she shook her head, feeling a stab of sympathy, as she started to undress. Their work would never end.

"You're perfect," Julianne said. She looked up at Emily, studying her body with an intensity that made Emily blush. "There isn't a scar on your skin, just..."

She indicated the rune between Emily's breasts. "What is that?"

"Protection," Emily said, shortly. "I carved it myself."

Julianne nodded, her eyes still sweeping Emily's body. Emily sighed, pushing her embarrassment aside as she looked in turn. Julianne was beautiful, but she was dangerously thin and she had a nasty-looking scar on her right arm as well as reddish pockmarks on her feet. She'd seen similar pockmarks before; they were almost always proof that their bearer hadn't been able to afford decent medical care. A dark patch was clearly visible just below Julianne's left breast, a purplish bruise that Emily hoped desperately was a birthmark. If someone had actually injured her...

Poor nutrition, she thought. She was hardly the tallest student in Whitehall in *her* time, but here she was amongst the tallest people in the castle. *Poor nutrition, and a lack of decent medical care.*

"I always thought I was too pale," Emily said. She started to wash herself, splashing warm water over her face. There was no soap, let alone shampoo or anything else she could use to wash her hair. "I didn't get enough sun when I was younger."

"You're perfect," Julianne said, again. She gave Emily an odd little smile. "What do you think of my father?"

"I think he's an interesting man," Emily said, after a moment. She was too tired for word games. "I'm grateful for the chance to study under him."

Julianne's expression twisted. "My mother died in childbirth," she said. "I never knew her."

Emily frowned. "I'm sorry to hear that..."

"He needs a wife," Julianne added. "You could..."

Emily had to fight down the absurd urge to start giggling. "Are you seriously suggesting I marry your father?"

Julianne colored. "It would give you a place..."

"Your father is old enough to be *my* father," Emily said. She had no idea how old Whitehall was, but if his daughter was nineteen, Whitehall had to be at least thirty-five. Not that old, not compared to Void or Grandmaster Hasdrubal...she shook her head. Even if she *was* inclined to marry someone, it wouldn't be a man nearly twice her age. "And I don't need a place."

A hint of bitterness flickered across Julianne's face. "Every woman needs a place," she said, sourly. "And I'm the only one in mine."

Emily frowned. "There are other young women here..."

"Yes, there are," Julianne interrupted. "But I'm the only magician's daughter. I have no place amongst the magicians and no friends amongst the other women."

"I would have thought that wouldn't matter," Emily said, after a moment. She tied her hair back as she splashed more water on her face. "You're all on the run, aren't you?"

"Yeah," Julianne said. Her face twisted, as if she had bitten into a lemon. "But it does matter."

"I know," Emily said.

She understood. She understood all too well. Julianne was isolated by gender, by birth, and by social status in a world where such status could be lost in a heartbeat. She was no serving girl, nor was she a magician. She had no place; she could not join the magicians any more than she could join the servants and camp followers. And she would never be anything other than her father's daughter—or, if she married Bernard, his wife.

Poor girl, Emily thought. *And yet, she's in the most progressive place in the world.*

Chapter Ten

THE DINING HALL WAS LOOKING RATHER MORE LIKE ITS OLD—OR NEW—SELF, EMILY decided, as she followed Julianne into the giant chamber. There were still no tables, but the servants had sorted out the rugs so there was a clear social hierarchy: masters at the top of the room, attached apprentices just below them, unattached apprentices in the middle and everyone else at the bottom. Emily hadn't realized just how large the commune actually was until she saw almost all of its members gathered in one place. Ten masters, seven attached apprentices, fifty unattached apprentices and over a hundred men, women and children serving as camp followers.

It's a start, she told herself. *And Whitehall School will be far larger.*

"You should be sitting with the attached apprentices," Julianne said, as they walked up towards the top of the room. Emily was uneasily aware of stares—not all of them friendly—following her every movement. "I'll...I'll be sitting by the domestics."

"Sit with us," Emily urged. It would be easy for Julianne to sit next to her, in the absence of tables and chairs. "You won't get into any trouble."

Julianne gave her a surprised look, then led the way over to where Bernard and Robin were sitting. The former gave Julianne a startled look, followed by a smile; the latter raised a glass of dark red liquid to Emily, then drank it in a single gulp. Emily frowned as she smelled the wine—she'd detested alcohol long before coming to the Nameless World—and silently warned herself to keep an eye on Robin. His behavior after summoning the demon had been quite worrying enough without adding alcohol into the mix.

"Lady Emily," Bernard said, as they sat down. "And Julianne."

Emily lifted her eyebrows. "Why am I a *Lady*?"

"My master—*our* master—commanded it," Bernard said. He shot Julianne a shy smile. "I did not see fit to question his reasoning."

"Oh," Emily said. She glanced towards the master magicians, but they seemed to be lost in their own conversation. The scent of magic hung thick in the air, threatening to overpower her senses. "Bernard...can you tell me who they are?"

"Of course he can," Robin said. "But is he going to?"

Bernard shot his friend a stern look, then nodded. "Master Whitehall and Lord Chambers you know, of course," he said. "They've been friends for...for longer than I've been alive, so they're pretty much the co-leaders of the commune. Lord and Master Incánus Wolfe joined them shortly afterwards, seeking out the last apprentice of Myrddin the Sane."

Emily nodded, tersely. "I know them," she said. "Who is the man next to Master Wolfe?"

"That's Lord and Master Alfred," Bernard said. "He's a little dotty, but he means well."

"I know the type," Emily said. Alfred could have passed for an older and balder version of Professor Dumbledore. His face was strikingly hairy, even though his head had been shaved clean; his eyes seemed to wander in all directions, as if he wasn't really controlling them at all. "He's a DemonMaster, right?"

"One of the oldest," Bernard confirmed.

Emily sucked in her breath. Lord Alfred was mentioned in a dozen textbooks, the star of a hundred different stories...none of which made sense. Professor Locke had practically driven himself mad by studying stories of terrifyingly advanced feats of magic and trying to work out how they'd been done. Lord Alfred was supposed to have plucked the moon from the sky, seduced a princess who'd been enchanted to deny men, battled a hideous monster that consumed virgins, tamed a dragon...

She shook her head. It was impossible to believe that the gentle-looking old man in front of her was responsible for *any* of those feats. The stories *had* to be exaggerated.

Unless a demon did them, she thought. *Unless...*

Bernard nodded to the grim-faced man sitting at the end of the rug. "That's Master Gila," he explained. "I believe I mentioned him to you."

Emily's eyes went wide as Master Gila *looked* at her. His face was scarred, but it was his eyes that caught Emily's attention. Even at a distance, she could see a hint of red light within his pupils, a red light she'd always associated with necromancy. The more she looked at him, the harder it was to get any real sense of what he *looked* like. There was something about his appearance that reminded her of Shadye in his last few seconds of life.

"You said he'd gone mad," she whispered.

"You don't want his attention," Julianne warned. "That's his wife down there."

Emily followed her gaze. An older woman—she looked around thirty—sat with the other women, her face contorted in absolute misery. Emily *knew*—knew beyond a shadow of a doubt—that her husband abused her, that he beat her and cursed her and did all manner of other horrible things to her, but there was no way she could escape. She was his property, as far as everyone else was concerned; there was nothing they could or would do to help her.

A good reason not to get married here, she thought, morbidly.

She looked back at Whitehall, who was still chatting with Master Chambers. How could he tolerate Master Gila? The man was a monster! But if he was steadily going mad, he might not have started out as a monster. The thought was no comfort. His poor wife would have watched, helplessly, as her husband degenerated, unable to do anything to save his mind from collapse. It wouldn't be long before he was gone for good.

And that might be a relief, Emily told herself.

"He used to be very skilled at healing," Bernard said. "But right now...he's losing his mind."

He closed his eyes for a long moment. "We might all go that way, one day."

"I won't," Robin said. He smiled. "You have to be optimistic about these things."

Emily kept her expression blank. She could still sense the lingering presence of the demon surrounding Robin, its magic tainting his very soul. And he wasn't the only one, either; three of the other apprentices had clearly summoned their own demons. Bernard might be frustrated at the slow pace Master Whitehall had set, but it was all that stood between him and outright madness. His magic was far from perfect, yet at least it wasn't *demonic*.

"Lord Drake is very skilled at transmutation," Bernard added. He nodded towards a tall, thin-lipped man chatting to Master Wolfe. "He's the only person I've met who has been able to turn people into frogs--" he winked at Emily "--as well as change lead into gold and a few other useful tricks. He's also incredibly conceited. His apprentices have to come up to his high standards..."

"Which is why he doesn't have one," Robin put in. He waved a hand towards the unattached apprentices. "Fifty young men, all growing older by the day, in search of someone to teach them how to handle their magic...and Master Drake refuses to teach them. They're not good enough for him."

Emily frowned. Changing lead into gold was tricky, although—according to Professor Thande—changing gold into lead was remarkably easy. And yet, without the solid base of knowledge she'd used in her own time, how did Lord Drake do it? Had he been the one to lay the foundations for what would become transfiguration?

She looked at Bernard. "Do you know how to transmute anything?"

"Of course not," Bernard said. "I don't even know the fundamental basics of transmutation."

"You know who you could ask," Robin pointed out.

Julianne paled. "My father would kill you."

Robin smirked. "Do it a long way from here..."

Emily tuned out the ensuing argument as she thought, hard. Transmutation would *have* to be the first step towards transfiguration, although she'd have to ask Lord Drake just how far he'd managed to progress on his own. She had a sneaking suspicion that putting Lord Drake and Master Wolfe together would actually lead to some interesting discoveries...but if Bernard was right, Lord Drake was unlikely to cooperate with anyone. Unless, of course, she could find something to use as a bribe...

"Tell me something," she said. "Does Lord Drake talk to anyone?"

"Hardly anyone," Robin said. "I once disturbed his studies and spent the rest of the day as an ass."

"Oh," Bernard said. "Why didn't he try to turn you back?"

Julianne giggled.

Emily sighed as the good-natured argument grew louder. If Robin was telling the truth, Lord Drake wasn't likely to talk to her...and *trying* to talk to him might prove fatal. Or, at least, embarrassing. Emily was confident that she could handle anything Bernard or Robin threw at her—although Robin's demons were dangerous wild cards—but could she handle a master sorcerer? *Whitehall's* magic was blunt and crude compared to the spells she'd seen Void or Sergeant Miles use, yet he was also immensely powerful. Lord Drake might be able to crush her defenses through simple brute force.

I'll have to think about it later, she told herself. *And keep working on ways to get home.*

Bernard sighed, loudly. "Lord Reaper is another DemonMaster," he said. "He shouldn't be here at all, but Lord Chambers insisted after his home was destroyed. Lord Keldor specializes in death magics, working with dead bodies...I think he's a DemonMaster too, but there's no actual proof. And Lord Bones is good at charms."

"There's a couple of others," Robin added. "Apprentice Sake will probably be raised to mastery soon."

"He's Lord Gila's apprentice," Julianne explained. "He's nowhere near as bad as his master."

"Poor bastard gets beaten every day," Robin said. "I don't know why he stays."

Bernard's face darkened. "A year ago, a skilled healer could live anywhere," he said, "and he would be welcome. Now...now I don't know what would happen if he tried."

Emily shuddered. If Gila was so far gone that he was taking it out on his wife and his apprentice...she glanced at the madman and winced, again, as he met her eyes. Just for a second, she felt an unpleasant pressure in her mind, as if Gila had just tried to break through her defenses and ransack her thoughts. She gritted her teeth as her head began to pound, tightening her shields even as she forced herself to break eye contact. Her headache rapidly faded as soon as she looked away, but she was grimly aware of red eyes staring at her as she turned her head.

Bernard frowned. "Emily?"

Emily shook her head. She'd had her mind ransacked once—by Grandmaster Hasdrubal—and she'd hated it, even though she knew the Grandmaster hadn't had a choice. No one had suggested that any of the magicians in the past could look into her mind...but she'd never thought to ask. Who *could* she ask? If Bernard didn't know...

Ask Whitehall, she told herself. *He might be able to answer any questions you have.*

She looked up as the servants entered, carrying large bowls of stew and placing them in front of the magicians. There was no formality, Emily noted; the diners filled their bowls as soon as the food was in front of them and started to eat with their fingers. Emily tested her own meal, just to make sure it was safe to eat, then started to pick at her food herself. The stew tasted faintly unpleasant, as if the meat was reaching the end of its life, but her spells insisted it was safe to eat. Beside her, Julianne ate so rapidly that Emily worried she was going to be sick.

"At least we have something better to eat," Bernard said. "And a whole castle to use as a base."

"Until the bastards get after us," Robin pointed out. "Do you think that *they* will find the forest impregnable?"

Emily frowned. She'd never been a good tracker—Sergeant Miles had said many sarcastic things about her ability to follow people through the forests surrounding Whitehall—but even *she* would have found it easy to track a group of two to three hundred men, women and children. Whoever—whatever—was hunting the commune wouldn't have any trouble doing the same, unless they were concerned about the nexus point. Perhaps they thought the commune *already* had the nexus point under control.

Or perhaps they think the nexus point will kill the commune for them, she thought. It wasn't a pleasant thought, but it had to be faced. *And if I hadn't been there, they would have been right.*

"Or the castle," Robin added, after a moment. "Can we defend the building?"

"We have magic," Bernard said.

"Magic hasn't been enough," Julianne warned.

Emily felt a shiver running down her spine. "We'll have to get the nexus point under control," she said, softly. "It's the only hope we have."

She forced herself to sit back as Bernard, making a determined effort to push away the gloom, started to introduce her to the other apprentices. The attached apprentices seemed more curious than doubtful, but the unattached apprentices regarded her with either open dislike or contempt. Emily sighed inwardly—the unattached apprentices would take months, perhaps, to get over their irritation at her presence—and nibbled on her bread as Bernard moved on to identifying the camp followers.

"It's a small village," she said, as Bernard pointed out the carpenters, the blacksmiths, the potters and even a couple of farmers. "You could set up a village of your own."

"Master Whitehall had a dream," Bernard said. "One day, there would be a whole *settlement* of magicians and the trades that support them. He thought...he thought that it would be one good way to increase our numbers."

Emily had to smile. Was that—*that*—the idea that had become Whitehall School?

"It didn't work," Julianne said, bitterly. "It *couldn't* work."

Robin snorted. "Magicians didn't want to do all the hard work themselves," he said, "so they needed a staff of mundanes to do everything from forging swords to growing crops. And then the mundanes didn't want to live near the wizards...the only way to keep them there was to enslave them, which made their work useless."

"The magicians picked on them," Emily said, flatly.

"Of course," Bernard said. He sounded tired, too tired. "Mundanes are raised, even now, to murder magical children before they become a threat. They won't want to live near us if they are given a choice."

Emily looked at him, then nodded to the blacksmiths, potters and carpenters at the bottom of the hall. "And now...?"

"And now they come with us because they're scared of what will happen if they go elsewhere," Robin said.

"And because they're loyal to my master," Bernard insisted. "He was good to them and they are loyal to him."

"No doubt," Robin said.

Emily sensed the magic field shifting behind her and turned, just in time to see Master Whitehall and Lord Chambers striding towards them. She hastily got to her feet and bowed, Bernard and Robin following suit. Julianne remained seated, her eyes downcast. It crossed Emily's mind, suddenly, that inviting Julianne to join them—even with her chaperoning the girl—might have offended her father. But he hadn't said a word when they'd sat down to eat.

"An eventful day," Whitehall observed. He looked straight at Emily. "Would you not agree?"

"Yes, Master," Emily said, formally. She wasn't sure *eventful* was the word *she* would have picked, but it suited. "I have learned a great deal."

Whitehall gave her a long considering look. "Tomorrow morning, you will report to me after breakfast," he said. "We have much to discuss."

Emily nodded. Beside her, Bernard cleared his throat.

"Yes, Master," Emily said, quickly.

"You will continue to assist in sweeping the castle," Whitehall added, looking at Bernard. "I will pick up your training tomorrow afternoon."

"Yes, Master," Bernard said. He sounded relieved. Emily didn't blame him. The thought of having his education pushed back still further clearly bothered him. "After lunch?"

"Report to me," Whitehall agreed.

"And Robin has a new spell," Lord Chambers said.

Whitehall's lips thinned in disapproval. Emily allowed herself a moment of relief. Clearly, the stories insisting that Lord Whitehall detested the Black Arts were true. Demons simply could not be trusted, particularly when the spells they offered tended to have dangerous side effects. And she was *sure* that the spell Robin had started to use so casually would cause all sorts of problems in the future.

"He can trade it to the other students, if he wishes," Lord Chambers added.

"*After* it has been checked carefully," Lord Whitehall insisted.

Emily tensed, drawing her protections around her as magic started to shimmer around the two older men, the scent of demons surrounding Lord Chambers only adding to the growing tension. She knew she could defend herself, particularly if she wasn't the target, but what about Julianne? Or Bernard, Robin and everyone else in the room? The two masters looked as if they were about to go to war, even though they were supposed to be friends...

There are cracks in the commune, Emily realized, dully. *And one of them could tear it apart.*

"We will check it together," Lord Chambers stated.

"Very well," Whitehall said. Emily relaxed, slightly, as the magic drained away. "But it will be checked *first*."

He looked at Emily. "You should go to bed early," he added. "Tomorrow will be a long day."

"Yes, Master," Emily said.

Chapter Eleven

JULIANNE TURNED TO EMILY AS SOON AS THEY WERE BOTH IN THE BEDROOM WITH THE DOOR firmly closed. "How much magic can you do?"

"A lot," Emily said. She eyed the door for a long moment. "Is this the sort of conversation that should remain private?"

"Yes," Julianne said. She paused. "*Can* you keep it secret from my father?"

"...Maybe," Emily said. She cast a privacy ward, reassuring herself that she hadn't seen anything like it from any of the commune. But then, if magicians of this era guarded their secrets closely, she might not have seen them use wards. "I don't *think* he can overhear us."

Julianne met her eyes. "I don't think he keeps *that* close an eye on me," she said. "But you never know."

Emily nodded. There were hundreds of spells that could be used to spy on someone, ranging from a very simplistic distance viewing spell to one that tracked its victim through blood. A magician could block most of those spells through wards and other countermeasures, but a mundane wouldn't have a hope of avoiding surveillance. If Julianne's father wanted to keep an eye on her, he certainly had the ability to do it.

"He doesn't appear to be watching now," she said. Her wards weren't detecting anything, save for the ever-presence *thrumming* of the nexus point. "What do you want to talk about?"

She sat down on her blanket and watched Julianne as she paced nervously around the tiny room, her eyes glancing from side to side as if she expected her father to pop out of the walls at any moment. Emily already had a good idea of just *what* Julianne wanted to talk about—there wasn't much else that Julianne would want to keep hidden from her father—but she knew she had to wait for Julianne to broach the subject herself. She waited, quietly keeping one eye on her wards. There were still no hints that someone was trying to break through her protections and spy on them.

Which is definitely a relief, she thought, wryly. *I'm the only girl here with any protections at all.*

"Father won't teach me magic," Julianne said, finally. She leaned forward, pleadingly. "Will you?"

Emily hesitated. She'd never taught anyone magic from scratch before, not even Frieda or the First Year students she'd mentored. They'd all had the benefit of training to show them how to tap their inherent magic and use it for spells. Emily knew, in theory, how to give someone that kind of training, but she'd never actually used it for real. Lady Barb had warned her, back when they'd traveled to the Cairngorms, that she wasn't to do anything of the sort unless there was no other choice. If something went wrong, she'd said, the consequences could be dire.

She looked up at Julianne. "Why do you want to learn magic?"

Julianne looked back at her. "Why did *you* want to learn magic?"

Touché, Emily thought.

"To defend myself," she said, after a moment's pause. Void had warned her, after all, that if she didn't learn to use magic she'd just wind up in more trouble. "And to..."

"Exactly," Julianne interrupted. "And I want to be something *more*."

Emily took a long breath. "And what about the curse?"

Julianne snorted. "How do you know the curse is *real*?"

She went on before Emily could say a word. "There aren't that many women with magic potential," she said. "For all we know, the handful who did have magic and couldn't have children had a run of bad luck."

"True," Emily agreed.

She frowned as she tossed it over and over in her mind. Experience told her that female magicians could and did have children, but it also told her that such beliefs tended to have a kernel of truth buried under the bullshit. Perhaps the curse *was* an excuse to keep girls from learning magic—primitive cultures did tend to be suspicious and fearful of powerful women—yet she knew better than to take that for granted. There might be a good reason to refrain from teaching magic to girls.

In this era, she thought. *But that clearly changes before my time.*

"I can't pay for training," Julianne said. "But I can offer you something in exchange."

Emily *looked* at her. "What can you offer me in exchange?"

Julianne picked up one of the bags she'd placed against the wall and opened it, revealing a handful of small tools. A stone mortar and pestle set, a handful of sharp knives, a couple of wooden spoons, a pewter jug and a large bowl...it struck Emily, suddenly, that she was looking at a very basic alchemical set. Professor Thande would have sneered at it—the knives looked stained, which was asking for trouble when unwanted ingredients were added to the mix—but it was usable. A second bag contained a number of dried herbs and seeds, carefully packed into cloth bags. Julianne spread out a third blanket, then started to lay them out on the floor.

"My mother used to brew up remedies made from herbs," Julianne said. She sighed. "Her family was supposed to have a reputation for producing potions from plants and other things they grew...she would have taught me, I suppose, if she'd lived."

Emily frowned. Was she looking at the birth of alchemy?

"I see," she said. She recognized some of the herbs, although a handful were new. "Who *did* teach you?"

"My aunt," Julianne said. She smiled, rather thinly. "My father dismissed it as quackery, but I've often found that her remedies worked."

They would have, Emily thought, *if magic was included in the mix.*

"Put those four together with water and boil them," Julianne said, pointing out a handful of herb bags. "You'll have a painkiller that numbs the body, if one is hurt. Add a couple more ingredients and you have a paste you can rub on the affected area."

She winked. "It is remarkable how many apprentices come to us and beg for it shortly after they begin their training."

Emily had to smile. "And you don't think this is magic?"

"It isn't *real* magic," Julianne said. "You can't..."

She sighed, sitting back on her haunches. "It isn't impressive," she added. "And I want to be something *more*."

"I understand," Emily said, quietly.

Julianne pointed to another cluster of bags. "You can mix them together and it will counteract the effects of most poisons," she said. "The results are messy, as you might expect, but the drinker will probably survive if he takes the potion quickly. Or you can alter the proportions to get a painless poison. A couple of magicians have asked to drink it before they lost their minds completely."

"It seems very useful," Emily said. She reached out and poked through the bag of dried ingredients. There didn't seem to be anything but herbs. No dissected animals, no ground minerals...it was definitely basic. "Do you experiment with the ingredients to see what you can do with them?"

"You need someone willing to drink the brew," Julianne said. She smiled, rather humorlessly. "There aren't many people who will volunteer."

"I suppose not," Emily said. *She* would have been reluctant to drink potions that might as well have been put together at random, knowing she risked stomach upsets at best and death at worst. And *she* knew spells that could test potions to make sure they were safe to drink, something Julianne lacked. "It would be tricky to convince them."

"And there are some brews I was taught never to use," Julianne said. "There's one you can use to make someone...*compliant*."

"Yeah," Emily said. She knew a couple of those too. "They can be dangerous."

Julianne leaned forward. "Teach me some magic and I will teach you this," she said, waving a hand at the small pile of ingredients and tools. "You will find it very useful."

Emily hesitated. On one hand, she didn't need to know how to brew potions—although she had to admit that it might be useful to know Julianne's recipes, particularly if she wound up spending the rest of her life in the past. Julianne clearly *didn't* have access to the ingredients Emily was used to using, ingredients that were harvested all over the continent and shipped to Whitehall. The recipes Emily knew might be worse than useless. *And* she would have a chance to encourage Julianne to invent the alchemical method...

But on the other hand, she thought, *Master Whitehall will be furious.*

She met Julianne's eyes. "Your father will be angry," she said. "Are you prepared to handle it?"

"I can cope with beatings," Julianne said, unflinchingly. There was a hard edge to her voice that reminded Emily of Whitehall. "And I'm not going to break his rules about demons."

"And what about Bernard?" Emily asked. She played with the snake-bracelet on her wrist, thinking hard. "Have you given any thought to how *he'll* react?"

Julianne looked down for a long moment. "He knows I want to learn magic," she said, finally. "And if he's unwilling to take me, after I do, I will live with it."

Emily sighed, inwardly. She'd been told, back in her time, that mixed marriages—marriages between magicians and mundanes—rarely worked. But Caleb's parents seemed quite happy together; they'd certainly produced five children. Now, though... whatever Bernard said, he might have doubts about marrying a sorceress. He certainly hadn't shown any sign of being interested in *Emily*.

But Robin is interested in me, Emily thought. *Even though he thinks I'm barren....*

...Or maybe because he thinks I'm barren.

She scowled at the thought. It was unlikely, very unlikely, that Robin or any of the other magicians could cast a contraceptive spell. Unless Julianne knew how to brew something that had the same effect—and she doubted any of the boys would *want* to ask her for a contraceptive—there was no way to use any kind of birth control. The little she'd heard about primitive condoms had been enough to convince her she *didn't* want to use them, despite the risk. Sleeping with a barren woman might be the only true contraceptive available to them.

"I know I'm asking a lot," Julianne said, quietly. She leaned forward, her voice pleading. "I would be very grateful if you taught me..."

Emily hesitated, thinking hard. Whitehall was *not* going to approve, when he found out about it—and he *would* find out about it. His magic sensitivity was nowhere near as good as Emily's—his own sloppy magic would drown out any traces of Julianne's magic—but when he was alone with his daughter, he might well pick up *something*. She wasn't scared of beatings either—Master Grey had battered her to a pulp during the duel—but being thrown out of the castle was a very real threat. Without the nexus point, there was no way to get back to the world she knew.

And yet, she knew one hell of an opportunity had been dropped in her lap. If this *was* the start of alchemy—and it certainly looked like it—she could work with Julianne to set the whole system on a solid footing. And if she taught Julianne a couple of spells to help her test her experiments before forcing anyone to drink them, it might help convince her father that women *should* learn magic. And if she could uncover the truth behind the curse...

"I can teach you," she said. She forced herself to think for a long moment. At least Julianne didn't have anything to unlearn, unlike Frieda. "But you'll have to give me a day or two to work out the best way to teach you."

Julianne leaned forward and gave her a tight hug. "Thank you, thank you," she said. "You won't regret it."

"Just get between me and your father if he decides to be furious," Emily said. "And now, I think we should go to sleep."

"Of course, Master," Julianne said. She was grinning from ear to ear as she packed up her tools. "Or...should I call you *Mistress*?"

"Just stick with *Emily*," Emily advised. She leaned back and pulled the blanket around her body. "And don't tell anyone until you've mastered a few tricks."

"Of course," Julianne said.

Emily had half-expected not to be able to sleep again, but darkness overwhelmed her almost as soon as she closed her eyes. The next thing she knew, it was morning and Julianne was shaking her awake. Emily resisted the urge to hex her—deliberately this time – as she stood and used the chamberpot, silently promising herself to discuss hot and cold running water with Whitehall and Master Wolfe as soon as possible. Tapping the nexus point would open up a great many possibilities.

"My father said you should meet him outside, after breakfast," Julianne said, as Emily dressed. The clothes were still itchy, but she was getting used to them. "Do you think he knows...?"

I hope not," Emily said. "We haven't *done* anything yet."

She ate breakfast quickly, then walked through the courtyard to where Whitehall stood by the grassy lawn. If he *did* know what she'd agreed to do with Julianne, he showed no sign of it as he demonstrated another couple of spells and watched, dispassionately, as Emily duplicated them. She couldn't help wondering just what was going through his mind—to him, her powers had to seem a form of outside context magic.

"I don't think there's much I can teach you," Whitehall said. "And you're still holding back."

Emily nodded. There was no point in trying to deny it, so she changed the subject. "Did you have a chance to look at Robin's new spell?"

"We found no unpleasant surprises," Whitehall said. "But with demons, one never knows."

Emily frowned. There *was* an unpleasant surprise—the spell used too much power, slopping magic everywhere. But to Whitehall, that was normal. He might not even see just how the spell could be modified to use less power, yet still have the same effect.

She looked up at him. "Why don't you trust demons?"

"My old master believed that demons were dangerous," Whitehall said. "They grant wishes—if the price is right—but the wishes always come with nasty surprises attached. He was fond of telling stories about fools who sold their souls to demons, only to discover that the demon kept the letter of the bargain and not the spirit."

He shrugged. "There was a man who sold his soul for the fairest beauty in all the land," he added, after a moment. "And the demon kept the letter of the deal—it brought the woman to him, as soon as the deal was made. But the woman was a haughty princess with five brothers and a very angry father."

"And so the man was killed," Emily guessed.

"Correct," Whitehall said. "I don't think that was *quite* what the young idiot wanted."

"No," Emily agreed.

"Demons will offer much in exchange for very little," Whitehall added. "Or so it seems. But the more you call upon demons, the more dependent you *become* on demons. Their magic becomes an addiction. You can perform fantastic spells by using demons, but *only* by using demons. And who's really in charge if the demon is the one performing the spell?"

"You're compelling the demon to serve you," Emily mused. "Aren't you?"

"A demon is a vastly powerful creature," Whitehall reminded her. "And it will take advantage of any loophole in the orders to wreak havoc."

He snorted. "And the DemonMasters *hear* their demons all the time," he added. "They tend to go mad quicker than other magicians."

"Oh," Emily said.

"There isn't much else I can teach you," Whitehall said, changing the subject again. "Your tutor appears to have given you an excellent grounding in magic."

"Thank you," Emily said.

"Master Wolfe has requested that you work with him," Whitehall added. His lips curved into a warm smile. "He has some theories he wishes to run by you."

"It would be my pleasure," Emily said.

Whitehall smiled. "Of course."

Emily took a breath. "I would also like to try to learn from the other masters," she said, carefully. For all she knew, it might be a touchy subject. If the apprentice system in the past was anything like the one she was familiar with, trying to learn from another master was a grave insult to *her* master. "They might well have something to teach me."

Whitehall gave her a long, contemplative look. "They may refuse to show you anything," he said. "Unless you have something you can show them in exchange."

Emily sighed. There was a *lot* she could show them. But unless she was very careful, she'd do a great deal of damage to recorded history. Perhaps she was *meant* to do everything she did...

...But what if she was wrong?

She shook her head. "They should share ideas," she said, instead. "How many spells are invented, lost, and then reinvented because the original inventor doesn't share them?"

"A long-standing problem," Whitehall said, dryly. Wolfe had said the same thing. "But trying to convince magicians to work together is quite hard enough *without* asking them to share their secrets too."

He sighed. "It's rare to have a commune with more than four masters," he added, "and even then they tend to keep their distance from one another."

Emily nodded. "But I can ask them?"

"Of course you can *ask*," Whitehall said. He sounded annoyed, although Emily wasn't sure why. It didn't seem to be directed at her. "But don't come crying to me when they refuse to share *anything* with you."

Chapter Twelve

A S SHE WALKED THROUGH THE CASTLE, EMILY WAS SURPRISED TO DISCOVER THAT MASTER Wolfe had moved into a much larger chamber near the nexus point. It was a dark room, illuminated only by a trio of lanterns hanging from the walls; three rickety-looking wooden tables had been placed in the center, surrounded by a couple of stools. They all looked as if they had been constructed overnight, Emily decided, as she knocked on the open door. The commune's carpenters were very efficient.

"Ah, Emily," Master Wolfe said, opening the door. "And you brought lunch!"

"Master Whitehall insists that you eat," Emily said. She'd carried the heavy tray herself, declining Robin's offer to carry it for her. "He said I was to force you to eat, if necessary."

She didn't dare put the tray on one of the tables—they were covered in parchment scrolls that were probably irreplaceable. Master Wolfe seemed to be the kindest of the masters in the commune—although she had to admit she hadn't spoken with many of the others—but she had a feeling he'd explode with rage if any of his parchments were damaged. And she wouldn't blame him, either. Parchment and vellum were both expensive, even in her time. It would probably be years before the Whitehall Commune could start producing it for themselves, if they were allowed to settle peacefully in the castle.

"I don't have time to eat," Master Wolfe said. His eyes were bright, too bright; his hands shook as if he were cold, even though the room was surprisingly warm. Emily suspected that he hadn't slept all night. "I have too much to do."

"You need to eat," Emily said, firmly. She picked up the bowl of stew and held it out to him, hoping he'd take it without further argument. "Please."

Master Wolfe sighed, but took the bowl and sat down facing her. "I've been dissecting Robin's spell," he said. "There are no surprises, as far as I can tell."

"Master Whitehall said as much," Emily said. She sipped her own stew thoughtfully, using a spoon to pluck out and nibble the meat. It tasted of lamb, but—as before—she didn't recognize the vegetables. "But it uses a great deal of power."

"Precisely," Master Wolfe said. He jabbed his spoon at her as he spoke. "I could devise a better spell, if I had time. But it won't be so easy to cast."

Emily shrugged. The spell drew on so much power that she suspected Robin was actually filling the holes in the spellware with raw magic. It was certainly possible—whatever his flaws, Robin was a powerful magician—but it was grossly inefficient. The light spells she'd been taught were commonly taught to First Years; Robin's spell would be tricky for a Fourth Year student to cast. Anyone younger probably wouldn't have the raw power to make it work.

"I've also been improving the nexus point spells," Master Wolfe said. He finished his bowl and dropped it back on the tray, then rose. "Tell me what you think of this?"

Emily put her bowl to one side and joined him as he stood by one of tables. A large roll of parchment had been unfolded, allowing Master Wolfe to draw out a set of complicated spell notations. Emily took a long look—and then sucked in her breath as she understood what she saw. Master Wolfe had taken the spells she'd used, down in the nexus chamber, and expanded on them. Each of his pieces of spellwork was designed to *grow*, rather than remain rigid: they would automatically adapt as the power ebbed and flowed through the nexus point. And the longer the spellwork remained in place, the more they'd be able to do with it.

Given time, Emily thought, *they'd be able to build up Whitehall itself.*

"I'm altering the spellwork so it expands outside our normal world," Master Wolfe told her, as he pointed to a cluster of elaborate notations. "Should something go wrong—and it might—the remainder of the system will compensate automatically. A major power surge will be shunted sideways..."

Emily frowned. "You'll still need a way to control it."

"I know," Master Wolfe said. "But crafting a genuine *mind* will not be easy."

The Warden, Emily thought. *We need to craft the first Warden.*

"I've been looking at ways to transpose my own mind into the spells," Master Wolfe added, after a moment. He picked up a large sheet of parchment and held it out to her. "This should be workable, if I could muster the power..."

Emily took the sheet and had to bite her tongue to keep from swearing out loud. Master Wolfe's notation was odd—there were runes she didn't recognize included within the bundle of notes—but there was no mistaking the proto-mimic. She'd done her best to duplicate what she'd seen, back in Second Year, yet she knew there had been pieces missing. Now...now she knew *what* had been missing.

Soul magic, she thought. *The Mimics don't just drain magic and life from their victims, they practically copy their very souls. And they don't even realize that's what they're doing.*

She shuddered. She'd had nightmares—everyone in Whitehall had had nightmares—about being replaced by a Mimic, utterly unaware of what had happened to her. She would be dead, but she wouldn't know it...until the Mimic ran out of power and reverted to its natural form, shedding what remained of her as it started to hunt for a new target. The proto-mimic didn't look like a hunter—indeed, it seemed designed to serve as a host for Master Wolfe's mentality—but it wouldn't be able to keep going indefinitely. How could it?

"This is madness," she said, softly. "How could you even power the spellwork?"

"Like this," Master Wolfe said. He held up yet another sheet of paper. "I devised this rite myself. It was so simple that I don't understand why no one ever thought of it before."

Emily took it—and blanched. There was no mistaking the necromantic rite, the simple spell that allowed a necromancer to use murder as a source of magic...at the price of everything from sanity to humanity. Shadye had been utterly insane, fighting desperately to find more and more sources of power as his mind collapsed in on itself, while Mother Holly had lost sight of why she'd sacrificed herself in the first place. Master Wolfe would be driven insane if he attempted the rite...if he was prepared to sacrifice someone to save his life.

"Madness," she breathed. "You'd go mad."

"All magicians go mad, eventually," Master Wolfe said, stiffly. "The smart ones kill themselves before it's too late."

Emily looked at him, then down at the sheet of paper. The necromantic rite *was* simple—and therein was the danger. *Anyone* with a tiny spark of magic could trade their sanity for power, if they were prepared to keep murdering people to stay alive. Grandmaster Hasdrubal had even told her, years ago, that particularly foolish magicians saw the necromantic rite as a shortcut, but it led right off a cliff. Shadye probably hadn't even *remembered* why he'd become a necromancer by the time he'd kidnapped Emily. All he'd cared about was remaining alive.

"You couldn't handle the surge of power," she said. "Your mind would snap at once."

Master Wolfe and Whitehall had looked for a sting in the tail, she thought, when they'd dissected Robin's spell. They'd even been surprised when they found nothing. But it had been hiding in plain sight. The sloppy magic spilling around, whenever the spell was cast, would damage Robin's mind. Each successive use of the spell would cause more and more problems, eventually driving him insane. And the more unstable he became, the more likely it was that he'd summon a demon without taking any precautions.

And it's true of all their spells, she thought. *They're slopping so much magic around that it's damaging their minds.*

She sat down, hard. Master Gila's eyes were going red, necromancer-red. Was that a side-effect of the slow descent into insanity? Mother Holly's eyes had gone red too. Perhaps someone *had* tried to use the necromantic rite before, only to discover that they couldn't find enough power to keep themselves alive. But it hardly mattered. Sparks of power burning through a magician's mind would be enough to eventually drive them mad.

And that explains the curse too, she told herself. *If they're slopping magic around, it might well make them sterile.*

"Emily," Master Wolfe said. "Are you sure?"

"Yes," Emily said. "You must *not* use that rite to empower yourself."

Her mind raced. Lady Barb had told her, back in Second Year, that there were curses that rendered women barren and men sterile. And while the latter could be reversed, the former were permanent. There was nothing that could be done, Lady Barb had said, to undo the destruction of a woman's eggs. The female reproductive system was far more delicate than the male...a female magician might accidentally render herself barren, simply by allowing her magic to slop around her body.

And if she believes it will make her barren, her own thoughts added, *it will.*

"Explain," Master Wolfe ordered.

"There will be a surge of power," Emily said. It would be worse for Master Wolfe, unless he had wards she hadn't sensed. "You won't be able to contain it. The surge will just burn through your mind. If it doesn't kill you, it will drive you insane. You'll be running around, lashing out at random."

They must have improved upon the spells they use, she thought, as Master Wolfe took back the parchment and stared at it. *If they learned to use less and less power, to focus it properly, they'd avoid doing any damage to their bodies or minds. And that's what I learned to do when I arrived at Whitehall.*

Master Wolfe looked dubious. "I can alter the spell matrix," he said, studying the proto-mimic. "It should be enough..."

"The surge would be an order of magnitude more powerful than anything you're used to handling," Emily warned. "A human mind would be unable to handle it."

"And if you're wrong," Master Wolfe said, "you're denying me the chance to boost my magic."

"I'm not wrong," Emily said. She took a breath. "You could rewrite some of the more common spells to use less magic."

Master Wolfe lifted his eyebrows. "Is that what you were taught to do?"

"Yes," Emily said, reluctantly. There was no help for it, not now. Professor Lombardi had taught her to always work out what the spell actually did—and rewrite it, if necessary—before trying to cast it. "You said that magicians always go mad?"

"They do," Master Wolfe confirmed. "Master Gila's eyes are already red. He is not long for this world."

Emily nodded. "He's probably used too many spells that have nasty side-effects. And that spell of Robin's will damage his mind, if he uses it extensively."

Master Wolfe cocked his head. "And how would you suggest rewriting it?"

Emily held out her hand and cast a light-spell. A glowing ball of white light hovered above her palm, casting an eerie radiance over the table. Master Wolfe stared at it with genuine fascination, then cast a spell of his own. Emily felt her magic waver, but the light globe merely flickered once before returning to normal. Master Wolfe reached out, very gently, and held his palm over the globe. It didn't seem to bother him.

"It's cool," he said, in wonderment. "There's no heat."

"It produces light," Emily said. Was Robin at risk of setting fire to something? His light globes had been quite warm, after all. "It doesn't produce anything else."

"Very clever," Master Wolfe said. He frowned, stroking his chin, as the light globe finally flickered and died. "I shall have to give the subject some thought."

"You could start rewriting some of the other spells," Emily said. "If you could get the same effect with less power..."

"If," Master Wolfe said. He sighed, heavily. "There are spells I could never get to work because I didn't have the power."

"Not casting those spells might have kept you sane," Emily pointed out.

She looked down at the necromantic rite, feeling a twinge of sympathy. Everyone had different levels of magic—she'd been taught—but how one used what one had was often just as important as their power reserves. A magician with vast power might throw it around carelessly, expending it until he was left drained; a magician with limited power might spend it carefully, hoarding it until it could be used for best effect. But here, where crudeness and brute force spells seemed to be the order of the day, Master Wolfe would be at a staggering disadvantage. No *wonder* he'd been willing to invent—perhaps reinvent—the necromantic rite, and then plan to use it.

Shadye might have been like that too, Emily thought. It still galled her that she knew little of Shadye's past, other than the simple fact that he'd been expelled from Whitehall in Second Year. Perhaps he'd been looking for ways to boost his power even then, rather than put in the hard work necessary to learn how to use what he had. *He wanted a shortcut too.*

Master Wolfe gave her a sharp look. "Why do I have the feeling you're not telling us everything?"

"I swore oaths to my tutor," Emily said, hastily. She'd given Master Wolfe too much, too quickly. "He wouldn't want me to share everything."

"I see," Master Wolfe said. Emily rather suspected he didn't believe her, not completely. "I will consider your words. But for the moment..."

He pulled out a new sheet of parchment and started to talk through what he'd already done, explaining his work on the nexus point. Emily was quietly impressed, although she had the feeling that it would be years before the spellware was firmly locked in place. Master Wolfe talked about spells that were only theoretical, spells that were beyond even the powers of the strongest magicians...spells that might become possible, once the nexus point was turned into a source of unlimited power. He was, Emily reminded herself again, a genius. His understanding of the nexus point, based on only a week of study, was far superior to hers.

"Some of the traps we found were quite odd," he commented, softly. "Did you have a hand in creating them?"

Emily shook her head. "I didn't place any traps here," she said, truthfully. "We never stumbled across any either, back when we first entered the castle."

"A shame we don't know how long it was between your arrival and ours," Master Wolfe mused. "It might tell us useful things about the nexus point's interaction with the local magic field."

He didn't seem inclined to keep studying the matter, to Emily's private relief. She had the feeling she'd said too much already, although she'd had no choice but to keep him from trying to use the necromantic rite. If he'd chosen to sacrifice someone to boost his own powers...Master Wolfe didn't seem like a monster, yet she knew that magicians rarely thought highly of mundanes. And now, when magicians were hunted by mundanes, who could blame him?

And if they do manage to devise spells that are less dangerous to human minds, she thought, *they could actually take their place in society.*

"Your magic is odd," Master Wolfe said. He rolled up two sheets of parchment as he spoke, not quite looking at her. "I can tell you're a magician, but you honestly seem less powerful than I. And yet I have been told that you turned Bernard into a frog, an act that requires staggering levels of power."

Emily sighed. She was surprised someone hadn't already asked her that question.

"I was taught to mask my power," she said, flatly. "My tutor...believed a magician shouldn't show off his power unless it was necessary."

Master Wolfe frowned. "To keep people from realizing that you were a magician?"

"Among other things," Emily said. In her time, deliberately showing off one's power was a challenge to a fight. "He believed that one should always conserve power."

"Because one never knows when one might need power," Master Wolfe said.

Emily nodded, and asked a question that had been nagging at her. "Why don't you have an apprentice?"

"Most apprentices prefer to apprentice themselves to someone who can show them more powerful spells," Master Wolfe said. "They don't appreciate the potential of my work."

"They should," Emily said. "Why don't you start teaching the basics to some of the unattached apprentices?"

"Because they wouldn't learn," Master Wolfe pointed out. He nodded towards the sheets of parchment. "They would assume this is useless."

He shook his head. "My master wouldn't have taken me on," he added, "if he'd had someone with more power who was also willing to learn. And now...many of the secrets he uncovered—the secrets he taught me—will die with me."

"They don't have to," Emily said. The thought of Master Wolfe being forgotten was horrifying, although she already knew that history had forgotten him. Every last discovery made during this era was credited to Whitehall. "You could share them..."

She paused. "And if you can work out ways to cast spells with less magic," she added, "you'll have many more potential apprentices willing to work for you."

"I'll think about it," Master Wolfe said.

He paused. "And now, if you don't mind, we need to tighten up the spells," he added. "I want to be sure we have everything under control before we start turning our dreams into reality."

Chapter Thirteen

THE DOOR LEADING TO MASTER GILA'S CHAMBERS FELT...OMINOUS.
Emily stopped outside the wooden door and hesitated, feeling oddly reluctant to lift her hand and tap on the wood. Bernard and Robin had both advised her not to approach Master Gila, no matter what Whitehall might have said; it had taken Emily two days to work up the nerve to walk down to his chambers and step into his power. The sense of standing far too close to a dangerous wild animal grew stronger, the longer she stood outside his door. And yet, trying to approach his apprentice had proved futile. Sake couldn't tell her anything without permission from his master.

And I killed two necromancers, Emily reminded herself, as she knocked firmly on the wooden door. *I can handle a single magician.*

"Enter," a voice called.

Emily pushed the door open and forced herself to step into the room. Master Gila was seated in one corner, half-hidden in the semi-darkness. And yet his presence dominated the room, a brooding sensation that made her hackles rise as she looked around. A light globe—one of Robin's—spun in the air, casting a flickering light over a wooden table. Leather straps hung down from the table, suggesting that patients—or victims—needed to be firmly tied down before Master Gila went to work. Emily knew enough about medicine—or what passed for medicine—in the Nameless World to know that might well be true.

Master Gila looked up at her, his red eyes pulsing with cold dislike. "What do you want?"

"Master," Emily said. Up close, his eyes weren't as bright as Shadye's, but it was clearly just a matter of time before Master Gila fell completely into madness. Maybe red eyes were a warning of madness in magicians. "I was hoping you could show me some of your healing spells."

Master Gila laughed, humorlessly. "Do you think I would offer a healing spell free of charge?"

"I can offer you a spell in exchange," Emily said, calmly. She cast a light globe of her own into the air. Master Wolfe's spell wasn't as flexible as the one she used, but it was vastly superior to Robin's. And it drew on far less magic. "Or we can discuss other terms."

"A little of your blood, perhaps," Master Gila said. He snickered. "Or would you give me an arm and a leg?"

Emily blanched. "I do know other spells," she said, slowly. "But I won't offer you blood."

"Smart girl," Master Gila said. He rose to his feet, moving with a ponderous grace that reminded Emily of a walrus. His magic sparkled around him, pushing against her defenses and driving her back. "Do you really want to see my healing spells?"

For a long moment, Emily hesitated. Master Gila was on the verge of utter madness. She had the feeling that trying to extract a secret from him might be a dreadful mistake. And yet, there was no one else who could show her healing spells. There was no other way to know what spells were currently used. Learning his secrets was worth a high price.

"Yes," she said.

"Then you shall," Master Gila said. He sounded affable, suspiciously affable. "Cast more light globes, if you please."

He raised his voice as Emily went to work. "Eldora!"

A door opened, a moment later. Master Gila's wife stepped into the room, her eyes flickering from side to side nervously. Emily blinked in surprise, then looked at Master Gila. His expression was contorted into a sadistic smile that sent a chill running down the back of her neck. She'd faced necromancers and a combat sorcerer, but the aura of utter madness surrounding the older man was worse. She had the feeling that his madness had reached a point where he would do anything, purely for his own amusement.

"I haggled intensely with demons to learn how to heal the sick," Master Gila said, as his wife stood in front of them. Her eyes were permanently lowered, her hands clasped in front of her as if she were a serving girl. "They were reluctant to show me many spells, at first; I had to force them to teach me the tricks. But it was worth it."

He looked at Emily. "A damaged body must be rebuilt," he added. "And that requires vast power and knowledge."

Emily frowned as he nodded to his wife. Eldora unbuttoned her dress and let it drop to the floor. Underneath, her body was scarred, brutally marked in a hundred places. Emily stared in horror. Eldora looked as though she'd been beaten savagely, time and time again; she hadn't even been given time to recover between beatings. She'd seen something like it, back in the Cairngorms, but this was far worse. Eldora, moving like a woman two or three times her age, climbed onto the table and lay on her back. Her husband snapped the leather straps into place with practiced ease.

Cold horror shivered through Emily's mind. What was he *doing*?

"Healing is a battle against the body," Master Gila added, as he placed the final strap around Eldora's neck. She was tied down so thoroughly that she wouldn't be able to move an inch in any direction. "The skilled healer must force the body to heal itself, even though it doesn't want to heal."

"It doesn't want to heal?" Emily asked, surprised. That wasn't what she'd been taught by Lady Barb. "The body..."

"Silence," Master Gila ordered. He made an odd gesture above his wife's body, preparing a spell. "You wanted to learn, and so you shall learn."

Emily started forward as she recognized the spell. But it was too late. Eldora gasped in pain as a series of cracking sounds echoed through the room. The bonebreaker curse was forbidden at Whitehall, where it was possible to practice on a homunculus rather than a living person...Master Gila had just broken his wife's legs, so casually that it took Emily a second or two to realize what had happened. And his wife was so used to the pain that she hadn't even cried out...

"Stop that!" she cried.

"Oh, do be quiet," Master Gila said. He gave her a quelling look. "You wanted to learn, did you not?"

He made a gesture in Emily's direction. A wave of force slammed into her defenses, picking her up and slamming her against the stone wall. It was crude, brute force on a staggering scale; it might not be able to break through her wards and crush her to a pulp, but it could keep her stuck firmly in place. She hastily started to adjust her wards, directing the power away from her so she could break free, yet it was like trying to stand against a tidal wave of raw magic. Her wards hardened desperately as the pressure grew stronger.

"We have here two broken legs," Master Gila said. His voice was oddly contemplative, even though his wife was whimpering quietly now. He didn't bother to look back to see if Emily was focusing on him. "Both broken in several places; internal bleeding and secondary damage a very real possibility. Repair work must be done quickly to prevent permanent damage."

Emily gritted her teeth as the pressure beat down on her. It wasn't threatening to break her defenses, but it *was* threatening to push them back into her body. Her chest was already starting to ache under the constant pounding, despite her protections...perhaps Master Gila *was* a necromancer. Or perhaps she'd just grown too used to subtle ward-cracking spells rather than brute force. Desperately, she fought to establish a second layer of protections she could use to redirect his power. She didn't dare try to break free without diverting it elsewhere...

She glanced up at him as a flicker of magic caught her attention. His hands glowed with a sickly yellow light, a pale version of some of the spells Lady Barb had taught her. A moment later, he plunged his hands *into* his wife's right leg. Eldora opened her mouth and screamed as the yellow light spread through her body, magic slopping in all directions so badly that Emily worried for her safety, even if she survived the *healing.* And yet, there was no let-up in the torrent holding her in place. Eldora's voice cracked as her leg twisted, then slipped back into place.

He's putting it back together by brute force, Emily thought. It was horrific—no better than any of the non-magical surgery she'd seen—and yet it was working. *He's actually healing her!*

"You should take a closer look," Master Gila said, as Eldora stopped screaming. He made another gesture and Emily found herself shoved upwards, against the ceiling. "As you can see, the right leg is already healed; the left leg remains broken..."

"You monster!" Emily shouted. Eldora's head flopped to one side and lay still. She'd fainted. "You..."

Master Gila smirked at her. "This art requires the willingness to do what must be done," he said, bluntly. "I've beaten and dismissed apprentices before for *not* being willing to push the spells as far as necessary. Clearly, you don't have the stomach to handle it."

His hands glowed yellow again as he thrust them into Eldora's left leg. She jerked awake and started to scream again, the ear-piercing cries tearing at Emily's heart.

Gritting her teeth, she thrust out all her protections, falling towards the ground. Something slammed into her chest, time and time again, before she managed to regenerate her protections an instant before it was too late. She thought, for a horrific moment, that she'd managed to crack a rib or two before she caught herself and stumbled to her feet. Master Gila was watching her with an amused smile.

"You don't have the stomach," Master Gila said. Absurdly, he sounded almost *kind*. "Not everyone does. But you will need to learn to overcome it if you are to be a healer."

He turned back to his wife. Emily stared at her in horror. Her eyes were glancing desperately from side to side, yellow liquid dripping from between her legs and splashing down to the floor. Master Gila didn't seem to care that he'd used her as a dummy—that he'd humiliated her in front of a younger woman—as he inspected her arms. And then he prepared to cast the bone-breaking curse again.

"No!" Emily screamed.

She threw herself forward, just as Master Gila cast the curse, knocking into his hand and sending the curse flying across the room. Master Gila bit off a word that sounded like glass breaking, then spun around to hurl a punch into her face. Emily barely managed to jerk backwards in time to avoid it, silently thanking Sergeant Miles and Mistress Danielle for teaching her how to dodge. A young woman *couldn't* trade blows with a man and hope to come out ahead, not without magic. She evaded a second blow, ducking as he hurled an unfamiliar curse at her. Her protections were too badly battered for her to take the risk of trying to catch and analyze it.

Shit, she thought, as he hit her with another curse. The blast threw her from him and left her crumpled against the far wall. *What the hell do I do now?*

"Bitch," Master Gila snarled. Red light flickered around his eyes as he drew on his magic, his power shimmering around him and hammering on the air with a savage intensity that chilled her to the bone. Perhaps, if Shadye had had more control, he would have felt like Master Gila. "Whitehall should have taught you respect."

Emily forced herself to think as she pulled herself upright. Her chest hurt badly; her legs felt wobbly, as if she was on the verge of collapsing. Master Gila was between her and the door—between her and the door leading back to the castle, in any case. She could try to dive through the other door, she thought, but she had no idea where it led. Or, for that matter, if there was another way out of the bedroom. Master Gila probably didn't want his wife free to walk out of the room.

And if I hurt him or kill him, she thought, *what then?*

"Girls shouldn't be using magic," Master Gila added. He glared at her as he started to walk forward. "I'll teach you respect."

He hurled a third curse at Emily. She caught it desperately with her wards, deflecting it into the far wall. Master Gila's eyes went wide; he threw another curse, then hurled himself forward, magic sparkling around his hands. There was a brilliant flash of light as soon as he touched Emily's protections, the force of the impact knocking her over backwards even as his magic started to dig into her wards, threatening to tear them apart. And yet, and yet...his work was terrifyingly crude. Emily braced herself, then threw back a spell of her own, knowing it was going to hurt her almost as much as it would hurt him. Master Gila was thrown upwards, slamming into the ceiling as Emily rolled over and over to get away from him. He fell back down and struck the ground with terrifying force. She thought she heard the sound of his nose breaking as she rose to her feet and started towards the door, then stopped herself as she heard Eldora cry out. There was no way she could leave Eldora with her husband. If he was anything like as bad as some of the men she'd seen in the Cairngorms—or Zangaria, for that matter—he'd take his defeat out on his wife.

And yet, what could she do with him?

Stop him now, she thought, numbly. She could take him, she thought, but what then? *And then let Whitehall decide what to do with him.*

Master Gila rose to his feet. Blood dripped from a smashed nose, but he seemed otherwise intact. Emily frowned, feeling the pain in her chest getting worse. Perhaps she *had* cracked a rib after all. Master Gila was clearly tougher than he looked—and he looked very tough indeed. The red light shimmering around him warned that he'd taken the final step into madness. She felt his mind pressing against hers—again— but she held him off with grim determination. He just didn't have the finesse to force his way through her defenses without inflicting horrendous damage to her mind.

Which won't bother him in the slightest, Emily thought. The pressure intensified, but there was nothing subtle about it. He could hurt her, yet he couldn't break in. *Having me go mad would suit him just fine...*

He started to chant, loudly. Emily didn't recognize the words, but she could sense their effect. The room darkened still further, *something* materializing in the far cor- ner, rapidly taking on shape and form. Emily risked a glance, then looked back at Master Gila, unwilling to risk what remained of her sanity by trying to make out the creature. Master Gila let out a high-pitched giggle as the power grew stronger, his chanting growing louder and louder...whatever he was summoning, it was *powerful*. And she didn't *dare* risk letting it materialize completely.

She summoned her magic and cast a force punch. The spell degraded rapidly, almost as soon as she cast it, the *mana* drained by the summoned presence, but enough remained to slam into Master Gila and throw him backwards. His chant- ing stopped; the summoned presence started to fade, folding back into wherever it had come from. Master Gila hit the wall, his head cracking against the stone, and crumbled to the floor. Moments later, Emily felt the magic field surrounding him fade out of existence.

He's dead, she thought. stunned. Master Gila was hardly the first person she'd watched die in the last five years, hardly the first one she'd killed personally, but it still bothered her to know that there was more blood on her hands. *He's dead and I killed him and...*

She forced the thought out of her head as she turned and hurried towards Eldora. The woman was staring at her with horrified eyes, trying to inch backwards—despite the straps—as Emily approached. Emily knew, all too well, that women sometimes stayed with abusive husbands because they couldn't bring themselves to leave, but

Master Gila had been sickeningly abusive...why hadn't she left? But the law—such as it was—would probably be on his side if she did.

Someone will have sensed his death, she told herself, as she struggled to undo the leather straps. They were far tighter than necessary, cutting into Eldora's skin as she struggled to escape. *And then they will come...*

Using the healing spells she knew was a risk—Eldora might well tell Whitehall or Wolfe what she'd done—but she was damned if she was leaving a badly-wounded woman to suffer and die when she could stop it. She touched the wounds gently, casting the spells one by one and watching, grimly, as the damage slowly healed. Eldora's eyes went wide, then she slumped backwards. Emily hesitated, then cast a gentle sleep spell. Eldora would have at least eight hours of rest before waking to start the rest of her life.

And may she have a better one, Emily thought.

She heard the sound of running footsteps outside and braced herself. Whatever came wasn't going to be pleasant, but she could survive it. And at least Eldora was free...

And I learned something new, she added, grimly. The door burst open, revealing Whitehall and Lord Chamber. *The spells Master Gila used opened his mind to damage. And they left his mind damaged beyond repair.*

Chapter Fourteen

"YOU LOOK A MESS," JULIANNE SAID.

Emily scowled as she struggled to remove her clothes. Whitehall had spoken briefly to her, but when it became clear she was in pain he'd ordered Bernard to escort Emily to Julianne so his daughter could see what she could do for Emily. The pain in her chest was fading slowly, but her fingers refused to work properly. Undoing the buttons holding her shirt in place was a real challenge.

"Let me help," Julianne said, briskly. "You need time to recover."

"Thanks," Emily muttered crossly, as Julianne gently undid the buttons and pulled her shirt open. "Do you have something for the pain?"

Julianne sucked in her breath. "What did he *do* to you?"

Emily looked down. Her chest was black and blue, as if she'd been punched repeatedly; the rune between her breasts had gone red, as if it had been branded into her skin. The pain was fading slowly, but she suspected the bruises would take longer to go. She winced as Julianne poked at her skin for a moment, feeling for broken bones, then held a small potions gourd to her lips. It tasted awful—Emily had to fight to keep from throwing up at the first sip—but the pain slowly faded away to nothingness.

"Rub this on your chest," Julianne said, passing her a small cloth. It smelled of wild flowers and herbs. "It should help the skin to recover."

She frowned. "What *happened?*"

"He was torturing his wife," Emily said, grimly. She shook her head as she outlined the whole story. Lady Barb might have turned injuries into learning opportunities, but she'd never tortured anyone to make a point. It wasn't as if the students had been short of people to practice on. "He wanted to show me what he could do, so he broke her bones just so he could heal them."

Julianne looked sick. "Bastard!"

She looked down at the stone floor. "There are others wounded in the castle," she added, bitterly. "He could have practiced on them."

Emily sighed, feeling oddly woozy. The combination of the potion—and whatever was on the cloth—made her feel disconnected from her body, as if she was mildly drunk. She didn't remember side effects like *those* from the potions she knew, although Julianne probably had to work with whatever ingredients were on hand. Emily just hoped that feeling woozy was the worst of the side effects. Some potions she knew forced their drinkers to stay near the toilets for hours until it had finally passed through their systems.

The wonders of modern medicine, she thought, as she pulled her shirt closed again. *But at least it's a step in the right direction.*

"Father wants to see you as soon as you're feeling up to it," Julianne said. She cocked her head mischievously. "Should I tell him that you won't be up to it for a few days?"

Emily hesitated. She didn't feel very good, but there was no point in trying to hide indefinitely. Lord Whitehall *might* understand that she wasn't at her best—or, more likely, he'd see her as a weak and feeble woman. The commune magicians simply didn't have much respect for women, although they did seem to make an exception for her. She didn't want to lose that merely because she needed time to recover.

"Give me a moment," she said, finally. Her legs felt wobbly, but they grew stronger the more she forced herself to walk around the room. "Are you going to be with me?"

"Father would probably prefer to talk to you in private," Julianne said. "You *did* kill one of his oldest friends, after all."

Emily sucked in her breath. She hadn't thought of that—and she should have. Master Gila hadn't always been a monster, had he? He'd been a great healer, once upon a time; he'd had friends and allies in the commune. No matter what he'd become, he'd still have friends and allies. And even those who didn't like him would start muttering angrily about *someone* having killed a healer, even though he'd been trying to kill her at the time. It would be hard to blame Whitehall for being unhappy...

He was torturing his wife, Emily reminded herself, sternly. *And that is utterly unforgivable.*

"I understand," she said, grimly. There was no point in trying to put it off any longer. "Let's go, shall we?"

Julianne eyed her doubtfully, then led her out of the room and down the stone corridor. The castle seemed empty, much to her relief, until they reached Whitehall's office. Bernard and Robin stood outside, talking together in low voices. Bernard gave Emily an unreadable look as she approached and then smiled broadly at Julianne. Robin grinned openly at her, then nodded towards the wooden door. *He* didn't seem particularly concerned by Master Gila's death.

"Good luck," he muttered.

Emily scowled, then tapped on the door. It opened a moment later, revealing a bare stone chamber. Whitehall was kneeling on the floor, his hands pressed together as if he were in prayer; he looked up, sharply, as Emily stepped into the room and closed the door behind her with an audible *click.* And then he rose to his feet in one smooth motion. Unsure what to say or do, Emily waited. His face was so impassive that she couldn't read his feelings at all.

"You killed Master Gila," Whitehall said. It was an observation, not an accusation, but Emily flinched anyway. She'd killed a man in mortal combat...and it bothered her that it *didn't* bother her. "What happened?"

"He was torturing his wife," Emily said, flatly.

Whitehall met her eyes, firmly. Emily felt a pressure at the back of her head and hastily tightened her shields, hoping she could keep him out if he tried to invade her mind. She hadn't realized that Whitehall could do that too...she cursed herself under her breath as the pressure intensified, then lessened. Master Gila might not have been in the habit of sharing his secrets, but Whitehall could have devised the technique for himself. He would certainly have known it was possible.

And he isn't mad, Emily thought, as the mental pressure vanished completely. *That works in his favor too.*

"Explain," Whitehall ordered.

He didn't seem pleased or displeased that his mental probe had failed, Emily noted, as she took a moment to gather her thoughts before launching into a full explanation. Whitehall showed no visible reaction to her story, starting from her talk with Master Gila to their brief and thoroughly savage duel. His face only tightened when she told him about the summoned presence—the entity Master Gila had tried to summon—and how she'd accidentally killed him in a desperate bid to stop him from raising a demon.

"An interesting story," Whitehall said, when she'd finished. "Perhaps you could answer me a question?"

Emily frowned. She hadn't lied to him...not this time, anyway. Did he think there was a hole in her story? Or...or what?

"Of course," she said.

"Of course, *Master*," Whitehall corrected. He sounded irritated. "I checked Eldora thoroughly, Lady Emily. And she does not appear to be wounded."

Lady Barb was right, Emily thought, sourly. *No good deed ever goes unpunished.*

She would have laughed, if it wasn't deadly serious. She'd healed Eldora—she'd made sure that the older woman survived, even to the point of repairing older damage and scars—and now there was no physical evidence to support her words! But what had she been meant to do? Leave Eldora with a broken leg and enough scars to practically guarantee she would die before winter? Or try to duplicate Master Gila's spells, despite knowing the risks?

"I healed her, Master," Emily said. She wondered suddenly if she was supposed to be on her knees, but it was too late. "I know a handful of healing spells."

"A handful of *remarkably good* healing spells," Whitehall said. He met her eyes. "Where did you learn *those* spells?"

Emily gritted her teeth as the pressure on her mind grew stronger. Her head started to ache, as if she were caught in a vice. Whitehall might not be able to crack her mental shields—Void's protections were still in place, even if her own defenses failed—but he could probably pick up on a lie. And he probably already suspected that she'd lied to him a few times. If he knew she was holding back, he'd have to start worrying about what else she might be capable of doing. Somehow, Emily doubted a normal apprentice would be capable of killing a master.

"My tutor taught me," she said. It was true enough, merely incomplete. "I was curious to see how they compared to Master Gila's spells."

"Were you?" Whitehall said. "And what did you conclude?"

"My spells are better," Emily said. "And my tutor less of a sadist."

Whitehall surprised her by laughing as he pulled back, the pressure on her mind fading away into nothingness. "He wasn't always a monster," he said, quietly. "But we knew it was just a matter of time until he needed to be put down."

Emily swallowed, hard. Master Gila had been mad. She didn't want to think about having to kill a friend because he was on the verge of losing control completely, but Whitehall—it was clear—had had no choice. And Master Gila wasn't the only magician in the commune who was losing it. Lord Alfred was clearly more than a little dotty.

"I'm sorry," she said.

"So am I," Whitehall said.

He shook his head. "I remember meeting him for the first time, Lady Emily," he said. "He had paid a high price for his knowledge, like so many others, but he tried to be good and cheerful despite it. I recall him mending Stuart's arm after he took a fall..."

Emily bowed her head, feeling a stab of sympathy. She couldn't imagine what it must be like to have to keep an eye on her fellows for madness—and to be prepared to kill them before they became a danger to everyone else. And it must be worse for friends. Jade and *his* friends had been strikingly loyal to one another—they'd worked well together—and *he* wouldn't have wanted to kill a friend. Hell, *she* wouldn't have wanted to kill a friend.

And in some ways, she thought, *he's almost grateful I killed Master Gila.*

"Madness is the price we pay for power," Whitehall said, morbidly. "And one day... Bernard may have to kill me."

"Yes, Master," Emily said.

She shook her head. The texts and tomes had said little about how Whitehall had died; indeed, save for the transition between Whitehall and Bernard as Grandmasters of Whitehall, there was almost nothing about Whitehall's later years. But she doubted that anyone would have wanted to record Bernard killing his master, even if he'd had no choice, even if Whitehall himself would have wanted to die rather than go mad. She wondered, darkly, if she'd be stuck in the past long enough to find out.

Whitehall clapped his hands, making her jump. "So we have two issues," he said, turning and striding over to pick up a bundle lying against the wall. "The first is this..."

He started to unwrap the bundle. The aura of evil surrounding the cloth told Emily what was in it, even before she saw the Book of Pacts; the runes and sigils on the front cover were steaming slightly, as if the book had been boiled before it had been wrapped in a cloth. She wrinkled her nose at the stench of burning human flesh—the book had to be made from human skin—and recoiled when Whitehall held it out to her.

"This is yours, by right," Whitehall told her. He sounded thoroughly displeased. "Some of the contracts are null and void with Gila's death, but others are still in effect and can be transferred to you..."

Emily shook her head, sharply. "No," she said. There was no way she wanted a Book of Pacts, certainly not one that had belonged to a madman. "Can you get rid of it?"

"There are people who would give their right arms for such a book," Whitehall said. His tone hadn't changed. "I am obliged to tell you that, Lady Emily."

But you'd rather the book was destroyed, Emily thought, *even though you're not allowed to mislead me about its value.*

She considered it for a long moment. Master Gila had wanted to bargain with her—and she didn't have much to bargain *with,* unless she offered spells she suspected hadn't been invented yet. The next master she talked to would want the book—perhaps—instead of spells or anything else she might offer. But on the other hand, the demons that had started Master Gila on the path to madness were bound within the book. She wouldn't have cared to bet that *their* sigils and contracts had been destroyed.

And that would just start another magician on the path to madness, she told herself. *It wouldn't be worth the cost.*

"Destroy it," she said, firmly.

Whitehall gave her a relieved smile. "As you wish, Lady Emily."

Emily met his eyes. "And the second issue?"

Whitehall looked back at her, evenly. This time, there was no pressure on her mind.

"The second issue," he said. "What, Lady Emily, are we going to do with you?"

He leaned backwards, his eyes never leaving her face. "Far too many of us," he added after a moment, "are going to say you shouldn't have killed him."

Emily forced herself to stand up straight. "He was torturing his wife," she said, "and he was on the verge of summoning something truly nasty."

Whitehall frowned. "And you believe that justifies killing him?"

"I believe he *shouldn't* have been doing either," Emily said. She knew she was being tested and forced herself to keep looking at him. "I regret the need for what I did, but I could not have walked away."

"No, you couldn't," Whitehall agreed. "And he was balancing on the edge of madness for years before he finally fell."

"On the edge," Emily repeated. "He was already insane."

"Perhaps," Whitehall said. "But there is still the matter of deciding what to do with you."

Emily waited, wondering just what sort of punishment awaited an apprentice who had killed a master. The past was far too much like the present—the victim's name and family mattered more than the reason he'd been killed. A peasant who killed a nobleman for molesting his preteen daughter could expect to be executed, even though he'd been perfectly justified in what he'd done. And Whitehall *had* to do something to assert his authority.

Because it will be seen as a sign of weakness if he doesn't, Emily thought. She couldn't help thinking that Lord Whitehall and King Randor had a great deal in common. *And if he can't control his apprentices, his enemies will start sharpening their knives.*

"There is a case to be made that you should be given your mastery," Whitehall mused, slowly. "I can teach you very little without you taking the oaths, which you refuse to do—and you *did* kill a master. Your punishment will be being denied your mastery for quite some time."

He smiled, rather dryly. "What do you make of *that?*"

Emily had to fight to hide her amusement. She had a sneaking suspicion that Bernard, Robin or any of the other apprentices would have begged for beatings or punishment duties like working in the kitchens, rather than being denied their masteries for a moment longer than absolutely necessary. But Whitehall, she suspected, had only taken her on as a semi-apprentice to allow him to keep an eye on her. Her punishment wasn't much of a punishment at all, but hardly anyone would *realize* it.

And I don't want to be given a mastery anyway, she added, in the privacy of her own mind. *I would be noted in the history books...*

She sighed, inwardly. It would be a great deal easier if she'd had an *accurate* account of everything that had happened—or would happen—in the past.

"A terrible punishment," she said. Whitehall's eyes sparkled with brilliant amusement. He knew she knew it was no real punishment. "Should I be begging for something else?"

Whitehall gave her a sharp look. "He was my friend," he said. "And while I know he had to die, I do not...*like*...the thought of losing him."

"I know," Emily said. "And I am sorry."

"You know healing spells that are unknown to us," Whitehall mused. "Why don't you try to teach them to Apprentice Sake? He has good reason to hate you."

Because I killed his master, Emily thought. *Does that mean he can't earn his mastery?*

"I will try," she said. She didn't know how Sake had felt about Master Gila—*she* wouldn't have cared to be so close to a madman—but he'd resent being kicked back to join the unattached apprentices. "Will he be denied his mastery?"

"That is a matter to be discussed," Whitehall said. He nodded to the door. "Go."

Emily bowed, then turned and walked out. Robin was waiting outside, keeping a sharp eye on Bernard and Julianne as they talked in hushed voices. He smiled at her as she closed the door.

"So," he said. "How bad was it?"

"I'm to be denied mastery for a while," Emily said, flatly.

"Ouch," Robin said. He sounded genuinely sympathetic. "That's bad."

"Yeah," Emily said. She yawned, despite herself. She wanted to go to bed and rest, but she knew she couldn't—not when there was too much else to do. "It's pretty bad."

Chapter Fifteen

Emily couldn't help feeling surprised, over the next few days, at just how calmly most of the commune took Master Gila's death. She'd expected to find herself hated, she'd expected to be ducking hexes and curses in the corridor, but hardly anyone seemed angry at her. Even Apprentice Sake—who was due to be tested after the funeral by the assembled masters—seemed torn between dislike and a kind of wary respect. On one hand, Emily reasoned, he had to dislike her for making it harder for him to gain his mastery, but on the other hand she'd saved him from constant beatings and death threats. Master Gila's wife, it seemed, was hardly his only victim. He'd abused his apprentice too.

She'd seriously considered not attending the funeral, but Bernard and Robin had practically dragged her out of the castle and forced her to watch as Master Gila's body—already decaying faster than it should have—was placed atop a funeral pyre and burned to ashes, while his friends spoke a handful of words each about his life. Emily couldn't help feeling a little guilty as Lord Chamber and Lord Alfred spoke about how Master Gila had saved their lives, more than once, but it made no difference. Whatever he'd been in the prime of his life, at the end Master Gila had been a monster.

"Lady Emily," Whitehall said, afterwards. "The Book of Pacts was burned with him."

Emily nodded, relieved. She'd half-expected to hear the screams of burning demons, to watch the flames flicker eerie colors as the book burned with its owner, but there had been nothing. Perhaps it was for the best. Robin had already asked her what she intended to do with the book and hadn't believed her when she'd told him that she had asked Whitehall to destroy it, although Bernard had looked relieved. He didn't feel so unhappy, Emily guessed, about not being allowed to play with demons when there was someone else under the same restriction.

"Thank you, Master," she said.

Whitehall looked tired. "Apprentice Sake will be tested in an hour," he added, after a moment. "Did you teach him some spells?"

"A couple," Emily said, carefully. She'd insisted on testing the spells on the mundanes who were still nursing wounds from their flight to the castle. "But I don't know if he mastered them."

"We will see," Whitehall said. He scowled at Bernard, who was sitting just a little bit too close to Julianne. It didn't look remotely indecent, not to Emily, but she knew Whitehall had different standards. "There will be drinking afterwards, Lady Emily, so we may bid Gila a proper goodbye. Take my daughter to your rooms and stay there until dinner."

Emily nodded, relieved. She wouldn't have wanted to join a wake, even if she'd been invited; Bernard and Robin had talked about it as though it was a celebration, an excuse to get drunk, rather than a final goodbye to a madman. Perhaps she should have protested, she thought, as Whitehall summoned Julianne to his side, but it wasn't worth the effort. She didn't *want* to get too close to a bunch of drunken magicians. There was a *reason* alcohol was largely banned at Whitehall, in the future.

The castle felt empty—it *was* empty—as they walked back to their room. They were still sharing, but they had been moved into a bigger room once Julianne started to unpack her tools and ingredients for brewing. There was no sign of a proper bed—they were still using blankets—but there was a table and a pair of rickety stools. Julianne could—and did—use the room as a workplace, despite the risks. Emily would hate to know what Professor Thande would have said about it.

"You promised me lessons," Julianne said, once the door was closed. "Are you going to keep your promise?"

Emily sighed, inwardly. Julianne had been very good about not nagging her, in the wake of Master Gila's death, but Emily *had* promised. She motioned for Julianne to sit down on the floor, then picked up one of the newer wooden spoons that a carpenter had carved for her. It wasn't quite a wand—and wands could be dangerous anyway, if the novice used them too often—but it would suffice. She cast a pair of privacy wards around the room and then sat facing Julianne. The younger girl's eyes were alight with anticipation.

This could go very badly wrong, Emily thought, grimly. *What if she doesn't have magic?*

It was a chilling thought. Lady Barb had told her, during their preparations for visiting the Cairngorms, that some students chose not to study magic. Sometimes, they could—and did—pick it up later, but at other times they lost the ability altogether. Julianne came from a powerful bloodline—Emily had no doubt that Whitehall was incredibly strong—yet she'd been denied the chance to practice. And she might have lost the ability through no fault of her own.

"If you want to learn, you have to do what I tell you," she said, firmly. She wasn't a teacher who *had* to put up with a disobedient student. "If you disobey me, for any reason, there won't be any more lessons."

Julianne nodded. "I understand."

Emily held the spoon up as she carefully embedded a spell into the wood. It didn't seem to work perfectly, much to her annoyance, but it would suffice. "Take this," she said, passing the spoon to Julianne. "Can you feel anything?"

"There's....there's a tingle," Julianne said, after a moment. "What is it?"

"Magic," Emily said. She braced herself. Julianne sensing the magic was a good sign, but it was only the beginning. This could *definitely* go very wrong. "Try to reach out with your mind and trigger the spell."

There was a pause. Nothing happened.

"I don't know," Julianne said. Her voice was level, but she was clearly worried. "How do I do it?"

Emily winced. "Imagine you're standing above the spell," she said. Lady Barb had talked her through a handful of procedures, but she'd never actually had to use them. "And then imagine power flowing through your hands and into the spoon."

There was a surge of magic. Emily barely had a moment to throw up a shield before the makeshift wand exploded into splinters. Julianne stared at the stub in her hand, then started to giggle helplessly as she dropped it. Emily joined her a moment later, shaking her head in amused disbelief. The wood hadn't been strong enough to take the magic.

"Well," Emily said. "At least we know you can do *something*."

"It feels like...like when I make some of the more complex potions," Julianne said. "But different, too."

Emily frowned. Alchemy and potions were sometimes considered separate subjects, although there was so much overlap that Professor Thande preferred to keep them together and ignore the times when they were separate. But she'd seen enough to know that while potions *could* be brewed by mundanes, alchemical concoctions needed a magician to brew them. The magician used his magic to force the ingredients to blend in a particular way.

"You may have been using magic all along," she mused. "Can *anyone* make your potions?"

Julianne shrugged. "Not everyone wanted to learn," she said. "Fanny was asked to study with her mother—my aunt—but she refused. She wanted to get married and have children."

Emily looked up. "What happened to her?"

"She got married to a magician and moved away," Julianne said. "I don't know what happened afterwards."

Of course not, Emily thought. *No email, no telephones...even letter-writing doesn't really exist here. Julianne's cousin might as well be on the other side of the moon.*

"I'm sorry," Emily said. She picked up a second spoon and turned it over and over in her hand, then embedded a spell into the wood. "Shall we try again?"

Julianne nodded and took the spoon. This time, the spoon merely cracked in two places before warming up so rapidly that Julianne yelped and dropped the remains on the floor.

"We're going to need better wands," Emily said, finally. "I'll work out something for the carpenters to do."

"Thanks," Julianne said. "But...what about my lessons?"

"They'll have to wait until we get the wands," Emily said. "You need to learn how to channel power properly."

She held up a hand before Julianne could say a word. "And you are *not* to experiment with anything on your own," she added. "You would run the risk of hurting yourself quite badly."

"Very well," Julianne said. She sounded disappointed. Emily just hoped she had enough sense to listen to instructions. But then, it hadn't taken Emily long between learning to use her magic and finding new spells to cast, with or without supervision. "Do you want to learn a recipe?"

"Yes, please," Emily said.

She watched, thoughtfully, as Julianne started to sort out her ingredients, naming them as she worked. Alfalfa and Chamomile, Fennel and Ginger, Burdock and Chaste

Tree...it was easy to work out that Julianne was trying to make a potion to comfort the drinker and provide mild pain relief. And as Julianne worked, Emily could sense sparks of magic crackling around her and flowing into the liquid. They were so subtle that she suspected Whitehall couldn't sense them—his senses were used to far more powerful magicians—but they were there.

"Done," Julianne said. She sniffed the brew, then left it to cool. "You'll probably need some of this yourself."

Emily frowned. The potion—she thought she'd seen something like it among the Travellers—was designed to help women cope with their menstrual cycles, dulling the cramps and making the experience easier to endure. It wasn't something she'd given any thought to—she'd taken a monthly potion at Whitehall and felt nothing—but she had a feeling it would be a problem soon. Her last dose of potion would be out of her system by the time that point in her cycle rolled around again.

And there aren't any sanitary pads here, she thought, grimly. *How the hell do they cope?*

"I'll have some later, when the time comes," she said. How *did* Julianne cope? "How...how do you handle the blood?"

Julianne gave her a sharp look—clearly wondering how Emily had managed to avoid the problem—and then launched into a clinical explanation that left Emily feeling dreadfully embarrassed. She'd never *liked* talking about it, even when some of the girls at school—back on Earth—had bragged about having their first period. For them, it was a step into adulthood; for Emily, it had been the start of her stepfather looking at her with lusty eyes...

"I can help," Julianne said, finally. She sighed. "I used to help quite a few people back in the village. Their parents didn't want to talk about it to them."

Emily rolled her eyes, although—if she was forced to be honest—her parents hadn't talked about it to her either. But then, she'd had the internet and largely-pointless classes on sex education. Villagers...she was surprised that village women didn't tell their daughters the facts of life. Imaiqah had definitely known how things worked long before she'd gone to Whitehall.

She put the matter aside for later consideration and leaned forward. "There's something you have to know," she said. "When you're making a potion, you're using magic."

Julianne stared at her. "I'm using *magic*?"

"Yes," Emily said. "You're using magic to encourage the ingredients to blend together to produce the effect you want."

"You..." Julianne slapped the table, making everything jump. "Are you...are you telling me that I've been using magic all along?"

"I think so," Emily said. "You were taught—accidentally—how to use magic to make potions. And you never realized this because you only met a couple of other brewers."

"There are people who do make potions without magic," Julianne said. "Aren't there?"

Emily met her eyes. "How would you know?"

"Father doesn't know," Julianne said. "He would have forbidden me from brewing if he knew."

"Probably," Emily agreed. "But you *are* the only brewer the commune has, aren't you?"

"Until I train someone else," Julianne said. "I never...I never thought it might need *magic*."

Emily shrugged. "How do you feel when you're brewing something?"

Julianne hesitated. "It depends on the potion," she said. "There are some recipes that are quite forgiving, ones you can throw together in a hurry if necessary; others that require intensive concentration, recipes that will go wrong very quickly if you take your eye off them or stir harder than strictly necessary. With them, I feel... intensely focused."

"Magic," Emily said. "You're not just producing magic, you're controlling its flow perfectly."

She picked up the third and final wooden spoon, embedded a spell within the wood and passed it to Julianne. "Pretend you're brewing a potion," she said, "and let the magic glide into the spoon."

Julianne nodded, holding the spoon as if she were about to dip it into the cauldron. Emily braced herself, hastily setting up a pair of protective wards, but this time the spell worked perfectly. The end of the spoon began to glow with torchlight, casting an eerie pale radiance into the air. Julianne stared at it, then started to laugh in childlike delight. Emily smiled as the light winked out, knowing that Julianne would treasure that memory for the rest of her life. She could do magic!

"That's wonderful," Julianne said. She sobered, sharply. "My father won't want to see it, will he?"

"I don't think so," Emily said, dryly. She reached out with her senses, but felt only hints of magic surrounding Julianne. Whitehall would probably miss them altogether as long as Julianne was careful. "Don't do it in front of him, all right?"

"I won't," Julianne said. She took a breath. "What else can you teach me?"

"Quite a bit," Emily said. She looked at the cauldron. "Have you ever considered experimenting with other ingredients?"

"I've never had the time," Julianne admitted. "When I wasn't brewing, I was tending the sick or injured, helping to cook food or clean the castle."

Emily felt a stab of sympathy mixed with guilt. Julianne had always been out of place, neither one of the magicians nor one of the wives or serving girls. Her father clearly hadn't known quite what to do with her. She made a mental note to convince Whitehall to ensure that Julianne could take an apprentice of her own, someone who could help take some of the burden of brewing off her shoulders and give her more free time to experiment. If this was the birth of alchemy, Julianne definitely needed more time to develop the scientific method...

"You could always try to teach Eldora," she said. "She'll need *something* to keep her mind off everything that happened to her."

"I could try," Julianne said. "But she's *old*."

"No one is too old to learn," Emily countered. Eldora was old, true, but she deserved a second chance at life. The thought of letting Master Gila cast a long shadow—even in death -- was unpleasant. "Ask her, if she's willing to learn."

Julianne didn't look pleased. Eldora was at least fifteen years older than her, perhaps more—she wouldn't take kindly to being taught by a young girl. And Julianne wouldn't carry the natural authority of her father or one of the other masters. But it was a good thought.

"My father may insist on selecting the candidate," Julianne mused. She frowned as another thought struck her. "Emily...what would happen if the candidate had no magic?"

"Some of the potions wouldn't work," Emily said. There *were* ways, Lady Barb had said, to use high-magic ingredients to kick-start the process, but she doubted Julianne could get her hands on dragon scales or basilisk eyes. "Others would, just not as well as they would have done with magic."

"Then we'd need a girl with magic," Julianne said. She shook her head. "Is there a test?"

There *was*, Emily knew, but that hadn't been developed—wouldn't be developed—for hundreds of years. Or so she thought...it was hard to say what had been developed and then lost between Whitehall's era and her arrival in the Nameless World. But anything created at Whitehall had a good chance of surviving the years to come.

And blowing a hole in the timeline, if it wasn't meant to happen, Emily mused. Not knowing was worse than knowing too much. *And what will happen then?*

"I don't think so," she lied.

"I could look for a girl fathered by a magician," Julianne said, finally. Emily nodded in agreement. Magic ran in the blood, after all; Julianne was very much her father's daughter. "If there are any reports of...odd things...happening around her, consider accepting her as an apprentice. If not...I can teach her the basics and see if she can do the more advanced brews. "

"Good idea," Emily said.

"Try to teach two or three girls at the same time," she added, thoughtfully. "The basic recipes should work for that—I think. And then those girls can teach two or three others, each."

Julianne stared at her. "But the secrets..."

"Will be useless if they die with you," Emily said. She knew it could be done. Professor Thande had taught fifteen to twenty students at a time, despite the risk of accidents. Emily suspected she'd go mad very quickly if she'd had to teach so many students in a large classroom. "This way, you will have dozens of apprentices instead of just one or two."

And, she added silently, as Julianne started brewing another potion, *the groundwork for teaching more than one person at a time will be laid.*

Chapter Sixteen

"I WAS WONDERING WHEN YOU WERE GOING TO COME VISIT ME," MASTER DRAKE SAID, AS Emily stepped into his office. He was seated behind a desk, studying a leather-bound book; he motioned to a chair on the other side of the desk and watched as she sat down. "You've visited Master Reaper and Master Keldor over the last four days, haven't you?"

Emily nodded as she took the proffered seat. She would have been surprised if Master Drake *hadn't* known she was moving from master to master, in-between helping Master Wolfe with his plans to tap the nexus point and teaching Julianne several new spells. Master Reaper hadn't had much to offer her—he'd barely spoken a word to her—but Master Keldor had been happy to teach her things she hadn't wanted to know about the uses and abuses of dead bodies, including how a magician could fake his death for a short period. Perhaps leaving Master Gila's body alone for several days before cremating him hadn't been a mistake after all.

She pushed the thought aside with an effort and studied Master Drake with interest. Bernard had admitted to being scared of him—not without reason—and Robin had outright told her that the man had an odd sense of humor. Emily wouldn't have cared to meet *anyone* who thought that turning people into animals was funny, particularly without the carefully-crafted prank spells she'd learned in her first year of studies, but she had no choice. She had a theory—and an idea she wanted to try—and she needed Master Drake to help her do it.

He was tall, easily the tallest person in the commune. His face was pinched and sallow, as if he were constantly sucking on a lemon; his eyes seemed fixed on her face, as if he was determined to see who would blink first. The magic surrounding him didn't feel anything like as tainted as Master Gila's—there was no trace of red in his eyes—but it was clearly powerful. And, if half of what she'd been told about him was true, he might well rival Whitehall for power.

"I've been told you practice transmutation," she said, carefully. "I..."

"A remarkable piece of intelligence," Master Drake interrupted. There was a faint, but clearly audible sneer in his voice. "Who could *possibly* have told you that, I wonder?"

"They say you can change lead into gold," Emily continued, ignoring the jibe. "How do you do *that*?"

"Magic," Master Drake said. He smirked. "You were expecting a different answer?"

"I would have liked to hear how you did it," Emily said.

"And I would like to hear how you turned Bernard into a frog," Master Drake said. "Was it something like this?"

He lifted his hand and threw a spell at her. Emily nearly fell backwards as her protections shivered under the impact, threatening to shatter into nothingness as they strove to break up and dispel the spell before it was too late. There was enough power, she sensed, to do much worse than merely turn her into a frog. Master Drake's spell would strip her of humanity too, trapping her as a frog until he chose to release the spell. It was hard, so hard, to deflect enough of the spell to take it apart, but somehow she made it work...

...And then the spell simply dissolved back into the ether.

Master Drake inclined his head, one magician to another. "Your protections are impressive," he said, sounding as if he would sooner have had teeth pulled without anesthetic than admit it. "I have never seen the like."

"Your spell was powerful, but blunt," Emily said. She refused to show him just how badly his spell had damaged her protections, even though she wasn't sure she could hold off another such spell. "My protections broke it into nothingness."

"So they did," Master Drake said. He gave her a considering look. "And you managed to turn Bernard into a frog?"

"Like this," Emily said.

She shaped the spell in her mind and hurled it at him, but she wasn't too surprised when he blocked it. Master Drake might not have her protections—indeed, she wasn't sure he had *any* protections—yet he did have a great deal of raw power. And her spell was actually quite fragile. It wasn't designed to survive almost any level of resistance.

"Impressive," Master Drake said. "And what do you have to offer me"—he gave her a lewd wink—"in exchange for a look at one of *my* spells?"

Emily felt her cheeks redden and reminded herself, sharply, that he was trying to get under her skin. She supposed she should be glad that his had been the only lewd suggestion aimed at her—she'd heard the serving girls being teased by the magicians—but it was still irritating, a reminder that she didn't quite fit in. He wouldn't have said that to Bernard, would he? Or to his own apprentice.

"I can show you something very interesting," Emily said. "And I believe it will be worth your while."

Master Drake studied her for a long moment. "And if it *isn't* worth my while?"

"It will be," Emily assured him.

"I will be making complaints to your master if it isn't," Master Drake said. He gave her a strikingly savage smile. "And you will not enjoy the consequences."

Emily nodded. "Show me your spell," she said. She reached into her bag and produced a piece of firewood she'd taken from the pile, placing it gently on the desk. "Turn this into gold."

Master Drake eyed her darkly, then held his hand over the firewood and cast the spell. Emily watched, tasting the spellwork, as the wood shimmered and turned to gold. The spell—like Master Gila's spells—drained a great deal of power, more than she would have expected. She doubted she could have cast the spell back in her fourth year, let alone her third. And casting it repeatedly would have been impossible without her boosted magic.

"Impressive," she said, finally.

She picked up the golden branch and examined it, thoughtfully. Permanent transfiguration was difficult, certainly when every magician in the world learnt how to cancel spells in their first year of schooling. It wasn't a bad idea—she knew she would have had real problems if she hadn't been able to cancel spells—but it could be frustrating. There were students from poorer families who could have made themselves better clothes, if they hadn't known the spells could be cancelled at any moment.

"One would hope so," Master Drake said. "It took me years to grasp that spell."

"I imagine it did," Emily said. "The sheer level of power you used..."

Master Drake preened. "I am very powerful," he said. "And I am hardly *insane*..."

It will come, Emily thought. She'd suspected it from the first spell and the second had confirmed it. Master Drake's spells had as much slop as anything she'd seen from Master Gila. She wasn't sure just how old Master Drake was—she'd have placed him in his thirties—but it wouldn't be long before the slop started to affect his mind. *And then you'll start losing your grip on reality.*

"I trust you found that interesting," Master Drake said. His voice hardened suddenly. "And what do you have to show me?"

"Master Wolfe has been working on the fundamental...*rules*...for casting spells," Emily said, carefully. "He's been using his work to rewrite spells."

"A pointless waste of time," Master Drake said, dismissively. "I *do* trust you have something more interesting to show me?"

"It is far from a waste of time," Emily said, nettled. She'd spent five years learning to analyze and rewrite spellware, knowing it would give her much more flexibility than merely casting and recasting common spells. "As you can see..."

She took a sheet of parchment out of her bag and carefully outlined Master Drake's original spell, then showed how it could be rewritten to use far less power. Master Drake watched expressionlessly—his eyes didn't blink once, as far as she could tell—as she finished her work, then cast the spell. The entire desk turned to gold.

Master Drake said a word she didn't recognize as he jumped backwards, then poked and prodded at the golden desk. Emily could sense the magic field leaping around him as he worked, testing the gold carefully. The golden stick suddenly reverted to wood, followed by the desk itself. Master Drake looked up, his eyes dark. There was something ugly in them that made Emily want to tighten her protections. And yet she didn't want to have to fight another master...

"Explain," he ordered.

"You're pushing far too much power into the spell," she said. Part of the reason she'd had so much trouble handling his spell had been because the spell was massively overpowered. He might not realize it, but there were dozens of redundancies -unnecessary redundancies—built into the spellwork. "You can cast it with much less power."

Master Drake reached out with astonishing power and caught her arm. "Why?"

Emily resisted the urge to pull back. "Because you are using brute force," she said. "And it is working, but it drains your power. The spells you use are grossly inefficient."

She sucked in her breath as Master Drake let go of her. Whitehall had kept her busy casting spells every morning, saving her from having to expend or store magic, but Master Drake might have the same problem if he managed to reduce the amount of magic he used for each spell. Perhaps Master Gila had had that problem too. Emily had suffered nasty headaches for several months after the duel, when her reserves had grown too high for her to handle them safely; she dreaded to think what would have happened if she hadn't kept expending magic.

It might have driven me insane, she thought.

"My master taught me how to perform these spells," Master Drake said. He sounded angry, but not at her. "He never suggested the spell could be modified..."

Emily looked at him. "Why not?"

"He always believed that the spells had to be cast with such force," Master Drake said. "And when I tried the spells as a young man, they didn't work."

"Because you didn't have the power to make them work," Emily said.

"I assume so," Master Drake said. "Why...why does this work?"

"Spells are structures," Emily said. "Like houses...spells are *structures*. You can take apart a large house and use the materials to build a smaller house..."

"And have enough for a second house afterwards," Master Drake finished. He tapped the wooden desk thoughtfully. "And I could make more gold."

Emily frowned. "How long does the gold last?"

"Not long," Master Drake said. "If you'd tried melting it down, it would have reverted to wood pretty quickly. But otherwise there would be no way to know."

"You're overpowering the spell," Emily mused. "And so some of the results are random."

She made a mental note to take the transmutation spell apart and see just what every last spell component actually *did*. It was possible that Master Drake was actually transfiguring the same thing time and time again—and equally possible, she supposed, that some parts of the spell were cancelling out other parts of the spell. If the transmutation didn't hold when the object was damaged...perhaps...

Perhaps some demon tempted his master with the idea of unlimited wealth, she thought, *and his master never noticed the sting in the tail.*

"I shall have to study Master Wolfe's work more closely," Master Drake said.

"And you could let him study your other spells," Emily pointed out. "Who knows what might happen when he starts looking at *them*."

Master Drake eyed her, sharply. "Secrets are secret for a reason."

"But trading knowledge would make it easier to come up with new inventions," Emily said, softly. "You could do a great deal more if you understood how the magic actually worked."

She rose to her feet and bowed, then headed for the door. She could *feel* his gaze on her as she walked, but managed to resist the urge to start running or to hurl back something nasty, knowing it would merely cause trouble. Robin was waiting outside, looking oddly amused about *something*. Emily closed the door behind her and then nodded at him. Where was Bernard?

"He's out with his master," Robin said. Emily blinked, then realized that Robin must have read the question on her face. "And I have nothing to do."

Emily sighed, inwardly, as he fell into step beside her. "You don't have more floors to clear?"

"We've cleared enough space for the moment," Robin assured her. He gave her a mischievous smile. "Didn't you kill him?"

"No, I did not," Emily said, realizing—a second too late—that she was being teased. "We had a very productive discussion."

"You don't *seem* to have been turned into a dog," Robin bantered. "Bernard won't have to do any of his chores for a week."

Emily frowned. "He won't?"

"Master Drake has a habit of turning apprentices into animals," Robin said. He didn't seem worried by the prospect, even though Master Drake's spells were far more powerful than any of the prank spells. "He turned Galveston into a chicken for babbling too much and Harold into a fish for..."

"You're joking," Emily said. Turning someone into a chicken was quite bad enough—particularly as there was a very real danger of someone mistaking the chicken for dinner—but a fish? Harold would have been lucky to survive. Hell, she wasn't sure if he *could* survive without being dropped into water. "Are you...?"

She shook her head. Of *course* he wasn't joking.

"So they all thought you'd be coming out of the room in some other shape," Robin said, ignoring her comment. "Or that you'd kill Master Drake. And Bernard bet on you and he's going to be pleased."

"Oh, *goody*," Emily said, with heavy sarcasm.

Robin didn't seem to hear it. "What do you plan to say to *my* master?"

Emily shuddered. Master Chambers was a DemonMaster. If he had any speciality, apart from summoning demons, no one had told her about it. And she didn't *want* to summon demons. It was just too difficult to keep them from finding a loophole in their instructions and exploiting it mercilessly.

Although finding a way to dismiss a demon would be useful, she thought. Aurelius had taught her a few Words of Banishment, but they didn't always work when she hadn't summoned the demon. *But do they know?*

She glanced at Robin. His magic field was tainted, but she didn't *think* there was a demon nestled within it. "Can you dismiss your demons?"

Robin frowned. "It depends on the demon," he said. "Some have to be summoned time and time again—they can be dismissed easily, if you keep your nerve. Others... others cannot be dismissed without destroying their sigil in the Book of Pacts. And once you destroyed it, you wouldn't be able to call on them again. They don't come when you call."

"I see," Emily said. She wasn't sure she wanted to ask more questions, but Aurelius's vast collection of books had included more speculation than hard facts. "Are there limits to what you can ask a demon to do?"

"Yeah," Robin said.

Emily waited, but he said nothing more. "And those are...?"

"I'm not permitted to talk about them," Robin said, after a moment. "My oaths..."

He cleared his throat. "All I can tell you is what my master told me, years ago," he added, slowly. His words were hesitant, as if he were choosing them carefully. "A demon will do anything for you—if you meet its price."

Emily nodded, slowly. A couple of Aurelius's books had discussed that, although the writers had written in such elliptical terms that it was hard to be sure. Demons were omnipotent—they'd insisted—but it had never made sense to her. If they could do anything they liked, why would they do favors for the DemonMasters? And if there was a *reason* they did favors for the DemonMasters, why weren't the DemonMasters ruling the world?

But if they need something from us, she thought, *it might put limits on their abilities. Or they might not be so powerful after all.*

"You offered the demon blood for a spell," she said, deciding not to point out the flaw in the spell. If Robin didn't already know, someone else could tell him. "What else do you trade?"

Robin frowned. Sweat was prickling on his brow. "I can't tell you," he said. "I..."

He cleared his throat. "You should ask my master," he added. "He could tell you."

"I'll consider it," Emily said. It was hard enough being close to Robin when his demon was clearly visible. She had no intention of walking into a DemonMaster's lair. Master Chambers might not want to let her go afterwards. "What are you doing this evening?"

"Just playing soccer with the lads," Robin said. "At least until the sun goes down..."

He gave her a wry look. "Do you want to come along?"

"Julianne insists on going to bed early," Emily said. It wasn't entirely untrue, but Julianne also insisted on spending half an hour practicing spells first. Besides, she'd never liked team sports. "We have to be up early in the morning."

"Yes, we do," Robin said. He frowned, wiping his brow. "I'm sorry I couldn't be more helpful."

"I wouldn't ask you to break a sworn oath," Emily reassured him. Even basic oaths could be unpleasant, if they were broken. And with demons involved, she was sure the consequences would be horrific. "Shall we go for dinner?"

Robin hooked his arm through hers. "Why not?"

Chapter Seventeen

EMILY WAS SURPRISED—PLEASANTLY SURPRISED—AT JUST HOW QUICKLY SOME OF THE SEEDS she'd planted began to bear fruit over the next few weeks. Master Drake joined Master Wolfe and herself as they worked out the spells for tapping the nexus point, Master Wolfe determined to rewrite Master Drake's spells so he could use them himself. Whitehall joined them too, abandoning his private sessions with Emily so he could throw himself into the new project. And Sake—now Master Sake—not only learned the spells she taught him, but—at her suggestion—taught them to four of the unattached apprentices.

"You seem to be encouraging us to share ideas," Whitehall commented, during one lunch break. Master Wolfe still had problems eating and sleeping, although he'd calmed down a little after Whitehall had started threatening to force-feed him a sleeping draught. "Is that deliberate?"

"The more minds working on a problem," Emily pointed out, "the greater the chance of finding a solution."

"Not with magicians," Whitehall countered. "Getting a bunch of magicians working on the same problem is worse than herding cats."

Emily concealed her amusement as they finished their lunch and prepared to head down to the nexus chamber. They said the same in her time, although magicians *could* work together if they learned the habit from the start—or if they liked each other. She recalled how much she'd enjoyed working with Caleb. The thought was bitter—being stuck in the past was enjoyable, but if she stayed she'd never see him again. And she missed him more than she cared to admit.

"This is dangerous," Master Chambers warned. He sounded pessimistic. "A single surge of raw magic would be enough to kill everyone."

"We've been through this already," Whitehall said, tiredly. He definitely sounded as though he'd had enough horror stories. "We *have* to tap the nexus point or we won't be able to remain here indefinitely."

Emily sighed, inwardly, as the two men kept sniping at each other. They were *meant* to be friends, according to their apprentices, but their arguments had grown more frequent over the past two weeks. Master Chambers seemed to like living in the castle—it was certainly better than a village—yet he didn't like trying to use the nexus point. And, she suspected, he didn't like *her* much either. He'd even scolded Robin for trying to spend so much time with her.

"The spells have been carefully worked out," Master Wolfe called back. He sounded confident—or at least trying to pretend he was confident. "We can handle any surges of magic."

"And if you're wrong, we're all dead," Master Chambers snapped.

Emily resisted—barely—the urge to point out that Master Wolfe *wasn't* wrong. Master Chambers wouldn't want to hear *anything* from her, not after he'd heard how Emily had convinced Master Drake to work with Master Wolfe. Emily had no idea why he disliked her so intensely—unless he was very wedded to the idea that women should be neither seen nor heard—but it hardly mattered. All that mattered was that he wouldn't listen to a word she said.

Maybe I should propose calling up a demon, she thought, as they walked into the nexus chamber. *He'd drop the idea in a hurry if it was my suggestion.*

She closed her eyes for a long moment as she felt the beating power surrounding her, then opened them and looked directly at the nexus. Her head started to swim a moment later as she tried to comprehend what she was seeing; the nexus point was tiny and yet immensely huge, pulsing with raw magic that made her hair want to stand on end. It was like staring into a terrifyingly bright light, one that could blind you if you looked at it long enough. None of the other magicians, even Whitehall, seemed able to look at the nexus point. Just being this close to it was unpleasant.

"I have the materials ready," Master Bones said. "Shall we begin?"

He sounded oddly amused, Emily noted; it was hard to blame him. Master Bones was an Elementalist, a magician who worked with the elements; he might be considered a master, but he was looked down upon by many of the other magicians. They didn't see any value in his work, from crystals that held spells to wooden wands and stone knives that could focus and direct magic. And yet, once Master Wolfe had started putting together the spells to control the nexus point, it hadn't taken him long to realize that something stronger would be required than mere spellwork. He'd pulled Master Bones into the research team shortly afterwards.

And there aren't any Elementalists in my time, Emily thought. Master Chambers had sneered at the whole concept, treating it as little better than potions or divination, but she'd had a different idea. *The discipline must have been folded into alchemy.*

She made a mental note to encourage Julianne to discuss the matter with Master Bones—if he would talk to her—and then watched as Bones and Wolfe carefully drew out the runes on the floor. Wolfe was a walking dictionary of runes and he was *delighted* to share, telling her what each of the runes did when they were drawn by a trained magician. Most of them worked on their own, like the rune on Emily's chest; the magicians had barely begun to consider the possibilities for using one or more runes in tandem. Emily had a private suspicion that Master Wolfe would end up with rather more apprentices than he could handle, after the nexus point was tamed. And *they* would be the ones who would work out how to use five or six runes per spell.

That might be why some of the runes went out of fashion, she told herself. The old runes weren't mysterious—or long-lost keys to power. Professor Locke would have been disappointed, if he'd been with her. *They were no longer necessary after newer techniques were developed.*

"This is a remarkable mess," Master Keldor said, as he slipped into the chamber. He smelled unpleasant, his shirt stained with blood. Emily didn't want to think about what he might have been doing, earlier in the day. "Are you sure it will work?"

"I'm betting my life on it," Master Wolfe said, waspishly. "You are welcome to check the equations, if you wish."

Master Keldor sniffed, exchanging a sharp look with Master Chambers. The masters had voted on Master Wolfe's plans and they'd been outvoted, five to four. It might have been a mistake, Emily privately considered, for Master Chambers to allow Sake to be raised to mastery. If Sake hadn't had a vote, it would have been tied. And somehow, she doubted Whitehall would have defied the others just to try to take control of the nexus point.

Master Wolfe stepped back from the network of runes he'd drawn and motioned for Whitehall to check them, which he did in clinical detail. Emily checked too, comparing the drawn runes to the notations Master Wolfe had scribbled on the parchment. There didn't seem to be any mistakes, as far as she could tell. Even Master Chambers, eying the runes balefully, didn't find anything. And *he* would have been delighted to have an excuse to demand a second vote.

"*She* shouldn't be here," Master Chambers said, instead. He didn't bother to look at Emily as he spoke. The disdain in his voice couldn't have been more obvious. "This is *master* business."

"I asked her to come," Whitehall stated, bluntly. He shot Emily a reassuring look. "And she *is* qualified."

Emily felt her cheeks heat. Masters, she'd come to realize, had near-unlimited authority over their apprentices. One master couldn't interfere with another's apprentice, even if the apprentice was being abused—or was taking advantage of his master. Whitehall had every right to keep her with him, if he wished, despite the near-certainty that it would cause resentment and nasty rumors. She was tempted to leave the chamber, for his sake, but she knew she needed to be present. It was the only way to ensure she was part of the group that held control over the nexus point.

"On your head be it," Master Chambers said, firmly.

Master Wolfe raised his voice. "Take your places," he ordered. He shot Master Chambers a sardonic look. "This is your last chance to back out, if you wish..."

Master Chambers strode forward and took his place along the edge of the runic circle. "I know my duty," he said. Emily shivered as she sensed the invisible demon sitting on his shoulder. It was hard to escape the feeling that the creature was staring at her. "And I will be there to support you."

Emily sighed, inwardly, as she took her place between Whitehall and Master Wolfe. It would have been better, she suspected, if Master Chambers had flatly refused to take part in the ritual, but he'd insisted on doing his part. Whitehall had told her, when she'd asked, that the masters had all sworn to honor the results when they'd voted, yet she would have been happier if Master Chambers had left. Not taking part in the ritual would have excluded him from the control group.

But he might not have realized that he will be part of the control group, she thought. *He certainly didn't pay much attention to the equations.*

She shivered at the thought, dismissing it as she prepared for the ritual. Maybe Master Chambers *hadn't* realized it, but she felt sure a demon would point it out, sooner or later. It would cause no end of trouble if Master Chambers started trying to control the planned wards, even if it didn't help the demons directly. And perhaps it would. If one had nestled within the school's wards...surely, another could do the same.

Demons exist outside the bonds of time and space, she reminded herself. *They may already know the outcome of whatever we do.*

She contemplated it while Whitehall and Master Wolfe made the final checks. If everything she did was *meant* to happen, the demons would definitely know the outcome. But if the future was still in flux, her intervention might have created an alternate timeline. And who knew how many problems *that* would cause? Logically, nothing she did in the past would erase *her* from existence—she'd been born on an entirely different world—but her past self might find a very different school...

If she gets kidnapped at all, Emily thought. *Shadye was a student at Whitehall, after all.*

"We will now begin," Master Wolfe said. Emily could hear the strain in his voice as he took one final look at the runic circle. "Join hands."

Emily was silently grateful she wasn't standing next to Master Chambers as she took Whitehall and Wolfe's hands. They both felt oddly calloused, although she wasn't sure why that surprised her. Even in her time, very few magicians enjoyed the luxury of only book-learning. Whitehall would have spent a *lot* of time working with his hands.

And he's scarred them too, when he experimented with magic, she thought. *Just like everyone else.*

"We begin," Master Wolfe said. "The spell starts...now."

Emily braced herself as the spellwork shimmered into existence, drawing power from all seven magicians. She half-expected the older magicians to find it hard to share power and awareness with her, just as her fellow students had done in the future, but none of them seemed particularly intimidated by her power reserves. Their magic required vastly superior reserves to anything taught at Whitehall School, certainly anything she'd seen before starting her fifth year at school. They might be surprised by her power, but they wouldn't be intimidated by it.

She wished, grimly, that there had been a way to hold a rehearsal before starting the rite, but they hadn't been able to devise a method to test their work without actually doing it. Wolfe had drilled them all mercilessly on what he wanted them to do, yet it had been nothing more than words. The reality...she gritted her teeth as a surge of power battered against her wards, the runes glowing with light as the spell grew stronger. Convincing Master Bones to work with Master Wolfe had been a lucky break, she told herself. The chalk drawings Master Wolfe normally used wouldn't have been able to handle the magic and would have disintegrated, leaving them exposed to the raw power of the nexus point. Even with it...

Someone grunted in pain as the magic grew stronger, the nexus point reacting to the spellwork and emitting a surge of power. She winced as Whitehall's grip tightened, but forced herself not to pull free. The nexus point *howled* in rage as more and more magic spewed into the chamber, only to be sucked up by the runes and directed into the spell. She couldn't escape the impression that the nexus point was actually *alive* on some level, as if it was a wild animal they were trying to tame. The howling grew stronger and stronger, power battering savagely against her shields...

...And then it was gone.

"Do not let go," Master Wolfe ordered. "We have to be ready to hold the spell in place."

Emily sucked in her breath. The spell—the ritual spell—was spinning in front of them, tapping the nexus's own power to keep it under control. She could sense Master Wolfe probing at the spell, hastily fixing cracks in the spellware before the nexus point burned through them and spat raw power into the chamber. The other magicians felt tired and drained, yet there was an exultation glimmering in the air that surprised and delighted her.

They've done something remarkable, she thought. *And they know it.*

"Very well," Master Wolfe said. "We will now commence the second stage..."

Emily's mind expanded, rapidly, as the spellwork reached out and sucked her into a whirlpool. She was suddenly aware—terrifyingly aware—of every nook and cranny within Whitehall, of every last remaining trap concealed within the castle. The traps themselves weren't linked *directly* to the nexus, but whoever had devised and emplaced them had designed the spellware so they drew on the higher levels of ambient magic surrounding the nexus point. She wasn't sure exactly how long it had been between their emplacement and Whitehall's arrival, but it looked as though the castle had been abandoned for nearly a hundred years.

And I will have to hope they believe I arrived before then, she thought, as she studied the castle's layout. *Or they'll be blaming me for the traps.*

She frowned, inwardly, as magic pulsed through the castle. It hadn't been apparent, based on the maps, but now she could see—all too clearly—precisely *why* the corridors were so poorly designed. Indeed, they hadn't been poorly designed at all! They were *runes*: the entire castle was a runic structure on an unimaginable scale. Whoever had built the castle had intended to use it as a spell-focus, but for what? If they were that advanced, why not tap the nexus point with spellware?

Unless there was a reason they couldn't tap the nexus point, she thought. *But what?*

Master Wolfe went to work, carefully locking the spellware in place while the other masters held themselves ready to intervene, if necessary. Emily watched glumly as a multitude of pocket dimensions sprang into existence, each one balancing the previous one and holding it in place. She'd hoped—prayed—that she could use the nexus point to craft a pocket dimension to allow her to jump forward in time, but it was becoming increasingly clear that it wouldn't be possible. Moving a few days— even a few *years*—forward might be doable, but nearly a thousand years...?

And if I keep popping out to check where—when—I am, she thought, *I might damage history still further.*

The thought wasn't reassuring. She had no way to know just how badly she was affecting history—if, indeed, what she was doing *wasn't* what was meant to happen. And linking the pocket dimension to the nexus would certainly attract attention...a Grandmaster, sometime between Lord Whitehall and Hasdrubal, might open the pocket dimension and pull her out...and who knew what would happen then?

There has to be another solution, she told herself, firmly. Staying in the past was not an option. Quite apart from just how badly she missed her friends, her mere presence was a danger to history. And she didn't want to slip into the forest and vanish. *I just need to find it.*

Yeah, her own thoughts answered her. *And if it involves calling on demons...?*

She staggered backwards as the spellwork came to an end, letting go of the masters' hands as she dropped to the stone floor. Her entire body was drenched in sweat, as if she'd been running for hours...she wondered, suddenly, just how long her mind had been lost within the spellwork. It might have been hours—or days. Her hands hurt badly: they'd squeezed her fingers so hard she couldn't help wondering if something was broken or dislocated. She heard someone grunting in pain and forced herself to sit upright, realizing dully that all of the masters had collapsed. If the spellwork failed, if there was a surge of raw power, they wouldn't have a chance to flee before it was too late. And yet...

We did it, she thought, as a handful of servants entered with food and drink. *We laid the groundwork for Whitehall School.*

And then she passed out.

Chapter Eighteen

"I THINK YOU IMPRESSED FATHER," JULIANNE SAID. "YOU CERTAINLY IMPRESSED BERNARD."

Emily shrugged, irritated. She hadn't been the only magician to faint after taking part in the ritual, but that hadn't stopped Master Chambers inquiring if women genuinely had the power to cast complex spells. He'd even suggested that it had been *her* presence that had made the other magicians faint, although Master Wolfe had insisted that it had been caused by disconnecting so sharply from the spellwork. And Robin had been absurdly solicitous over dinner, offering to walk her back to her bedroom afterwards. Emily still wasn't sure if he was trying to help—and had no idea how to go about it—or if his master had put him up to it.

Better to be mocked openly than talked down to, she told herself.

"That's something, I suppose," she said.

She leaned back in her chair and watched as Julianne chopped up a piece of ginger root, preparing to put it in a potion. The castle *felt* different now, the magic pulsing through the stone reminding her of her first days at Whitehall School. Master Wolfe had needed to be talked out of going straight back down to the nexus chamber after dinner and starting a whole series of experiments. Emily supposed *she* would have wanted to play with a new toy too, if she had one, but Whitehall was right to be cautious. The spellwork—and crystal structures—she recalled from *her* Whitehall were in their infancy.

"Yeah," Julianne said. "And Master Bones was bragging about the value of his work to anyone who would listen."

"He's right," Emily said. "You should listen to him."

Julianne shot her a sardonic look. Emily understood. Master Bones might have attracted a few new apprentices—he'd definitely played a vitally important role in controlling the nexus point—but it would be a long time before he considered a *female* apprentice. And yet, Julianne could listen, learn, and experiment herself. She'd already started teaching a handful of girls how to brew potions. Emily had hopes that two or three of the girls had enough of a talent for magic to brew even the more complex potions.

"Maybe if I bat my eyelashes at him," Julianne said. She smiled, humorlessly. "But Father would not be amused."

"No," Emily agreed. It was hard to be sure, but she was fairly certain that Master Bones was old enough to be Julianne's grandfather. He was definitely surprisingly *sane*, compared to Chambers, Keldor or even Drake. "Your father would definitely not be amused."

"Nor would Bernard," Julianne said. She sprinkled the ginger root into the cauldron, then added water and several herbs. "But he might teach me more himself."

Emily hid her amusement. Bernard hadn't been remotely sure what to make of the sudden changes in the commune, from Master Drake working with Master Wolfe to Master Bones actually knowing something useful. Emily rather suspected that he—and Robin—had their doubts, perhaps even wondered if their extensive education was about to become obsolete, although neither of them had said anything to *her* about it. Bernard was completely focused on Julianne, and Robin spent half of his time trying to flirt with Emily.

"He might," Emily said, finally. "But he will be worried..."

She sighed, inwardly, as Julianne cast a spell, lighting the fire under the cauldron. She'd grown more and more willing to use spells over the last few days, rather than struggle with tapers or ask one of the boys to light the fire for her. Emily didn't blame her for *that*, but she did worry about Julianne absent-mindedly using magic in front of her father. She had no idea what Julianne intended to *say* to Whitehall, when he caught her, yet Emily knew he wouldn't be pleased. And even if her theory about the Curse was correct...

"Yes, he will," Julianne said. There was a new firmness in her tone. "But he will just have to get used to it."

There was a loud banging at the door. "Open up, now," a voice snapped. "Julianne, open the door *now*!"

Emily's blood ran cold. That was Whitehall's voice.

Julianne glanced at Emily, her face suddenly very pale, then stood and walked towards the door. Emily realized, just as Julianne pulled back the latch and opened it, just how badly they'd screwed up. She'd grown too used to casting spells without any monitoring at all—without fearing that someone was going to complain about her practice—and forgotten that Master Wolfe had designed a ward to track magic within the castle. Locating the traps so they could be removed wasn't its *only* use.

Shit, she thought.

Whitehall stepped into the room and shut the door behind him, his face icy cold. He'd probably missed the earlier traces of magic on Julianne—just as he had problems detecting Emily's magic—but he could sense them now. Julianne had just used a very simple spell, after all, and the residue hung in the air. Emily wondered, numbly, just *how* he would react to Julianne's magic. He had to believe—he still had to believe—that Julianne would pay a high price for her powers.

"You used magic," Whitehall said. It wasn't really a question. "Didn't you?"

"Yes, Father," Julianne said, tonelessly.

Whitehall rounded on Emily. "Is this how you thank me? By teaching my daughter magic?"

"I asked her to teach me," Julianne said, pleadingly. "Father..."

"Be *silent*," Whitehall snapped. The anger in his voice made Emily flinch. "Emily..."

"I will not be silent," Julianne said. She met her father's gaze evenly, resting her hands on her hips. "Father, I asked her to teach me magic..."

Whitehall's face fell. No, he wasn't really angry, Emily realized; he was too numb to be *really* angry. She'd expected everything from threats to beatings and banishments from the castle, but instead...there was a dreadful numbness that left her feeling sorry for him, despite the certainty that they were both in big trouble.

"I hope you know what it will cost you," Whitehall said, quietly. "Your mother would have been furious..."

"She wouldn't have been," Emily said. "Master..."

"I am your master," Whitehall said. His voice hardened. "I accepted you as an apprentice, over the objections of my commune. And you repay me by costing my daughter her chance at children."

The betrayal in his voice stung. He was wrong—Emily *knew* he was wrong. But it still stung. He had gone out on a limb for her, she knew all too well, and he had good reason to be angry at her. By his standards, if nothing else, she had betrayed him.

"I don't believe I have," she said, keeping her voice low. It would be easy to puff up and shout at him, but somehow she knew that would be disastrous. "Master, please will you let me explain?"

Whitehall eyed her for a long moment, then took a step backwards with visible effort, crossing his arms in front of him. "Explain."

Emily took a moment to gather her thoughts. "The spells you use—the spells *most* of you use—are very poorly designed," she said. "I believe Master Wolfe said as much."

"He did," Whitehall confirmed. "Continue."

"Every time you cast one of those spells," Emily added, "you get...you get *slop*, magic spilling out from the spell in all directions. Many of the spells are actually designed to *encourage* slop. You're...you're always doing things the hard way."

Whitehall didn't look pleased, but he nodded curtly for her to continue.

"That magic has an unfortunate effect on the human mind and body," Emily continued, hoping desperately that he believed her. She knew it, but it was hard to explain. "Mentally, using such spells has an unfortunate effect on the caster's mind. Magicians like Master Gila start going insane because they're constantly using the same spells and damaging their minds. They may snap completely, one day, when they can no longer handle the magic."

And when they try to take too much power at once, she added, silently. She had no idea what had happened to Master Wolfe's necromantic rite, but she knew—all too well—that it wouldn't remain buried forever. *A single touch of necromancy is enough to drive anyone insane.*

"At first, it has a lesser effect on the body," Emily added. "For men and women, the effects are seemingly minimal. But for both sexes, the magic damages their reproductive systems..."

Julianne cleared her throat. "Emily, my father has a daughter," she said. "Me."

"Yes," Emily said. She tried hard to be clinical. "But the male reproductive system is less fragile than the female system."

Whitehall met her eyes. "In what way?"

Emily winced, inwardly. Just how much did they know already? Master Gila had never given the impression that he knew much about how the human body, male or female, actually *worked*. She might accidentally tell them something that altered history...

She shook her head. She was well past the point where it mattered.

"The male...constantly refreshes his supply of sperm," she said. Lady Barb had told her that she might be called upon to explain the facts of life—despite her lack of experience—but she'd never envisaged explaining them to the founder of Whitehall School. "The damage may be quite considerable, yet the male may still be capable of fathering children."

She took a breath. Julianne jumped in.

"I only know one magician who has more than two children," she said. "Father..."

"Be quiet," Whitehall snapped. "Emily? Continue."

"The female only has a limited supply of eggs," Emily said. She forced her voice to stay even, despite Julianne's incredulous look. She'd probably never realized that she laid eggs like a chicken. "Once they're gone, they're gone. And the sloppy magic is damaging them, rendering the woman infertile."

"I see," Whitehall said. His voice was deadly cold. "And you have rendered *my daughter* infertile?"

"No, Master," Emily said. "The spells I taught her have no slop."

Whitehall met her eyes. She felt the mental pressure a second later and concentrated on projecting impressions of sincerity at him. He would want to believe her, she was sure, yet he wouldn't be too trusting. She *had* betrayed him, even if she didn't want to admit it. It wouldn't have been *that* difficult to go to him and ask, before she started.

But he might have said no, she thought.

"I was taught how to build up my magic from the moment it developed," Emily said. She was fairly sure that only *very* strong magicians, at least by her standards, ever learned how to use their powers without proper training. "There was never any *slop*, therefore there was no danger to...to my ability to have children."

Whitehall looked her up and down. "You have had no children," he stated, bluntly.

Emily colored. "No," she said. "But I could have children."

"It will be true of Bernard too, Father," Julianne said. "He might not be able to sire children."

Whitehall rounded on her. "And are you sure," he asked sharply, "that he will still want you if you have magic?"

"She's been using magic for a long time," Emily said, as Julianne's face crumpled. Whitehall turned back to glower at her. "Many of those potions she makes require a trickle of magic to get them to work."

Whitehall rubbed his forehead. "You're sure?"

"Yes, Master," Emily said.

"I see," Whitehall said. He glanced at Julianne. "Go back to your bedroom and wait for me there."

Julianne shot Emily an unreadable look as she hurried to the door and vanished into the corridor, closing the door behind her. Emily met Whitehall's eyes as best as she could, trying to calm herself. Whitehall had every right to be angry at her—and so did Bernard, perhaps—and if he wanted to punish her, she supposed he had that right. But at the same time...

"You should have brought it to me," Whitehall said, quietly. And yet she could hear an edge in his tone that told her he was keeping himself under strict control. "You are an apprentice. You had no right to teach anyone without my permission. And yet..."

He sighed. "You're no ordinary apprentice, are you?"

"No, Master," Emily said.

She tasted a hint of despondency in his voice and shivered. Whitehall...she thought Whitehall *wanted* to believe her. He *needed* to believe her, perhaps, if he wanted to cling to the idea of having grandchildren. But it wouldn't be easy for him to acknowledge that the shortage of magical children might have something to do with the men, as well as the women.

"I think you'd better explain," Whitehall said.

Emily swallowed hard. She didn't dare tell him the truth. But what *should* she tell him?

"My tutor believed in following more than one branch of magic," she said, finally. "He insisted on me learning everything he had to teach, ranging from spells like yours to potions and even runic alphabets. I used what he taught me to combine the different disciplines and keep my magic under control."

Whitehall lifted an eyebrow. "Indeed?"

"Yes, Master," Emily said. It was true enough. "Brewing potions is excellent practice for using magic. Potions—the more advanced potions—simply don't work unless you control the magic perfectly."

"Getting male students to learn potions might be difficult," Whitehall observed. He gave her a brilliant smile. "They see them as women's work."

"Then the students who do learn will have an advantage over those who don't," Emily said.

She took a breath. Did she dare? She'd already laid the groundwork...

"Your problem, right now, is that you have only eight masters to service fifty apprentices," she continued.

"*Nine* masters," Whitehall corrected.

Emily nodded, acknowledging the mistake. "It can take five to ten years to tutor an apprentice properly," she said. "In the time it will take for Bernard to gain his mastery, some of the other apprentices will have lost their powers or grown desperate enough to turn to demons and ask for help. And even if they don't, they will have a great deal to unlearn before you can make something of them."

She paused, just for a moment. "Matters aren't helped by the fact that not all masters are equal," she added. "Sake is already dealing with several apprentices because he can teach healing, but Master Wolfe and Master Bones have fewer candidates because most apprentices want to learn something *useful*—something they *see* as useful. Realistically speaking, you only have *six* masters because the remaining two have no apprentices."

Whitehall frowned. "And you have a better idea?"

"I was taught the basics of several disciplines," Emily said. "Do the same here—you have enough room, in this castle, to house an entire school. Name it after yourself! Get five or six apprentice students studying the same discipline, then move them to the next class and let them study a different discipline. Those who want to study healing have to spend an hour or so a day studying runic alphabets and spell circles too. It should give them a way to use one discipline to assist them in others."

"I could see a number of masters refusing to teach several students at once," Whitehall mused, thoughtfully. "I wouldn't want to teach more than two or three apprentices at once."

"You'd have to keep demons out," Emily added. She rather suspected that would appeal to him. "They couldn't be allowed into the school."

Whitehall scowled. "And why not?"

"Robin summoned a demon and asked for a light-spell," Emily said. "The demon gave him a spell he didn't understand—couldn't understand, because he didn't study spellwork—and let him use it, unaware that it was slopping magic everywhere. Robin...is likely to go mad sooner rather than later because he's been using that damned spell."

"Master Wolfe rewrote it," Whitehall said.

Emily met his eyes. "Is the rewritten version the one Robin is using?"

"...No," Whitehall said.

Emily nodded. "Demons offer shortcuts to power," she reminded him. "But their gifts come with a terrible price."

Whitehall held up his hand. "I will take your words under advisement," he said. "They will certainly need to be discussed with the other masters. Not all of them will want to share their secrets."

Master Chambers, Emily thought. *He won't want to share anything.*

"I'm sure you can talk them into it," Emily said.

"We will see," Whitehall said. His voice hardened. "There is, however, a different matter to discuss. You taught my daughter magic."

"It won't harm her," Emily protested.

"That's not the point," Whitehall said. "You are an *apprentice*. You should not be teaching *anyone* magic. There are rules, Lady Emily, and those rules exist for a reason. My master would not have forgiven me if I had taken on an apprentice myself, certainly not before I was granted my mastery. It doesn't matter *who* you were trying to teach. All that matters is that you *were* teaching magic."

Emily nodded. "I understand."

"Glad to hear it," Whitehall said. "You—and Julianne, once I have spoken to her—will spend the rest of the afternoon harvesting herbs and other ingredients from the forest. I'll be sending Bernard and Robin with you. And I don't want to see you back in the castle before twilight."

Emily blinked. She'd expected something worse. Masters had complete power over their apprentices. Whitehall could have beaten her to a bloody pulp and no one would have given a damn, let alone tried to stop him. And maybe he should have. It was the second time she'd done something that could—that should—have gotten her in real trouble. The other masters would give him a hard time...

...And sending her out of his sight would give him some time to think.

"I expect to see four full baskets of supplies by the time you come back," Whitehall added, darkly. There was a hint of amusement in his voice. "I'm sure the boys will be happy to assist you."

"I'm sure they will too," Emily lied. Whitehall snorted, rudely. Apprentices—attached apprentices—were excused from chores. Bernard and Robin would be furious when they realized what they'd been signed up to do. "And thank you..."

Whitehall scowled. "I hope you're right about this, Lady Emily," he said. "Because, if you're wrong, it isn't you who is going to pay the price."

Chapter Nineteen

"I'M SORRY I GOT YOU IN TROUBLE," JULIANNE SAID, AS THEY WALKED DOWN TO THE COURT-yard. "I...I just wanted to learn."

Emily shrugged. She'd had to wait outside while Whitehall spoke to his wayward daughter, but Julianne looked fine. "What did he say to you?"

"Just said I should be very careful," Julianne said. "And that I should tell Bernard before he hears it from someone else."

"Rumors have a tendency to grow," Emily agreed. Whitehall had taken it remark-ably calmly, she thought. Had he been delighted to hear of something that could end the curse—or had he merely realized that there was no point in being angry? "You do have to tell him the truth."

"They're going to be annoyed enough at coming into the forest with us," Julianne warned, ruefully. "And to think it would be enjoyable without them."

Emily hid her amusement as they reached the courtyard. Bernard and Robin were standing in the open, looking up at the bright blue sky. Four large wooden baskets rested by their feet; a small knapsack, open to reveal a gourd of water, reminded her that they'd been ordered to remain out of the castle until twilight. Judging by the position of the sun, they wouldn't be allowed back for at least seven hours, perhaps longer. She sighed, inwardly, as the boys noticed them. It was going to be a long day.

It could be worse, she told herself, firmly.

"Lady Emily," Robin said. His demon didn't seem to be nearby, much to Emily's relief. "I hear we're meant to be sticking to you like a weasel that's just..."

"Thank you," Bernard said, cutting him off. "Julianne...are you all right?"

"Yes," Julianne said. She sounded oddly exuberant—but then, Emily knew, she had reason to be. Her father might have been furious, yet he hadn't outright banned her from using magic...yet. "I'll tell you the rest once we're in the forest, if you don't mind?"

Bernard shrugged, picked up two of the baskets and started towards the open gates. Robin smiled at Emily, made a show of picking up the remaining two baskets, then motioned for Emily to follow Bernard and Julianne. Emily sighed—she wasn't sure she wanted Robin behind her—but followed the other two anyway. The air grew warmer—and sweeter—as they walked down towards the forest; she couldn't help noticing that there didn't seem to be a path leading away from the castle. But then, Whitehall had admitted that they'd hacked and slashed their way to the castle when they'd first arrived.

No Dragon's Den here yet, Emily thought. She looked back towards the Craggy Mountains and smiled. *And no Blighted Lands, either.*

The forest was...odd, she discovered, as they walked into the trees. She'd expected darkness, but instead enough light burned through the overhead canopy to illumi-nate their path. Flowers—many unrecognizable to her—grew everywhere; she could hear birds and insects buzzing through the trees, the sound rising and falling from a faint background note to an almost overpowering racket. And magic...magic was everywhere. She could feel it tingling along her skin, see flickers of blue light at the corner of her eyes...

She found herself smiling as the sensation grew stronger and glanced at Robin. He was smiling too, an open, honest smile that set off an odd flutter within her heart. Robin was...sardonic, sharp-edged, when he wasn't trying to flirt with her; now, there was something gentle and relaxed about him that she found far more likeable. He reminded her, just a little, of Caleb. And, up ahead, Bernard and Julianne were holding hands. Emily couldn't help being touched by the way they held one another. They walked in silence, the magic humming around them. Butterflies flew beside them for a long moment before vanishing into the distance.

Robin cleared his throat. The spell was broken. "So," he said. "To what do we owe the pleasure of our afternoon walk?"

"I was studying magic," Julianne said. She turned to face Robin and Emily, still holding Bernard's hand. "I...I convinced Emily to teach me."

Bernard's eyes went wide. "And your father didn't disown you?"

"He didn't," Julianne said. "But he wasn't too pleased."

"He's secretly pleased," Bernard said. He sounded as if he wasn't quite sure what to make of it. "If he wasn't pleased, you would have been severely punished—or disowned."

"This *is* a severe punishment," Robin said. He held up the baskets. "Do you realize how long it will take to fill these?"

"It could be worse," Bernard pointed out.

Emily nodded. Julianne could have been beaten—or disowned. And being disowned would be a fate worse than death. Julianne would have to leave the castle and make her way to the nearest settlement—wherever that was—and hopefully find a place there. She had magic—and her potions—but would it be enough to keep her alive? Emily wouldn't have cared to try it in this time period and she had *far* more magic at her disposal than Julianne.

"Yeah," Julianne said. "It could have been."

She looked at Bernard. "I'm going to keep studying magic," she said, softly. "Is that a problem?"

Bernard shook his head. "I promised to teach you magic," he said. "And I don't mind if you learn from someone else."

"But what about children?" Robin asked. The look Julianne gave him, by rights, should have blasted him into ashes. "You want someone to carry on the family name, don't you?"

"It shouldn't be a problem," Emily said. "Julianne has been doing magic for a long time."

Robin gave her a disbelieving look, so Emily explained what she'd discovered about potions and how they tied into elemental magic and alchemy. Bernard seemed to believe her when she explained the dangers of using overpowered spells—although he wasn't happy with the suggestion he might be sterile—but Robin seemed much less inclined to accept it. Emily wasn't too surprised. Robin had moved ahead by leaps and bounds, at least in part, because he'd used demons. The idea that he might have made a terrible mistake was unacceptable to him.

And the idea he might be sterile is worse, Emily thought. There had been husbands in the Cairngorms—and Zangaria—who'd beaten their wives for not getting pregnant or for giving birth to girls. None of them had wanted to face up to the fact that it might be their fault. *He won't want to admit it at all.*

"If that's true," Bernard said, when he'd finished, "we should all be learning potions."

Robin snorted. "Good luck trying to teach them to the others."

Bernard nodded, ruefully.

Julianne cleared her throat. "You don't mind?"

"I don't mind you learning magic," Bernard said. "I can swear that as...as an oath, if you wish."

He swallowed, hard. "Will you marry me?"

Emily had to smile as Julianne wrapped her arms around Bernard and kissed him, hard. The magic seemed to grow stronger as the kiss became deeper and deeper, Bernard's hands running up and down Julianne's back. They separated, just for a moment, their eyes shining as they kissed again and again. Robin caught Emily's arm and pulled her back, quietly encouraging her to give the couple some privacy. It was unlikely they'd go much further than kissing in the forest...

But Whitehall will probably explode with rage if she loses her virginity before the wedding night, Emily thought. *And Bernard...Bernard may have to be released from his apprenticeship before he can marry her.*

"They won't do anything too stupid," Robin assured her. His face twisted into a warm, unguarded smile. "Or at least nothing more than they've already done."

He shook his head. "I cannot *believe* her father took it so calmly. My master would have screamed the place down."

"He's a calm man," Emily said. "And we opened up a whole new field of magic."

She sighed inwardly. Whitehall had been careful not to use any of the demonic spells. *His* spells were still sloppy, compared to the spells Emily had been taught in her first year, but they did far less damage. She rather suspected that the *lack* of mental damage explained why Whitehall was nowhere near as unpredictable as some of the other masters.

"If you can teach apprentices to brew potions," Robin said. "Do you think many will want to learn?"

"It's a good way to learn how to control your magic," Emily said. She glanced towards Bernard and Julianne, still kissing deeply, and sighed. "They need it, I think."

"Perhaps," Robin said.

He looked at her. "I could teach you how to summon a demon...?"

Emily blinked. Where the hell had *that* come from?

"I wouldn't want to know," she said. She'd learned how to summon two demons at Mountaintop, but she had no intention of doing it ever again. Demons simply could not be trusted. And, no matter how smart the DemonMasters were, the demons were probably smarter. "Why are you offering?"

"You've taught me something useful," Robin said, evasively. "And I wanted to teach you something too."

"Learn to brew potions and I'll call it even," Emily countered. She wondered, suddenly, if Master Chambers had ordered Robin to make the offer. Whitehall would be furious if he caught her experimenting with demons—and he'd be right. "You'll find it very useful."

"I suppose," Robin said. The magic surged again, humming around them. She couldn't help wondering if it was responding to Bernard and Julianne. "You're a very interesting person, Lady Emily."

"Just Emily, please," Emily said. She understood why Whitehall and the other masters addressed her as *Lady Emily*, but Robin was only a year or two older than her. "And I'm not that interesting."

"You are," Robin said.

Emily shook her head, keeping one eye on Bernard and Julianne. How long could they keep kissing? But then, there was something strikingly romantic in the air. Her heartbeat started to race as she turned back to Robin. When he was silent, when the magic was billowing around them, she couldn't help finding him attractive. And yet there was Caleb, waiting for her in the future. She didn't want to betray him.

And then the tingle rose up around them, stronger than before. Robin took a step forward, leaning forward to kiss her. Emily felt her body respond, her lips parting slightly as they kissed. She *wanted* him suddenly, wanted him with an intensity she couldn't explain; she wanted him to kiss her again and again...

Emily shook her head, firmly. "No."

She stepped back, breaking the embrace and crossing her arms under her breasts. Robin stared at her, a conflicting mixture of emotions crossing his face.

"No?"

"No," Emily said. She readied herself, unsure just what he would do. Some men could turn very nasty if they were rejected: Robin might, particularly after she'd kissed him for a handful of seconds. Her lips tingled, mocking her. She *still* wanted to kiss him. "We can't..."

Robin stared at her for a long moment, then turned and stalked away. Emily was torn between going after him—no one should be on his own in the forest—and honoring her commitment to Whitehall and staying near Julianne. And yet, being on his own was probably what he needed. He wouldn't want to see her and he wouldn't want to see Bernard making out with Julianne, not when he'd been denied the chance to make out himself.

Men, Emily thought.

She took a deep breath, focusing her mind. Her body was sweaty, although she had no idea when she'd started to overheat. There was *definitely* something odd about the forest, an aura of raw magic that she didn't recall from her time. But then, she'd sensed more magic when she'd stood on the battlements and peered into the darkness. Had something happened, between Lord Whitehall and her time, to drain the magic? Or...

The nexus point, she thought. *It's no longer oozing magic into the world.*

Bernard and Julianne finally separated and started to make their way back towards her, holding hands. Emily wondered, ruefully, if she'd need to create a glamour for Julianne; her lips were puffy and swollen. And Bernard's weren't much better. Whitehall would have to be blind to *not* realize that Bernard and Julianne had been kissing. He might take a dimmer view of that than Julianne learning magic.

"You need to watch your lips," she teased. "You've been kissing."

Bernard didn't rise to the bait. "Where's Robin?"

Emily hesitated. "He decided to go off on his own," she said, finally. Robin wouldn't thank her if she told his friend the truth. "I thought I should stay with you."

"Silly bastard," Bernard said. He peered into the forest, looking for Robin. "I'll get after him if you two start hunting for herbs."

Julianne caught his arm. "Should you be alone?"

"*He* shouldn't be alone," Bernard said. "And if his master *catches* him alone, out here, he'll regret it."

He strode off before Emily could point out that Master Chambers was likely to be busy—Whitehall would probably be telling him about the planned school—leaving Emily and Julianne behind. Emily glanced at Julianne and frowned, inwardly, at the odd little smile crossing Julianne's face. She looked like the cat that drank the cream... her face flushed, her shirt rumpled, and her short hair in disarray. Whitehall wouldn't have any trouble noticing that she'd been...*intimate*...even if he *was* blind.

She leaned forward. "Are you all right?"

"Just feeling a little strange," Julianne said. She touched the space between her breasts thoughtfully. "Is that normal?"

Emily shrugged. She knew that some of her friends—male and female—bragged about their conquests, but it wasn't something she intended to do. Besides, she was very far from *normal*.

"He made me feel so good," Julianne burbled. Emily couldn't help wondering if she was a little high. There was so much potent magic in the air that it had to be having *some* effect on them. "I never wanted him to stop."

She looked up, suddenly. "Robin tried to kiss you, didn't he?"

"He did kiss me," Emily said. She touched her lips, feeling a pang of guilt. Her boyfriend might be nearly a thousand years in the future, but she still loved him. Caleb would be heartbroken if he knew Robin had kissed her and, just for a moment, she'd kissed him back. "This place...it has that effect on people."

Julianne shrugged. "He's definitely interested in you," she said. "But if you don't want him, make that clear. You have no protector."

"I don't need a protector," Emily said, stiffly.

"No," Julianne said, after a moment. There was a wistful note in her voice. "I don't suppose you do."

She picked up one of the baskets as they heard the sound of approaching footsteps, then motioned for Emily to start picking herbs. Emily did as she was told, keeping her eyes down as Bernard and Robin rejoined them. Bernard gave her a thoughtful look; Robin, behind him, refused to meet her eyes at all. Emily wondered, rather darkly, just what he might have told his best friend about her. That she'd led him on? Or that the kiss had gone badly wrong?

Don't worry about it, she told herself firmly. *Nothing is going to happen between you and him.*

"Make sure you leave the seeds behind," Julianne said. She glanced into Emily's basket and frowned. "They'll grow the next crop of herbs."

Robin looked up, still refusing to look directly at Emily. "What can you do with these herbs?"

"Brewed into a tea, you can put someone to sleep," Julianne said, briskly. "Boiled together with four other herbs and plenty of water, you can keep someone awake for hours."

"That will be very helpful," Emily said.

"It catches up with you," Julianne said. "I once drank a potion to stay awake for several days—there was a particularly difficult childbirth—and afterwards I was completely out of it for three days. My tutor had to pour water into my mouth just so I would have something to drink."

"Everything has a price," Robin muttered.

Emily *looked* at him. "What do you pay for each demonic spell?"

Robin's eyes flashed. "None of your business, you..."

He caught himself. "I beg your pardon, Lady Emily," he said. He made a visible effort to calm himself. "This place brings out the best and the worst in people."

Emily shrugged as they moved to the next clearing and began harvesting a bundle of moon flowers. Professor Thande used them in several potions, yet—from what she recalled—there were several other herbs that could be used in their place. Moon flowers weren't actively poisonous, he'd said, but they did have irritating side effects. Julianne, she assumed, didn't know about their replacements yet.

She's already halfway to inventing the alchemical method, Emily told herself. Julianne had taken to the concept like a duck to water. *She doesn't need any more help.*

The air suddenly blew cold, so cold she shivered as she straightened up. Julianne's eyes were wide with fear, while the two boys—their disagreements forgotten—were glancing from side to side, their hands held up in casting gestures. Emily stared at them as the temperature continued to drop, sensing the magic field flickering and changing. She could *feel* it.

Something was coming...

"Stay very quiet," Bernard hissed. Emily shivered, again. She could hear the fear in his voice. He was absolutely terrified, too terrified to try to hide it. "And start inching back towards the castle..."

Emily glanced towards the other side of the clearing, just in time to see the trees part, as if something had pushed them aside...

...And then a monstrous creature scuttled into the clearing.

Chapter Twenty

EMILY FOUGHT THE URGE TO INCH BACKWARDS AS THE CREATURE SLOWLY ADVANCED ON them. It was hard, so hard, to get a clear idea of what it *was*. There was something about it that her mind refused to grasp, as if there were parts of it that existed in other dimensions. And it was faintly translucent, as if it wasn't truly solid; she could see trees and bushes *though* it, if she peered carefully. She found herself catching impressions of teeth and claws, long spider-like legs and flickering eyeballs...oddly, the trees were bending *around* the creature, rather than being broken or pushed aside by its bulk. She couldn't help thinking that the creature was being *pushed* into her reality, rather than being native to the Nameless World. There was something about its multidimensional nature that made it very alien.

She tried to look closer, but her head started to pound. The creature seemed to draw her thoughts towards it, tugging at her mind; it was a compulsion, she realized dully, every bit as dangerous as subtle magic. She bit her lip hard, using the pain to focus her thoughts, then poked Bernard in the back. He jerked, then elbowed Robin while Emily did the same to Julianne. They'd been entranced so thoroughly that they hadn't even noticed!

And yet, her rune was still. There was no burning sensation in her chest.

Whatever that creature is, Emily thought, *it isn't natural.*

The boys motioned for Julianne and Emily to slip backwards while they blocked the creature's path. A typical giant spider could be killed by a sword, if magic wasn't available, but the creature in front of them was no true spider. Her mind, she realized numbly, was trying desperately to match the morass of impressions to something she could accept. And yet, the more she looked at it, the harder it was to escape the idea of a dozen spiders melded together and turned into a single entity.

"Get ready to run," Bernard hissed. He never took his eyes off the creature. "Go straight back to the castle. Don't worry about us."

Robin glanced at him. "If it found us here, it could follow us back to the castle," he objected, bluntly. "We can't let it find the others."

Emily swallowed, hard. If the spider-*thing* was one of the creatures hunting the magicians...no wonder no one had ever been able to give her a good description. There was something about it that slipped from her mind, the moment she looked away. It was wrapped in a power that concealed it, she suspected, a spell that was *very* like subtle magic, in that it stole thoughts and memories without the victim ever suspecting they were gone. If they escaped, they might even forget what had happened and slip back to the castle, unaware that they were being followed. And then the castle itself would be invaded.

"No," she agreed. Her throat was very dry. "We can't lead it back to the castle."

The creature moved forward in eerie silence. Even the birds and insects were still. Emily saw the grass bending around the creature, as if it wasn't really there, as if reality itself was being parted to allow the creature to exist. Bernard swore savagely and hurled a fireball right at the creature, only to see the fireball flicker out of existence long before it reached its target. The local magic field was shifting, Emily realized, as the creature picked up speed, flowing towards them with all the inevitability of a tidal wave. It was drifting towards the creature...

"Go," Bernard ordered. "Go, you..."

He pushed Julianne back, throwing a stream of fire towards the creature as he ran away from the girls. Emily thought, just for a second, that he was running away and abandoning them; then she saw the creature shift, turning to chase him. He was leading it away from them.

The creature sprang forward. Robin let out an oath and threw a spell of his own, striking the creature in the chest. The creature stopped and spun around, flickering impressions of malicious eyes focusing on Robin. It lunged forward, the ground shifting rapidly as it advanced, only to stop again when Bernard hit it with a fireball. Emily pulled Julianne back—the younger girl was staring in horror—as her mind worked desperately, trying to think of an angle. The creature seemed immune to spells, all spells. And yet it was only going after the boys. Didn't it realize that Bernard and Robin were probably faster on their feet than Emily and Julianne?

Not that it matters, Emily thought, as the creature flowed forward. *At that speed, it won't have any difficulty catching any of us.*

She reached what she devoutly hoped was a safe distance, then turned to stare as the creature sprang forward, lashing out with translucent legs—or tentacles— towards Robin. Robin was picked up and thrown across the entire clearing by *something*, landing badly and hitting the ground. He snapped a word Emily didn't recognize, releasing one of his demons. For a long, chilling second, there were two utterly inhuman creatures in the clearing...and then the demon flickered out of existence, as if it had never been there at all. Robin stared in disbelief, his mouth dropping open as the creature reached for him. And then Bernard threw a fireball into the creature, drawing it back towards him.

It banished a demon, Emily thought, stunned. Beside her, Julianne seemed no less astonished. From what little she recalled, a demon released in such a manner had to defend its master before returning to the darkness. But Robin's demon had lost, spectacularly. *The...the creature just kicked its ass out of our world.*

"That's not possible," Julianne breathed.

Emily was just as shocked. It clearly *was* possible, even though she had no idea how it had been done—or why. Perhaps the creature ate magic. The spells Bernard and Robin were hurling into the semi-translucent monster, draining their power at a terrifying rate, didn't even seem to be *touching* it. Instead, they were breaking up and fading back into the ether. The creature didn't even seem to have *noticed* Emily and Julianne.

"It hunts by using magic," she mused. Bernard and Robin had made it clear that the hunters—whatever they were—had gone after the master magicians first. They were the ones covered with sloppy magic, the most tempting targets. "Perhaps it can't *see* people without magic."

Julianne yelped in horror as Bernard was thrown back against a tree. The creature advanced slowly, opening its mouth as it reached out for Bernard.

Emily pushed Julianne away as hard as she could, then carefully cast a fireball of her own, trying to minimize the magic traces that would point directly to her. The fireball struck the creature's rear and it whirled around, eyes searching for the caster, but it didn't seem to see her. Emily held her breath, silently praying that Bernard would have the wit to crawl away while the creature was distracted. Her spell was weaker than the fireballs Bernard and Robin had been hurling about, but it should still be strong enough to blind the creature to Bernard's presence.

If, of course, she was right.

The creature advanced forward. She couldn't help thinking that it was sniffing the air, looking for traces of her magic. The world had to look very different to a magic-hunter, she thought; Bernard and Robin had to be bright, easy to see, while Emily and Julianne were barely even visible. She sensed the magical field shifting around the creature, flickers of raw magic flowing towards the translucent bulk and flickering out of existence. Could it be, she asked herself, that the creatures had *drained* the ambient magic field until it was too weak to support them? Did they explain why she'd never seen or heard anything like them in her own time? Or...

She staggered as the memory struck her. There had been...*something*...in the tunnels below Whitehall, something they'd seen just before encountering the statue. And there had been warnings of spider-like creatures carved into the walls...was she looking at one of those creatures in the flesh? Or whatever it had that passed for flesh? And then there was the statue, the vanishing statue...

Dear God, she thought. *The statue*!

The creature sprang forward. She recoiled in shock—she saw a whole series of flickering impressions of tentacles, claws, teeth and a stomach that went all the way to infinity—and then screamed in pain as...*something*...lashed across her face. She'd been hurt before, more times than she cared to imagine, but this was different. The pain slashed all the way to the very core of her being, tearing at her, and...

A spell struck the back of the creature and it recoiled, magic billowing around it and sliding *towards* the creature. Emily flew backwards and hit the ground, barely managing to brace herself a second before she landed. Bernard was blasting raw magic at the creature, trying desperately to overwhelm it; Robin joined him a second later, throwing wave after wave of raw magic into its gullet. But it wasn't anything like enough. Emily pulled herself to her feet, somehow. Her face hurt so badly that it felt as if she'd been punched, repeatedly.

"Help us," Bernard shouted. His power was already draining rapidly. "Emily..."

"It won't help," Emily shouted back. The creature, whatever it was, seemed more interested in *eating* the magic than anything else. They might as well try to drown a fish. "It won't stop it..."

She forced herself to think—and think hard, despite the pain. Drawing power from the nexus point *might* be enough to stop the creature, by overfeeding it if nothing else, but there was no way to get it to the castle without putting everyone else at risk. The creature would see the commune as an all-it-could-eat buffet. She didn't dare take the risk, but what else could she do? Julianne and she *might* be able to sneak away; Bernard and Robin, magic tainting the very air around them, would have no such option.

I could try to teleport it, she thought. *Maybe send it into orbit or scatter its atoms across the world...?*

She shook her head a moment later, dismissing the thought. There was no way the spellwork would hold up long enough for her to complete the spell, even if she managed to muster the power to make the spell work. The damned creature would simply drain the magic and then turn on her. And there was nothing else she knew that could overload the creature. The more she looked at it, the more certain she was that nothing short of the nexus point could *hope* to stuff it to bursting point.

If it eats magic, Emily thought suddenly, *maybe it can be starved.*

"Keep it busy," she yelled. "I've had an idea!"

She picked up a stone, cast a locomotive spell and hurled it directly at the creature. There was enough power to smash the stone right through a person's chest, but the stone didn't even *touch* the creature. It seemed to bend *around* the creature, as if it was still part of the real world, and slam harmlessly into a tree on the other side of the clearing. Emily cursed—the creature, whatever it was, probably wouldn't be harmed by physical attacks—and then turned and ran towards the forest. She needed a place to work.

Julianne caught up with her as she hurried into the trees. "Where are you going?"

"I've had an idea," Emily repeated. She glanced from side to side, looking for another clearing. "But we need a clearing..."

"There," Julianne pointed.

Emily nodded in relief as they ran into another clearing, silently thanking whoever might be listening that there was no grass growing nearby. A pool of water rested in the exact center—Emily eyed it suspiciously, noting the absence of animal tracks near the water's edge, then dismissed the thought. There was no time to worry about what might be lurking in the water, waiting to grab an unwary passer-by. She just hoped it couldn't get *out* while she worked desperately to set up her plan, drawing out runes in the soil. Julianne watched from the edge of the clearing, clearly puzzled. Emily had no time to explain.

"All right," she said.

Bracing herself, she shot a beam of raw magic back through the trees towards where she'd left the boys. It wasn't strong enough to do more than serve as a spotlight, but if she was right about how the creature saw the world it should be enough to draw it towards her. She heard Bernard shouting in the distance, just before the trees started to warp and twist around the creature as it charged through the forest. Emily would have been impressed with the sheer level of power it was displaying if it hadn't been trying to kill them. She had a series of impressions of teeth and claws as it approached, flowing towards her on translucent legs...

She forced herself to stand still, careful to keep the runes between her and the creature, as she extruded magic into the air. The creature seemed to find the bait irresistible, but Emily was all too aware that—if the plan failed—she was dead. There was no way to get the taint of her magic off her before it was too late. She heard Julianne cry out in horror as the creature emerged into the clearing, allowing the trees to slip back into place. The boys had been left far behind.

Come on, you monster, Emily thought. *Come on...*

The runes blazed with blue light as the creature crossed the line. Emily readied herself to jump, as if she had any hope of escaping. The creature stopped dead, as if it was suddenly blind and deaf. The runes were designed to push magic *away* from the circle, erasing all traces of ambient magic...Emily was surprised it had worked as well as it had. But then, the magic field seemed stronger in the past. The nexus point had only just been tamed.

Bernard ran into the clearing, one hand raised to cast a spell. "Don't do anything," Emily snapped. She hoped the creature couldn't hear normally. "It's trapped."

"Trapped?" Robin repeated, following Bernard. "What have you done to it?"

"Drained the *mana*," Emily said. It was hard to be sure, but the creature seemed to be getting smaller. It was hunching down, curling its legs like a giant spider. "I'm trying to starve it."

Robin gave her an incredulous look. "And you believe that will kill the creature?"

Emily looked back. "Did anyone else think to try?"

She regretted it instantly. If there had been more than one creature, they would have been screwed. A horde of magic-eating monsters swarming through a settlement would have been more than enough to slaughter the communes, going after the masters first and making sure the apprentices never had a chance to rebuild. And the masters would have tried to fight back with magic, which would have done nothing more than draw the creatures to them. Physical force didn't seem to have any effect at all.

"No," Bernard said, slowly. "No one thought to try."

Emily rubbed her face, gritting her teeth as she touched the wound. The creature had scarred her left cheek. She couldn't feel blood, thankfully, but the wound was still aching. And it was tainted with wild magic. It would take weeks for it to fade enough for her to heal the scar. By then, the scar might have healed on its own.

She pushed the thought aside as she watched the creature shrinking rapidly, growing weaker and weaker until it finally twisted out of existence. Her head swam as the creature unfolded from reality, her eyes unable to follow where it was going. It *definitely* hadn't been part of the natural world, she realized numbly. Its multidimensional nature had been more than just a defense against physical attack.

"It's gone," Bernard said.

"It could be a trap," Julianne warned. "The...the *thing*...might be toying with us."

"I felt it go," Emily said. "But I'll leave the runes in place, just in case."

Robin sat down hard. "They found us," he said. "We're going to have to run."

"But we have a defense," Bernard objected. He nodded to Emily. "Don't we?"

"Against one," Emily said. She sucked in her breath tartly. "You and Robin are *covered* in magic. It found you the most desirable targets."

"They never attacked mundane villages," Bernard said. He sounded very tired. He'd pushed his reserves to the breaking point. "The monsters only ever go after magicians."

"They eat magic," Emily said. "The spells you were throwing at it...you might as well have been hurling food into its belly."

"...Shit," Robin said. He sounded tired—and stunned. "And...and I wasted a demon."

"It just fled," Bernard said. "You overpaid it, clearly."

He cleared his throat before Robin could come up with a rejoinder. "And we'd better head back to the castle," he said. "Master Whitehall needs to know that they're still tracking us."

"They might have trouble *finding* us," Emily commented. The creatures definitely hunted using magic. Their hunter would have killed them all if it could see normally. "There's so much raw magic in the air that we might not stand out so much."

But that won't last, her own thoughts reminded her. *And once the level drops a little more, we'll stick out like sore thumbs.*

Chapter Twenty-One

THE WALK BACK TO THE CASTLE TOOK LONGER THAN EMILY HAD EXPECTED, IF ONLY BECAUSE Bernard insisted on keeping a careful eye out for signs of pursuit. Emily didn't blame him, even though the birds and insects could be heard, once again, as they buzzed through the trees. It was their first close look at one of the hunters—Bernard hadn't had a good look at them earlier—and they were all shocked. Julianne was shaking so badly that Emily couldn't help wondering if she needed a sleeping potion and a few hours of uninterrupted rest.

She kept her thoughts to herself as she walked, remembering the statue. It wasn't just a statue of *her*, she realized now; it *was* her. Or would be her, after she petrified herself and waited away the years in a hidden chamber within Whitehall. Her own touch—her past self's touch—would be enough to break the spell, just slowly enough to ensure that her past self didn't see her future self before it was too late. And she had to have—or would have—taken the books from the hidden library. She smiled, rather humorlessly, at the thought. Professor Locke had been right all along when he'd accused her of stealing them.

I might need to write all this down, she thought, darkly. *And then diagram out how it's supposed to work.*

Her blood ran cold as another piece of the puzzle fitted into place. She'd been summoned to the nexus chamber, pulled out of bed by blood magic. And she'd wondered just who had enough of her blood to summon her. But she knew the answer to that too—*she'd* summoned herself. No, she *would* summon herself. She and her past self were the same person, after all, just existing at different points along the same timeline. All her defenses, already dangerously weak against blood magic, were useless against a person who knew her defenses as intimately as she knew her own.

Because they—we—are the same, she thought, morbidly. She rubbed the cut on her cheek. *And the statue had the scar that would develop from this too.*

She tossed the idea round and round in her head as they finally walked out of the forest and up towards the castle. Turning herself to stone would be easy—she'd just have to cast the spell on herself—but shutting down her own thoughts would be tricky. If she didn't remain awake and aware, breaking the spell from inside would be impossible, yet if she *did* remain aware she'd go mad within weeks or months. Being turned into an animal wasn't too bad, once the victim got over the shock; she could still move and signal for help. But remaining a statue for centuries...? She'd been a statue for a week, back in her second year, and the experience had almost broken her.

And it would have, too, she thought, *if they hadn't been trying to keep me entertained.*

She shook her head, grimly. She'd need to devise the spell very carefully, just to make sure it awoke her at the right moment...without dooming her to madness. On one hand, she *knew* the spell had worked; logically, her future self had pushed her past self into the nexus. But on the other hand, who was to say her future self was sane? Someone worse than Shadye could have been unleashed on the Nameless World, after centuries trapped in stone. The idea of surrendering to stone—of gambling everything on remaining in suspension for centuries—was terrifying. It was hard enough to willingly drink a sleeping draught. Trapping herself in stone, freezing her thoughts, was worse.

"Master," Bernard called. Whitehall was standing by the gates, chatting to Master Keldor. "I have to speak to you."

Whitehall looked surprised to see them—Emily belatedly remembered that they weren't meant to be back until twilight—but he nodded as they hurried towards him. They had to look a sight, Emily realized; Julianne was terrified, while Emily and the boys were wounded, tired and muddy. Whitehall tensed when he saw his daughter, then turned his head and called for a serving girl. When she appeared, he ordered food, drink and blankets for the apprentices and then gave Julianne a tight hug. She clung to her father as if she had feared she would never see him again.

"Master," Bernard said. "They've found us."

Whitehall blanched. "Already?"

"One creature," Emily put in, tiredly. The servant returned with food and drink and she nibbled gratefully. She hadn't drained herself as badly as the boys, but she still needed to replenish her reserves. "There was no sign of any others."

"Which means nothing," Robin muttered.

Emily nodded. Robin was right. There could be a small army only a day or two away—or, perhaps, waiting in the next dimension. If the creatures—whatever they were—could bend reality so easily, neither teleporting nor building portals would be much of a challenge. And what *were* they? The Faerie? In her time, the remnants of the Dark City were two or three days away on foot, but as far as anyone knew there were no settlements for nearly a hundred miles around Whitehall.

But the Faerie would have ample time to build the Dark City, she thought. *If, of course, they're planning to build it now, before the first war.*

She cursed her own ignorance under her breath. If only the historical records had been accurate! She had no idea when the Dark City had been established, nor when it had been abandoned in the wake of the Faerie Wars. And, realistically, she had no idea what was happening beyond the forest. For all she knew, the war might already be well underway—or the creatures might merely be the first in a series of terror weapons. She touched the bracelet at her wrist, wondering if the Death Vipers existed yet. Sergeant Miles had been fairly certain they were as unnatural as the Faerie themselves.

And the creature we saw was very unnatural, she thought. *A manavore, perhaps?*

She pushed the thought out of her mind as Bernard and Robin explained what had happened, starting with the arrival of the creature and ending with its destruction. Whitehall looked very pale up until they told him what Emily had done, whereupon he turned to her, looking as though he had a hundred questions he wanted to ask. There was a calculating expression on his face that Emily didn't like, although it was hard to blame him. He was one of the most powerful magicians in the world and yet he'd been forced to flee by the creatures, which had casually destroyed his home and butchered his friends.

"Emily," he said. His eyes flickered over the gash on her cheek. "What did you do to it?"

"I drained the local magic around it," Emily said. In hindsight, she'd read a couple of books where gods and monsters had flickered out of existence when the *mana* levels dropped too low to support them. It was both good and bad, she thought, that something akin to the Warlock's Wheel couldn't work on the Nameless World. "And once the level dropped too low to sustain it, it died."

Whitehall frowned. "Are you sure it died?"

"She got rid of it, My Lord," Robin said. "Does it matter if it's dead or merely gone?"

"Yes, it does," Whitehall said, flatly. "If it's dead, then there's no need to worry about it reporting back to its comrades. But if it's alive, then it could be telling the rest of its people about us right now."

"Yes, My Lord," Robin said.

"But we stopped it," Bernard said. He hesitated, then leaned forward. "A demon couldn't stop it, but we did!"

Whitehall's eyes narrowed. "Explain."

Bernard looked at Robin, who scowled. "I unleashed a protective demon, My Lord," he said, slowly. He was clearly reluctant to say anything, but it was obvious that he didn't want to defy Whitehall. "The demon should have torn the creature into little pieces. Instead...it just died."

"It fled," Bernard said.

Robin's face flushed angrily. "With your permission, My Lord, I would like to seek out my master," he said. "He needs to be informed."

"You may inform him," Whitehall said, after a moment. "And then inform him that I would like the pleasure of his company."

He looked at Bernard as Robin hurried off. "Escort my daughter back to her bedroom," he ordered. "And then hunt down the other masters and ask them to meet me in my office, one hour from now."

Bernard looked surprised, but he bowed anyway and took Julianne's hand. Emily didn't blame him for being astonished. Normally, he wouldn't have been left alone with Julianne under any circumstances. She wondered if Whitehall knew that Bernard and Julianne had grown closer, then realized that Whitehall knew that Julianne had magic too, now. Bernard would be in for an unpleasant surprise if he tried anything stupid...

Which he isn't going to do, she thought, as Whitehall led her back into the castle. *He's almost sickeningly sweet on her.*

The thought nagged at her mind, tormenting her. *She'd* kissed Robin—and she'd *wanted* to kiss Robin. The forest had been romantic...no, it had been *more* than merely romantic; there had been something in the air that had encouraged romance. Julianne and Bernard did have feelings for one another, thankfully, but had the forest pushed them together? Would they come to regret it in time?

"Emily," Whitehall said. They stepped into his office and sat down. "What happened?"

"The Manavores hunt by using magic," Emily said, flatly. "They..."

"Manavores," Whitehall repeated. "Is that what they're called?"

"I named them," Emily said. She brushed her hair out of her eyes as she leaned forward, hoping to convince him. "It went after the boys first, Master. It didn't seem to notice me until I used magic and it completely ignored Julianne. When they attacked your village..."

"They went after the powerful magicians first," Whitehall finished. "The ones covered in...*slop*."

"Yes, Master," Emily said.

She paused, taking a moment to gather her thoughts. "I hit it hard enough, physically, to kill a man," she added. "I don't think it even *noticed* the blow. The only way to stop them seems to be to drain the surrounding magic field."

"I see," Whitehall said. He looked like a man who had bitten into a particularly sour lemon and forced himself to keep chewing. "Should we abandon the castle?"

Emily shook her head, without thinking. Whitehall *couldn't* abandon the castle. The school *had* to be established—and she'd been laying the groundwork for it all along. She didn't dare let him simply walk away, but how could she stop him? And the rest of the Whitehall Commune? She'd earned some respect from him, she felt, yet not all the masters saw eye-to-eye with him. Master Chambers disliked her personally and she rather suspected that Master Reaper felt the same way.

And I killed Master Gila, Emily thought. *They'll hold that against me, even if it had to be done.*

"You don't think we should go," Whitehall said. "Why not?"

"The current system of learning magic is doomed," Emily said, grimly. "Those creatures—the Manavores—are going to be hunting you for the rest of time, until they run out of prey or you learn to kill them. Each apprentice raised in the old system is going to be prey, as far as those creatures are concerned. Their magic will draw the hunters like moths to a flame."

"Which is why they kept discovering our villages," Whitehall muttered. "But our apprentices cannot abandon magic."

"You don't have to," Emily said. "The creature ignored me *until* I used magic. And even after I did cast a spell, it had problems seeing me. You have to teach your students to mask their powers."

"Like you do," Whitehall said. He cocked his head, thoughtfully. "How very convenient for you."

Emily flushed. "I didn't set out to..."

"I know," Whitehall interrupted. "But this is not going to go down well."

"Yeah," Emily said.

She sat back in her chair, suddenly feeling very tired. Logically, if she already had the scar on her cheek, it couldn't be long before she petrified herself. The scar couldn't be allowed to heal...it crossed her mind that she could *keep* the scar from healing, but she'd definitely not looked very much *older* than she was when she started her trek back to the future. She hadn't spent as much time admiring herself in the mirror as some girls she could mention, yet she didn't *think* she'd put on too many years...

I need to work out the spell, she thought. *Then I need to find my hiding place.*

"And Robin's demon was banished," Whitehall mused. "It didn't turn on him?"

"No, Master," Emily said. "It just vanished."

She leaned forward. "What *was* it?"

Whitehall frowned. "A protective demon? Robin would have bound the demon to one task—protecting him. When released, the demon would attack the person threatening Robin and then return to the darkness. DemonMasters prefer not to use them because they're completely indiscriminate. There's rarely any time to get them targeted before they have to be unleashed."

"And they could lash out at everyone," Emily mused.

"They could," Whitehall agreed. "And their presence can make it harder to summon some of the other demons."

And the demon simply flickered out of existence when the Manavore attacked it, Emily thought. *Does that mean that demons are made of magic?*

She pushed the thought aside for further consideration as she met his eyes. "It should be possible to use the nexus point to safeguard the castle," she said. "And now that the nexus point has been tamed, the level of ambient magic in the vicinity should drop sharply."

"That might have been what brought the creature here," Whitehall said. He looked back at her, thoughtfully. "Can you show me how to cast the runes you used?"

Emily hesitated, briefly. The runes *had* come from the future, after all. But realistically...it wouldn't be long before Master Wolfe duplicated them, once he knew they were possible. He was already halfway towards building up a comprehensive outline of runes, sigils and other rituals that would eventually lead to subtle magic. And Whitehall *needed* them. If the Manavores were on the prowl, he'd have to prepare to defend the castle.

"On one condition," she said. "You teach the girls how to use them too."

Whitehall gave her a sharp look, but nodded. "Very well," he said. "You might have to do the teaching, though."

"I know," Emily said. "Julianne will learn quickly, I am sure."

She sketched out the runes for him, briefly explaining how they diverted magic around the circle, leaving the interior isolated from the ambient magic field. The Manavore had starved very quickly, suggesting that it desperately needed *mana* to survive. And yet, there was the nagging doubt over precisely what had happened after it had been trapped. Had it died—or, as Whitehall had warned, had it merely gone home? The implications worried her more than she cared to admit.

"There's no reason why mundanes can't draw out the runes," she finished. "You could surround the castle with traps designed to catch and kill the monsters."

"This is something that should be spread far and wide," Whitehall said. "And something that I should discuss with the other masters."

He shrugged. "And unfortunately, I cannot ask for you to attend."

Emily felt oddly conflicted. On one hand, she would have liked to be there, standing and watching as history was made...but, on the other hand, she knew that Master Chambers wouldn't welcome her presence. And some of the others would probably agree, pointing out that Emily was no master. *And* that she'd only been with the commune for a few short weeks.

"You have to propose changing how to teach apprentices," Emily said. Could she spy on the meeting? It might have been possible before the nexus point was tamed, but now...she had a feeling her spells would be detected. "And you have to try to bring other apprentices here."

Whitehall smiled, humorlessly. "We will see," he said. He rose. "Go to your bedroom and wait; have a wash, if you like, but don't try to sleep. I may have to summon you to answer questions."

"Yes, Master," Emily said. She rose and bowed. "Please make sure they all know how to cast the runes."

"Of course," Whitehall said, dryly. His smile grew warmer. "That will be the first order of business—once we finish hearing the protests, of course."

"Of course," Emily agreed.

She turned and walked out of the office, then paused by the air vent, glancing up and down the corridor before removing the snake-bracelet from her wrist and undoing the spell, freeing Aurelius from his confinement. The Death Viper curled on her palm, sniffing the air; a barrage of impressions slammed into her mind as the familiar bond returned to life, leaving her feeling oddly guilty for keeping Aurelius in suspension for so long. But what other choice did she have? No one else in Whitehall had a familiar that was utterly lethal to everyone else.

Gritting her teeth, she introduced Aurelius to the air vent and watched as he crawled inside, slithering up the pipes. The castle was threaded with tiny air vents, all far too small to allow a human to use them to move from room to room. But a snake would have no difficulty in finding a place to listen, spying on the conversation. And they'd have no way to know that they should be watching for him.

And I'll know what they're saying, she thought, as she hurried to her bedroom. *And then I might know who truly understands what is at stake.*

Chapter Twenty-Two

JULIANNE LOOKED HALF-ASLEEP WHEN EMILY ENTERED THE BEDROOM, BUT SHE STILL INSISTED on cleaning the wound on Emily's cheek and disinfecting it before lying down on her blankets and downing a foul-smelling potion of her own. She fell asleep moments later, leaving Emily sitting on the blankets, watching her. Emily allowed herself a moment of relief—she'd been considering casting a sleep spell on Julianne to make sure she couldn't interfere, then checked the potion before lying down and closing her eyes. It was strange to see through her familiar's eyes—the world always looked weird—but she'd grown used to it. Void had made her practice, back when they'd shared a house.

And I really should spend more time with him, she thought, as the snake slid into a vantage point. *Other familiars spend all their time with their partners.*

She shook her head, dismissing the thought. Aurelius was just too dangerous to be left off the leash, no matter how she felt about him. His poisonous skin wouldn't cause *her* any harm, but anyone else who touched him would be lucky if they *only* lost a hand. She still shuddered when she heard the horror stories, including a number Lady Barb had told her when she'd been trying to convince Emily to turn Aurelius into alchemical ingredients. But the thought of slaughtering her familiar had been unbearable.

I'll just have to give him more time in my bedroom, she mused, as she watched Master Chambers and Master Reaper step into the chamber. *And when I get home, I can take him to the house for a few days.*

She couldn't help feeling oddly dirty as the remaining masters gathered in Whitehall's office, even though they weren't doing anything naughty. Magic provided hundreds of ways to spy on one's foes—hell, Emily had heard that trying to crack the spells protecting the girls changing rooms and bedrooms at Whitehall kept a number of male students gainfully occupied when they weren't actually studying. She *knew* she'd be in real trouble if she was caught spying on another student, let alone a tutor... she felt, despite herself, that she shouldn't be doing anything of the sort. And yet, she wanted desperately to know what was going to be said. She *had* to know.

At least I'm not spying on the boys, she told herself. It wasn't a convincing argument. *And the discussion concerns me.*

"We have a problem," Whitehall said, once the door was closed. "They've found us."

"*One* of them has found us," Master Chambers corrected. "And it was destroyed."

"By *her*," Master Keldor said.

"She gave me a copy of the runes she used," Whitehall said. He passed the parchment to Master Wolfe. "I have no reason to doubt her story."

"My apprentice confirms it," Master Chambers said, grudgingly. "The hunters *have* found us."

"None of us had any warning," Master Reaper said. "I have been attempting to divine the future. None of my...*contacts*...gave any warning about this."

Demons, Emily thought.

"Nor mine," Master Chambers confirmed. "Are we sure it was one of *them?*"

"Your apprentice said so," Master Drake snapped. "And so did Whitehall's apprentice. Apprentices."

"They could have been fooled," Master Chambers said. "And encountering the creature could have been nothing more than bad luck."

Master Wolfe leaned forward. "I questioned young Bernard extensively," he said. "There is no reason to doubt their story."

He paused. "The creature was extremely resistant to magic," he added. "It shrugged off both direct and indirect attacks, as well as...*snuffing out*...a demon. If it was not related to the hordes that destroyed our settlements and slaughtered dozens of magicians, we will have to come to terms with the fact that there are *two* forces out there hunting us."

Logical, Emily noted.

"Emily believes that the creature actually *eats* magic," Whitehall said. "Our... *sloppy*...magic draws the creatures to us."

Master Chambers snorted. "First you argue that uncontrolled magic causes madness," he said, sharply. "And now you argue that sloppy magic lures the hunters."

"The hunters have targeted magical villages almost exclusively," Master Drake said. "I have only heard of a handful of attacks on mundane villages and all of them housed at least one magician."

He paused. "And we have learned, in the last few weeks, that many of our spells are overpowered," he noted. "We can achieve so much more with less, if we knew better what we are doing."

"And you may be giving up some of your power," Master Chambers said. "Have you considered the possibility?"

"When we came to this castle, turning someone into a frog for a few hours would leave me tired and drained," Master Drake said, curtly. "Now, I can cast the spell several times in a row without feeling so rotten afterwards. And a couple of apprentices can *also* cast the spell without constantly casting smaller spells to build up their reserves."

Emily shivered. *She'd* boosted her reserves, after the duel with Master Grey, but it had come with a price. And Void had admitted, openly, that he'd worried about her sanity. Whitehall and his commune didn't know about the dangers of pushing themselves too hard, tacitly accepting the risk of either driving themselves mad or burning out their magic. But they didn't know what they were doing to themselves.

Master Wolfe nodded. "And there's another point," he added. "Apprentice Bernard was very clear on the important matters. It was he and Apprentice Robin who were targeted first, even though there were two other magicians present..."

"You need to control that girl," Master Chambers said, to Whitehall. "There's nothing more disruptive than a disobedient apprentice."

"Particularly one who involves herself in the affairs of her betters," Master Keldor added, darkly. "If I had talked to my master the way she talks to you..."

"She is clearly unused to living in a commune," Whitehall said.

"She is clearly unused to being brought to account for her actions," Master Chambers thundered. "She taught your daughter *magic*! The curse will strike them both."

"They believe the curse can be handled," Master Wolfe said. Emily honestly wasn't sure if he believed his own words. "And we need to know if..."

"It *can* be handled," Master Chambers said. "By not learning or using magic."

"I worked my way through the figures," Master Wolfe said. "There are no incidents, as far as anyone can recall, of a witch giving birth..."

"We *know*," Master Chambers interrupted.

"...But there are also creditable reasons to worry about men too," Master Wolfe continued, ignoring the interruption. "I have no children; *you* have no children...the largest number of children born to any magician, any *male* magician, is *three*. And *that* father was a notorious seducer: his three children were born to three different mothers."

He nodded to Whitehall. "And Whitehall, who never uses demonic spells, still only has one child," he added. "He..."

"Should have married again," Master Keldor said. "So should the rest of us."

Whitehall cleared his throat. "We have three problems," he said, cutting off any further digressions. "First, the hunters—the Manavores, as we have termed them—are clearly sweeping the area for us. Second, we now understand both the true nature and the *cause* of the curse—and that it affects men as well as women. And third, we have rather more apprentices than we can hope to teach.

"At the same time, we have also discovered--" he nodded to Wolfe and Drake "--that combining the different magical disciplines leads to more useful and versatile spells. Spells, I might add, that we don't need to draw from demons."

"And how to tame the nexus point," Wolfe said. "We are constantly expanding the control structure under the school."

Emily felt a thrill of excitement. Wolfe had taken her ideas and run with them, creating what would eventually become the control room she recalled. How long would it be, she asked herself, before the first Warden was ready to take his place? Maybe not long, now that some of Master Keldor's work had been integrated into the growing structure. He knew more than anyone else about how the human body worked.

Whitehall pressed his fingers together as he surveyed the room. "I believe we need to rethink our approach," he explained. "And that we should...expand the commune to the point we can teach multiple apprentices at once."

"Out of the question," Master Chambers snapped. "Do you have any idea of the *dangers*?"

"We can prepare for the dangers," Whitehall said. He kept his voice calm, but Emily caught the underlying edge. "There's enough power in the nexus point to protect the apprentices from harm."

"He does have a point," Lord Alfred said. Emily was surprised. Lord Alfred had always struck her as a doddering but kind-hearted old man. "Teaching one student at a time does allow us to catch their mistakes before it's too late. Trying to teach even two or three students will make it harder to save them from themselves."

"We will be encouraging the apprentices to develop their powers gradually," Whitehall said, firmly. "And that will also allow them to mask their powers."

"Our students would have a great deal to unlearn," Master Drake said. "But if I had learned some of the runic structures before I started studying transmutation...it might have made me a better magician."

"And apprentices would no longer be bound to one master," Sake said. "They'd be able to free themselves from a bad master."

"Not *all* masters are bad," Master Chambers snapped. "And what about the secrets?"

He took a breath. "I have secrets I will not share with anyone, save for my apprentices," he said. "Do you expect me to share them with everyone in the commune?"

"You may make your own choice in such matters," Whitehall said. "Personally, I intend to put the basics on the table for everyone."

"And I," Master Wolfe added.

"I do not believe this," Master Chambers said. He glared at Whitehall. "This is *her* idea, isn't it?"

"It is a logical solution to our problem," Whitehall snapped. "Or do you have a better idea of how we can teach fifty apprentices with only nine masters?"

"This is her idea," Master Chambers repeated. Emily winced at the scorn in his voice. "Do you trust her *that* much?"

"Tell me," Master Keldor added. "Do you know if she's even *human?*"

"She could be a succubus," Master Reaper said. "My...*contacts*...will not be drawn on her."

Emily felt her cheeks heat with embarrassment. A succubus, her? There had only been a handful of mentions of succubae in the books she'd read, all hints and innuendo rather than hard facts. She'd certainly never *met* one. Any magician stupid enough to try to create one -the books had insisted they needed to be *created*—had to be out of his mind. It was a great deal easier—and safer—to find a village girl to impress. There was no shortage of commoner girls who would happily marry a magician, knowing it would mean they would never have to be poor or hungry again. Creating a succubus was nothing more than a way to die happy.

"She is human," Whitehall said, flatly.

"She is unusually pretty," Sake countered.

"And you're ugly," Drake snarled. "Let's not confuse the issue, shall we?"

"I've traveled far," Lord Alfred said, suddenly. "I have met and bedded girls with skin as black as coal, girls with almond eyes and yellow skin, girls so pale that the merest blush made their faces glow. There were girls so strong that they could have passed for men and girls so weak that they had to be carried around in wagons. And yet they were all *human.*"

Master Keldor sneered. "The pieces fitted, did they?"

"Yes. Yes, they did," Lord Alfred said. "Lady Emily is human."

"And yet she is just an apprentice," Master Chambers said. "We should not be taking *her* suggestions..."

"She should be classed as a master," Master Wolfe countered. "Or have you forgotten that she saved our lives? We would be dead without her and don't you forget it!"

"I have forgotten nothing," Master Chambers said. "But I have also not forgotten..."

He broke off for a long moment, clearly gathering his thoughts. "Tell me," he said, looking at Whitehall. "Are you really prepared to throw out hundreds of years worth of tradition on the say-so of a girl you barely know?"

"I wouldn't have said *hundreds* of years," Lord Alfred commented.

"Shut up," Master Chambers hissed. "I want an answer."

"Tradition is failing us," Whitehall said. "The demons are untrustworthy. And establishing a...a *school* is the best solution to our problems."

He took a breath. "Yes, she helped inspire the concept. And yes, I understand that you don't like her. But that doesn't mean that her concepts are invalid. We've already seen proof that some of them work very well."

"She's certainly got your ear," Master Chambers snapped.

"I hope she hasn't got another part of your anatomy," Master Keldor added, darkly.

Emily blushed, furiously. Did they really think that she would...?

Probably, she thought. *They're not used to powerful women.*

"I believe I have stated my case," Whitehall said. "Are there any other objections before we move to the vote?"

"You want to throw away a tradition that has served us very well," Master Chambers said. "I think you will boost your own position at our expense."

Whitehall scowled at him. "Any *relevant* objections?"

Emily winced. She hated political discussions and did her best to avoid them, but even she could tell that had been a mistake.

"You will be leading a pack of hundreds of semi-apprentices," Master Chambers snapped, sharply. "And we will have *no* apprentices."

And the more apprentices a master has, Emily thought, *the greater his prestige.*

"Then we vote," Whitehall said. "All in favor, say aye."

Emily scowled as the vote was taken. Whitehall, Bones, Alfred and Wolfe voted in favor; Chamber, Keldor, Drake and Reaper voted against. Sake, apparently, had abstained—or, perhaps, he was waiting to see which side would make the better offer. She thought she understood why Chamber and Reaper had voted against— they were both DemonMasters who stood to lose a great deal if demons were officially banned—but Drake? He'd *benefited* from the new arrangement.

Whitehall clearly shared her disappointment. "Drake?"

"I am not blind to the advantages that come from sharing secrets," Drake said. "But I am also not blind to the need for apprentices—and for private tuition, later in life."

You want to have your cake and eat it too, Emily thought. *And you might just have scuppered the entire school.*

Sake cleared his throat. "I did not vote," he said coolly, "because I was only recently raised to mastery. And I believe that both sides have valid arguments."

"Really," Master Chambers said.

"I would like to propose a compromise," Sake continued. "We will give all the new apprentices basic training, the training any of us would have to give a *true* apprentice before starting his proper training. At that point, we would have plenty of time to choose our apprentices *after* they start showing their specific talents for magic."

Drake stroked his chin. "Which would have the advantage of ensuring that the apprentice is genuinely interested in the discipline he wants."

"As well as a firm grounding in everything else," Wolfe added.

"And yet, those apprentices will not be *true* apprentices," Master Chambers objected.

"I would not have stayed with Master Gila," Sake said, bluntly. "I intended to leave as soon as I gained my mastery. There was no argument that could have convinced me to stick with the constant beatings, the fits of rage, the willingness to test new and unpleasant ideas on me...I was obedient, but he had done nothing to earn my loyalty."

He paused. "If there had been options, a way to leave ahead of time and find another master, I would have taken them," he added. "And if your apprentices are ill-suited to your branch of magic, do you really want to *keep* them?"

Drake looked at Whitehall. "Compromise," he said. He didn't seem to have listened very closely to Sake. "All apprentices get the basics—from us, from any other masters we can recruit. And then we choose our apprentices from among the trained magicians."

"Agreed," Whitehall said. He silently canvassed the other masters. "Sake?"

"Then count my vote in favor," Sake said. "I believe that is six votes to three."

Master Chambers snorted. "This isn't just a break with tradition," he snapped. "This is a slap in the face of the DemonMasters. It will not stand."

"Then go," Whitehall snapped back. "Your pet demons have been luring us into madness for hundreds of years."

"I found this place with the rest of you," Master Chambers reminded him. "I have a claim to it too."

He marched to the door, then stopped. "I believe this will go badly wrong," he added. "And when it does, I will laugh."

Emily wasn't sure if she should laugh or cry as he stalked out of the door, followed by Master Reaper. Keldor exchanged a handful of words with Whitehall, then left the room too, closing the door behind him. Whitehall...Whitehall looked tired. Emily couldn't help wondering if he'd readied himself for a fight.

"We'll start work tomorrow," Whitehall said. "If we are lucky, we should be able to head to the Gathering in a week or so."

"Unless the Gathering has been interrupted," Wolfe pointed out. "The Manavores are on the prowl."

"All the more reason to tell them about the runes," Whitehall said. "And to invite them to join us here."

He dismissed the rest of his group, then looked up towards the vent. "I should tell you," he said wryly, "that those who eavesdrop rarely hear well of themselves. But I imagine you've learned that lesson for yourself by now."

Emily recoiled in shock. How the hell had he known the snake was there?

"And you can report to me after dinner," Whitehall added. "I'll be wanting your input too."

Chapter Twenty-Three

EMILY COULDN'T HELP FEELING NERVOUS—VERY NERVOUS—AS SHE APPROACHED Whitehall's office after dinner. There had been no sign of him or any of the other masters in the Great Hall, leaving her fretting over the mystery of just how he'd known she was eavesdropping. No matter how she looked at it, she just couldn't figure it out. Aurelius hadn't made a sound—hell, the Death Viper should have been effectively invisible. And yet Whitehall had known she was watching through the snake's eyes.

She recovered the snake from the vent, then tapped on the door, wishing she was somewhere—anywhere—else. Whitehall had trusted her and she'd betrayed him, simply by peeking on his secret meeting. It was expected, in *her* school, that students would try to spy on each other, or their tutors, but she had no idea how Whitehall would react. He might applaud her skills or evict her from the castle... the door opened a moment later, allowing her to slip into the room. Whitehall was sitting behind his desk, scribbling notes on a piece of vellum. He glanced up at her and smiled.

"Eavesdroppers rarely hear well of themselves," he said, as he nodded to a chair. "I trust you're not *too* offended?"

Emily colored as she sat down. "I've heard worse," she said, although that wasn't entirely true. No one had accused her of trying to seduce King Randor—or Void. "Why are they so...so angry?"

"There are always winners and losers in anything," Whitehall said, sardonically. He gave her a sharp look. "I would have expected you to know it."

"Yes, Master," Emily said. "But Chambers and Reaper don't stand to lose *that* much."

"They will lose the prestige that comes with being DemonMasters," Whitehall said. "We have already determined that our new apprentices will *not* be taught how to summon and use demons. Without that, their ability to win apprentices and gain influence will be severely limited. They're too old to learn new tricks."

"They could," Emily insisted.

"I doubt it," Whitehall said. "They have grown too reliant on using demons."

Emily nodded. That made sense, she had to admit. Master Chambers had grown far too used to taking spells from the demons and casting them, without any awareness of how the spells actually worked, let alone how they could be modified by capable students. His demons might have given him insights in some areas, but they'd left him terrifyingly blind in others.

She took a breath. "How did you know I was listening?"

Whitehall gave her a rather crooked smile. "You have until the end of this discussion to work it out," he said. "And if you do, we'll forgo punishment for both spying on us and getting caught."

Emily swallowed. "Yes, Master."

Whitehall smiled. "We'll be spending the next four or five days organizing the teaching patterns," he said. "If nothing else, the apprentices will have to learn how to draw the runes you devised—you'll be willing to help teach them, won't you?"

"Yes, Master," Emily said. She wondered, vaguely, if the apprentices would actually listen to her. *Bernard* listened, but she'd beaten him in a duel. "If that is your wish."

"We'll be traveling to the Gathering in six days, depending..." Whitehall added, and paused. "I'll be taking you, Julianne and Bernard. Lord Alfred may be in attendance too. Have you ever attended a Gathering?"

Emily shook her head.

"Dozens of masters and hundreds of apprentices—and would-be apprentices—will be gathering, nearly two hundred miles from here," Whitehall explained. "We will have ample opportunity to tell them about the castle and our planned new approach to magic."

"Oh," Emily said. She frowned. "Is it safe to travel?"

"It's *never* safe to travel," Whitehall said. "But we need additional masters and apprentices."

Emily nodded, sourly. As interesting as the Gathering would be, there was no way she could look forward to the trip. Two hundred miles was nothing on Earth—a car could travel two hundred miles in less than a day—but it was a significant trip on the Nameless World. At best, it would take several days...and if they were expected to walk, it would take a great deal longer. Whitehall *did* have some horses...she shuddered at the thought of riding a horse for several days. Alassa might be horse-mad, but Emily had never liked the smelly beasts.

And the Manavores were out there, somewhere.

She leaned forward. "Master...won't the Gathering make a very tempting target?"

"Yes, it will," Whitehall said. "It may even have been cancelled."

Emily shook her head in disbelief. But then, there were no communications spells in the past, no way to get a message from one place to another instantly. Whitehall might arrive at the Gathering only to discover that it had been cancelled, or that the camp had already been attacked and destroyed by the Manavores. It was just another thing she'd had to get used to after her arrival, although there *were* spells, in her era, that could get a message from place to place. She'd just never learned them until she'd had a reason to learn.

"And we're going," she said. "Is there no way to check if it's still taking place?"

"Not really," Whitehall said. "I was hoping that some of the other communes would find their way to the castle, but we haven't seen them."

He sat back in his chair. "You will be coming, won't you?"

Emily rather suspected it wasn't a request. She was his apprentice, as far as he was concerned; he couldn't leave her alone in the castle. Who knew what sort of mischief an unsupervised apprentice would get up to? And besides, she was still a young girl in his eyes. Whitehall knew—intellectually—that she could look after herself, but emotionally it was a very different matter. He felt responsible for her safety.

"If you wish me to come," she said, silently resigning herself to a long and uncomfortable trip, "it will be my pleasure."

Whitehall gave her a look that suggested he *knew* she wasn't happy about the trip, but said nothing. She wouldn't have been surprised if he'd been a little perplexed by her reluctance to go. For most villagers, going to the next village was hard enough—traveling to the nearest town or city was the trip of a lifetime. And for a young girl, who wouldn't be expected to travel at all, the opportunity to go on a trip was not to be missed.

Julianne will love it, she thought.

She took a breath. "Is it wise to leave Lords Chambers and Reaper here alone?"

"They will not be unsupervised," Whitehall said. "Drake and Wolfe will keep a close eye on them."

Emily had her doubts. She'd always had the impression that Chambers simply didn't respect Wolfe—or Bones. Even now, with their disciplines becoming increasingly useful, he didn't think highly of them. But they would definitely respect Drake—and perhaps Sake too. And their ability to tamper with the nexus point was very limited.

Unless they want to cause an eruption of raw magic, she thought. *The results would be quite disastrous.*

"They will honor the commune," Whitehall added. "A vote, once taken, cannot be overruled."

"Yes, Master," Emily said. She didn't believe it—Master Chambers had good reason to be annoyed at the way the vote had gone—but there was no point in arguing further. Whitehall still saw Master Chambers as a friend. "I understand."

Whitehall nodded, curtly. "I trust you have been keeping an eye on Julianne?"

Emily kept her face blank, refusing to allow the sudden shift to throw her.

"She's been behaving herself," she said, slowly. "Apart from sleeping through dinner, I suppose."

"Understandable," Whitehall said. He met her eyes. "But that wasn't what I meant, and you know it."

Emily hesitated. She knew *precisely* what Whitehall meant. "She and Bernard are drawing closer," she said, flatly. "But they haven't gone further than kissing."

Whitehall gave her a sharp look. "Are you sure?"

Emily fought down a flicker of irritation. She understood Whitehall's concerns, but she found it hard to accept them. Julianne was nineteen, by her own reckoning; hell, if she'd been born to a normal village family, she might have had two or three children of her own by now. She had the right, as far as Emily was concerned, to decide what to do with her own body. But Whitehall would feel very differently.

"To the best of my knowledge," she said stiffly, "she hasn't been alone with him long enough for anything to happen."

She paused. "You *did* send them off together."

"I did," Whitehall said, curtly.

Emily leaned forward. "Do you...do you *object* to the relationship?"

"If I did not approve of Bernard, I would never have taken him as an apprentice," Whitehall said. He sounded irked, although Emily suspected he wasn't angry at *her*. "But their relationship will cause her problems if they do not get married."

"And it won't cause *him* problems," Emily said. "How...*unfair*."

"The world is not fair," Whitehall said, rather sarcastically. "And rumors will destroy a young woman's reputation even as they enhance a young man's."

Emily looked at him. "You don't have a problem if they get married," she said. It was hard to keep the sarcasm out of her voice. "But you do have a problem if they *don't* get married."

"Quite," Whitehall said. "Did your family not have such problems?"

No, Emily thought. *Because no one would have given a damn.*

She shook her head in frustration. If Julianne lost her virginity outside wedlock, or if there were prevalent *rumors* she'd lost her virginity outside wedlock, it would reflect badly on her father. And if she'd had siblings, it would have reflected badly on them too, making it harder for them to find a good match. Hell, the mere *suggestion* that Bernard had seduced her purely to *marry* her wouldn't do her any good either.

"I am surprised," Whitehall said. He lifted his eyebrows. "Are things so different where you were born?"

"I never paid much attention," Emily said. It was true enough—and it saved her from having to tell another lie. As absurd—as oppressive—as the system seemed, she knew it existed for good reason. The potions that might have changed that were simply unavailable, at least outside the fragmented magical community. "There was little hope of me marrying anyway."

Whitehall didn't look as though he believed *that*, although he didn't seem inclined to challenge her words. An unwanted girl could always be sold off, if there was no one willing to marry her. Frieda would have faced such a fate if she hadn't developed magic. Hell, she practically *had* been sold to Mountaintop. The harsh demands of survival insisted she be sacrificed so that others might live.

"It is of no matter," Whitehall said. He smiled, rather wanly. "Although you should be aware that Robin has already asked for your hand."

Emily shook her head, hastily. She had no idea why she'd been overwhelmed in the forest—her protections would have sounded the alarm if Robin had cast a love or lust spell on her—but she didn't want to marry him. Her personal history said she would make it back to her future—she rubbed the scar on her cheek—and see Caleb again. She was damned if she was doing *anything* with Robin.

"I told him that I didn't have the right to *offer* your hand," Whitehall added. "I should say he's shown more nerve than Bernard."

"I'm not your daughter," Emily said. She was the first female apprentice, as far as anyone knew. It was unlikely there were any provisions in the apprenticeship oaths for arranging their marriages. "And I don't want to marry him."

She shook her head in wry amusement. Bernard had to be *terrified* of approaching Whitehall and asking for Julianne's hand in marriage. Whitehall could say no...

and where would Bernard be then? How could he even continue as Whitehall's apprentice?

"Noted," Whitehall said, pleasantly.

Emily looked at him. "Would you object if Bernard and Julianne were to marry?"

Whitehall looked back at her. "Are you asking on his behalf?"

"No," Emily said. "I'm...I'm just curious."

"I see," Whitehall said. He shrugged. "If Julianne is willing to be his wife, then I have no objection. But she's been learning magic and he may object to that. The curse..."

"Is no longer a concern," Emily said.

"It is," Whitehall countered. "You might well be wrong—and even if you're *not* wrong, Julianne might already have damaged herself."

"She was using magic to brew potions," Emily said.

"Quite," Whitehall said.

He pushed the vellum aside and leaned forward, resting his elbows on the table. "And now as we approach bedtime," he added, "it's time for you to tell me how I caught you spying on the meeting."

Emily swallowed hard. She had no idea. None of the wards she knew from her studies surrounded the office...indeed, she could have spied on Whitehall without using the snake, if she'd been prepared to take the risk. And yet he'd *known* she was spying on him. A dozen options ran through her mind, but none of them quite made sense. Somehow, she doubted Whitehall would let her *guess*.

He didn't try to block me, Emily thought. It was possible that Whitehall had *wanted* her to listen, but he could have made the order explicit. He couldn't reasonably have expected her to guess that was what he wanted her to do? *And he had no way to know what issues would be raised ahead of time.*

Whitehall smiled, rather coolly. "Have you figured it out?"

Perhaps I should just take whatever punishment is coming, Emily thought. She'd been taught, time and time again, not to guess, that it was better to admit ignorance than pretend to know more than she did. *And then maybe he'd explain...*

She gritted her teeth in frustration. There were no wards designed to block spying spells, no protections that would have kept her from peeking on him. Whitehall's protections were brutally unsubtle...there was no way he should have been aware of the snake's presence, let alone that she could peer through its eyes. And yet he'd caught her.

Or had he?

"You didn't catch me," she said. Perhaps she was wrong, but it was worth a try. "You just gambled, you *assumed*, that I'd be trying to spy on the meeting. And you were right."

Whitehall smiled. "And your reasoning is?"

Emily pushed onwards, despite the doubts nagging at her mind. "If I had been listening, and I was, I would hear your order to report here," she said. "If I came, you'd know I was spying on you; if I didn't come, you'd know I wasn't spying on you."

"Clever," Whitehall said. "And what if you'd decided to call my bluff?"

"I couldn't have," Emily said. "If I'd assumed you were bluffing, and I was wrong, I would be in worse trouble. I'd have to gamble that I was right to call your bluff—if I was right, you'd never punish me because you wouldn't know there was anything to punish me *for*, but if I was wrong you would."

She met his eyes. "Am I right?"

"I am not going to tell you," Whitehall said. "But I will give you a word of advice."

Emily tensed as he rose and started to pace the room. "I have given you a great deal of leeway because of your...origins," he said. "I have—perhaps—not disciplined you as harshly as I would a male apprentice. But you have been pushing the limits very hard, Emily. If things had been different, teaching my daughter magic would have been the very last straw."

"Yes, Master," Emily murmured.

"And spying on me was unwise too," Whitehall added. "If you did that to any other master, you would be in deep trouble. Do *not* do it again. Do you understand me?"

"Yes, Master," Emily said.

"They are already questioning our relationship," Whitehall warned. "I have tolerated far too much from you, as far as they are concerned—and they may well be right. And while they may not openly challenge *me*, they are more than happy to challenge *you. And* you cannot defend yourself against whispered insinuations."

"I know, Master," Emily said.

"I would suggest you keep a low profile over the next few days," Whitehall added, as he opened the door. "But as we are going to need you to help teach runes, Emily, it would be largely pointless. Just be aware that I cannot afford to turn a blind eye to your...oddities any longer."

Emily nodded. He wasn't the first person to say that to her. "Yes, Master."

She stepped through the door and headed back to her bedroom, feeling torn between irritation at having fallen so easily for his trick and a gnawing concern about the future. She knew, beyond a shadow of a doubt, that she couldn't stay for much longer, but far too much could happen before she managed to craft the spells that would get her home. Master Chambers had good reason to hate her, she had to admit, and Reaper and Keldor probably felt the same way...

And she hadn't been making Whitehall's life any easier, she admitted, privately. Perhaps it would have been better to tell him the truth, despite the risk to the timeline. He would have believed her if she'd teleported—or shown him something else beyond his skills...wouldn't he? She had no way to know.

And if I fall into the trap of believing that I am destined to return home, she told herself as she reached the bedroom door, *I might well make a mistake that will cost me everything.*

Chapter Twenty-Four

"I DO NOT BELIEVE THAT THESE RUNES WORK," APPRENTICE TAMA SAID. HE WAS A TALL MAN, two or three years older than Emily; his hair, like nearly everyone else in the castle, had been shaved close to his scalp. "They're useless."

Emily scowled at him. Tama was precisely the kind of boy—a young man, really—that she would have hated and feared on Earth: strong enough to be threatening, stupid enough not to care. And Tama was far less inclined to listen to a girl than anyone she'd known on Earth. An hour of trying to batter runes into his head had left her feeling more irritated than she could recall, even when she'd been tutoring other students. At least they'd wanted to learn.

"They may save your life," she said, tartly. Her head was starting to pound. Whitehall *had* to have known that Tama wouldn't listen to her, hadn't he? Perhaps he'd envisaged tutoring the idiot as a subtle punishment for spying on him. "The Manavores will consume you if you don't know how to defend yourself."

"I am mighty," Tama said. He struck a pose that showed off his impressive muscles, then cast a spell to summon a fireball. "My fists are strong and my magic is..."

"Useless against a Manavore," Emily pointed out. "Bernard and Robin hit it repeatedly with spells and it just absorbed the magic."

Tama snorted. He'd heard the stories, Emily was sure; Bernard and Robin had been telling everyone what had happened two days ago. *And* he'd been part of a group that had been forced to flee the creatures. But he clearly didn't realize that it wouldn't have made any difference if he'd stood and fought, rather than following the other apprentices away from the disastrous battle.

It would have made a difference, she thought, as she sketched out the next rune. *It would have added his name to the list of the dead.*

"This is not real magic," Tama objected. "And it isn't what I want to learn."

"It's what you *have* to learn," Emily said. Tama's former master had died, just before the remains of his commune had been absorbed into the Whitehall Commune. He knew enough to be dangerous, but not enough to be useful. "Your master died because he didn't know how to defend himself."

"My master was a very wise man," Tama snapped. "But I suppose you wouldn't know anything about *wise* masters."

His gaze lingered on Emily's chest. "What did you give him in exchange for training?"

"I learned," Emily said. She wondered, briefly, if she should hex Tama into next week. He had a considerable amount of raw power—and he was certainly physically stronger than her—but she had far more training. Clobbering him with magic would be very satisfying, yet she doubted it would make him listen. "And you are going to learn, too."

Tama picked up the vellum and tore it in half. Emily stared in shock. Parchment and vellum were *expensive*, even for magicians. Whitehall and Wolfe had only brought a limited supply to the castle and it was already running out. A common peasant would take *months* to earn enough money to replace the destroyed vellum.

"I don't kneel to *girls*," Tama said. He smirked at her. "Girls kneel to me."

Emily opened her mouth to say something cutting, then stopped as Robin stepped into the room. "You should listen to her," Robin said. "She beat *Bernard* in a duel."

Tama sneered. "So he says."

"And if you *don't* listen to her," Robin added, sharply, "*I'll* teach you respect."

Tama scowled at Robin, gave Emily a thoroughly nasty look, then rose to his feet and stalked out of the workroom, slamming the door behind him. Emily shook her head in disbelief as she picked up the pieces of vellum, wondering if she could use a spell to bind them back together. Tama hadn't said much about his past, but his disdain for women and book learning suggested a commoner background. He probably didn't give a damn about reading and writing—or the fiddly spellwork Master Wolfe used.

And reading would be a useless skill, if there were no books, Emily thought. *What could he do with it?*

She sighed. Robin might think he'd done her a favor. But to Tama? He'd just looked like a white knight defending someone who couldn't defend herself.

"He lost his master during the rout," Robin commented. He didn't seem aware of her ambivalence. "And since then, he's been forbidden to practice magic."

"I can see why," Emily said. Tama had too much to unlearn, if he wanted to continue to study magic. She didn't blame him for being frustrated, but there were limits. If she'd managed to learn from Master Grey, who had planned to kill her, Tama could learn from a woman. "He didn't learn anything from me."

"I'll have him beaten for you," Robin offered. He sat down facing her, taking the seat Tama had vacated. Emily could sense the demon sitting on his shoulder, even though it was invisible to the naked eye. "Your master will not tolerate such impertinence."

Emily cocked her eyebrows. "And is that what you—or Bernard—would do?"

"We'd curse him into a pulp," Robin said. "But no one expects that from you."

"I suppose you wouldn't be *beating* him into a pulp," Emily said. Robin was hardly a weakling, but Tama was clearly stronger than him. "And it isn't me he has to worry about."

"He's got a chip on his shoulder," Robin agreed. "He was an apprentice—his master was training him up to be a real magician. And then he lost his master and his chance of gaining his own mastery."

Emily sighed. She would have felt sorry for Tama if he hadn't been such an asshole—and a sexist prick, at that. People could and did lose something they'd worked for through no fault of their own—as an apprentice with some training, Tama should have found it easy to attach himself to another master. But there were forty-five other unattached apprentices in the castle and his attitude worked against him. Emily probably hadn't helped by allowing herself to be attached to Whitehall right from the start.

Which probably explains why he was so unpleasant, she thought. *It's easier to believe I cheated—which I suppose I did—rather than accept I might be better.*

She scowled down at the vellum as her spell repaired the damage. Tama would have to learn, sooner or later. It wouldn't be long before the Manavores returned—or, perhaps, the magicians set out to hunt them down. The simple fact she'd never heard of anything like them in her time suggested that they had been exterminated—if, indeed, they were natural creatures. She knew enough about the coming years to fear for her friends among the commune. There was no way to tell who might die, years ahead of their time, and who might be forever changed.

"I'm sure he'll get over it," she said, curtly. "And if he doesn't, he will wind up dead."

"Yeah," Robin said. "We could all be dead soon."

He leaned forward. Emily had to fight the urge to move back.

"I asked your master for your hand," he said, after a moment. "And he said I should ask you."

Because I have no family, Emily thought, darkly. *And because a girl with no family is horrifyingly vulnerable.*

She sighed, taking a moment to study him. Robin...didn't quite make sense; he seemed to look down on her, yet he *wanted* her. His behavior veered backwards and forwards in a way she would have unhesitatingly called bipolar, if they'd been on Earth. He could be charming one moment and demanding the next. And he might well be just a little bit insane. Even now, he didn't seem to have toned down his magic. She could sense the power boiling through him without any effort at all.

And he's defying his master by talking to me, she thought. *Master Chambers would not be pleased if he caught us together.*

"I don't want to marry you," she said, finally. A dozen weaselling excuses came to her mind, but she pushed them aside. "I have..."

Robin gave her a pleading stare. "I know you felt something, in the forest," he said. He leaned forward, pressing into her personal space. "I felt it too."

Emily winced at the memory. "It wasn't *real*," she said. She took a deliberate step back, unsure what else to do. "What happened there didn't happen because I like you..."

"It *was* real," Robin said. His voice hardened. "Or are you trying to deny your own feelings?"

"I am aware of what I felt," Emily said, stiffly. She clamped down hard on the flash of anger that threatened to overwhelm her. "But it was not *real*. I regret kissing you..."

"Bernard doesn't regret kissing Julianne, you know," Robin said. There was a hint of envy in his voice. "And I don't think *she* regrets it either."

"They already had feelings for one another," Emily said. "I don't have any feelings for you."

"You kissed me," Robin protested.

"I know," Emily said. She resisted the urge to shout at him, then held up her hand as he took another step towards her. "And I regret it."

Robin glared. "Why?"

"I have a...a prior relationship," Emily said. "I don't..."

"You were trapped in the nexus point for years," Robin snapped. He sounded, just for a moment, as if he thought she was being stupid. Perhaps he did. "You have no idea just *how* long you were trapped or how to return to your home, if it even exists. Your...former partner will have found someone else—if he isn't already dust! There is no reason for you to wait for him when there is no hope of you seeing each other again."

His voice hardened. "I'm going to be a master soon," he added. "I have contacts with masters both inside and outside the castle and a number of relatives who have married into other communes. And we have feelings for each other. You should consider me..."

Emily cut him off. "Because you're the best offer I'm likely to get?"

"You need someone who will protect you," Robin said. "And someone who will overlook your...eccentricities. Or any...prior relationships you might have had."

He met his eyes. "Why should you not consider me?"

Emily felt her temper snap. "Because you are a rude and pushy young fool?"

She sensed his magic blazing with fury and hastily strengthened her protections, unsure if he would try to lash out at her or merely lambast her with angry words. Robin's demon seemed to flicker into visibility for a long second—a concentrated mass of malice sitting on his shoulder—before vanishing again. Emily braced herself, unwilling to back down and yet unwilling to fight. If Robin lost control completely...

Somehow, he calmed himself. "Explain."

Emily was tempted to point out that he had no right to give her orders, but refrained.

"I don't need your protection," she said, instead. "And I should not have to seek a match based on whoever will tolerate me."

Robin looked blank. "Why not?"

He met her eyes. Emily tensed, half-expecting an attempt to invade her mind, but felt nothing. "You are a woman who has been trained as a magician," he said. "You have no family, no friends; you are surrounded by rumors that will shadow your foot-steps until the day you die. Any man interested in courting you will wonder, deep inside, if those rumors are true, if he's not the first man to..."

Emily felt a hot flash of anger. "To have sex with me?"

"Yes," Robin said. He lowered his voice. When he spoke, he sounded oddly sincere. "Your prospects for a good match are minimal."

It was hard, very hard, not to either laugh or cry. The hell of it, Emily knew, was by his lights it was a very good offer. An apprentice magician—an apprentice who would be a master soon—was a very good catch, even if his wife could expect mood swings and bouts of insanity that would only grow worse as he grew older. And yes, someone with such an uncertain past and present as Emily couldn't expect many suitors. Bernard might have accepted her as an equal, of sorts, but he wasn't inter-ested in *marrying* her...

And he honestly believes I left Caleb in the past, Emily thought. *As far as he knows, I have no family ties.*

She shook her head, gently. Even if she had been trapped in the past, even if what she'd told them about her origins was true, she wouldn't have wanted Robin. She'd met too many people like him, too many people who were charming and likable as long as they got their way. Being his wife would be an unpleasant experience. The best she could hope for from him would be being treated like a china doll, someone to dress up in finery and clean regularly, but not a person in her own right. And at worst...she remembered, all too clearly, the look on Eldora's face.

I would have poisoned my husband if he'd treated me like that, she thought. *But Eldora would have nowhere to go afterwards.*

"I thank you for the offer," she said, formally. "But I must decline."

Robin peered at her, as if he were trying to see into her mind. "Is there someone else?"

"You would not find me a comfortable wife," Emily said. "And we would fight as much as anything else."

She watched him, wondering how he would react. Her magic shimmered below her skin, ready to shield her and strike back...she could sense his demon *looking* at her, even though it was still invisible. Perhaps she should have mentioned *that* as a reason to reject him, even though he wouldn't have accepted it. And then he rose to his feet and walked to the door.

Emily blinked in astonishment, staring after him as he left the room. She'd expected everything from a quiet apology to violent screaming and shouting, not... not Robin just *leaving*. Did he feel too ashamed to push the issue any further? Or did he think he'd embarrassed himself enough? Or...no matter how she looked at it, she didn't understand what was going through his head. But if he was already unstable, thanks to the demons, his reactions might be unpredictable anyway.

She returned the vellum to her pocket and rose, heading to the door. Her watch hadn't come through the time warp with her, but it *felt* like she had an hour to go until lunch and she wasn't scheduled to meet any other apprentices until afterwards. No doubt Tama was busy complaining to the rest of them about what a bitch she was, just for making him try to learn to draw runes. Such stupidity wouldn't last long in *her* Whitehall, she reminded herself. A stupid magician would be a dead magician very quickly.

And no one would have said any of that to Mistress Irene or Lady Barb, she thought, as she made her way back to the bedroom. *Neither of them would have tolerated it for a second.*

"Emily," Julianne said. She was sitting at the table, working her way through a basket of herbs. "Did you have a good time?"

Emily shook her head. "Is Tama always such a pain?"

"He's worse to the serving girls," Julianne said. "He didn't want to learn from you?"

"Yeah," Emily confirmed. "How did you know?"

Julianne snorted. "I've been trying to teach a couple of the boys," she said. "One—a servant who wanted to learn potions—did well, but the other—a former apprentice—flatly refused to learn from me."

"Oh," Emily said. "And what did you say to him?"

"Said if he didn't want to learn, it was his problem—not mine," Julianne said. "And he just up and left."

Emily had to smile. "And then Robin asked me to marry him," she added. "I said no."

Julianne frowned. "He's really taken with you, isn't he?"

"I know," Emily said. Since when had *she* become a desirable girl? She hadn't realized that Caleb was interested in her until her friends had told her. "But I don't want him."

"I'm sure he took that very well," Julianne said, sarcastically. "His master was not pleased with him sniffing around you."

"I imagine he wasn't," Emily said. If Master Chambers believed—genuinely believed—that she'd seduced Whitehall, of all people, he might assume she was trying to seduce Robin and lead him astray. Or he might fear that she would teach Robin how to use magic without demons. "What happened?"

"Bernard said that Robin was beaten for it," Julianne said. Her face twisted in sympathy. "I don't know for sure, but he *did* take a couple of healing and painkilling potions afterwards."

Emily snorted in surprise. Robin's master had put his foot down—and Robin had carried on anyway? "Is it really that bad?"

Julianne frowned. "The beatings, or you saying no?"

"Me saying no," Emily said.

"There was a time when he could have had any girl he wanted," Julianne said. "He was young, powerful, had excellent prospects...there were quite a few girls who looked on him with favor. But now...the only marriageable women here, apart from you and me, are the serving girls."

"So he wants me because I'm the only candidate," Emily said. She supposed she should be relieved that the other apprentices hadn't started asking her to marry them too, although Robin had probably intimidated them. "Apart from you, I suppose."

Julianne nodded. "We'll be trying to bring more women into the castle during the Gathering," she said. "And if they happen to be of magical blood, so much the better."

"Stupid," Emily muttered. If Robin believed in the curse, Robin would be better off trying to court one of the serving girls. *She* wouldn't have any problem bearing children. "Robin isn't exactly of noble blood—and Tama definitely isn't."

"Men can be very stupid," Julianne agreed. She sighed, rather melodramatically. "But then, women can be stupid too."

Chapter Twenty-Five

"A ND UPON THIS CRYSTAL," MASTER BONES SAID, AS EMILY ENTERED THE CHAMBER UNDER the nexus point, "we will build our base."

She sucked in her breath as she took in the crystals, growing rapidly until they branched up to the nexus point and throughout the castle. The control room—the control room she'd discovered under Whitehall School—was taking shape in front of her, the pieces of spellwork growing organically into something that would last the ages. A humanoid figure lay on a table, magic bubbling around it as Master Keldor and Master Wolfe made the final preparations. The Warden, too, was coming to life.

A voice-activated control system, Emily thought. *It would take time for the Warden to evolve, but she knew it would happen. And an intelligence that will be far too close to human—without ever quite crossing the line—to exist anywhere else.*

"Ah, Emily," Master Wolfe said. "Please wait in the next chamber, will you?"

Emily nodded and walked out of the control room, feeling the odd sensation of someone walking over her grave as she passed the tiny library. A handful of scrolls were already resting within, waiting to be consulted; others, she knew, would be added in the weeks and months before the underground tunnels were sealed. She watched a gaggle of workmen hurry past her, then followed them down into the next chamber. The map room was already taking shape.

Another shiver ran down her spine as she walked through the map room—the maps on the walls were clearly going to be updated, sometime in the future—and into the room beyond, empty save for a handful of runes on the walls. She stopped, reaching out with her senses to feel the magic running through the stone; she knew, centuries from now, her past self would discover her future self in the chamber. And her touch would be enough to bring her future self out of stasis, *slowly*. She would need to hide—or jump into a pocket dimension—as soon as she was awake. There was no way to know what would happen if her past and future selves met ahead of time, but she doubted it would be good. She already knew they *hadn't* met until she shoved herself into the nexus point.

She turned and strode back to the library, silently running through the spells she'd devised as she took a seat and waited for Master Wolfe. Tapping the nexus point to power the spell—and conceal it from everyone else—wasn't going to be hard. Keying the spell so it would start to come undone at the touch of her past self's hand was a little harder—her past self's magical signature was identical to her future self's—but it could be done. The *real* problem lay in shutting down her mind, rather than merely petrifying her body. There was no way she could endure nearly a thousand years as a statue...

...And yet, she couldn't find a way to avoid it.

My future self did it somehow, she thought. *I only have to figure out how.*

Master Wolfe stepped into the library, looking tired. "Lady Emily," he said, taking a seat facing her. "I trust you had a pleasant few days?"

Emily shrugged. She'd tried to teach five male apprentices and only one of them had *listened* to her, although none of them had been *quite* as rude as Tama. And Robin had refused to face her, while Bernard had eyed her oddly...it made her wonder just what Robin had said to him, after she'd turned down the proposal. No doubt he'd blamed everything on her.

"I've been expanding the wards." Master Wolfe added. "The castle will be safe in Lord Whitehall's absence."

"I hope so," Emily agreed. Thankfully, neither Master Chambers nor Master Reaper had shown any interest in learning how to maintain the wards. *She* would have preferred to quietly lock them out of the command system, but that was impossible without tearing the whole network apart and starting again. "Did you find a way to keep demons out?"

"I can keep new ones from being summoned," Master Wolfe said. "But keeping old ones out may be impossible."

Emily scowled. It was possible, she knew, but she didn't know *how*.

"It's the Manavores that pose the real problem," Master Wolfe added. "There's too much ambient magic flowing through the castle to starve them."

"We could try overfeeding them instead," Emily offered.

"There'd be an explosion of raw magic when they reached capacity," Master Wolfe pointed out, thoughtfully. "And the wards might not be able to handle it."

"Particularly if they're already being drained," Emily mused. Perhaps they could start creating the multidimensional interior, then simply reconfigure and delete entire sections to trap and kill the Manavores. She'd done something similar to Shadye. "Or we could try to cut them off from their power source."

"Perhaps," Master Wolfe said. "I cannot account for them."

Emily bit her tongue. She was almost sure the Manavores were merely the first of the terror weapons the Faerie would unleash, in the not too distant future. But she could think of another possibility. If some enterprising DemonMaster had asked for a weapon he could turn against his enemies, a conniving demon might have taught him how to produce a Manavore in the certain knowledge that it would get out of hand. And they *had* gotten out of hand. It was impossible to be *sure*, but everyone agreed there was definitely more than one. Perhaps they'd been breeding when they hadn't been hunting magicians.

"Setting that concern aside for the moment," Master Wolfe said. He produced a large piece of folded parchment, placing it on the table and carefully unfolding it. "What do you make of this?"

"It's...*complex*," Emily said. In truth, she was reminded of the spells Master Wolfe had crafted to make use of the nexus point. "And it's..."

She sucked in her breath as she realized she was looking, for the first time, at a complete Mimic. No, at the spellwork that would *become* a Mimic. It was *fantastically* complex, perhaps the most complex piece of spellwork she'd ever seen...she'd thought her work with Caleb was complex, but this was an order of magnitude greater. No single magician could *hope* to cast such a spell...

And yet, if Master Wolfe was right, it should be possible.

She forced herself to think through it logically, dissecting the spellwork into its component subsections. First and foremost, there was the necromantic rite: ready and able to consume enough power to fuel the spellwork. And then there was a complex mixture of soul and illusionary magic, the former providing the framework for the latter. She'd assumed that the Mimic merely *copied* its victims—an impressive feat in its own right—but in some ways it *was* its victims. The intelligence that underlay the whole framework was both staggeringly capable and yet very limited. It was smart enough to take command and hunt for new prey when it found itself running out of power.

"I don't understand," she said. "You could make it smarter."

"I could transfer myself into the spellwork," Master Wolfe explained. "It doesn't *have* to be smarter."

Emily shook her head. "The power demands would be staggering," she said. "And what would happen when you targeted someone new?"

"I wouldn't," Master Wolfe said. "I'd be drawing power from the nexus point."

"Clever," Emily said. "But what happens when you get it wrong?"

"I'm an old man," Master Wolfe said. "And I want to live to see the coming generations."

You'll be seeing more than that, Emily thought. Transferring himself into the Mimic wasn't a bad idea, but the power requirements would eventually force the hindbrain to take control and start hunting for a new victim. *And when something goes wrong...*

She frowned as she considered the implications. Clearly, *something* had gone wrong along the way. By her time, everyone had forgotten that the Mimics were spells. They'd assumed they were just odd creatures. And in a world where dragons flew through the skies, it wasn't a bad assumption.

Just wrong, she added, silently.

She closed her eyes in pain. She could tell him to stop. She could try to tell him to accept his death, knowing that his place in history was already assured. And Whitehall would listen to her, she thought, if she went to him and urged him to forbid Master Wolfe from experimenting further. A plague—a terrible plague—would never be released. But history said that the Mimics *would* escape, *would* become a nightmare...

...And there was nothing she could do to stop it.

"Test everything," she urged, finally. "And be *careful.*"

Master Wolfe snorted. "If we were careful all the time," he said, "would we get anywhere at all?"

Emily shrugged.

"I'm going to be keeping the notes in this chamber," Master Wolfe added. "You'll have access, of course. I trust you won't abuse it?"

"No, Master," Emily said. She already knew she'd be taking the books from the tiny library later, centuries in the future. And then...she'd have to have a careful look at the books before deciding what to do with them. There were already secrets within the tomes that Professor Locke would have sold his soul to see. "It will never be abused."

Master Wolfe launched into a long and complicated explanation of the spellwork he and his team were slowly slotting into the Warden. Emily listened, injecting the occasional suggestion, as Master Wolfe described how *replacing* the Warden could be done by inputting the correct string of commands into the growing spellwork. Building a homunculus was tricky, he admitted, but the nexus point made animating it a great deal simpler. Given the right materials, the Warden could practically be replaced overnight.

As long as there's nothing interfering with the process, Emily thought. *How long did it take us to replace the last Warden?*

Her head was pounding by the time she was finally dismissed. Master Wolfe was definitely a genius, an *eccentric* genius. He'd already invented a prototype analysis spell that new apprentices could learn, one that she was sure would eventually turn into the spell she'd been taught by Mistress Irene. Emily was honestly nervous about saying *anything* in front of him, just because he had a habit of taking wild ideas and running with them. He was already halfway towards devising more and more wards to sweep the castle for dark magic.

And it will give whoever is in control vast power over the school, she thought, as she made her way up to the bedroom. *They'll be able to see into every last nook and cranny.*

She tensed as she turned the corner and saw Tama, standing next to two other apprentices and scowling fiercely. He balled his fists, then muttered a couple of words as he hurled a spell towards her. Emily felt too tired to try to catch and dissect it, so she stepped aside and allowed the spell to splash harmlessly against the stone wall. Tama grunted and tossed another spell at her, a lightning bolt that flashed through the air and spent itself uselessly against her protections. There was no shortage of power in his magic—although he was nowhere near either Bernard or Robin—but he had almost no control at all.

The apprentices are going to go mad, she told herself. She didn't want to fight, but she was so *tired*. Tired of being treated either as an inferior or someone who needed to be protected, someone who couldn't look after herself. *They're slopping magic through their brains...*

"Fight me," Tama snapped. He hurled another lightning bolt at her, brilliant flashes of light dancing off her wards and making her hair want to stand on end. "Robin's not here to defend you, *bitch.*"

Emily fought down the urge to throw a lethal curse—or something too far out of place—back at him. Instead, she shaped a spell in her mind and cast it, hurling it right towards him and his watching friends. He was going to hate her more—they were all going to hate her—but she found it hard to care. The spell she'd hurled wasn't powerful, nowhere near as powerful as the lightning spells he'd cast at her, yet that hardly mattered. He'd underestimate the spell...

Tama's eyes went wide as his lower body suddenly froze, sending him and his friends tumbling to the ground. Emily felt a flicker of sympathy for one of them—he'd cracked his head against the stone floor—but he didn't look to be seriously injured. Tama stared at her, then let loose a flurry of inventive curses as he cast another spell. He didn't even seem to be trying to *free* himself.

He thinks my spell won't last, Emily thought. Against Robin or Bernard, he might well have been right. He hadn't even tried to ward the spell off because it had been weak, but that had been a fatal error. *He's trapped and he doesn't even know it.*

She lifted a hand and cast a prank spell on all three of the boys. Their hands were suddenly glued to their sides, held in place by an invisible force. A second spell shut their mouths, holding their lips together...Tama's eyes went wide with shock. He'd genuinely thought she wasn't a true magician, she realized. And his friends hadn't even *talked* to her...

"You underestimated the spells I used," she said, "because they weren't very powerful."

Tama glared at her, his magic field flaring around him. Emily watched him warily for a second, then decided he didn't have the power or the precision to break the spells ahead of time. He'd definitely learned far too much for his own good before losing his master and fleeing to the commune. What had he *thought* would happen? He'd overwhelm her magic and then have his way with her? Or merely humiliate her in front of his friends?

"Their power doesn't matter," she added. Tama had definitely not been trained in casting spells without using his hands. "All that matters is that the spells are designed to make it impossible for you to break free. Your power is nowhere near sufficient to break free before I cut your throats."

She felt a stab of guilt at the sudden panic on his face and told herself not to be silly. He probably hadn't planned to rape her—Whitehall would have killed him, quite literally, if he had—but humiliating her would have been a different story. Would Whitehall have reacted *quite* so badly if she'd been stripped naked and displayed to the world?

But if he was right about how I became his apprentice, she thought, *my master would be insane with rage.*

She shook her head. Tama was an idiot. It never seemed to have occurred to him that he might have been wrong...and the consequences of actually being *right* would be a great deal worse. Village boy or not, he should have known better. Perhaps his father had been the headman, like Hodge. The bastard hadn't had the wit to think twice before trying to rape a magician either.

"You need to learn how to use your power more efficiently," she added, forcing the thought aside. "Right now, even a weaker magician with more skill can tie you up in knots. I could kill the three of you, right here, and you couldn't hope to stop me. I *suggest*, very strongly, that you go to Master Wolfe and beg him to teach you before it's too late."

She walked past them, resisting the urge to kick Tama while he was down. "The spells will wear off, sooner or later," she told them. "When they do...learn from the experience. Or die, the next time you challenge a more capable magician."

Gritting her teeth, she kept walking, feeling sweat running down her back. It was hard to walk slowly—she wanted to run—but she forced herself to keep going at the same pace until she was round the corner and heading up a flight of stairs. God alone knew what Master Whitehall would say, when he heard about what she'd done. But then, it was quite possible that *no one* would stumble across the trio until the spells had worn off. Would they make a complaint?

They'll be laughed at if they do, she thought.

She couldn't help smiling at the thought, even though it wasn't particularly funny. It was one of the ironies of a world that was blatantly sexist, if not misogynistic. She'd seen it in Cockatrice. A man might beat his wife—perfectly legally—and she might complain to her father or the local headman, but no self-respecting husband would dare complain about his wife beating *him*. He'd be a laughingstock. And while a man could be punished for excessive beating, a wife couldn't be punished without making her husband the butt of countless bad jokes.

And I'd better tighten up my protections, she told herself as she entered the bedroom and closed the door behind her. Thankfully, Julianne was somewhere else. *Tama might just learn a lesson—but he might also take another shot at me.*

She shook her head as she started to put the spellwork together. The past had always fascinated her, but living in it...that was a different story. And she wanted to go home.

Chapter Twenty-Six

"OPEN YOUR BAG," LORD ALFRED ORDERED, AS EMILY ENTERED THE SMALL CHAMBER. "Lord Whitehall insists that I need to see what you've packed."

Emily scowled, but opened the knapsack without comment. A change of clothes, a couple of potion gourds, a handful of pieces of vellum...there wasn't anything else. She would have liked to bring a book or two with her, but there *weren't* many books in the castle and those that were there were literally irreplaceable. It would be nearly a thousand years before the printing press was invented, allowing them to be copied easily. Master Wolfe's small collection of books was a treasure beyond price.

"Good," Lord Alfred said. "I trust you have *everything* you might need?"

"Yes, My Lord," Emily said. "Julianne assured me that we should be able to get our clothes washed at the Gathering."

"Of course," Lord Alfred said. "We have to look our best."

Emily hid her amusement with an effort. Alassa wasn't quite as obsessed with cleanliness as Emily herself, but she'd insisted on changing her clothes every day. Emily didn't really blame her, either. But then, Julianne had only a handful of outfits and she'd already loaned two of them to Emily. Thankfully, altering borrowed dresses to fit her was the work of a few hours.

And there will be hardly anywhere to wash along the way, Emily thought, morbidly. *We'll going to be smelly by the time we arrive.*

"We won't be coming back to the castle for at least a month," Lord Alfred warned. "If you leave something behind, we won't be able to go back for it."

Emily nodded as she started to repack her bag. There was no way she could take any reading matter along—she would have been glad to have *anything* to read—and everything else was in very short supply. Whitehall and Bernard intended to hunt for food along the way, she'd been told, if they failed to buy it from nearby villages. And if they failed to catch anything...

We can eat plants, if necessary, she reminded herself. *We just have to be careful what we put in our mouths.*

She watched as Lord Alfred hastily packed his own bag. He seemed to be bringing more clothes than Emily and Julianne combined, although she supposed he was going to be carrying his bag. Whitehall had made it clear that they wouldn't be bringing servants along with them. Emily would have suspected that she and Julianne would be expected to do all the work, but Whitehall seemed to have accepted his daughter as a promising magician in her own right. Perhaps she, Julianne and *Bernard* would be expected to do all the work instead.

"It will be an interesting journey," Lord Alfred commented. "I haven't been on the far side of the mountains for *years*."

It took Emily a moment to realize he meant the Craggy Mountains. They'd be heading into the Blighted Lands—or what would *become* the Blighted Lands, in her time. She tensed, recalling the long walk from Whitehall to the Dark Fortress, then dismissed the thought. The Faerie Wars had yet to begin, let alone the rise of the

Necromancers. There was no reason to worry about walking into the Blighted Lands.

But then, the Manavores are on the prowl, she reminded herself. *We might never make it to the Gathering.*

"It should be interesting," she agreed, neutrally. "Do you think..."

She stopped as she saw Lord Alfred open a drawer and pick up a heavy book. An aura of pure evil filled the room. She took a step backwards reflexively as he placed the book on the table, its *malice* so powerful that it dominated the room. It was suddenly hard to remember that there was *anything* else in the room. The book was... it was just *there.*

"That's a Book of Pacts," she said. She hadn't touched it, but merely being so close to the book made her want to hurry to the shower and scrub her skin raw. "You..."

Lord Alfred gave her an affable smile. "I *am* a DemonMaster," he said, reprovingly. His fingers traced the sigil on the cover. "And I have fifty-seven under my command, bound to my name and my blood."

Emily found her voice. "Does Lord Whitehall know?"

"Of course," Lord Alfred told her. There was a reproving tone to his voice. "We have been partners for decades, young lady."

"But you voted against bringing demons into Whitehall," Emily said. "You..."

She cursed herself a moment later. The book had rattled her more than she cared to admit—and she'd practically just confessed to eavesdropping on the fateful meeting. Unless Whitehall had told her afterwards...she knew she didn't dare claim that was true, if Lord Alfred asked. He might well check it with Whitehall.

"Demons are tools," Lord Alfred said. If he noticed her slip, he gave no sign. "And like most such tools, they are best used once the user actually knows what he's doing."

Emily frowned. "You intend to teach your apprentices how to summon demons?"

"If they ask," Lord Alfred said. He smiled, thinly. "I haven't survived so long by being careless, my dear. My apprentices will be made *very* aware of the dangers before they draw out their first circle."

"They might not *want* to summon demons," Emily pointed out. "They'd be able to do everything themselves."

"Perhaps," Lord Alfred said.

He sighed, heavily. She couldn't escape the impression that he was suddenly a great deal older. "When I was a young man, there was an...incident," he said. He leered cheerfully at the book. "I had seduced and bedded the daughter of a local headman—she wasn't much of a lay, but it was quite a challenge. She was devoted to the Crone, you see."

"I'm sure she was," Emily said, disapprovingly.

"The headman sent out his goons to capture me," Lord Alfred added. He didn't seem to notice her disapproval. "I fled into the night, knowing that it wouldn't be long before they tracked me down. And so I summoned a demon and bargained for my life. I wanted to be hidden from the trackers and guided to the nearest safe town. A thunderstorm sprang up, hiding my tracks; the demon told me that the next town was only a mile away. It didn't take me long to reach it."

He looked up at her. "Now tell me," he said. "Did the demon cause that thunderstorm to take place...or was it going to happen all along?"

"I don't know," Emily said, after a moment.

"Nor do I," Lord Alfred told her. "Demons are cunning, my dear. They will take whatever loophole you offer them and turn it against you. I might well have reached that town anyway, if I'd just continued down the path. Was it really worth the price I paid?"

Emily shrugged. "And what happened to the girl?"

Lord Alfred ignored the question. Instead, he packed the book into his knapsack—the aura of evil vanished as soon as the book was out of sight—and slung the bag over his shoulder. He seemed younger, somehow, as he headed for the door, even though there was something wrong with the way he walked. But then, if he hadn't been reasonably healthy for his age, he wouldn't have lasted long in any case. The Nameless World was not kind to the elderly.

Unless they happen to be magicians, Emily thought, as she followed him through the door and down to the courtyard. *I wonder how old he really is.*

She puzzled over the problem for a long moment, then pushed it aside as they stepped into the courtyard. Four horses were waiting, Whitehall and Bernard brushing them down while Julianne checked and rechecked her potions bag. Emily had watched her put it together the previous evening and she'd been quietly impressed by just how much Julianne could do with a few herbs and a little water. She could brew cures for a dozen ailments if necessary, without needing to harvest anything else from the surrounding forest.

"You'll be riding behind Julianne," Whitehall said, as he nodded to the nearest horse. The beast gave Emily a disdainful look. "We have to leave the remaining horses here."

Emily nodded, privately relieved. She could ride, but she didn't *like* it. She'd half-hoped there would be a carriage—there was no hope of anything better—yet Julianne had pointed out, when she'd asked, that there were hardly any roads near the castle. The network of Roman-like roads Emily had seen in the future simply didn't exist. And she had a private suspicion that what few roads there were would be nowhere near as good. The peasants had no particular desire to make it easier for royal officials and tax collectors to make it around the kingdom.

"It's better this way," Julianne whispered, as her father walked back into the castle. "I don't have to be trapped behind father—or Bernard."

Emily nodded in agreement. She was mildly surprised that Julianne knew how to ride—women were rarely taught how to ride unless they were nobility—but she had no hesitation in taking advantage of it. Julianne felt the same way too, she suspected. Being forced to ride behind her father would have been bad enough, but riding behind her boyfriend would have been indecent. And Emily would have had the same problem if she'd ridden behind Whitehall...

"Just try not to gallop too fast," she muttered back. "I think the horse hates me."

Julianne gave her an incredulous look as Whitehall re-emerged from the castle and ordered them to mount up. Bernard climbed into his horse's saddle with admirable skill, but Emily had to scramble up after Julianne. Alassa had taught her how to get onto a horse without using a stand, forcing her to do it again and again, yet she'd never been very good at it. The horse twitched uncomfortably as she settled, wrapping her arms around Julianne, then started to amble towards the gates. Bernard and Whitehall cantered past, while Lord Alfred seemed to be bringing up the rear. His horse snorted unpleasantly.

It probably senses the Book of Pacts, Emily thought, darkly. *And really doesn't want to be anywhere near it.*

"Here we go," Julianne said. "Hang on!"

Emily swore out loud as the horse lunged forward, galloping out of the castle and towards the forest. There *was* a path, she saw now; the commune had hacked and slashed their way through the foliage, clearing their way to the castle. But it had already started to close, the trees and bushes pressing closer and casting long shadows over the path. Emily hunched low as the horses rode into the forest and cantered along the path. She couldn't escape the sense that it was only a matter of time before she cracked her head against a low branch and tumbled off the back of the horse.

"You don't need to hold on *so* tightly," Julianne teased. She didn't seem bothered as the horse picked up speed. "What happened to the girl who killed Master Gila?"

Emily felt her cheeks heat. "She doesn't like riding horses," she said. She thought she saw something moving, within the shadows, but they were past before she could get a clear look at it. "And she would prefer to walk."

Julianne laughed. "And would she prefer to spend months traveling to the Gathering?"

"No," Emily said.

She cursed under her breath. If she'd known where the Gathering was going to be—or if she'd had a decent map—she could have tried to teleport. But no one—not even Whitehall—knew that teleportation was possible, at least without the help of a demon. The spell—and the spell for portals—was far too advanced for her to introduce, at least until Master Wolfe had built up enough expertise with spellware to make it work. Coming to think of it, she hadn't read *any* reference to teleporting before the Second Faerie War. It was possible that the spells wouldn't be invented until then, centuries after Whitehall.

The horse seemed to move faster and faster as they plunged through the forest and out onto a muddy track. Emily realized, to her shock, that they were actually approaching the Craggy Mountains, heading towards a pass that had long since been closed in her time. The mountains grew closer and closer, the horses slowing as they picked their way through the stony ground; the temperature fell sharply as they made their way through the pass, then out into the far side. Emily silently tried to match up the geography to what she'd seen in the future, but rapidly decided it was impossible. Too much was going to change in the next thousand years.

"It isn't so bad," Julianne called back. "Is it?"

Emily shrugged.

She would have enjoyed the trip, she admitted privately, if it hadn't been on horse-back. They found a campsite when the sun started to set and stopped for the night, sleeping under the stars, but when she awoke her body was aching so badly that she had to swallow one of Julianne's potions before she could climb back on the horse. She was all too aware that she was sweaty and unclean—and she'd slept in her clothes, which hadn't helped—but the stream they'd found was nowhere near large enough for a proper wash. Indeed, she found herself wishing she'd remained at the castle, even though Master Chambers had been left in charge. It couldn't have been worse...

Don't be silly, she told herself, as the horses started to gallop again. *Of course it could have been worse.*

The countryside blurred into a mixture of trees, cropland and tiny villages that looked little different to the villages she recalled from her own time. None of them were bigger than a dozen or so houses—she had the impression that Whitehall was deliberately skirting the larger towns—and the peasants seemed worn down and tired by their constant backbreaking labor. Their masters, whoever they were, would be just as greedy and rapacious as any of the aristocrats she'd met in her own time, although the handful of bigger houses didn't *look* strong enough to resist a deter-mined assault. No doubt the peasants were too tired and worn to revolt.

Castles are still in their infancy, she thought, dully. *Which leads to the question of just who built Whitehall?*

She frowned as she contemplated the problem, using it to distract herself from the trip. No one in the commune knew who'd built the castle; indeed, they hadn't even *known* about the castle until Lord Alfred's demon had pointed them in its direction. Emily would have wondered at such ignorance, if she hadn't known that a combina-tion of concealment spells and sheer isolation—and the slow spread of news—would have made it harder for anyone more than a few miles away to know the castle existed. Dragon's Den certainly didn't exist, not now. There might be no settlements for hundreds of miles on the other side of the Craggy Mountains.

But that raises the question of just how they built it, she thought, *and why?*

It was possible, she supposed, that something had been forgotten in the last few hundred years. Lord Alfred was the oldest member of the commune, but she doubted he was any older than seventy—and there wouldn't be many others who reached his age. For all she knew, the area surrounding the castle had been heavily populated a mere couple of hundred years ago, before *something* had caused the population to flee. Perhaps there had been a violent surge of raw magic from the nexus point. The villages she'd seen wouldn't last long without constant maintenance, even if they survived whatever had happened to their inhabitants. There might be hundreds of villages buried under the forest.

They stopped at another campsite for the night, then proceeded onwards the following morning. Emily rapidly found herself growing bored with the monotony, although none of the others seemed to share her feelings. Julianne didn't get to make many trips away from the commune, while Bernard was enjoying Whitehall's undivided attention. Emily felt a stab of envy when he was sent to the nearest town to buy supplies, but her attempt to convince Whitehall that she should accompany him fell on deaf ears. She found herself seriously considering sneaking away from the campsite, just out of boredom. Only the very real risk of getting lost kept her from following Bernard to the town.

And Whitehall would be angry, she thought, privately. *And he'd have a point.*

"We'll be there tomorrow," Whitehall said, as they reached the final campsite, five days after leaving the castle. "I want all of you to be on your very best behavior."

Lord Alfred chuckled. "Even me?"

"Yes, even you," Whitehall said. "I would have thought you were too old to cause trouble."

"There's no such thing," Lord Alfred said.

Whitehall scowled, then reached into his pouch and produced a handful of coins. "I want you and Julianne to stay together," he said, passing the coins to Emily. "Purchase a couple of things for yourself, if you wish, but stay together."

"I don't get pocket money?" Lord Alfred asked. He struck a shocked pose as Whitehall laughed. "Horrors!"

"You might also want to go for a bath," Lord Whitehall added. "There's usually a communal bathhouse for women as well as for men. If not...we'll have to make other arrangements."

Emily nodded. "What do you want us to do after that?"

"We'll see how things go," Whitehall said, thoughtfully. He looked from one to the other, his eyes grim. "And *do* try to stay out of trouble."

"Of course, Father," Julianne said. Her father passed her a handful of coins, too. "We'll do our very best."

Chapter Twenty-Seven

A S SHE RODE UP TO THE GATE WITH THE OTHERS, EMILY COULDN'T HELP THINKING THAT the Gathering was very much the predecessor of the Faire. A number of tents scattered around a large field, surrounded by a wooden fence that was decorated with a dozen protective and concealment runes; hundreds of men and women milling around, the former wearing fancy outfits while the latter wore either long dresses or servant clothing. She tensed, despite herself, as the horses cantered to a stop outside a guardhouse, where a trio of men carrying swords eyed them nervously. None of the men looked very pleasant.

But they're not even looking at Julianne or me, she thought, torn between astonishment and amusement. The sellswords—she couldn't detect any magic surrounding them—probably thought she and Julianne were both Whitehall's daughters. *They're actually trying to behave themselves.*

She pushed the thought out of her mind as Whitehall spoke briefly to the guards, then to a grim-faced man who looked as if he were pushed to the limits of his endurance. The organizer, Emily guessed; he looked too tired to be surprised when Emily and Julianne were introduced as magicians too, rather than relatives or servants. She couldn't help wondering if telling the entire Gathering that Julianne and she were both magicians was a mistake, but she thought Whitehall knew what he was doing. And yet...far too many of the men in front of them were not inclined to accept female magicians.

"You've got Tent Seventeen," the organizer said, after some coins had changed hands. "I'll have the boys take care of your horses."

Whitehall scrambled down. Julianne followed him, then helped Emily down to the muddy ground too. Bernard and Lord Alfred looked more reluctant to dismount, but joined Whitehall as a trio of stable boys appeared to take charge of the horses. Emily was surprised that Whitehall was prepared to just let them take the beasts, yet she had to admit it made a certain kind of sense. No one in their right mind would try to steal from a magician, certainly not in the middle of a Gathering. Whitehall could do whatever he liked to the thieves and the rest of the crowd would only cheer him on.

"This way," Whitehall said. "We'll leave our bags in the tent before you can go exploring."

Emily couldn't help thinking, as they walked through the crowd, that the atmosphere was distinctly nervous. There was no way to know *just* how many magicians were in attendance, but there were definitely enough to make a *very* tempting target for the Manavores. She wasn't sure just how far the rumors had spread—getting from the castle to the Gathering hadn't been easy—yet the magicians had to know they were being hunted. A nasty undertone of fear echoed in the air; hundreds of sellswords manned the fence, ready to sell their lives dearly in defense of their masters.

And they won't stand a chance, Emily thought, *if the Manavores attack.*

"I've been in better places," Julianne said, as they stepped into the tent. "Father..."

"I've been in worse," Lord Alfred said.

"So have I," Whitehall agreed. "You did *want* to come."

Emily couldn't help agreeing with Julianne. The tent was hot, stuffy and dark; the bedding was nothing more than a pile of blankets on the ground. Were they all expected to sleep together? Probably, her own thoughts reminded her. No one in the Nameless World would bat an eyelid at Whitehall and Lord Alfred—and Bernard— sharing a bed. They certainly wouldn't see anything sexual—or *wrong*—with it. She would have expected better...

There isn't better, she told herself, numbly. *We'll just have to cope with it.*

"You can find the bathhouse, if you wish," Whitehall said, once they'd stowed away their knapsacks. "Meet us in the cooking pits at sunset for dinner."

"Yes, Father," Julianne said.

There were two bathhouses, they discovered as they walked towards the handful of permanent buildings: one for men and one for women. The female section—and she assumed the male as well—actually had three baths, each one large enough to pass for a small swimming pool. They undressed and washed themselves clean in the first one, then moved to the second pool for a long soak. Emily was so relieved just to be *clean* again—the servants had even taken their clothes to be hastily washed and dried—that she didn't find it embarrassing to be naked in front of Julianne and several other women, even though the women eyed her oddly.

I do look odd here, Emily thought. She was easily the tallest woman in the pool, her skin practically unblemished. *And I don't look half-starved either.*

She could have stayed in the pool for hours, allowing the warm water to work the kinks out of her body, but Julianne insisted on leaving after an hour. They splashed quickly through the third pool, then dressed hurriedly and stepped back into the outside world. She glanced around and saw a line of young men waiting outside another building, but Julianne grabbed her arm and led her away before she could ask what they were doing. Emily guessed, as they made their way over to the stalls, that they were waiting to enter the brothel. It couldn't be anything else.

"Yeah," Julianne confirmed, when she asked. "And if I see Bernard going there, I'll cut off his balls."

Emily kept her thoughts to herself as they moved from stall to stall, inspecting the merchandise. There was very little she wanted, she had to admit; the only items of interest were a handful of parchment scrolls and bound manuscripts, all priced so highly that she couldn't even *begin* to afford them. She dreaded to think just how hard a common laborer would have to work, just to make the down payment...if there was such a thing. She rather doubted it. And there was no way to check if the spells were actually *genuine* without paying hard cash first.

"Father might buy one, if you convinced him it was worth his while," Julianne said, after the stallkeeper flatly refused to allow Emily to examine one of his books. "It wouldn't be easy to fake the spells."

"I suppose," Emily said. The seller would have to be insane to try to con a magician, but a couple of his books were advertised as being written in an unknown language. There were no translation spells yet. "But I don't think he'd buy one for me."

She followed Julianne as she moved from stall to stall, picking up a handful of rare ingredients and chatting to some of her fellow brewers. They were all women, Emily noted; Tama and his friends weren't the only ones, it seemed, who considered brewing to be women's work. And they all looked remarkably sane, even though Emily could sense flickers of magic surrounding them. Julianne told them a little about what they'd discovered at the castle and promised to tell more later, if they agreed to listen to her. Emily couldn't help wondering just what would happen when they heard the truth.

Will they be pleased to hear that they have been doing magic all along, she asked herself, *or will they be worried about the curse?*

Bernard joined them, holding Julianne's hand as they slowly made their way towards the cooking pits. Emily couldn't help comparing it to a barbeque, although it was much larger, smokier and smellier than anything she'd seen on TV—or, for that matter, in the Nameless World. A giant ox was roasting over an open fire, dozens of pigs and chickens being roasted or fried next to it; vast barrels of beer and bottles of juice were being distributed to all and sundry. She couldn't help noticing that there was no water, although *that* made a certain kind of sense. The water in such a place wouldn't be very safe to drink.

They don't know spells to purify it yet, she thought. *Do they even know to boil water before they drink it?*

They took their food—bread and meat, without a trace of vegetables—and walked over to join Whitehall and Lord Alfred. Whitehall was chatting to an older man who eyed Emily and Julianne disdainfully, then obstinately ignored them for the remainder of the meal. Emily was tempted to join in the conversation, but instead she merely listened as Whitehall explained what they'd discovered at the castle and how they planned to proceed. When he'd finished, the older man stood and walked away. He didn't look pleased.

"The younger magicians are interested," Whitehall commented. "But the older magicians are too wedded to demons."

Emily glanced at Lord Alfred. "What do you think?"

"I think that the old rarely want to change," Lord Alfred said.

"*You* want to change," Bernard said.

"I'm *old*," Lord Alfred pointed out. "It's quite likely I won't see the next summer."

Emily frowned. "So you don't care?"

"Emily," Whitehall said, warningly.

"It's quite all right," Lord Alfred said. "I have never settled down, never chosen to stay in one place and build a reputation. Being in the commune...that's the longest I've stayed anywhere. It doesn't matter to me if things change or not."

He sighed. "But for someone who has built a reputation, young lady, it can matter a great deal."

"A reputation based on a fundamental misunderstanding of magic," Whitehall said.

"Yeah," Lord Alfred said. He rose, slowly and ponderously. "But do you think that matters to them?"

Emily watched him stride away into the darkness, remembering all the stories that had been told about Lord Alfred. She was almost sure that none of them were true, although it was clear that he was neither a super-magician nor a charlatan. Perhaps his travels—she recalled him bragging about sleeping with girls from all over the world—had given him an odd reputation that had only grown in the telling. She knew, all too well, just how rapidly rumors could change until they were almost unrecognizable.

And history gets retold by the winners, she thought. *It might have suited them, later on, to portray Lord Alfred as a freakishly powerful magician—or a fraud.*

"I've organized a meet for tomorrow morning," Whitehall said, as they finished eating. He was drinking from a tankard of ale, although he'd banned Julianne and Bernard from touching a drop. "I will expect all three of you to attend."

"Yes, Father," Julianne said.

"Master," Bernard said. "Will they not raise eyebrows?"

"Probably," Whitehall said. "But I've spoken to enough magicians to know that nothing has really changed. I don't know if the Gathering will even last the full ten days."

"We came all this way," Julianne protested.

"Others came from further away," Whitehall pointed out. He rose, too. "I expect you to behave yourselves, tonight. Don't go wandering off alone."

"We'd better get to bed," Julianne said, once her father had gone. "Tomorrow is probably going to be a very long day."

Emily was surprised that Bernard didn't object, as they slowly made their way back to the tent, but he said nothing. Perhaps he was tired too. They evaded a handful of spluttering light globes, walking around fires lit in front of a number of tents. Emily couldn't help noticing the shadows flickering around the edges of some of the tents, casting jagged shapes that flickered and flared at the corner of her eyes. Protective wards, she speculated, or protective demons. She hadn't sensed many demons in the Gathering itself, but Lord Alfred was hardly the only DemonMaster in the vicinity. They wouldn't be too pleased when they heard what Whitehall had to say.

"I'll be sleeping on the far side of the tent," Bernard said, as Emily covertly cast a handful of anti-vermin spells. "That should satisfy decency, I think."

He gave Julianne a quick kiss which rapidly developed into something more. Emily pretended not to see it until Bernard's hands started wandering, whereupon she cleared her throat loudly. She found it hard to hide her amusement as they both stared at her nastily. If Bernard had asked for Julianne's hand...

"Goodnight," Emily said. She lay down next to Julianne, realizing she was going to have Whitehall or Lord Alfred on her other side. She'd just have to endure it. "See you in the morning."

The blankets were scratchy and the ground was uncomfortable, but she surprised herself by falling asleep almost at once. She remembered nothing more until a gentle hand shook her awake what felt like seconds later. But bright sunlight was streaming in through the flap and Lord Alfred was snoring loudly. Emily allowed herself a moment of relief at having fallen asleep before Lord Alfred returned, then followed Julianne out of the tent. Whitehall and Bernard were standing outside, drinking something that smelled like spiced tea.

"Get some *tarik* for yourself, then get changed," Whitehall ordered. "We'll be meeting in the big tent in two hours."

Bernard nodded. "Have you thought about what you're going to tell them?"

Whitehall looked grimly determined. "The truth," he said.

He grew quieter as the minutes ticked away, even though Bernard tried to distract him by asking questions about magic and Lord Alfred told tall tales about crazy adventures on the other side of the continent. Emily realized, to her shock, that Whitehall was nervous. He *knew* he was right, but he also knew he wasn't going to make himself popular. And here...he only had Bernard and Lord Alfred for support.

And me, Emily thought.

She shook her head as Whitehall led them towards the big tent. If they wouldn't listen to Lord Whitehall, one of the greatest magicians of the era, they certainly wouldn't listen to an uppity little girl. They'd wonder why she wasn't barefoot and pregnant in the kitchen instead of learning magic. It still galled her to be dismissed so easily. Even the nobles of Zangaria, the ones who had disliked her, had respected her power.

The fear was almost palpable, she discovered, as they stepped into the tent. Julianne and she were the only women in the chamber. The remainder were all men, ranging from DemonMasters in bright red robes to apprentices—attached and unattached—standing at the rear, their eyes flickering from side to side nervously. There was an ugly feel to the air, a sense that something could happen at any moment, that chilled her to the bone. And, for the first time, she could sense the presence of demons. She could feel invisible eyes watching her as she followed Whitehall up to the front row. The organizer was already standing on a box, pitching his voice so it could be heard throughout the tent.

"Wait here," Whitehall ordered, as they reached the front. Emily was all too aware of other eyes—human eyes—studying her. It was hard to resist the urge to turn her head and look around to see who was looking at her. "I'll be at the front."

He stepped up to stand next to the organizer, who introduced him briefly—Emily wasn't too surprised that not everyone knew who Whitehall was—and then stepped down, allowing Whitehall to speak. Whitehall took a long moment to look around the tent, then cleared his throat. He didn't seem to need any spells to project his voice right across the chamber.

"For uncounted years," Whitehall said, "it was rare—truly rare—for a magician to survive long enough to gain control of his powers. He would either be killed by his fellows, out of fear of what he would do to them, or accidentally kill himself. Even when he was lucky enough to find a master willing to teach him, it was very hard for him to survive. It was not until my master, Myrddin the Sane, laid the groundwork for actually casting spells that magicians could be fairly sure of gaining control over their powers, allowing the novice to eventually become a magician in his own right."

He discussed—briefly—the problems of the master-apprentice system and the madness caused by demonic spells, then talked about the castle and the nexus point. Emily couldn't help thinking that some of the listeners seemed suspicious—or downright angry—when demons were mentioned. Myrddin the Sane had been strongly opposed to demons, she knew, and Whitehall had continued that tradition. And yet he was close friends with at least two DemonMasters...

"We have a unique opportunity," he concluded, after outlining the planned school. "Instead of one master to one apprentice, we can teach the basics of magic to a much larger number of apprentices simultaneously. Each apprentice will have a grounding in *all* of the magical disciplines, allowing masters to select the best of them for future training..."

"Enough," a voice thundered.

Emily turned. Who would dare to interrupt?

A fat man—easily the fattest man in the chamber—was stalking towards the stage. She could *sense* the demons surrounding him, invisible eyes glinting madly. He cast a nasty look at Emily as he strode past and stopped in front of Whitehall, glaring at him.

"This is nothing more than an attempt to win all the apprentices for yourself," he snapped, loudly. "And to deny us the right to use demons."

A low mutter ran through the crowd. Emily shivered. Some of them clearly agreed.

"This cannot be borne," the newcomer thundered. He tugged on his beard, warningly. "I..."

Lord Alfred moved forward. "It must be borne, Lord Fire," he said. "Demons have proved themselves to be horrifically dangerous. Magicians who wish to use them must be prepared to deal with the consequences..."

Fire slapped him across the face. "Traitor," he snapped. "I challenge you to a duel!"

"And I accept," Lord Alfred said, calmly. "Should we have the circle prepared?"

"Yes," Fire snapped. "We will meet after lunch, so the circle can be drawn properly. And may the best man win."

Chapter Twenty-Eight

Emily wanted to talk with Whitehall about what had happened, after Fire and a good third of the other magicians stormed out of the tent, but he snarled at her to shut up and then practically dragged Alfred in the other direction. The remaining magicians seemed just as confused as Emily, although they did seem convinced that the duel would settle the question of following Whitehall or not. Bernard caught Emily's hand and led both her and Julianne out of the tent, just in time to watch a trio of apprentices drawing out a large protection circle on the ground.

"I'm sorry Father snapped at you," Julianne said. "He's desperately worried."

"Yeah," Bernard agreed. "Lord Alfred could *lose*."

"And it will be very unpleasant for him if he loses," Emily finished. Fire had called Lord Alfred a traitor, after all. One DemonMaster had betrayed the others, as far as he was concerned. He wasn't going to hold back. "What happens if he does lose?"

Bernard gave her an odd look. "Dead—or wishing he was."

"I meant to us," Emily corrected. "What happens if he loses?"

"I don't know," Bernard said. "Fire can probably convince a majority of the others to kick us out of the Gathering."

Emily frowned as they made their way towards the cooking pits. Something was nagging at the back of her mind, a memory from her studies. But it refused to come to her as she took a plate of meat and bread, then sat down to eat with her friends. Whitehall and Lord Alfred were talking some distance away, but she didn't dare try to eavesdrop. She didn't think she wanted to know what they were saying to one another...

...And besides, she'd promised Whitehall she wouldn't.

"I was expecting them to demand proof that you could cast spells," Bernard mused, drawing her away from watching the older magicians. "Or perhaps proof you could have children."

Julianne giggled. "And how would you prove *that?*"

Emily shrugged. "It would take nine months for me to give birth, even if I got pregnant now," she said. She wasn't quite sure where she was on her cycle—Julianne's potions were nowhere near as efficient as the ones she used in the future—but she was damned if she was trying to get pregnant just to prove she could. "There's nothing wrong with my cycles, though."

She smiled as Bernard reddened, then watched grimly as Whitehall and Lord Alfred ate their food. It had to be a nightmare for Whitehall, she realized; his friend might well die, yet he could do nothing. And even if Lord Alfred won, he'd have won through the use of demons. It would be a slap in the face to everything Whitehall had planned to achieve—and to the lessons he'd learned from his master. She couldn't help wondering just how much of it Fire had calculated before issuing the challenge to a duel.

"He could have challenged Whitehall," she muttered. "Why not?"

"He wouldn't have been able to use demons," Bernard said. Emily flushed. She hadn't realized she'd spoken loudly enough for him to hear. "And without them, our master would have the advantage."

Emily felt sick, sick at heart, as she slowly finished her dinner. Lord Fire had appeared at the far end of the dining area and was holding court, bragging loudly and boastfully about just what he intended to do to Lord Alfred. He wasn't making any preparations, as far as Emily could tell; he just seemed confident of victory. She wondered, despite herself, if he'd asked the demons for a vision of the future, one that 'proved' he was bound to survive the coming duel. Oddly, the thought gave her hope. A demon might well have deliberately misled its master.

She looked up as Whitehall walked over to join them. He looked to have aged twenty years in an hour. Emily silently forgave him for snapping at her, even if it had been a shock. She wouldn't have liked to lose a friend either. Caleb had chosen not to watch her duel with Master Grey and she didn't blame him. Watching his girlfriend die—and being unable to do anything to stop it—would have torn him apart.

"The duel will be held after we finish eating," he said, quietly. "Whatever happens, whatever you see or hear, do nothing."

"Yes, master," Bernard said.

Emily merely nodded, then listened absently as Whitehall talked them through the dueling rules. They didn't seem too different from the ones she knew, save for a warning that no one was to cross the circle once the umpires announced the start of the match. Anyone who did would be unceremoniously killed, if they were lucky enough to survive the energies unleashed by the magicians.

"It's time," Whitehall said, finally. "Let's go."

This is going to be bad, Emily thought. She glanced at Julianne and noticed, to her surprise, that she was holding hands with Bernard. Her father seemed to be ignoring it. *This is going to be very bad.*

Lord Alfred and Lord Fire stood within the dueling circle, both hastily drawing smaller circles of protection around themselves. That was new—old, she corrected herself—but she supposed it made sense, if both contestants intended to use demons. Lord Alfred held his Book of Pacts in one hand, chanting under his breath as he marshalled his forces; Lord Fire placed his on the ground, then used a wooden cane to turn the pages. Emily wondered, absently, if there was some advantage in not carrying the book...

Maybe it's so vile even he can't touch it, she thought. It seemed unlikely—Robin had never shown any reluctance to touch his Book of Pacts—but magic constantly surprised her. *Or maybe he thinks it will give him some safety if one of the demons breaks free.*

She wished, suddenly, that she had someone to hold as the umpires took their places, one of them announcing the duel while the others checked and rechecked the protective wards. The gathered crowd fell silent, watching and waiting to see what happened. Emily glanced at Whitehall—his face was completely expressionless—and then back at Lord Alfred. He was smirking, an insolent pose that made her want to smile, despite the seriousness of the situation. Lord Fire's face was quivering with anger, clearly believing that he was being mocked. And then the lead umpire spoke a single word.

"Begin."

For a long moment, nothing happened. The two combatants eyed each other, clearly waiting to see who would move first. And then Fire spoke a single word. A wave of *malice* flared through the air—Emily had to force herself not to look away—as a demonic...*thing* launched itself out of Fire's Book of Pacts and hurled itself towards Lord Alfred. Another creature materialized in front of Lord Alfred, catching the first creature and holding it at bay. There was a brilliant flash of light and both creatures vanished.

Lord Fire hissed out a string of words, each one sounding like breaking glass. Emily had a flurry of *impressions* as more and more creatures materialized; flashing teeth, sharp claws, evil eyes gleaming with malice...she remembered, suddenly, the Manavore and wondered if there was any connection between the demons and the Manavores. Perhaps the Manavores were demons that had been allowed to go free.

Julianne turned, her eyes streaming with tears, but Emily refused to look away as the impressions grew stranger and stranger. Thunderstorms flashed and flared in front of her, each seemingly huge and yet tiny; brilliant flickers of inhuman eyes growing stronger for long seconds, then flickering away into the ether. She saw a creature that looked like a particularly demonic raptor, its semi-translucent jaws dripping with blood, lunge towards Lord Alfred. Alfred raised his hand and spoke a single word. The creature snapped out of existence with a thunderclap.

The Books of Pacts were steaming slightly, Emily noted, as more and more creatures joined the fray. It struck her, deep inside, that she was only seeing the tip of the iceberg, that most of the conflict was taking place at a level beyond her perception. And she knew she should be grateful. The flickers she did see were enough to make her eyes water, as if she was looking into a bright light. Each half-seen impression was terrifying to the imagination.

Flames burst into existence, roaring towards the combatants and only flowing back when they touched the protective circles. The crowd murmured and fell backwards as the heat began to rise—Emily felt sweat trickle down her back—but neither of the combatants seemed to notice. She saw faces within the fire, evil twisted faces that laughed and laughed as they grew larger, feeding on the energies unleashed by the duel. More and more creatures flared into existence, charging forwards and slamming into the protective circles. And then Emily knew, beyond a shadow of a doubt, what she was seeing.

This is the last great duel, she thought, numbly. She already knew the outcome. *And both of them are going to die.*

She started forward, unsure what she intended to do, but Whitehall caught her upper arm and dragged her back towards him. His grip was strong enough to hurt, yet she didn't dare try to do anything to break free in the middle of the crowd.

She refused to look back at him as the noise grew louder, as still more creatures materialized...

...And then the protective circles broke.

Lord Fire screamed, in horror and fear and pain, as the demons lunged at him, dragging him down into the pits of hell. There was a flash of light and then he was gone. Emily turned, just in time to see Lord Alfred's body crumple into dust. And then the demons vanished too.

"It's over," the umpire said, quietly. "They both died."

Emily winced as Whitehall squeezed her arm tightly and then let go. "That was stupid," he hissed. "You could have died."

He marched past her and over the outer circle. Emily rubbed her aching arm— Whitehall had probably bruised her—and then watched as he picked up Lord Alfred's Book of Pacts. No one came forward to claim Lord Fire's, so he picked that one up too. Emily couldn't help noticing, as Whitehall turned to speak to the umpire, that both books were still steaming. The red sigils on the front covers had turned black.

Their owners are dead, she thought. *And the books themselves can pass to another owner.*

Bernard glanced at her. "What were you thinking?"

"I was thinking I didn't want him to die," Emily said, quietly. But history clearly recorded that both men had died. "Did you?"

"He knew the risks," Bernard said. "He could have backed down."

Julianne looked as if she wanted to cry. "He was always good to me, you know," she said, softly. "He never talked down to me."

Whitehall's voice echoed over the field. "Lord Fire summoned a demon and asked who would win the duel," he said. "And the demon told him—the demon told him— that Lord Alfred would not survive the day. And the demon was *right*! Lord Alfred did not survive, but nor did Lord Fire. Do we really need such creatures?"

There was a long, chilling pause. "I say that we do *not* need such creatures," he said, his voice growing louder. "We can learn to use magic—we can learn to *develop* magic—without them. And I intend to lay the foundations for a whole new approach to magic at the castle, where all will be taught the basics before they can proceed. I invite all of you—masters, attached apprentices, unattached apprentices—to join us. The one condition is that you do not bring your demons with you."

He lowered his voice. "The demons have never lied to us," he warned. Emily felt an odd thrill as his words echoed on the air. "But they have frequently misled us, as Lord Fire could attest, if he wasn't dead. They have ensured that we have learned spells that damage our minds, spells that make it harder for us to have children, spells that will eventually destroy us. How many of our finest minds have fallen to madness?"

Emily's gaze swept the crowd. Many—far too many—of the older magicians had eyes that were going red. Others looked unstable—or displeased with Whitehall's words. And yet, the duel had strengthened his hand. Lord Alfred had died for

Whitehall's cause. The other DemonMasters had to respect his decision, even if they didn't understand it.

He knew he didn't have long to live, she thought. If Lord Alfred had kept his mouth shut, he would have survived. Instead—and she felt a strange mixture of awe and grim sadness as she realized what he'd done—he'd made his death serve a greater purpose. *And he wanted to go out in a blaze of glory.*

"We will be returning in two days," Whitehall concluded. "Those of you who wish to study with us, to learn how to master your powers, are welcome to accompany us. Those who wish to come later will also be welcome. But those who bring demons will be turned from our walls. There will be no further warnings."

Emily let out a sigh as the crowd began to disperse. A handful of servants were already dispensing drinks, pouring tankards of beer in honor of the two dead magicians. Several gamblers were threatening to curse the bookies because hardly anyone had bet that both magicians would end up dead. Bernard was staring at where Lord Alfred had been with a contemplative expression as Whitehall returned, carrying both books under his arm. Emily quailed at his forbidding expression.

"Back to the tent," he ordered, curtly. "We'll join the wake later."

"Master," Bernard said. "I..."

"Later," Whitehall snarled.

Emily rubbed her arm and then followed him, wondering just what Whitehall intended to do with the books. Master Gila's Book of Pacts had been priceless, she'd been told, even though he'd only harnessed a handful of demons. Lord Alfred had claimed to have over fifty demons under his control. His book had to be even *more* priceless. She would have smiled at the thought, if she hadn't just watched a man die. DemonMaster or not, Lord Alfred had been a good man.

"I'm putting both of these books in Alfred's knapsack," Whitehall stated, as soon as they were inside the tent. His voice hardened. "Emily, as punishment for gross stupidity, you will remain to guard the books while the rest of us attend the wake."

"Yes, Master," Emily said. It could easily have been a great deal worse. She could have crossed the circle before Whitehall caught her. "I understand."

"You must have driven your tutor insane," Whitehall commented. "Do you know what would have happened if you had stepped into the circle?"

"Yes, Master," Emily said. "I just didn't want Lord Alfred to die..."

Whitehall gave her a long, considering look, then placed both of the books into the knapsack, tying the string tight before adding a nasty protective curse. Emily was fairly sure she could dismantle it, given time, but she had no intention of opening the bag, let alone removing the books. Even *looking* at them was difficult. Perhaps it was her imagination, but there was a faint sense of pulsing evil surrounding the knapsack.

"Stay here," Whitehall ordered. "There's a chamberpot, if you need it."

"Yes, Master," Emily said.

Bernard took a breath. "Lord and Master," he said. "Please, may I plead for the hand of your daughter in marriage?"

Whitehall's eyebrows rose. "You're asking *now*?"

Emily had to smile, despite her concerns about being alone with the books. Bernard really *should* have asked earlier. Whitehall had practically done everything but tell him that it would be all right. And Julianne had started to wonder if he would ever have the nerve.

"Yes, Master," Bernard said. "I'm asking now."

Whitehall gave him a contemplative look. "Marriage is a holy state," he said, bluntly. "You and Julianne will be tied together for the rest of your lives—and beyond. Your children will carry your names into the next generation. You will be charged with her protection, even from herself; you will be charged with power over her, power you must never abuse. Are you willing, truly, to take on such a responsibility?"

Power over her, Emily thought. *But she's a magician now...*

"I am," Bernard said.

"Julianne," Whitehall said. "Will you marry him?"

"I will," Julianne said. "Father..."

"Very well," Whitehall said. "You will be married when we return to the castle. One would not wish to deprive your friends of a chance to make merry before you become a respectable married man."

"No, Master," Bernard said. "And thank you."

"We will discuss your precise responsibilities later," Whitehall added. "Until then..."

He looked at Emily. "Remain here," he reminded her. "And don't let *anyone* near the books."

Emily sat down on the blanket as they walked out of the tent, leaving her alone. It was hot and stuffy, rather like she envisaged a prison; there was no light, save for what came through the flap. She cast a handful of spells to cool the air and illuminate the tent—and provide warning if anyone tried to break in—then closed her eyes and forced herself to meditate. And yet, the mere presence of the books made it impossible. She could *feel* them calling to her, promising power, if only she would make them her own.

You could take the books and be well away by the time Whitehall returns, a voice said, within her mind. She wasn't sure if it was her own thoughts or a demon, perhaps one still bound to a book. *And you could be great.*

"Shut up," she snarled.

She bit her lip, hard. It wouldn't be long, she was sure, before Whitehall returned. Hell, Julianne would probably be sent back while Whitehall had a long chat with his future son-in-law. And then...

But it's going to feel longer, she thought, grimly. *And I can't wait to go home.*

Chapter Twenty-Nine

EMILY HADN'T EXPECTED MUCH FROM THE REMAINING TWO DAYS AT THE GATHERING, BUT she was pleasantly surprised as Julianne dragged her from meeting to meeting with her fellow potions brewers and a number of other young women related to magicians. Julianne made her show off a handful of spells, then explain—repeatedly—the nature of the curse and how it could best be avoided. By the time the party was assembling, ready to return to the castle, Julianne had managed to convince nine other potion brewers and thirty-seven young women to join a small army of unattached apprentices. Emily couldn't help thinking that it wouldn't be long before they started pairing up.

"We only recruited a handful of masters," Bernard said, as they made their final preparations to depart. "We should have been able to get more."

"They're not ready to embrace change," Whitehall said, darkly. He'd been his normal self, when speaking to potential recruits—as well as spreading news of the Manavores far and wide—but he'd brooded in the tent. "And there's no way to avoid the simple fact that we're threatening their power."

"But building up more for later," Emily added. "They'll have influence over hundreds of magicians rather than a handful."

"Influence," Whitehall stated. "Influence, not *power.*"

He picked up his knapsack and strode out of the tent, walking over to where the convoy was waiting. Emily followed, silently relieved that someone had provided horses and carts—and even a couple of carriages—to transport the volunteers home. A number of carpenters, blacksmiths and other tradesmen had requested permission to join as well and Whitehall had gravely accepted. It wouldn't be long before the castle was surrounded by a small township of its very own.

Which doesn't exist in my time, Emily thought, morbidly. *Either it was destroyed during the wars...or they moved down the road to Dragon's Den.*

She scrambled into one of the carriages and sat back, forcing herself to relax. Someone—she had no idea who—had assigned most of the girls to the carriages, either in an attempt to make their trip easier or separate them from the men. The carriage rattled to life moments later, shaking so heavily that she almost regretted her decision not to ride on horseback. She quickly cast a handful of spells, in the hope of making the trip easier, but they didn't seem to be particularly effective. The roads— or what passed for roads—were uneven and thoroughly unkind to the posterior.

The trip back took longer than she'd expected, although she supposed it really shouldn't have been a surprise. There was no way they could take the carts and carriages through the mountain pass or the forests surrounding the castle. They needed to go the long way around, just to get back to the forest. And then a number of the mundanes had to be detailed to hack open the path to the castle before they could pull the carts and carriages to the gates. A couple of dozen workers found themselves carrying vast quantities of supplies from the stalled carriages to the castle.

"We really need a proper road," she said to Bernard, as they walked slowly up towards the castle. The sense of being watched nagged at her, although she couldn't see or hear anything in the undergrowth. "People aren't going to come if it's a difficult trip."

"It'll take a good long time," Bernard said. He'd been happier since Julianne had accepted his offer of marriage. "But you're right. It does need to be done."

Emily nodded to herself. By her count, the commune had occupied the castle for just under two months, but the path they'd hewed through the forest was almost completely gone. It would have vanished completely, she suspected, if the workers hadn't been chopping trees and bushes down for firewood. The wild magic loose in the forest clearly made it grow faster—indeed, she couldn't help wondering if it was a defensive mechanism to hide the entire castle. No one would come probing into the forest if they had no idea there was anything to find.

She allowed herself a sigh of relief as the castle finally came into view. The nexus point was a constant presence in the background—it seemed stronger, somehow, than it was in her time—yet there were no wards designed to keep them out. Whitehall might have faith that Master Chambers and Master Reaper would honor the vote, but Emily had her doubts. Leaving the castle unattended might have been a dangerous mistake.

But we have access to the command spellware too, she reassured herself. *Getting back in wouldn't be that difficult.*

"Whitehall," a voice called. Emily looked up to see Master Chambers standing by the gates, glaring at the newcomers. "What is the meaning of this?"

"Get everyone up to the field," Whitehall ordered Bernard. "We'll assign rooms and suchlike after we've had this little chat."

"Yes, Master," Bernard said.

Emily wasn't sure what *she* should do, but Whitehall motioned for Julianne and her to follow him as he strode up to the gates. Master Chambers looked forbidding, his arms crossed over his chest as he sneered at Whitehall. She could sense a pair of demons, both invisible, sitting on his shoulders. Technically, he wasn't defying Whitehall's ban on summoning demons, but it was very much a gesture of defiance. Master Chambers was throwing down a gauntlet.

"Whitehall," Master Chambers said. He cast a sharp glance at Emily, then looked back at Whitehall. "What have you done?"

"Invited others to the castle," Whitehall said. "Enough apprentices and tradesmen came with us to make a start on a *real* community. We even recruited three new masters."

"I do not recall granting permission to recruit other masters," Master Chambers said. "Is it not traditional that masters may only be admitted to the commune with the agreement of every *other* master?"

He looked past Whitehall, frowning. "And where is Alfred?"

"Dead," Whitehall said. "He fought a duel with Lord Fire."

Master Chambers' face flickered with an emotion Emily couldn't read. "Lord Fire?"

"Their demons broke loose and killed both of the combatants," Whitehall said, stiffly. He'd kept his grief to himself, but Emily had been able to tell he *was* grieving. "They lost control of their...*tools*."

"I will mourn his death," Master Chambers said, slowly. He gazed at Whitehall for a long moment. "But accepting other masters..."

"They will not have access to the nexus point," Whitehall said. "And they have agreed to teach magic to multiple apprentices."

Master Chambers scowled. "Do you imagine they will be satisfied with an inferior position?"

Whitehall sighed. "I imagine we will have time to...*discuss* accepting them fully into the commune," he said, tartly. "Or are you going to insist that they leave?"

"No." Master Chambers said. "I would lose that vote, would I not?"

Hopefully, Emily thought. She was still surprised that Master Drake had sided with Master Chambers, at least until a compromise had been worked out. *But every new master reduces the influence and power available to the other masters—and they know it.*

Whitehall raised an arm to indicate the rest of the travelers. "We have enough apprentices—untrained apprentices—to make a genuine start," he said. "And enough workers to build a small township, if we can't fit them into the castle. We can make our dream real."

"We can make *your* dream real," Master Chambers said.

"Yes," Whitehall said. "And with your permission, we will start organizing their sleeping arrangements for the night."

Master Chambers stepped aside, his face unreadable. Emily glanced at him as she followed Whitehall into the school, but he didn't respond to her. Julianne shadowed her as they walked into the Great Hall, where Master Wolfe and Master Drake were waiting. Whitehall took the Books of Pacts out of his knapsack and placed them on the nearest table. The aura of evil and malice, once again, filled the room.

"Lord Alfred and Lord Fire are dead," he said, bluntly. "Their books survived."

"Destroy them," Master Wolfe urged.

"I doubt they can be destroyed so easily," Master Drake said. He opened one of the books and turned the pages, inspecting the sigils. A number were still blood-red. "They didn't expend all of the contracts."

"They didn't make their orders precise enough," Whitehall said. "And so the demons broke free."

He wrapped the books up again, then handed the knapsack to Master Wolfe. "Put these somewhere safe, then use the nexus point to protect and conceal them," he ordered. "We'll try to destroy them later, once we have integrated the newcomers into the commune, but for the moment they will just have to be hidden."

"Understood," Master Wolfe said. He took the knapsack and glanced at Emily. "I have some ideas I want to show you..."

"Later," Whitehall said. "We will be holding a ceremony for Lord Alfred this evening."

He dismissed Emily and Julianne, ordering them to head back to their bedroom, then hurried to the courtyard. Emily didn't envy him, she decided. Master Chambers was not going to be welcoming to the newcomers—and, as a master who had helped take control of the nexus point, his opinions could not be easily dismissed. Maybe Whitehall had pushed a little too far by recruiting masters as well as apprentices, although he'd made no secret of his plans to do just that. Master Chambers had a perfect opportunity to undermine his position amongst the rest of the original commune.

She pushed the thought aside as she caught sight of Robin, walking down the corridor towards them. He lowered his eyes theatrically, pretending to stare at the stone floor as they walked past. Emily sighed, then told herself that it was for the best. She wasn't sure just *what* had happened in the forest, but she didn't have any feelings for Robin. Besides, she'd have to make the jump to the future soon. She felt the weight of history pressing down on her.

"I'm sorry the two of you couldn't be together," Julianne said, as they stepped into the bedroom. "It would have made matters so much easier."

Emily barely heard her. She'd had neatness and tidiness hammered into her head almost from the very day she'd entered Whitehall to the point it was almost second nature. It was impossible to be *sure*, but she thought someone had entered the bedroom while they'd been away and searched it thoroughly. The more she looked from place to place, the more certain she was that *someone* had broken into the room. Too many things were out of place. She hesitated, cursing her own caution under her breath. Warding the room as carefully as she would have done back home would have been far too revealing, if someone had tangled with the wards.

"Check your stuff," she ordered, grimly. "Someone was in the room while we were gone."

She cast a spell, searching for traces of magic, but found nothing apart from the background hum of the nexus point. It wasn't as if anyone would have *needed* vast amounts of magic to break into the room. Besides, if someone had entered shortly after they'd left the castle, there would have been plenty of time for any traces to fade into nothingness. She checked her small collection of clothes carefully, half-expecting to find a nasty jinx or hex hidden within the cloth, but found nothing. Perhaps she was just being paranoid.

"My supplies were turned over," Julianne said. "But nothing was taken."

Emily puzzled over the mystery as they unpacked, wondering just what the mystery intruder had actually *wanted*. If he'd wanted to make it clear that her privacy had been violated, surely he would have ransacked the room; if he'd wanted to take something, surely he would have taken it. Unless, of course, he hadn't found it...but what had he wanted? Master Gila's Book of Pacts had been destroyed and she didn't have anything else worth the effort, save perhaps for the snake-bracelet. But she'd worn that on her wrist, taking it with her to the Gathering.

"I don't get it," Julianne said. "They took nothing."

"Me neither," Emily said. "Do we even have anything worth stealing?"

Bernard tapped on the door a minute later, inviting them back down to the dining hall. Emily followed Julianne out of the door, taking the time to set up a hex that would surprise anyone who made it into the room, then walked behind them as they hurried down the corridor. Bernard and Julianne held hands, even though Whitehall couldn't turn a blind eye to anything they did in front of his fellow masters. Perhaps Whitehall had already informed the rest of the commune that they were engaged.

Robin was standing by the door, handing out tiny glasses of wine. Emily took one, sniffed it doubtfully and then held it, rather than drinking. Robin still refused to meet her eyes as Bernard led her further into the room, pushing through the gathered crowd until they stood at the front. A large bier sat in front of them, a wicker effigy of a man placed on top. She realized, with a chill, that it was meant to represent Lord Alfred.

"Lord Alfred was a remarkable man—and a talented liar," Whitehall said. "I have never known anyone so full of contradictions. He would happily tell a story about his early life—and then tell another, the day after, that contradicted the first story completely. I know nothing about his birthplace or about his early life. And I know nothing about which of his stories are true, which are merely exaggerated and which are outright lies. The only thing I know for sure is that he was a DemonMaster.

"He would, I think, find it amusing that we would tell lies about him after his death," he added, "even though it flies in the face of tradition. And yet, we have no way to know what *is* a lie. One of his stories might be a lie; another might be true. We have no way to know which ones should be told and which ones should be politely forgotten. But there is one of his stories that has always stayed with me. And I tell it now because it speaks, I think, to the person he was.

"Many years ago—or so he told me—there was a king in a far-distant land. And that king was very—very—fat. He was so grossly overweight that he looked like an immense slug. His health had suffered so badly that it took five strong men to help him in and out of his bed each day. And every time a magician came to his city, the king would demand a cure. But how many magicians would dare to tell the truth? That the king was so fat because he ate and drank his fill, without working it off afterwards? How many would dare tell such a man that he was a lazy slug?"

Very few, Emily thought.

"Lord Alfred tricked him into exercising, so the story goes," Whitehall continued. "He told the king that he could cast a spell to help him regain his health, but the king would have to follow his instructions precisely or the spell would not work. And the king, so desperate for a cure, did as he was told. He forced himself to walk every day, then to run, then to climb hills and dig ditches...eventually, one day, he looked in the mirror and saw a healthy man looking back at him.

"Lord Alfred never saw magic as the be-all and end-all of his life. He saw it as nothing more than a tool, one of many. And it is that approach, I think, that preserved him from the fate of so many other DemonMasters. He went to his death knowing that his death would serve a greater purpose. And for that I honor him."

Emily found herself blinking away tears as other masters—even Master Chambers—rose to add their own recollections of the dead. Lord Alfred had helped a young man win the love of a good woman, Master Drake said; Master Chambers insisted that Lord Alfred had been involved in a project to tap the power of the moon by dragging it down to the planet. Emily doubted *that* was true—dragging the moon down would have destroyed the entire world—but she had to admit it was a good story. And there were more...

No wonder there are so many stories about him, she thought. *They just kept growing in the telling.*

"Life goes on," Whitehall said, once the bier had burned to ashes. "It gives me great pleasure to tell you that my daughter Julianne will marry Apprentice Bernard in five days, when the summer is at its height. Their children will carry on our legacy. Life goes on."

"Life goes on," the crowd echoed.

"Tomorrow, we will start organizing formal lessons," Whitehall concluded. "But tonight, we will remember the man who gave his life to allow us to proceed."

He lifted his glass in a silent toast, then drank the wine. Emily hesitated, then took a tiny sip from her own glass. It tasted smoky and left a burning trail down her throat, as if someone had distilled fire. She cursed herself under her breath. Alcohol and she didn't mix, even if it was a wake.

"We'd better go back to bed," Julianne said, as the crowd started to disperse. "We have a long day ahead of us tomorrow."

"I know," Emily said. She remembered trying to teach Tama and scowled. "But at least the rest should have less to unlearn."

Chapter Thirty

A N APPRENTICE RAN AROUND THE CORNER AND STOPPED DEAD AS HE STEPPED ON A RUNE, his entire body frozen in place. Another followed, running straight into the first apprentice and winding up stuck too. Emily wondered, as she watched from her position, if all eight of her pupils were about to wind up stuck together, but the *third* apprentice was a little more careful and managed to avoid the trap before it was too late. He walked around the trapped apprentices and hurried down the corridor, eyes scanning right and left for more traps. Emily smiled to herself as he neatly avoided a second trap just before running right into the *third* trap and finding himself stuck to the wall.

And he doesn't seem to have considered the virtues of freeing the others, she thought, as the fourth apprentice ran right into the first and second, winding up stuck too. The fifth, who seemed to have actually *listened* when Emily told them they needed to work together, took the time to destroy the rune, freeing all three of the trapped apprentices. They landed in a heap, stunned and disoriented. *But at least they've learned something useful.*

She put her fingers in her mouth and whistled loudly as she stepped out of concealment. It had been Bernard's idea to teach the apprentices through playing games and, Emily had to admit, it was working surprisingly well. But then, most of her pupils had almost no formal training at all. They had nothing to unlearn. Tama and his ilk were still reluctant to admit that she had anything to teach them.

"As you can see," she said, "runes may not look flashy, but they pose a danger to even experienced magicians."

A bell rang, the sound echoing through the corridor. "It's time for you to proceed to your next class," she added, after a moment. "And I strongly suggest you concentrate hard on your brewing."

She watched them go, feeling a twinge of sympathy for Julianne. Even the inexperienced apprentices still believed that brewing was women's work, although Emily had a feeling that would change once it became obvious that skilled brewers were also better at casting spells. And they would be, too. Potions—and alchemy, when it came into being—taught students how to modulate the flow of magic into the cauldrons as well as how to brew miracles.

Turning, she strode along the corridor and down the flight of stairs into the underground chambers. Master Wolfe had rigged up a complex set of wards to keep unwanted guests—including the new masters and apprentices—out of the area, but Emily had a private suspicion that she could have hacked her way into the network even without being one of the school's founders. Wolfe's spellwork was nowhere near as complex as Professor Lombardi's.

She glanced into the library as she passed—Master Wolfe had rigged up another set of complex wards to protect the books—and then made her way into the statue chamber. It had taken her three days—she'd started the day after they'd returned from the Gathering—to isolate the chamber from the rest of the complex, then ensure that she—and only she—could walk through the wards and into the room. It wouldn't do to have her vanish from the castle, only to be replaced by a statue of herself. *Someone* was bound to ask a few awkward questions. She grinned at the thought as she sat on the stone floor, then slowly started to input her spells into the wards. If they drew power from the nexus point—and they would—they should last long enough for her past self to touch the statue.

And no one will be able to enter without me, she thought. *I'll remain isolated from history until my past self comes along.*

She cursed under her breath as the spellwork took shape and form. There was no escaping the simple fact that she'd used far too much guesswork. Turning herself into a statue was easy; freezing her own thoughts, so she wouldn't have to endure nearly a thousand years of complete immobility, was a great deal harder. If she wasn't very careful, there would come a time when she literally *became* a statue, her thoughts evaporating into nothingness. It had been hard enough keeping her thoughts together when she'd turned herself into a rat...

And none of the prank spells can be adapted to fit the situation, she told herself. *I'd spend too long trapped in stone, unable even to scream.*

An hour later, she rose to her feet, testing and retesting the spells. They *should* work, she told herself, although the only way to be sure was to *do* it. If she said her goodbyes after the wedding, perhaps after Bernard and Julianne had a week together, she could slip down to the chamber and freeze herself in stone. History would add its own gloss to the Dark Lady, she was sure; there would be nothing to suggest, by her time, that the Dark Lady had been a traveler from the future. And some of the stories she'd read had been quite shocking, when the storytellers even admitted that the Dark Lady had *existed*. The first female apprentice...or Whitehall's wife or lover...

"It should do," she muttered, pushing thoughts of posterity aside. "And if it doesn't..."

She cursed under her breath as she headed for the door. She knew from her own recollections that a statue would be found, but she had no way of knowing just how sane she'd be. The only hopeful sign was that the books from the library chamber had gone missing, just before the collapse began, and that her contemporary self had been lured down to the nexus point and shoved into the past. But that didn't prove that her future self would be *sane*. Perhaps she should cast some compulsion spells on herself to make sure she actually did as history required...

Don't be stupid, she told herself, sharply. *That would be absolutely insane.*

Master Wolfe was standing just inside the library as she passed, inspecting one of the parchment rolls. Emily hesitated, then stepped into the room. One of the carpenters had put together a protective box for the Books of Pacts, trapping their aura to ensure they couldn't be sensed by any passing magicians. Emily still felt her skin crawl, every time she looked at the box, but she had a feeling it was purely her imagination. She still didn't understand why Whitehall hadn't destroyed the books immediately.

"Emily," Master Wolfe said. "I trust that lessons are going well?"

"They're making progress," Emily said. If a Manavore showed up, her students should be able to destroy—or banish—it. "And yours?"

"Much the same," Master Wolfe said. "And they're gaining in enthusiasm after discovering just how useful it can be."

They shared a smile. She hadn't been surprised to discover that the strongest apprentices—Robin and Bernard—were at the top of the totem pole, dominating and bullying the weaker apprentices. But now, with the weaker apprentices learning how to use their powers more effectively, the balance of power was slowly shifting towards the *smarter* apprentices. Those who weren't smart enough to learn how to use their powers properly would fall by the wayside...

Or turn into necromancers, she thought. She wasn't sure she wanted to know what had happened to Master Wolfe's copy of the necromantic rite, but it hardly mattered. Anyone with a working knowledge of spellwork could reinvent the rite in an afternoon. *The necromancers are so powerful that there is a limit to what smarts can do against them.*

"They're also putting forward suggestions of their own," Master Wolfe added. "And so we are advancing in leaps and bounds."

Emily nodded. It was all crude, but the bare bones of the system she'd been taught, right from the start, were already taking place. Julianne's work on alchemical experiments, she suspected, would eventually lead to genuine alchemy...she just hoped Julianne was careful enough to avoid an accident. Potions were reasonably safe, as long as one knew what one was doing, but alchemy was far more dangerous.

She looked at the boxes and frowned. "When are they going to be destroyed?"

"Once we figure out how," Master Wolfe said. "Master Gila's Book of Pacts was easy to destroy, but these will be a little bit harder. There are still demons attached to them, you see."

Emily winced. "What would happen if we just threw the books in the fire?"

"It would depend on what protective spells were layered on the books," Master Wolfe admitted. "It's possible the books would be destroyed, but equally possible that they'd be unharmed or the demons would be released. DemonMasters are always very protective of their books."

"Because if they lost their book they'd lose their power?" Emily guessed. "Or is that too simple?"

"It depends on just what spells they used to protect the books," Master Wolfe said. He turned and led the way into the control room. "But most DemonMasters would prefer not to take chances. Removing a demon's sigil from a book might just be enough to break the contract."

The Warden had grown, Emily noted, as she followed Master Wolfe. Master Keldor was standing behind the homunculus, putting together the finishing touches. There was no way the entity would ever pass for human, but history said that wouldn't matter. The Warden would be tied into the control network and serve as an interface, as well as the school's future disciplinarian.

"It should be ready soon," Master Keldor said. "And once it is linked to the nexus point, it should be effectively autonomous."

"Quite," Master Wolfe said.

Emily studied the Warden for a long moment. It was hard to escape the impression that he—it—had been made out of mud and then baked in a kiln, although there was a leathery feel to its skin. There were no genitals, no sign of any muscles...but then, they wouldn't be necessary. The Warden was not human. He would never be able to outgrow his programming—or his purpose.

And yet he will develop an intelligence, of sorts, Emily thought. She couldn't help wondering when and where that would happen. Master Wolfe had programmed an adaptability into the spellwork—his spells would adapt to new circumstances—but there were limits. And yet, at some point, the Warden would cross the line. *I wonder who did that—and why.*

Master Wolfe glanced at her. "What do you make of him?"

"He seems suitable," Emily said. "He'll just need a cloak and cowl to hide his true nature."

"We'll be keeping him out of sight," Master Keldor said. "We don't want *too* many people looking at him."

Emily had to agree. The discipline of wardcrafting was still in its infancy—if that—but most magicians would assume that whoever owned the castle had a direct link to the wards, allowing them to control it at will. Letting outsiders know about the Warden would tempt them to try to *destroy* the homunculus, even though it would be practically impossible as long as it was linked to the wards. It was a risk, she admitted, but the benefits outweighed the disadvantages. The wards could be passed from Grandmaster to Grandmaster without using blood magic.

She bid them a polite farewell and headed back to the stairs, walking up to the inhabited levels. Master Chambers stalked past, giving her a look that suggested she was something nasty he'd scraped off his shoe, but said nothing. Emily wondered just what Robin had said to him, if anything. It wasn't as if they hadn't brought plenty of young and unattached girls back to the castle. Robin might be on his way to becoming a DemonMaster, but he was still a very good catch.

Whitehall is planning to grant Bernard his mastery, Emily thought, as she walked towards Julianne's classroom. *Robin won't be far behind, I think.*

Julianne was seated behind a desk, peering dubiously into a simmering cauldron. The other desks were empty. Emily stepped inside, feeling her stomach rumble. Lunchtime had become a matter of opinion over the last few days. She'd been too wrapped up in her work—and then assisting Master Wolfe—to bother to eat. And yet she *needed* to eat to replenish her reserves...

"I'm not sure what he managed to do to this one," Julianne said, as Emily closed the door and walked over to the desk. "It seems to be doing something, but *what?*"

Emily frowned. "What were you trying to brew?"

"Painkilling potion," Julianne said. "As you can see, the consistency is all wrong."

Emily nodded. Julianne's painkilling potion was green, but the bubbling mixture in front of her was a sickly yellow color. Her spells insisted that the potion would be safe to drink, yet that only meant it wouldn't kill her outright. Professor Thande had sometimes encouraged his students to drink their brews, even knowing they'd be spending the next few hours throwing up everything they'd eaten for the last few days. He'd insisted, when his students had complained, that it taught them to be careful. Just because something wasn't poisonous didn't mean it was safe to drink.

"I think you should be very careful," she said. "You're getting married in two days, remember?"

"I might *just* have forgotten," Julianne said. She giggled. "Do you mind sleeping alone?"

Emily shrugged. She wouldn't be in the castle long enough for it to get wearying. Besides, she *liked* sleeping alone. It had been hard enough to get used to sharing a room with two other girls, let alone sharing a tent with male and female classmates. Julianne thought she was letting Emily down, but the truth was very different.

"I've been writing and rewriting the vows," Julianne added. "Bernard's agreed to let me continue to study magic—and *teach*."

"Good for him," Emily said. "And what will *you* be vowing?"

"To be a good wife," Julianne said. "But it's not going to be easy, is it?"

Emily shrugged. It *wasn't* going to be easy. Bernard had been raised in a culture that expected the wife to stay at home and raise the children while the husband worked for a living. It wasn't as if they were farmers, with everyone expected to work the land, or nobility, with servants to do all the work. Bernard would have problems, she suspected, adapting to a woman who wanted a more public role. But he'd just have to get used to it.

"You'll need a lot of respect," she said, instead. Even if she'd *liked* Robin, she wouldn't have married him. Not when it meant putting everything in the hands of a man. Her mother had made that mistake and it had been disastrous. "And you'll have to be prepared to stand your ground."

She wondered, absently, just what else she should say. Bernard was a trained magician—and Julianne was heading down the same road. The dynamics of their relationship would be very different to anything either of them would have seen, not in a time when female magicians were almost unknown. Bernard might be stronger, physically, than Julianne—she would have been surprised if he wasn't—but magic would even the odds. The near-equality of male and female magicians in her time stood mute testament to just how *much* magic evened the odds.

But it won't be easy for them, she thought. *Bernard will be expecting to dominate her if they have a fight.*

"Marriage is never easy," Julianne said. "There was a time when I thought I would never marry."

Emily shrugged. She'd felt the same way too.

"There were wives—Eldora, for example—who had a purely beastly time of it," Julianne said, softly. "And there were others who wore themselves out though having as many babies as they could. Their husbands wanted sons and more sons...some of them even asked me for potions that would guarantee sons. And others...had a good time with their husbands, but their mothers-in-law were absolute bullies. That won't be a problem for me."

"I know," Emily said.

"And I *do* want children," Julianne admitted. "And if you're right, I can have children *and* practice magic."

"I am," Emily said.

She leaned forward as Julianne put out the fire and left the mixture to cool. "Are you going to be doing anything the night before your wedding?"

"I'm supposed to hold a vigil," Julianne said. "But I don't know if I really want to."

Emily frowned. "What would your father say?"

"He'd say that I should follow my heart," Julianne said. "And I already *know* I want to marry him."

No hen night then, Emily thought. She was almost relieved. Alassa's hen nights had been events she wouldn't forget in a hurry. *Just...just a rush to get married.*

She took a breath. "Do you...do you need any other advice?"

Julianne laughed. "I've had *plenty* of advice," she said. "Do you know how frank some of the older women become when they know you're going to get married?"

"No," Emily said, honestly.

"They do," Julianne said. "I learned more about men and sex in two days than I learned in nineteen years."

"That's good to hear," Emily said. Lady Barb had given her the talk—and she'd seen a handful of pornographic movies—but she was still a virgin. She would have felt odd telling Julianne how to do something she'd never done herself. "And I hope it works out for you."

Julianne gave her an odd look. "Are you not planning to stay?"

Emily cursed herself under her breath. "I'm not sure," she lied, reluctantly. "But you and Bernard will need some time alone."

Chapter Thirty-One

EMILY HAD SEEN TWO WEDDINGS SINCE COMING TO THE NAMELESS WORLD, MELISSA'S MAR-riage to Markus and Alassa's marriage to Jade. She'd wondered just what Julianne's wedding to Bernard would look like, but it seemed to be remarkably similar to the very basic ceremony they'd held for Melissa and Markus. There was, in fact, a surprising *lack* of ceremony; Bernard and Robin stood on one side, in front of Master Chambers, while Julianne and her father stood on the other. The men wore white shirts and pants; Julianne wore a long white dress that fell loosely to the stone floor. Emily stood next to Master Wolfe and watched, curiously, as the ceremony began.

"Master Whitehall, father of the bride," Master Chambers said. "Do you consent to this union?"

"I do," Whitehall said.

"Apprentice Robin, speaker for the groom," Master Chambers continued. "Do you testify that the groom is fit to be a husband?"

Robin reached down to hold his hand over his crotch. "I swear it by my manhood and my power," he said. "May it wither if I lie."

Emily had to fight to keep the disgust from her face. She'd known the root of the word *testify*, but she'd never seen it in practice. To swear by one's manhood...Robin must be *very* sure that Bernard was a good man. It made her wonder, deep inside, if a woman could testify as well. There had been courts—and not just in the Nameless World—that considered a woman's word to be far less than a man's.

Master Chambers produced a small silver knife from his robes. "Master Bernard," he said, calmly. Whitehall had granted Bernard his mastery yesterday. "Are you willing to pledge yourself to Julianne, Daughter of Whitehall? To be her husband and protector, to father her children and raise them as your own?"

"I am," Bernard said.

He held out his hand. Master Chambers cut it once, then held it up so everyone could see red blood welling up from the wound. Emily felt sick, despite herself. The dangers of blood magics weren't well understood yet—wouldn't be understood for hundreds of years—yet watching them use such magics with abandon chilled her to the bone. It was dangerous, far too dangerous...

"Julianne, Daughter of Whitehall," Master Chambers said. "Are you willing to pledge yourself to Master Bernard. To be his wife and helpmate, to bear his children and raise them?"

"I am," Julianne said.

Emily forced herself to remain still as Master Chambers made a cut in Julianne's hand, held it up for everyone to see, then motioned for them to join their hands, allowing their blood to mingle. There was a pulse of magic, echoing through the air for a long second; they stared at each other with faintly soppy expressions, then kissed. The apprentices cheered and whistled loudly; the masters, more restrained, merely looked on approvingly. Emily couldn't help feeling cold, even though she was happy for her friends. Julianne had just bound herself to Bernard permanently.

And vice versa, she told herself. *He's bound to her, too.*

Master Chambers turned Bernard and Julianne around, then shook Whitehall's hand before walking over to Master Reaper, who was leaning against the wall and watching with a faintly amused expression. Master Keldor stood next to him, his face unreadable. Emily turned back to Julianne as she and her new husband approached—they were *still* holding hands—and gave her a tight hug. Bernard merely nodded to her as a gaggle of male apprentices hooted and hollered.

The hall was quickly cleared as a band began to play, allowing Bernard to lead Julianne onto the floor for the first dance. Emily made her way to the wall and watched, missing Caleb more than she cared to admit, as other couples joined them, whirling around the dance floor with more enthusiasm than skill. Not, she supposed, that it mattered. There was no *need* to follow strict rules, no *need* to dance perfectly. The only thing that mattered was having fun...

...But she would have felt bad about dancing without Caleb.

She caught sight of Whitehall, standing on the far side of the hall and made her way over to him. He was a good catch himself, she knew—a trained magician, probably still capable of fathering children—but he hadn't made any attempt to take any of the women, young or old, onto the dance floor. Instead, he watched his daughter and his new son-in-law with a weary expression, as if he was too tired to think straight. Emily felt a stab of sympathy for him. It couldn't be easy to know his daughter was now a wife, even though he liked and trusted Bernard.

"Lady Emily," Whitehall said.

Emily met his eyes. "Are you all right?"

"Just tired," Whitehall said. Emily could have kicked herself. Whitehall might be fantastically progressive, by the standards of the time, but he wouldn't unburden his heart to a young girl. "And thinking about the future."

Emily looked at Bernard and Julianne. "*They're* the future."

"Yes," Whitehall agreed. There was an odd edge to his voice. "They are."

He looked past Emily. Emily turned, just in time to see Robin walking up behind her. His eyes were still downcast, as if he was reluctant to even look at her.

"Emily," he said, gravely. "Please, would you dance with me?"

Emily was tempted to refuse. She didn't share the general attitude towards dancing that was so prevalent on the Nameless World—the *future* Nameless World—but dancing with another man felt just a little like being unfaithful. And Robin could have danced with any of the girls, if he'd had the nerve to ask them onto the floor. Surely, a man who had summoned demons and bent them to his will wouldn't be nervous of a girl...

And it might help, she thought, *if I do dance with him.*

"Just one dance," she said. "And then I should be gone."

Robin took her hand and led her onto the dance floor, keeping his eyes low. Emily would have wondered if he was trying to keep his eyes on her breasts, if it hadn't been clear that he was peering at the floor. Robin wasn't a bad dancer, she had to admit, but there was something about the way he moved that suggested she wasn't holding his attention, as if he was constantly distracted with a greater thought.

"I need to show you something," he muttered, as the dance came to an end. "It's to do with the *future*."

Emily tensed. She'd assumed that no one could or would guess the truth of her origins. It wasn't as if anyone knew about alternate worlds, let alone time travel. And yet, Robin seemed to know the truth. She didn't want to be alone with him, not after their last private conversation, but what he had to say couldn't be for anyone else's ears.

"We can talk in the classroom down the hall," she hissed. "That's far away enough to allow us to talk in private."

She allowed him to pull her off the dance floor as she looked around for Bernard and Julianne. They'd already slipped off, probably to consummate the marriage. Unless the traditions were very different from the ones in her time, the match would not be legal—blood magic or no—until they'd actually slept together. A number of other couples were already forming up, it seemed. Emily couldn't help wondering if the masters were going to be prowling the corridors, reminding youngsters that they shouldn't be getting intimate before marriage. There was no welfare for unmarried mothers on the Nameless World.

And contraception may not be reliable either, she thought. *Did all of the newcomers have a chance to take a potion?*

The classroom was dark and shadowy. Emily cast a light globe into the air as Robin closed the door and turned to face her. His eyes were *still* fixed on the ground. He was breathing heavily, his mouth opening and closing rapidly. She felt herself tense again as she readied defensive spells. If he had something unpleasant in mind, and she was starting to suspect he'd lured her away under false pretences, he was in for a nasty shock.

"They wouldn't talk about you," Robin said. She was suddenly very aware of the presence of an invisible demon, perched on his shoulder. "Nothing I could offer them was enough to get them to talk about you."

Emily frowned. "The demons?"

"I kept asking them about you," Robin said. His voice was light and breathy. "They wouldn't say *anything*."

"You talked about the future," Emily said, carefully.

"*Our* future," Robin said. He looked up. Emily saw glints of red within his eyes. "We are destined to be together."

He's mad, Emily thought. Robin's eyes weren't quite the same shade as Master Gila's, before his death, but it wouldn't be long before the madness consumed him. *He's spent too long summoning demons -- and they've tainted him.*

"They wouldn't show me visions of my future either," Robin continued. He'd tricked her, she realized; no, she'd effectively tricked herself. Robin, quite by accident, had stumbled on something that had been bound to make her pay attention. "And that means that your future and mine are entangled."

"Or that you don't *have* a future," Emily snapped. She readied herself. She'd have to blast him out of the way, then run through the door and escape. Whitehall could decide what to do with him. "Maybe *neither* of us has a future."

"We do have a future," Robin said. "Together."

He spoke a word she didn't recognize. There was a surge of power...she tried to raise her defenses, only to discover that the spell was already *inside* her defenses. It felt like blood magic, but it wasn't blood magic. Her body quivered as she tried desperately to muster her resistance, her mind racing as she tried to analyze and counter the spell. It was an order of magnitude more powerful and complex than anything she'd seen from any of the commune, even Master Wolfe. She would have thought, if she hadn't known better, that it was tied directly into the nexus point.

The spell won. Her hands dropped to her sides, helplessly. A dull feeling enveloped her mind, making it hard to feel fear, or panic, or anger. She felt almost as if she were drifting over her body, looking down helplessly as it waited, at Robin's mercy. The spell pulsed around her, holding her in thrall. She knew she should feel terrified—she knew how easily such a spell could be abused—but she felt nothing.

"I knew it." He clapped his hands together in glee. "I knew it would work."

Emily forced herself to think, despite the dull lethargy slowly infesting her thoughts. Had a demon given Robin the spell, even though it was vastly more complex than anything he'd been able to coax out of them before? Or was there another visitor from the future? *She'd* never seen such a complex piece of spellware, but Void or Professor Lombardi would probably have been able to cast it. Robin...Robin was nowhere near their level. It just didn't make sense.

Robin giggled. "And we are meant to be together," he said, his voice becoming terrifyingly unhinged. "And now you are mine."

He leaned forward. "Kneel."

Emily struggled, desperately, but it was useless. Her body dropped to its knees, the long dress she'd borrowed from Julianne bunching up around her legs. He couldn't mean to force himself on her, could he? *Of course he did*, her own thoughts responded. Robin was mad enough to believe they were meant to be together and so everything he did to win her was justified. His trembling fingers started to struggle with his fly as he leered down at her.

"Open your mouth," he ordered. He seemed to be having trouble unbuckling his trousers, but she knew it wouldn't last. "Open and..."

Rage blasted through her, so powerful she quite lost control. The rune on her chest blazed with fire, the pain shocking her out of her trance. Void's protections, part of her mind recalled; they'd been pushed back, but they hadn't been beaten. The spell evaporated into nothingness, her magic growing stronger and stronger as her anger grew into a hurricane of pure energy. She opened her mouth and screamed in rage.

Robin's eyes went wide with shock and fear, a second before she rose and lashed out at him with a burst of raw magic. His shields were formidable, more powerful than she'd realized, but they crumpled like paper under her rage. How dare he? How *dare* he? He stumbled to one side, her power tearing through the walls and cracking the stone; she was dimly aware, on some level, of the castle's makeshift wards trying to suppress her rage before it was too late.

But it was already too late.

She turned, fire building behind her eyes. Robin was staring at her in absolute horror, his weakling magic starkly revealed by her rage. The demon on his shoulder was clearly visible, but utterly unmoving. She should have felt its malice, yet all she felt was her own overpowering rage. Hot fury burned around her as her anger built into a crescendo, a tidal wave of fire that fell on Robin like the hammer of God. His body exploded into bloody fragments, her power streaming on and smashing through the walls. She was dimly aware of someone shouting, the voice so tiny that the shouter seemed miles away, as the entire building shook. The wards Master Wolfe had worked so hard to build seemed to have vanished...

...And Robin was dead.

She sank back to her knees and closed her eyes as all the energy started to fade away into the ether. Her eyes *hurt*, power pulsing behind them; her entire body felt tired and drained. Only the grim certainty that she didn't dare fall into the darkness, that she didn't dare let herself be rendered helpless, kept her awake and aware. She hadn't felt so vulnerable, even after facing Master Grey for the final time. Even *Whitehall* might choose to slit her throat while she was helpless.

There was a dull ringing in her ears, as if someone was whispering to her from a far distance; she gritted her teeth, then forced herself to open her eyes. A demon, a faintly-translucent demon, was standing in front of her, the form too indistinct for her to make it out clearly. It shimmered a moment later and was gone, but she could still feel its presence at the back of her mind. And yet, Robin was dead. Surely his demon should have returned to the darkness by now. Unless it was still tied to his Book of Pacts...

It was hard, so hard, to think clearly. Where *was* Robin's Book of Pacts?

He couldn't have been carrying it, she thought, numbly. *There was no room for a book.*

She looked up, suddenly very aware of just how much damage she'd done to the castle. The room had practically been shattered, the rear walls smashed and broken... she was privately surprised she hadn't brought the roof down. She looked up and winced at the cracks and scars in the stonework. Whoever had designed the castle had designed it to channel raw magic, she was sure, but they hadn't expected a magician to start lashing out at the wards...

"Emily," Whitehall called. Emily realized, in her dazed state, that the door was gone and the doorway was nothing more than a pile of stone. "Emily, what happened?"

They'll all have sensed the surge of magic, Emily thought, numbly. *They'll know it was me.*

She tried, desperately, to think of a convincing story. But there was nothing, nothing that wouldn't be exposed as a lie within seconds. She'd tried to hide her true power...

...But that was now nothing more than a waste of time.

"Robin," she managed. She wanted to be sick. He'd intended to dominate her, humiliate her, rape her...and he would have, if she'd not broken his control. And it had been sheer luck that she'd managed to escape his spell. "Robin...he tried..."

She stumbled, the world spinning mercilessly around her. Whitehall put out a hand to help her regain her balance, but she shook him off angrily. Her eyes were still hurting, as if she'd stared right into a bright light for an instant too long. She was suddenly *very* aware that everyone who'd been on the dance floor had probably sensed the surge of magic. No, there was no *probably* about it. They *would* have sensed the surge of magic. She wondered, as she fought down the urge to giggle, just what Tama was thinking now. He'd never imagined she might be able to do real damage to the *castle*, let alone a young man on the verge of mastery.

"Julianne, take Emily back to her bedroom," Whitehall ordered. Where had Julianne come from? Emily wanted to argue—she'd interrupted Julianne's wedding night—but she knew there was no point. "Everyone else, clear off. The party is over."

"Yes, Father," Julianne said.

"Sorry," Emily murmured, through the haze. Julianne didn't deserve to lose her wedding night. "I'm sorry."

"Don't worry about it," Julianne said, briskly. "Just come with me."

Emily did as she was told, feeling her head starting to pound. The demon was still there. She could *feel* it. Whitehall could probably feel it too...he wasn't going to be pleased. What was it *doing*? She hadn't summoned it...*Robin* had summoned it. And it should be gone.

"Go back to Bernard," she managed, when they stumbled into the bedroom. Julianne should have been sharing a room with her husband. "Go..."

"I'm staying," Julianne said, firmly.

Emily nodded, then—with the last of her strength—warded the room as thoroughly as she could. It was hard to make the spells work through the pain, but she had no choice. Julianne would be trapped until she awoke, she knew, yet there was nothing she could do about that, not without weakening the wards...

And then the darkness reached up and pulled her into blessed, merciful, sleep.

Chapter Thirty-Two

"E MILY," A VOICE SAID. "ARE YOU ALL RIGHT?"

Emily fought her way back to awareness. Her memories were jagged, her head was pounding like a drum, her body felt dehydrated...she pleaded for water, honestly unsure if she was thinking or speaking until someone held a glass of cool liquid to her lips. It crossed her mind, a second later, that she should be careful what she drank, but it was already too late. She *needed* the water.

Her eyes sprang open. Julianne was kneeling beside her, holding a glass of water in one hand and a potions gourd in the other. And there was something at the corner of her eye...something sitting on her shoulder. She turned her head, despite the throbbing pain, but saw nothing. And yet there was something there, just out of sight...

Shit, she thought, numbly. It was hard, so hard, to form a coherent thought. *What happened?*

Memory returned in fits and starts as she drank the remaining water, too thirsty to care about the possible risks. Robin had...Robin had...she felt the remains of his spell surrounding her, too complex and powerful to fade quickly even though she'd torn it to ribbons when she'd broken free. It was an order of magnitude more complex than anything she'd seen in the past, more powerful than any compulsion spell she'd studied in the future. She wasn't quite sure how it had managed to get though her defenses—she didn't *think* Robin had managed to get a sample of her blood—but it had clearly succeeded. If Void's protections hadn't been in place, she would have...

She gagged, her stomach heaving, as she remembered what he'd wanted her to do. Hodge had merely wanted to rape her; Robin would have turned her into a helpless slave, a helpless observer trapped in her own body as he did what he willed with her. And the spell he'd used would have bound her permanently. Even if someone else had come to her aid, freeing her would have been beyond their abilities. She honestly wasn't sure if the spell could have been undone, if she could have been freed to live a normal life, in her own era. Robin would have crippled her.

He's dead, she told herself.

"I think Father will want to talk to you," Julianne said, nervously. "Are you fit to walk?"

Emily frowned. Julianne was acting skittish...she felt a stab of guilt as she remembered that it should have been Julianne's wedding night. But instead of consummating her marriage to Bernard, she'd been trapped in a warded room with Emily. And she might not know what had actually happened. She might have wondered, deep inside, if Emily was a murderess...or if she was trapped permanently, if Emily died. Whitehall *might* have been able to muster the raw power to tear down Emily's wards, but the surge of power might well kill Julianne as the wards collapsed.

"I don't know," Emily managed, finally.

She waved off Julianne's attempt to help as she stumbled to her feet. Her body *ached*, pains everywhere, but nothing actually seemed to be broken. Julianne held out a gourd; Emily took a sniff, then declined the offer of painkilling potion. It would make the pain go away, if only for a few hours, but it would also make her sleepy. And she needed water desperately. Her legs felt wobbly and pains ran up and down her arms, but nothing seemed to be broken. She could move.

"I'm sorry," she managed, as she dismantled her wards. *Someone* had probed the edges of them, she noted; thankfully, they hadn't been able to break the wards down. "This should have been your night."

"Don't worry about it," Julianne said, shortly. There was an edge in her voice that told Emily she *should* worry about it. "We were taking it slowly."

Emily felt another stab of guilt as they opened the door and walked out into the corridor. If Julianne and Bernard didn't consummate their marriage within a few days, it wouldn't be legal or binding. Or, at least, that would be true in Zangaria. She had no idea if that was true in the past. But then, Julianne and Bernard could simply lie. No one would know if they consummated their marriage immediately or had waited a couple of days.

There was no one outside when they emerged, much to her relief; they made it down to the kitchens without incident. Julianne asked Emily to remain outside as she hurried into the kitchens and picked up a large gourd of water and some bread and ham. Emily ate and drank quickly, feeling ravenous; Julianne, standing beside her, ate more delicately. They had just finished when Bernard appeared, striding along the corridor towards them. The look he bestowed on Emily was far from friendly.

I interrupted his wedding night, she thought, morbidly. *And I killed his best friend.*

"Lord Whitehall wants to see you," he said, curtly. Emily couldn't help noticing that he was keeping one hand on the pommel of his sword, although he shouldn't have needed it to defend himself. "Come with me."

Emily exchanged glances with Julianne, then followed Bernard down the corridor. The...*thing*...at the corner of her eye seemed to twitch in and out of view, although she couldn't get a good look at it. Two other apprentices—two of the newer apprentices—were standing outside the office doors, looking nervous. Their eyes went wide when they saw Emily and they started to sidle backwards, as if they were terrified of her. Emily groaned inwardly at their expressions, wondering if people would *always* be scared of her. She didn't *want* everyone to be scared of her.

Let them hate, as long as they fear, the cynical side of her mind noted. *You keep turning their world upside down.*

"Julianne, wait here," Bernard ordered. "Emily, come with me."

Emily clenched her teeth at his tone—he'd barely been married a day and he was already bossing his wife around—but Julianne showed no reaction. Emily hoped—prayed—that she'd make Bernard pay for his tone later, then followed Bernard through the door and into the chamber. Whitehall, Master Chambers, Master Wolfe, Master Keldor and Master Reaper were sitting behind a stone desk, their expressionless faces chilling her to the bone. She could feel the wards growing stronger, pressing down on the magic in the room. Master Wolfe had been busy, Emily thought, as she fought to keep her own expression under control. She doubted she could summon enough magic to do real damage.

"Emily," Whitehall said. For a second, his eyes went very wide; a moment later, the expressionless mask snapped back over his face. He indicated a stool placed in front of the desk. "Please, be seated."

"Yes, Master," Emily said.

She sat, gingerly. The stool was barely large enough for a child half her age. It forced her to look up at them, as if she came as a supplicant. She supposed they wanted to use it to put her in her place. Lady Barb had discussed such tricks time and time again, pointing out that one didn't need to use magic to make an impression. It was why King Randor had such a magnificent—and crowded—throne room. The chamber was *designed* to make the man on the throne the center of attention.

"Emily," Whitehall said. There was a note of cool disapproval in his voice, although it didn't seem to be directed at her. "Please could you tell us what happened?"

Emily took a breath. Master Wolfe looked friendly—he'd relaxed after she sat down—but Master Chambers, Master Keldor and Master Reaper were eying her nastily. She could sense a demon sitting on Master Chambers' shoulder, the sense of cool malice making her jittery as she hastily pulled her senses back. The...*thing*... at the corner of her eye seemed to respond to the other demon, although she could never have put the feelings into words. Panic threatened to overwhelm her as she realized she might just have picked up a demon herself. And yet, she'd never tried an unsupervised summoning rite...

"Robin tried to rape me," she said, bluntly. Her skin felt dirty, even though he hadn't actually touched her. She wanted to fill a bathtub, then scrub herself until her skin was raw. "He used a spell to try to *control* me."

She outlined the entire story, starting with Robin luring her out of the hall and ending with his death. Master Whitehall listened, his face expressionless, as she described the spell Robin had used, but neither Chambers nor Reaper seemed to believe her, even though the fragments of the spell were still present. Wolfe showed no visible reaction, although she had the feeling he was quietly analyzing the remains. She hoped—prayed—that the spell wouldn't go any further. If Wolfe put it together, if it got out of his hands...

Robin won't be the last person to use it, she thought, grimly. *And its next victim will not have hidden protections.*

"Absurd," Chambers said, when she finished. "Apprentice Robin could *not* have cast such a spell."

"His magical signature is all around her," Master Wolfe pointed out, coolly. "Who *else* could have cast the spell?"

"There isn't enough of the spell *left* to tell what it was designed to do," Chambers countered, sharply. "Have you ever heard of a spell that controlled someone so completely?"

"No," Wolfe said. "And until I came to this castle, I hadn't heard of a transmutation spell I could use either."

Chambers ignored him. "Your apprentice," he said, addressing Whitehall, "killed *my* apprentice. I demand the Rite of Blood."

"Out of the question," Whitehall said. "If your apprentice was experimenting with demons..."

"He *was* going to become a DemonMaster," Chambers snarled. "Calling up and using demons was his life!"

"He was already staggering towards madness," Whitehall snapped back. "For his eyes to change at such a young age..."

"And we have only *her* word his eyes *were* changing," Chambers insisted. He glared at Emily, nastily. "For someone to develop red eyes at such a young age is completely unprecedented. The youngest person I know to even develop a *hint* of red eyes was easily twice Robin's age!"

His eyes hardened. "And she has taken his demon," he added. "How could that have happened if he had not opened himself to her?"

Emily staggered as she was suddenly aware—very aware—of the demon sitting on her shoulder. It felt as though she was balancing something that was both impossibly heavy and feather-light. Panic surged through her as she realized that the demon had done *something* to her, just to make sure she didn't react badly to its presence; she reached up with her hand to try to push it away, but felt nothing. The waves of malice she would have expected to be emanating from the creature weren't there. Instead...there was nothing.

Chambers was still speaking. Somehow, she dragged her attention back to him.

"She has concocted a tissue of lies," Chambers said. "It is true that my apprentice found her attractive and attempted to court her, despite my orders, but he would not attempt to bind her to his will or force himself on her. He could not have hoped to keep such a deed hidden indefinitely and, when he was caught, his punishment would be remembered for generations to come. Robin was not *stupid*."

"Young men can be very stupid when they are in lust," Wolfe said. "And Robin was already teetering on the verge of madness."

"He was not mad," Chambers said. "Does anyone honestly believe that we would not have thrown him to the demons if he'd assaulted *her* in such a manner?"

But you have to defend him, Emily thought, coldly. *He was your apprentice. His behavior reflects badly on you.*

She cursed under her breath. No one could deny she'd killed Robin, not after her magic had damaged the castle itself. But it would take a skilled magician to put the traces of the control spell back together...and even if Master Wolfe succeeded, Master Chambers could insist that it hadn't been *Robin* who'd cast the spell. He might just manage to convince the others of it too. Robin hadn't shown the same ability as Bernard, Julianne or Emily herself. Hell, *Emily* wouldn't have believed him capable of casting such a spell if she hadn't seen him do it.

And there's a monster sitting on my shoulder, she thought. The demon's presence seemed to flicker in and out of her mind. There were moments when she was very aware of it and moments when it was almost gone. *That doesn't make me look very good either.*

She tensed, wondering if Master Chambers had set the whole thing up. Robin had been a disobedient apprentice, at least if he'd been telling the truth when he'd claimed that his master hadn't approved of him trying to court Emily. Chambers might just have decided he wanted to be rid of him. Or, perhaps, to use him as an unwitting tool against Whitehall or Emily herself. She had a nasty feeling that Chambers wouldn't have been too unhappy if Robin had succeeded.

"I demand the Rite of Blood," Chambers said. "Blood calls for justice."

Whitehall steepled his fingertips. "I believe she is telling the truth."

"You would," Chambers snarled. "She's *your* apprentice—an apprentice you cannot control!"

"Robin would hardly be the first young man to believe he could just take something he wanted," Whitehall added. "And with demons whispering in his ear, he might have been in no state to understand the difference between right and wrong."

Chambers took a long breath. "This...this...*girl*...has bewitched you," he snapped. "How many more are going to die?"

He waved a hand at Emily, who stared back defiantly. "She killed Master Gila," he added, darkly. "And then Lord Alfred dies too. And now Robin De Bold is dead. Who is next?"

His gaze bored into Emily's eyes. "Who will be next?"

Emily gritted her teeth as she felt his mind pushing against hers, the pressure growing rapidly as he tried to break through her defenses and ransack her mind. Void's protections were in fragments, she realized suddenly. She had to hold him out completely on her own, without additional help. Her head started to pound as she felt her defenses giving way...

...And then Whitehall reached out and punched Chambers' arm, hard.

"That will do," he said. "I am convinced she is telling the truth."

"Her or me," Chambers snapped. The tension between the two masters, Emily saw now, had been growing for weeks. Their friendship was dying right in front of her. "Put her out of the castle or I will leave, today."

Whitehall rose. "Do you think I would condone applying the Rite of Blood to an innocent girl?"

"People *die* around her," Chambers said. "Who will be next?"

He rose and stalked around the table. "Your grand project is doomed to fail," he said, as Master Reaper rose and followed him. "And it will all be because of *her.*"

Emily braced herself, half-expecting a curse or a physical attack as he passed, but Master Chambers merely scowled at Keldor.

"You should come too," he snapped. "How long do you think it will be before you too are isolated?"

"There's too much to do here," Keldor said. "Master..."

"Then we are no longer companions," Chambers said, cutting him off. He jabbed a finger at Emily. "How many people will die because of this snake in the grass?"

He strode out of the room, followed by Master Reaper. Emily was surprised they didn't slam the door as they left.

"Go make sure they don't do anything stupid before they leave," Whitehall ordered. It took Emily a moment to realize he was talking to Wolfe and Keldor. "Or try to take something that doesn't belong to them."

"Of course," Wolfe murmured.

Emily allowed herself a moment of relief as soon as Whitehall and she were alone. "Thank you."

"You are my apprentice," Whitehall said. "Standing up for you is one of my duties." His face tightened, noticeably. "And you have a demon on your shoulder."

Emily shuddered as another stab of panic ran through her. "*Get rid of it!*"

Whitehall didn't seem to notice her tone. "I don't know how," he said. "Did you summon it?"

"No," Emily said. "I wouldn't dare!"

"The person who might be able to give us some advice has just stormed out," Whitehall said, curtly. "And I'm not sure I could trust his answers in any case. Demons may not be able to lie directly, but they can be very misleading."

He frowned. "I'll have to give the matter some thought," he added. "If you beat Robin so thoroughly, his demon might have transferred itself to you...I've never seen it happen, but some demons have been reported to trade masters when they have a chance. Or something else might be at work."

Emily saw—again—the demon at the corner of her eye. "Will it try to hurt me?"

"I don't know," Whitehall said. "But you would be well-advised not to listen to a word it said."

"Yes, Master," Emily said, tiredly. "And I'm sorry..."

She cleared her throat. "I'm sorry," she repeated. "I should never have left the hall with him."

"Perhaps not," Whitehall said. "But Robin made the choice to rely on demons, rather than try to develop his own magic."

Emily swallowed. "I meant about Lord Chambers," she said. "I knew the two of you were friends."

"I will mourn in my own time," Whitehall said. He met her eyes, gently. "And be kind to Bernard, if you can. He'll be mourning his friend too."

Chapter Thirty-Three

WHITEHALL, EMILY DISCOVERED OVER THE NEXT FOUR DAYS, HAD BEEN ENTIRELY CORRECT. Bernard rarely spoke to her, even when she was in Julianne's company. He certainly made no attempt to seek her out or try to include her in any of the commune's activities. Emily had little inclination to play games or go roaming through the forest, but she couldn't help feeling oddly disconcerted by his sudden lack of attention. And yet, she knew Bernard was mourning his friend. Robin and he had been friends for years before Robin's fall.

"He'll start talking to you again soon," Julianne reassured her. "He's just a little..."

"Mad at me," Emily finished. "And I don't blame him."

She shook her head in annoyance. She'd tried talking to some of the other apprentices, but they had very little in common. The boys needed to see her as a teacher, while the girls were so different from her that it was hard to hold any sort of conversation with them. It would need at least a generation, she was sure, before the girls were ready to learn on equal terms with the boys. Indeed, from what she remembered learning in history, it would be Bernard—as Grandmaster—who would drop most of the gender barriers at Whitehall.

It did have its advantages, she had to admit. Her classes proceeded well—she taught the Manavore Runes to everyone, male and female—and no one, not even Tama, gave her any trouble. Tama practically hid at the back of the classroom, never daring to look up and meet her eyes. Emily had quietly checked, wondering if he too was hiding red eyes, but it seemed he was just reluctant to be noticed. If she'd killed an apprentice who was on the verge of gaining his mastery, she would have no trouble doing the same to him.

But being so isolated—Julianne wanted to spend most of her free time with Bernard—was wearying. None of the distractions she would have enjoyed at *her* Whitehall were available in the past. There was no library, save for the collection of books Master Wolfe had hidden near the control chamber; there was little to do, save for wandering around the castle looking for secret passageways. Emily had seriously considered walking down to the statue chamber and making the jump into the future—she would have done it, if the demon hadn't been bound to her shoulder. She had no idea what would happen if she triggered the spells while the demon was there, but she doubted it was anything good.

She rubbed her eyes tiredly as she walked down the stone corridor. The demon had done *nothing*. It hadn't tried to speak to her, it hadn't tried to warp her mind—she'd erected new mental defenses, just to make sure—and it hadn't done anything to her friends or enemies. It was just sitting there, biding its time. She'd had nightmares, curled up in her bedroom, but she didn't *think* any of them had anything to do with the demon. Robin's attempt to take control of her had brought many of her old fears back to light.

A pair of apprentices were chatting in an alcove as she passed, both falling silent as soon as they saw her. She nodded to them politely and hurried on, uneasily aware

that she might be the topic of conversation. It seemed to be her *fate* to have everyone scared of her, although in the past she was largely unique. A trained magician,
a *female* trained magician; a magician of rare power. She wondered, absently, what
Whitehall made of her now. He hadn't been unfriendly, but he hadn't been very
communicative either. He'd certainly forgotten his promise to teach her how to fly.

He has been occupied with setting up the school, she thought. *And he has been inter-*
viewing new masters.

She sighed under her breath as her feet took her into the Entry Hall. Word had
been spreading ever since the Gathering, naturally; hundreds of masters, apprentices
and mundane tradesmen had been making their way towards the castle. Whitehall
had put most of the latter to work on widening the path to the castle, cutting back
the foliage daily just to make sure the castle was never forgotten again. It would
probably be years before they had a proper road leading to the castle, but they were
on their way. And the castle was starting to teem with life.

Eyes followed her as she peered towards Whitehall, who was chatting to a pair
of men in fancy robes. She reached out with her senses and picked up two magical
signatures, one clearly Whitehall's. One of the guests was no magician, she decided,
unless he was better at masking his magic than anyone she'd met, either in the past
or the future. She wondered if Whitehall knew—his senses were nowhere near as
developed as hers—then decided it was quite possible. Wolfe's fiddling with the
wards had allowed him to identify and track every last magician who came into the
castle.

She frowned as a handful of men stepped through the doors, all but one of them
sellswords or lifeguards. Probably lifeguards, she decided, as their master strode
towards Whitehall with a grim expression on his face. They wore livery, rather than
makeshift armor or leather pads; their weapons were clean and shiny, suggesting
they took the time to clean and maintain them. Sergeant Miles had said some nasty
things about lifeguards, in the future, but Emily had to admit that this group looked
competent. Looking nasty was probably the best way to avoid a fight.

And they're not trying to ogle me or any of the women, she thought, as the nobleman
broke into Whitehall's conversation. *They're keeping an eye out for threats.*

Whitehall didn't look very pleased, she noted; she couldn't help wondering if the
nobleman was suicidal. He wasn't a magician and, as far as she could tell, nor were
any of his bodyguards. Whitehall could have killed them all in an instant. But he
merely asked his guests to wait, then waved to Emily. The nobleman stared at her as
she walked over to join Whitehall. She had to look very different than the women
he was *used* to seeing.

"Emily," Whitehall said. "Please escort the Brothers Suram to the dining hall and
make sure they have something to eat."

"Yes, Master," Emily said. She nodded to the brothers, who smiled at her. "If you'll
come with me...?"

She led them through the corridors and into the dining hall, where a number
of other guests were being fed as they waited to learn if they would be allowed to

stay or not. Emily was tempted to ask why they were traveling together, if one was a magician and the other a mundane, but she somehow managed to resist the urge. Magic was nowhere near as strong as it would become, in the future; a family might easily produce one magician and one mundane without finding it odd. And it wasn't as if being a magician in this era was a bed of roses...

"Thank you," one of the brothers said. "Your master is very welcoming."

"Lord Whitehall is a great man," Emily said. It was hard to push enthusiasm into her voice, but she tried. "This is his dream."

She nodded to them both, then hurried away. There was nothing for her to do until dinnertime, so she wandered down the stairs to the underground passageways and made her way into the statue chamber. Her wards remained active, keeping everyone out, but she didn't dare start casting the spells that would freeze her, within the chamber, until her past self came along, nearly a thousand years in the future. The demon was still there, its presence silently mocking her.

Emily twisted her head, trying to *see* the creature. But it was always just at the corner of her eyes.

She gritted her teeth. "What do you want?"

Whitehall had told her not to try to talk to the demon. She had the feeling that it would be the very last straw. Even the kindest man in the world would have had some doubts, after Master Chambers had pointed out just how many people had died, since they'd met Emily in the nexus chamber. Whitehall might have accepted her as an apprentice, but an apprentice could be dismissed for disobedience...

But she had to know what the demon wanted.

There was no answer. She reached out with her senses, probing where she knew the demon to be, but felt nothing beyond the bare fact of its existence. She'd wondered how the DemonMasters had coped with having a demonic presence looming over them...now, she thought she knew the answer. The demonic aura must specifically exclude the magician who had summoned it. Perhaps it was deliberate on their part, she noted. It would be harder to manipulate someone into screwing up if there was a constant reminder of ever-present hostility surrounding the demon.

It's just sitting there, she thought. *And waiting.*

She puzzled over it as she strode towards the control center. Whitehall hadn't known *much* about demons, but he'd been fairly clear that demons couldn't remain in the mortal world without *something* binding them in place. A Book of Pacts was dangerous because demons were bound within its pages. And yet, the demon should have been trapped as long as the book itself was intact, not tied to Emily. No one had found Robin's Book of Pacts...

And if I destroyed it when I killed him, she thought, *the demons should all have been thrown back into the Darkness.*

It made no sense. And that, in her experience, generally meant that she was missing something. A piece of information, perhaps, or a loophole that only made sense to a demonic mind. She doubted demons changed allegiances so quickly. Demons didn't *have* allegiances, not really. They resented being used by humans and were quick to take advantage of any mistakes their masters might make. Robin could have done something that allowed the demon to slip itself to Emily...

...But if that was the case, why was the demon still sitting there?

"Emily," Master Wolfe said. He stood by one of the crystal columns, watching the spellware slowly bubbling into place. "I was wondering when you would make your way down here."

Emily had to smile. Master Wolfe seemed to be the only person who wasn't intent on treating her as a freak, a monster, or an unexploded bomb. *And* he'd stood up for her more than once.

"I've been busy," she said. She strode over to join him, then frowned as she spotted Master Keldor bending over the Warden. "Master."

"Emily," Keldor said, gravely.

He didn't seem inclined to say anything more, which was something of a relief. Emily had thought Keldor was definitely part of Master Chambers' faction. He'd certainly voted *against* the plan to turn the castle into a school. But then, *his* brand of magic wasn't under threat, although Emily knew there would come a time when death magics were banned at Whitehall. Perhaps that would happen long after Keldor's death.

There was an odd twinge of magic around Master Wolfe, she discovered as she stepped up to stand next to him. It felt familiar, although she couldn't place it. He'd been experimenting heavily with the nexus point, using it to prove that certain spells worked before he started to modify them so a magician could cast them without needing a boost. Maybe he'd started work on something she'd use herself, in the future. He certainly seemed as excitable as ever.

"I thought this might interest you," Master Wolfe explained. He jabbed a finger at the crystal, where a piece of spellware was slowly taking shape. "This will respond to any burst of magic above a sustained level."

Emily nodded. Whitehall and his peers could *sense* magic, but they were largely blinded by their own slop. Emily half-suspected that Master Chambers couldn't sense her at all, which might explain the contempt he felt for her. He *knew* she'd helped with the nexus point—and dozens of other things—but he still couldn't sense her power. She had no *reason* to slop her power everywhere, just to show off.

"Clever," she said. It was basic, compared to some of the detection spells she'd used in her own time, but it was an order of magnitude more advanced than anything she'd seen in the past. "And what does it do?"

"It automatically absorbs such a burst of power," Master Wolfe explained. "The prospect of someone accidentally unleashing a blast of raw magic will thus be eliminated."

And you added it after I blasted Robin, Emily thought. *And you, of all people, know you don't need vast power to be dangerous.*

She looked at him, sharply. "And what if someone casts a killing spell with less power?"

"That will be harder," Master Wolfe admitted. "I can track bursts of magic throughout the castle, as you can imagine, but stopping it will be difficult. The background noise from the nexus point--" he nodded up towards the sound of *thrumming* "--makes it harder to separate the real spells from the random flashes of magic."

"That will change," Emily said. "At least you could prove what happened if there was a...a disagreement."

Master Wolfe gave her a sympathetic look. "I was trying to analyze the remains of his spell," he said. "But there wasn't enough to *prove* what it was designed to do."

Emily winced. She *had* managed to take enough of the spell apart—with the aid of a couple of memory charms—to allow her to fill in the blanks. If anything, she'd *underestimated* the danger of the spell. Using it on someone—anyone—would do more than cripple them for life; it would shatter them. She would have sooner dosed someone with love potion than cast that spell on them. It was unforgivable.

And if he'd managed to work out how to cast the spell, she thought, *he'd probably wind up using it himself.*

She pushed the thought out of her head as Master Wolfe started to show her his other projects, moving around the room as he pointed to pieces of parchments and scraps of notes scattered everywhere. Plans for expanding the interior of the school, plans for crafting wards so strong that even the most powerful magician couldn't dent them, plans for rooms that would become spellchambers, given enough time... she couldn't help thinking, with a twinge of pity, that Professor Locke would have been disappointed. And yet, what she was seeing was genuinely wonderful. The birth of a whole new world.

"It's interesting to see how different materials respond to magic," Master Wolfe said. "I've actually approached Bernard to see if I can take Julianne for an apprentice. She's starting her own project, testing and retesting the plants taken from the forest. If we put our heads together..."

"I'm sure Bernard will like the idea," Emily said. Master Wolfe wasn't anything like as old as Lord Alfred—and she knew there were some old men married to very young girls—but Julianne was already married. "And Master Whitehall and I set the precedent."

"Both you and Julianne already have some training," Master Wolfe said. "Anyone without that training will require a more...intimate...relationship until they master their magic. It may cause complications."

Emily shrugged, but she had to admit he might have a point. She'd taught Frieda and Julianne some magic, yet both of them had already been using magic before she came along, although Julianne hadn't realized it. Someone starting completely from scratch...Mistress Irene had taught her, but Mistress Irene was an experienced teacher. It would take time for Master Wolfe and his fellows to develop the techniques she'd used so carefully.

"I've been working with human...*materials* in potions," Master Keldor commented. He looked oddly nervous as he walked over to join them, an odd twitch visible—just for a second—on his face. "Adding human blood to some concoctions seems to have a striking effect."

"A dangerous effect," Emily said. Was she looking at the start of blood magic? But then, she had a feeling that *some* blood magic was already in common use. Bernard and Julianne's wedding rite suggested it. "You might discover that you had cursed someone—or yourself."

"True," Master Keldor agreed. "But normally I work with the freshly dead."

"There is magic in murder," Master Wolfe mused. "But the surge of power is uncontrollable."

Emily gave him a sharp glance. History said that the necromantic rite would be discovered and rediscovered, time and time again, but it didn't have to be born *here* and *now*. Master Wolfe had the nexus point. He didn't *need* necromancy. And if it stayed buried, it wouldn't taint Whitehall's early days...

"My master used to caution me against working too close to a murder scene," Master Keldor commented. He glanced upwards, just for a second. "He said there were black auras surrounding murder, even though working with materials from a murdered body could be quite rewarding."

"I see," Emily said. She'd never heard of that in her time. But then, what little she'd learned of death magics hadn't been pleasant. "Was he right?"

"I never had any problems," Master Keldor said. "But the remains lose their potency very quickly."

He glanced upwards again, then shrugged. "I might just have been unlucky," he said. He looked back at the Warden, lying on the table. "And now I have a chance to study something entirely new."

Emily frowned. "Are you modifying him?"

"A little," Master Keldor said. "But it's quite a frustrating process."

He picked up a hammer. "I'd like to fiddle with his intelligence. And probably smack him on the head with this."

"I don't think that will help," Master Wolfe said.

"No," Master Keldor said. "I don't imagine it will."

He hefted the hammer and smacked it into Master Wolfe's head, hard.

Chapter Thirty-Four

MASTER WOLFE DROPPED LIKE A SACK OF POTATOES, HIS BODY HITTING THE GROUND WITH a thud.

Emily gaped in shock, then snapped up her hand to cast a spell. But she felt the wards pressing down on her as soon as the magic came to her fingers, threatening to turn her own power back against her. Master Keldor let out an odd little giggle as she started backwards, then waved his hand at the door. It slammed closed and locked with an audible thump.

"Not bad," he said. He smirked at her as she kept backing away. "Master Wolfe does good work, doesn't he?"

Emily swallowed, hard. "What have you done?"

"Nothing," Master Keldor said. "Master Wolfe thought it might be a good idea to program the wards to keep your magic under control, should anything...*unfortunate* happen. And as long as I keep *my* link to the wards, you have no magic. *What* a good idea, would you not say?"

Fuck, Emily thought.

She tested the wards, then cursed under her breath. Master Wolfe, for once, hadn't tried to be subtle. He'd just tied the wards into the nexus point, raw power on a scale no living magician could hope to match. There were no weak points for her to exploit, no glitches in the spells she could use as a starting point as she began to unravel them...nothing, but a solid wall of magic pressing down on her. The merest attempt to cast a spell would see it rebound on her.

"No," she said, trying desperately to think of a plan. If she kept him talking, she might just be able to think of something. "It was a very bad idea."

She glared at him as a piece of the puzzle fell into place. "You're working for Chambers, aren't you?"

Keldor moved forward with lightning speed and slapped her hard, right across her scarred cheek; she tasted blood in her mouth as she used the blow to throw herself to the side and try to get away from him. But he jumped forward and landed on top of her, shoving her body to the floor and holding her down with his weight. She tried to cast a spell anyway, despite the risk, but the magic refused to form. She couldn't even release Aurelius! A moment later, he caught her hands, yanked them firmly behind her back and tied them tightly together. The knots were so tight she could feel the blood refusing to flow into her hands.

"I do not work *for* Chambers," Keldor said. His voice was suspiciously affable as he hauled her to her feet and pushed her against the wall. "I am a *master magician*. I work *with* my fellow masters, not under them."

"But you're working with him," Emily said. She tested the bonds as carefully as she could, but they refused to weaken. Master Keldor was clearly very good at tying knots. "Why?"

Keldor shrugged. "It won't be long before Lord Whitehall bans the practice of death magics too," he said, dryly. "He's already turned on some of his most loyal friends, purely because he regards their magic as an abomination. How long will it be before I too am forced to knuckle under or flee the castle?"

"You don't know that's going to happen," Emily said, pleadingly. "Death magics don't involve demons..."

"They can," Keldor said. "And they can be uniquely dangerous."

He smiled. "If a master is judged by the number of apprentices under his thumb—the number of apprentices who become masters in their own right—what will Whitehall be after he starts teaching hundreds of apprentices at once?"

Emily stared at him. "You're scared that Whitehall will become the most powerful magician in the world?"

"Among other things," Keldor said. "Whitehall has shown himself willing to upend tradition for his own purposes. Taking you as an apprentice, allowing his daughter to learn magic, taking a whole bundle of apprentices at once...and evicting magicians because they practice spells he regards as dangerous."

"And those magicians don't want to be sidelined," Emily finished.

"Of course," Keldor said. He waved a hand towards the crystal columns. "This place is the most important magical discovery since Myrddin the Sane convinced his students never to call on demons. Allowing Whitehall undisputed control would be wrong."

"And you think you'll never be able to outvote him," Emily said. *Whitehall* had been wrong, she saw now. Master Chambers and his ilk had never intended to abide by the vote. They'd even made sure to leave Keldor in place to lower the defenses for them. "He'll listen to you..."

"No, he won't," Keldor said. "He's monomaniacal on many subjects. I'm surprised he didn't throw you out because of that demon on your shoulder."

Emily scowled at the demon, still at the corner of her eye. It did nothing.

"He's a good man," she said.

"He's a manipulative conniving bastard," Keldor said, flatly. "He seduced Lord Alfred to his side, then convinced Master Drake to join him. And then he convinced Master Wolfe to join him too, probably because he felt a weak magician could be useful."

"It's not what you've got that's important," Emily said, pleadingly. "It's how you use it. And Master Wolfe knows how to use it."

"*Knew* how to use it," Keldor said. He knelt down to Master Wolfe's body and felt for a pulse. "He's dead, Emily."

Emily blanched and looked away, hastily blinking back tears as they welled at the corner of her eyes. Master Wolfe hadn't deserved to die. He'd been a genius, a man who had taken the clues she'd provided and run with them until he'd managed to jump-start the process that would become Whitehall School. He hadn't deserved to die...he would have lived, she was sure, if he hadn't been too close to her. He'd used so little raw magic that madness would never be a real threat to him...

"There, there," Keldor said. "I'm sure you'll join him soon enough."

He turned and strode towards the nearest column, leaving Emily staring after him as she fought to undo her bonds. But the ropes remained firmly in place, making it impossible to weaken them even slightly. Her hands were starting to ache, no matter what she did. It wouldn't be long before they went numb completely.

It hurt her pride to beg, but perhaps it would work. "Please, could you loosen my bonds?" she pleaded. "I..."

"No," Keldor said. He didn't look back at her. "And I suggest you keep your mouth closed if you don't want a gag stuffed in it."

Emily gritted her teeth in frustration. Master Keldor was no Master Wolfe, but he'd been intimately involved with crafting and empowering the Warden. He might well know how to disrupt the castle's wards, perhaps even turn them against Whitehall and his loyalists. And it might not be just him, either. Master Chambers could easily have recruited others from the commune to fight beside him.

They could have hidden out in the forest, she thought. *As long as they were careful, they wouldn't be spotted. Unless...*

She looked at him. "And what will you do," she asked, "when the Manavores return?"

Keldor stiffened, but he didn't look round. "Shut up."

"They will," Emily pressed. "The one I killed wasn't the only one, was it? Assuming they're actually intelligent, they'll already know they lost one of their number somewhere around here. And they sense the ebb and flow of magic. How long will it be before they realize that *something* has happened to the nexus point and put two and two together?"

"You are a stupid little girl," Keldor said. He turned to glare at her, keeping one hand on the crystal. "We already know how to kill them."

"That doesn't mean you're bound to win," Emily pressed. "The discoveries made here might just tip the balance in your favor."

She cursed under her breath as Keldor abandoned the crystal and stalked towards her, one hand pulling a filthy rag from his pocket. Emily clamped her mouth shut as he held it up towards her, but he caught hold of her nose and squeezed it tightly until she had to open her mouth to get in some air. Keldor stuffed the rag in her mouth, then shoved her hard against the wall. Emily struggled to breathe for several seconds, trying desperately to push the rag out of her mouth before it choked her to death. But all she could do was breathe through her nose and watch him helplessly.

The wards were shifting around her, she realized, as she sensed flickers of magic moving through the school. She tried to cast a third spell of her own, but nothing happened; the magic simply refused to form. And her connection to the nexus control spellware seemed to be blocked completely. She scowled at Master Wolfe's body as she worked hard to focus her mind, trying desperately to think of a plan. For once in the short time she'd known him, why couldn't he have made a mistake?

"They're entering the castle now," Keldor informed her. He shot her a smirk. "Soon, we will see."

Emily closed her eyes for a long moment. She'd never felt so helpless in her life, not even when Shadye had held her in his grip or Master Grey had pushed her right to the edge. She knew how to fight without magic, but she knew there was no way she could best him in a physical fight, even if her hands weren't tied. He was stronger than her and smart enough to know she didn't need magic to be dangerous. She was mildly surprised he hadn't trussed her up like a chicken.

There has to be a way out, she thought, desperately. History said she'd make it back—or did it? Perhaps she'd been wrong all along. *Or should I try to use the demon?*

She tried to look at the creature, but nothing happened. It just sat there, waiting. But waiting for what? Her mind raced, desperately, as she tried to consider her options. She couldn't do magic, she couldn't break free, she certainly couldn't kick him hard enough to make him reconsider...she was screwed.

The door opened. She looked up, desperately hoping that Whitehall or Bernard or even Drake was about to walk into the chamber, but her heart sank as Julianne appeared, shoved into the chamber by Tama. Her hands were bound behind her back and her dress was rumpled, suggesting that Tama had taken advantage of the situation. And there was a bitter hopelessness in her eyes that chilled Emily to the bone. Bernard couldn't be dead, could he?

And if he is dead, she thought, *history as I know it is screwed.*

"Put her next to Emily," Keldor ordered. "And then keep an eye on the door."

"Yes, Master," Tama said.

He dragged Julianne over to where Emily was leaning against the wall and shoved her face-first against the stone. Emily fought the urge to recoil back as he leered at her, then reached out, grabbed hold of the gag and pulled it out of her mouth. She choked, wishing desperately for water as Tama dropped the gag on the floor, his leer growing bigger as he loomed over her. He no longer seemed to be afraid of her at all.

"So," he said, pushing her back against the wall. "Not so clever now, are you?"

He kissed her hard, forcing his lips up against hers. Emily opened her mouth, then bit his lip as hard as she could. He stumbled backwards, gasping in pain; she took advantage of his distraction to bring her knee up as hard as she could and strike him firmly in the groin. Tama doubled over, howling with shock, then collapsed to the ground. Emily stepped forward, intending to bring her foot down on his throat, but a wave of magic slammed her back against the wall.

"How...inconvenient," Keldor said. He sounded amused, rather than outraged. "How annoying it is to have a stupid apprentice."

Emily found her voice. "You took him as an apprentice?"

"We *did* have to promise him *something*," Keldor said. He strode over to stand above Tama, then kicked him into blissful unconsciousness. Emily couldn't help thinking that it had probably come as a relief. "But clearly it wasn't enough to keep him from being an idiot."

He inclined his head to Julianne. "I'm sorry about his misbehavior," he added. "Rest assured that he will be punished."

"Go curse yourself," Julianne said. She sounded sullen. "And my father will turn you into a pig and dine on your hams."

"Your father will not be a problem for much longer," Keldor said. He didn't seem to mind the threat. "And you will be under my personal protection. Nothing will harm you."

"But it will harm me," Emily said. A thought crossed her mind as she gathered herself. If Master Wolfe had designed the wards to suppress *her* magic, was there any reason for them to suppress Julianne's? "Chambers is not going to let me live."

"Probably not," Keldor said. "Quite a few others will also need to be purged."

Emily swallowed, hard. Whitehall would die, of course; Bernard and Drake would probably follow him into the grave. And her, of course. Chambers hated her so much that she could expect to die in the most horrific manner he could devise. The other masters would be given a flat choice between respecting the DemonMasters or leaving, if they weren't killed out of hand. Chambers had had plenty of time to convince some of the apprentices to support him, while Whitehall had been at the Gathering. And the others would not be able to resist, if they didn't want to join the plotters...

But Julianne? Julianne might be allowed to live, under the proper conditions. God knew she could bear magical children, after all. And she was a talented potions brewer.

And they'll underestimate her because she's a girl, Emily thought, vindictively. *And one day they might wind up discovering that she's poisoned them.*

Keldor smirked at her horrified expression, then turned back to the crystal and resumed his work. Emily met Julianne's eyes, wishing she knew how to communicate silently though eye contact, and motioned for her to turn away so she could see the knot tying her hands behind her back. Tama hadn't done such a good job of tying Julianne up, she noted. The bastard had probably been so keen to start groping her that he'd accidentally used a weak knot. Julianne couldn't escape, not from the inside, but it was an easy knot to undo.

She glanced at Keldor, still fiddling with the spellware, then mouthed an order to Julianne to stay quiet. The younger girl nodded as Emily slipped closer, turning to bring her bound hands to bear on the knot. Her fingers felt numb, but she managed—somehow—to start loosening the knot. Julianne started, very slowly, to pull her hands free.

"No mercy," Emily mouthed, silently. Julianne couldn't cast spells without moving her hands, not yet. Keldor was a far more powerful and experienced magician. They were only going to get one shot at breaking free. "Hit him as hard as you can."

Julianne nodded, her expression grim. She might have liked Keldor, Emily thought; he'd certainly been close to her father, back when the commune had been making its run towards the castle. But he'd betrayed Whitehall and threatened his daughter—and his apprentice—with a fate worse than death. And Julianne's husband might be dead. Emily hated to think about what Bernard would do to Tama, if he were still alive. Molesting Julianne wasn't just sexual assault, not in his culture. It was a deliberate insult to her male relatives.

Sickening, she thought. She made a private resolution as the seconds ticked away. *No matter what, Tama will not survive this day.*

"They're thrusting into the Great Hall," Keldor said. Emily froze. If he saw Julianne tugging at her bonds, they were dead. At the very least, he'd tie Julianne's hands himself and do a better job of it. "We'll go up to meet them there."

"I could outbid Chambers," Emily said, moving forward. It was a desperate ploy, but it might just work. "I could offer you so much..."

"I'm sure you could," Keldor said. He took her upper arm and pulled her forward, motioning for Julianne to follow him. "But I think it would come with a pretty high price."

Emily hesitated. If Julianne was ready...and if she wasn't, she was making a fool of herself.

"It doesn't have to," she said, as she dropped to her knees. "I can make it worth your while."

"Get up," Keldor snarled. The sudden flash of anger surprised her. He jabbed a finger at Tama. "Do you think I'm *him*?"

Emily cringed at her own words, shaking her head at the irony. A culture full of misogynists, a culture full of people who thought nothing of women...and she just *had* to be held prisoner by the only one who wouldn't be tempted. Maybe she was just doing it wrong. She had next to no experience in being seductive. And what she'd done to Tama would cool the ardor of *any* man.

"No," she said, trying to keep him focused on her. "I don't think you're him."

She ducked her head as she sensed the surge of magic. She'd taught Julianne the spell, cautioning her that it was only to be used in desperate circumstances. Keldor's protections were no match at all for a spell that had been invented, in its base form, seven hundred years in the future. He flew backwards, flickers of balefire crackling over his chest, and hit the wall with a thump. Emily let out a sigh of relief as her magic returned to her. It was the work of a moment to undo her bonds and start rubbing life back into her wrists.

Julianne caught her in a tight hug and held her, just for a second, before leaning back.

"What now?"

"Now?" Emily asked. "Now we go save your father."

Chapter Thirty-Five

JULIANNE STARED AT HER. "THERE'S...TAMA SAID THAT HUNDREDS OF MAGICIANS HAD invaded the castle."

"If Tama told me it was going to be a dry day," Emily said tartly, "I would make sure to wear my cloak."

She contemplated the problem for a long moment as she touched the crystal column. If she could get access to the wards, she could turn them against the invaders. But nothing happened. Either the wards had been programmed to reject her—Wolfe could have done it, if he'd feared her power—or something else had scrambled them. And it would have been hard, if not impossible, to separate the two sides.

And Chambers was one of the founders, she thought, grimly. *The wards might refuse to turn on him in any case.*

"We have to get back upstairs," she said, after a moment. "Are you ready?"

Julianne looked nervous, but nodded shortly. Emily felt a stab of sympathy—*she* disliked fighting and she'd had much more training—as she walked towards the door and peered out into the corridor. There was no sign of anyone, male or female. She wondered, as she glanced into the library, just how many of the newcomers had been influenced by Chambers or Reaper. Hundreds of people had visited the castle over the last few days and dozens of them had stayed. If even a third of them worked for Chambers, as part of a Trojan Horse operation, Whitehall and his loyalists had a serious problem.

"Keep very quiet and stay behind me," she hissed. Master Wolfe had configured the wards to keep unwelcome guests out of the underground tunnels, but Chambers could probably tell his allies how to defeat the protections if necessary. Who knew what else Keldor might have done? "And get ready to cast a spell if necessary."

She glanced at Julianne, worried. If she had someone—anyone—else along, she would urge Julianne to remain in the control chamber. Julianne might have grown up in a harsher world than herself—although she *had* had a father—but she had no experience whatsoever in actually *fighting.* Sergeant Miles had made *Emily* sneak through the forest and the castle until she could move like a ghost...

But it has its limits, she thought, as they reached the bottom of the stairs. *And the demon might be detectable too.*

She glared at the creature, a flickering impression at the corner of her eye. It hadn't moved at all, even when she'd tried to touch the control system. What was it *doing?* She rubbed her scarred cheek as she slipped up the stairs, reaching out carefully with her senses in hopes of detecting any waiting magicians before it was too late. How long would it be before the scar healed? And how long did she have left in the past? She could practically *feel* time pressing down around her, insisting that she needed to sneak back to the statue chamber and begin her trip to the future.

Or maybe I'm imagining it, she told herself. *There's no way to be sure.*

She held up a hand, stopping Julianne, as she sensed a knot of magic at the top of the stairs, just in front of the wards. There was a magician standing there, a magician practically spewing wild magic in all directions. A DemonMaster, perhaps? Emily couldn't *sense* any demons, but that meant nothing. He might just be powerful enough not to have to carry one around with him all the time.

He'd be down here if he could see the gates, she thought, grimly. *Chambers must have told him where to look, but he doesn't have the mental discipline to see through the first line of defense.*

Or he's just there to keep us penned up, her own thoughts countered. *They may already know that Keldor's plan went awry.*

"There's a magician lying in wait for us," she hissed. Julianne paled. "Stay here. I'll deal with him."

She wished, absurdly, for a sword or a dagger as she stepped through the wards. Her magic was far stronger than any mundane weapon, but Keldor had reminded her—again—that she could not depend upon it. The magician looked up, surprised—from his perspective, she had practically materialized out of nowhere—and then jerked up a hand. She slammed a hex into him before he could cast a spell, heedless of the dangers of using modern spellware in the ancient castle. The magician slammed back against the wall, then crashed to the ground, leaving a trail of blood behind. She was relieved, deep inside, to realize that she didn't recognize him.

Stunned, she thought, as she checked his pulse. *But he'll probably live.*

She beckoned Julianne through the gates, then searched the magician thoroughly. He had five small pouches at his belt, each one filled with....*something*...that had an evil aroma, but nothing else. Julianne looked revolted and muttered something about death magics and blood-based potions, then leaned away from the fallen man as Emily carefully took his pouches and dumped them through the gates. Whatever they were—and the magic surrounding them had felt *evil*—they wouldn't play any further role in the battle. She cast a spell on the magician, just to make sure he would remain asleep for the next few hours, and reached out with her senses. Flashes and flickers of magic were darting through the castle.

"There's a battle going on," she hissed. Chambers had probably planned to turn the nexus point against the loyalists. Keldor would have done it too, if Julianne hadn't managed to surprise him. Any hope of a quick victory had died with him. "But I don't know who's winning."

Julianne stared at her. "Can you sense my father?"

Emily shook her head. "Not at this distance," she said. "But we need to get up there."

She contemplated possibilities as they made their way towards the stairs, cursing under her breath as she realized just how few options there were. Sergeant Miles had taught her that castles—and *this* castle was no exception—were designed to make it harder for the attacker to break in, but their interiors tended to be double-edged swords if the attackers actually *did* get into the castle. A couple of magicians guarding the stairwell would be quite enough to keep the defenders pinned down, at least before the attackers started hurling fireballs or other spells into the bowels of the castle. She *might* be able to punch her way through, but it would reveal her presence to everyone else.

We could go up the side of the castle, she thought. *But can we get outside?*

It didn't seem likely. She had no idea how much experience Master Chambers had of warfare, but she'd seen bows and arrows at the Gathering. A handful of bowmen could keep the defenders from making a sally, let alone trying to scramble up the stone walls and crawl into an upper window. And Julianne probably couldn't get up the walls in any case. Emily wasn't entirely sure *she* could. Whitehall—*her* Whitehall—was charmed to make that difficult.

We could teleport, she thought. *But how would the wards respond to that?*

She cursed Master Wolfe under her breath as she reached the bottom of the stairs and peered up, her senses probing for trouble. A surge of magic—and a teleport spell was easily powerful enough to qualify—would trigger the wards...and then what? She doubted he'd been able to program them to dump her into the oubliette, if there *was* an oubliette. But merely preventing the spellwork from forming would be quite bad enough. She'd waste a great deal of her reserves for nothing.

And that's the good option, she thought, tartly.

There were no magicians at the top of the stairs, according to her senses, but that proved nothing. Chambers might well have hired sellswords, although she found it hard to imagine that he'd found many willing to attack a magician's home. Even the lowliest of the apprentices could pose a serious risk to mercenaries. But then, Chambers could have promised them magical protection and enough money to make them independently wealthy for life. It wasn't the sort of offer that could be sneered at easily, despite the risks.

She pushed the thought out of her mind as she motioned Julianne to stay back, then slowly inched her way up the stairs. The flickers of magic from high overhead were growing stronger all the time, suggesting that the battle was intensifying. Both sides would have realized that neither one was going to get an easy victory. And they were committed. Neither Chambers nor Whitehall could just walk away from the castle, not now...

"All right, girl," a voice growled. "Come on up."

Emily looked up. Four men were standing at the top of the stairs, carrying swords and peering down at her with disdainful expressions. Sellswords, she decided; none of them had any trace of inherent magic surrounding them. They *did* have *some* protections, she realized, as she slowly walked towards them, doing her best to seem both obedient and fearful. But their protections simply weren't very good.

Chambers should have listened to Wolfe, she thought, gathering her power. *His protections are full of holes.*

She cast the spell, pushing it forward as she reached the top of the stairs. The four men froze completely, utterly unable to move. Emily smiled, even though she knew they would probably have raped her and Julianne if they'd had a chance. Clearly, Chambers' warning about female magicians—if he'd bothered to issue such a warning—had fallen on deaf ears.

He probably didn't, she thought. *Convincing the sellswords to join the fight would have been hard enough without it.*

"Come on up," she called. "Hurry!"

Julianne ran up the stairs, her eyes going wide when she saw the frozen men. Emily nodded to her, then led the way down the corridor. The sound of fighting grew louder, the flickers of magic stronger and nastier. It sounded as through the enemy had secured the entrance hall, but not managed to push much further into the castle. Sergeant Miles would not have been impressed.

She sucked in her breath as she stuck her head into the dining hall. Several magicians were fighting savagely, brilliant spells smashing into wards or exploding uselessly against the stone walls. It didn't *look* as though either side was thinking *tactically*, she noted; they stood, gathered together, blasting away at the other side. A child with a machine gun could have killed everyone on both sides within seconds. And it was hard, so hard, to tell just who was on which side.

And then she saw Bernard, standing with his fellow magicians.

Emily braced herself, gathering her power, then threw a spell towards the opposing side, shaping the spell to tear through their defenses. Their position wavered and broke as her spell struck them, utterly unprepared for an attack from the side or a spell designed to pick its way through the weak points in their protections. She saw Master Reaper turning to face her, his face contorted with hatred; he made a gesture towards her, a second before a fireball slammed into his chest and incinerated him. A demon rose up from his body and glided towards Emily, its face twisted with malice...

She froze, numb horror rooting her to the spot. The demon was so powerful that its mere presence blanked everything else out, as if it were *realer* than *real*. It was hard, so hard, to get a clear impression of what it *looked* like, but its mere presence was like trying to stare into the sun. She suddenly found it impossible to muster a spell or run for her life...

"Down," a voice shouted.

Emily staggered backwards as the spell snapped. *Something*—another demon—flashed past her and dove into the first demon. Moments later, they both blinked out of existence, leaving nothing but a malign stench in the air. Emily turned. A young man was standing behind her, his face tried and worn. She had barely a second to recognize him as one of Master Wolfe's students—a magician of so little power that he would never have amounted to anything, without his understanding of spellwork—before he turned and hurried away from her. He'd had a demon, she realized numbly. And he'd unleashed the demon to save her life.

Bernard ran past her and grabbed Julianne, hugging her tightly. Emily rolled her eyes as she cast spells to cover them—making out in the middle of a fight was crazy—and watched the loyalists as they began mopping up the room. The remaining attackers were swiftly killed by the defenders, without even a hint of mercy. It would have sickened her a year ago, she knew, and in some ways it still did. But it was their world.

And they cannot be allowed to escape, she told herself, numbly. *Or continue the fight elsewhere.*

"Emily," Bernard said. Emily turned back to him. He was flushing and Julianne, holding his hand tightly, refused to meet her eyes. "What happened?"

"Keldor betrayed us," Emily said, shortly. "He did something to the control system, weakening it. I...it needs Whitehall to retake control."

"Understood," Bernard said. He looked grim. "I don't know what happened to him."

Emily closed her eyes, reaching out with her senses, but there were so many magical traces in the hall that she couldn't sense anything useful. Whitehall couldn't be dead, could he? She had read a number of accounts of the founding of the school that insisted Whitehall lived to a fine old age, but she had good reason to know that most of the history books were either inaccurate or flat-out wrong. And yet, they all agreed that Whitehall lived for decades before turning the school over to Bernard.

But all of the books are intensely focused on him, she thought, numbly. *Master Chambers and Master Drake are barely mentioned...and Julianne isn't mentioned at all.*

"We have to find him," she said. "Come on."

Bernard looked astonished as she led the way towards the door, then hurried past her and into the corridor. Emily was surprised he didn't send Julianne back to her room, although she supposed he might just have believed that Julianne was safe with him. Tama was in for a horrific time, Emily was sure, when Bernard realized what he'd done to his wife. She just hoped he didn't blame Julianne for it too. She'd known men who'd done just that...

Because they believe it's impossible to rape a good woman, she thought, grimly. It had made her sick when she'd had to stand in judgement, knowing that the law of the land and her sense of right and wrong were in conflict. *And because they think a woman can only get pregnant if she enjoys herself.*

She pushed the thought aside and reached out, again, with her senses. There was another battle going on in the Great Hall. She tapped Bernard on the shoulder and muttered advice, then followed him as he slipped down towards the hall. The waves of magic were getting stronger, mingled with flickering bursts of concentrated malice that sent shivers down her spine. There were demons ahead of them, waiting. And she knew she couldn't ask anyone to sacrifice themselves on her behalf, not for a second time.

There has to be a way to banish them, she told herself. *But how?*

Whitehall was standing, his back to them, as they entered the Great Hall. Master Chambers was standing at the other end of the room, his eyes burning with red light as he hurled spell after spell towards his former friend. Emily felt sick as she tasted the magic, grimly aware that Master Chambers was working demonic power into his spells. It made her wonder if it had been Chambers, rather than Robin, who'd bargained for the control spell. He might have nudged Robin into using it in the hopes of provoking a confrontation.

"You," Master Chambers howled. Emily shuddered as she saw the rage and hatred on his face. His sanity was gone, gone completely. The invisible presences surrounding him were laughing at her. "You..."

She threw herself to the side as a wave of magic lashed out at her, but she couldn't move fast enough to escape. The magic slammed into her protections, crawling along them as it searched for weaknesses. There was no elegance to the spell, but it hardly mattered. The demonic malice—and his madness—gave it power. She thrust the wards away from her, hoping that it would be enough to keep the spell from touching her. Master Chambers would never be satisfied with merely killing her.

"Enough," Whitehall said. "Chambers..."

"*Die*," Chambers screamed.

Dear God, Emily thought, as another wave of magic slammed into Whitehall's shield. *He's a necromancer!*

She threw a spell of her own, hoping Master Chambers hadn't been using necromancy long enough to start the transformation into an eldritch abomination. Perhaps he'd had enough experience controlling his own mind, after using demonic magic, to avoid the first bouts of outright madness. But the spell merely glinted off him, as if he was already too far gone to be stopped. Emily shuddered as Bernard, Julianne and the other magicians started pouring spells into Chambers' wards. She knew with a sick certainty that it wasn't going to be enough.

A wave of pain almost drove her to her knees as the door behind Master Chambers bulged in a direction her eyes couldn't follow, a creature slipping into a room. Master Chambers turned, letting out a terrible scream as he saw the Manavore; magic boiling around him as he readied himself to attack...

And then, quite casually, the Manavore opened its mouth and swallowed him.

Chapter Thirty-Six

A BSOLUTE SILENCE FELL.
The Manavore stood there, looking at them with semi-translucent eyes. Once again, Emily found it hard to even *look* at the creature, as if there was something about it that defied her imagination. It was a spider, but it wasn't a spider; it was a mangled construct of a dozen different animals, her mind desperately trying to make sense of something completely beyond its comprehension. The walls were faintly visible *through* the translucent creature, but they were bent and twisted, as if the mere *presence* of the Manavore was enough to bend reality around it.

Master Chambers unleashed a vast amount of magic, and Master Keldor took down most of the wards, Emily thought. In his bid to prevent Whitehall from reshaping the magical community, Master Chambers might well have destroyed it. There had been nothing about *this* in the history books. *We might as well have been announcing our presence to every last Manavore in the world.*

The magicians seemed entranced. Emily glanced from side to side; Bernard and Julianne were staring at the Manavore in horror, but most of the others were just stunned, as if it had cast a spell over them. *None* of them had seen a Manavore before, not directly. Even when they'd fled, they'd seen nothing beyond flickering impressions that had rapidly faded from their minds. But now...now they were looking straight at their foe. They would have been safer staring into the face of a medusa.

She gritted her teeth in pain as the magic field shifted and tilted towards the Manavore. The shock jerked the others out of their trance; they started casting spells, only to watch helplessly as their spells struck the Manavore, broke apart into glistening flickers of magic and vanished into its aura. It was feasting, she realized; there was so much magic in the air that it was blinded to their presence. But that wouldn't last...

"Emily," Julianne screamed.

Emily turned and swore as she saw the doorway bulging, distorting out of shape until a second Manavore entered the hall. Something nagged at her mind—the Manavores seemed to need to use doors, despite their transdimensional nature—but she had no idea how to make use of it. She glanced at Whitehall and cursed again. The older magician was staring around him, his eyes wide with shock. His dream was dying, and he could do nothing. And then he snapped out of his trance.

"Get out of the room," he bellowed. "Set up the runes in the corridor!"

The magicians turned and ran towards the final door. Emily couldn't help noticing that several of the younger men and women were panicking, their faces utterly terrified. She didn't blame them. They'd grown used to being powerful, to being unstoppable...and then the Manavores had shown them that they were small fish in a very big ocean. They'd watched helplessly as a DemonMaster, who also happened to be a necromancer, had been destroyed in passing.

She glanced back and swallowed, hard, as more Manavores swarmed into view. They'd consume the stray magic from the battle, then come hunting more. Stopping one or two with the runes she'd devised might be possible, but stopping five or six...?

She had no idea if they were smart enough to recognize the threat and avoid it—if they didn't already know what had happened to the first Manavore—yet it didn't matter. One Manavore might be trapped, while the others killed the trappers and then fought their way onwards, hunting down the remaining magicians.

Whitehall caught her arm and yanked her forward, slamming the door behind him. Emily rather doubted it would stand up to a good kick, let alone a Manavore. Perhaps they *needed* an open door—the laws of magic governing magical creatures often made no sense—but even if they did, there was no reason they couldn't go out through one of the other doors and scuttle around the corridors until they found their prey. And their distortion effect *probably* meant they could fit down even the narrowest corridors...

"Every magician for a hundred miles is here," Whitehall snarled. "Even those who opposed me were brought here by Chambers!"

Emily swallowed, hard. Had history been derailed beyond repair? *Both* sides in the conflict were on the verge of being wiped out. The nexus point—and the castle—would be forgotten soon enough, an experiment that had failed. And her? Would she simply blink out of existence, or would history rewrite itself to allow her to exist? She glanced at the demon on her shoulder, but no answers were forthcoming. Maybe it was just waiting until she died before returning to the Darkness. None of the books she'd read had said much about the demonic realm, but she found it hard to imagine that it was a very pleasant place.

"Bernard," Whitehall snapped. "You need to set up the runes. Organize teams to slow them down."

"Yes, Master," Bernard said. He was *still* holding Julianne's hand. "What about...?"

"If you find any of *his* supporters, put them to work," Whitehall ordered. "Hurry." He glanced at Emily, tightening his grip on her hand. "Come with me."

Emily nodded as he pulled her down the corridor. "We need to retune the wards!"

"If we can get control," Whitehall snapped. "What happened?"

"Keldor betrayed you," Emily said. She caught one last glimpse of Bernard and Julianne, then followed Whitehall down the corridor. "He damaged the control systems."

Whitehall looked pained. "How badly?"

"I'm not sure," Emily admitted. "He locked me out, somehow."

She met his eyes. "Did you order Master Wolfe to prepare wards to stop my magic?"

"Yes," Whitehall said. He had the grace to look ashamed. "I'm sorry."

Emily sighed. "I survived," she said. She ran through the rest of the story as they passed the frozen sellswords and hurried down the stairs. Whitehall glanced at them, but said nothing. "And the school itself has to survive."

"Because of the *future*," Whitehall said.

"Yeah," Emily said. She allowed herself a moment of bitter regret. "You know, don't you?"

"It took me a long time to figure it out," Whitehall said. He reached out and squeezed her hand, gently. "You're from the future."

Emily nodded. "You can't make a record of that," she said. How had Whitehall figured it out? "And you mustn't tell *anyone.*"

"Of course," Whitehall said.

"Thank you," Emily said. She gave him a sidelong look. "How did you figure it out?"

"You were too good," Whitehall said. "You spoke with too much assurance. You knew spells Wolfe insisted were too advanced for anyone, even him, yet there were also odd gaps in your knowledge. And the demons Master Chambers summoned to interrogate insisted that you hadn't existed prior to the moment you fell out of the nexus point."

"And so you knew I was lying," Emily said.

"I knew you were lying about *something,*" Whitehall said. "And there were too many odd discrepancies in your story, things that didn't quite make sense. And eventually I patched it all together."

He leaned forward. "How far back did you come?"

"I'm not sure," Emily admitted. They reached the nexus chamber and paused to allow Whitehall to inspect the wards. "Our records aren't that good."

"I see," Whitehall said, tartly. "Do they remember me?"

"Yes," Emily said. "But that's all I'm going to say about it."

Whitehall scowled, but nodded reluctantly. "Do you want me to do anything for you? I could leave a note for my successors..."

Emily considered it, briefly. Would she have fewer troubles with Gordian if he'd had a note, purportedly from Lord Whitehall himself? One telling him, perhaps, to listen to her? But she doubted that any such note had been found. It had been nearly a thousand years, after all; there was no way they could be *sure* that such a note would survive. And she didn't *know* that one *had* survived.

"No," she said, slowly. "Just...try to forget the details."

Whitehall nodded as they walked into the nexus chamber. She knew he had to be brimming with questions, but he held his tongue. Emily knew *she* wouldn't be able to avoid asking questions about the future, despite the risk of damaging the timeline still further. Whitehall seemed more capable of controlling himself.

He asked if they remembered him, she thought. *And that was all he wanted.*

"He didn't damage the spellware that much," Whitehall said, thoughtfully. The nexus point glittered in front of them, waiting. Emily couldn't help wondering just how long it would be before the Manavores came down to consume it. "But it will take some time to expel the creatures completely from the castle."

"Chambers inadvertently called them," Emily said. "The magic he unleashed...it summoned them."

"So I gathered," Whitehall said. "And he was killed before he could do anything."

Thank God, Emily thought.

She nodded as Whitehall went to work. For the first time, she sensed a flicker of motion from the demon on her shoulder, a sense that it had turned its head to watch Whitehall at work. She eyed it warily, wondering if she should make her way down to the statue chamber while Whitehall was working on the nexus point. It would be simple enough to take advantage of his work to ensure that the chamber remained undiscovered, at least until her past self came along. The demon might have its own plans for the nexus point.

"I want you to do something for me," Whitehall said. Emily glanced at him, worried. "You remember the Books of Pacts? I want you to take them into the future and destroy them there."

Emily gave him a sharp look. "Are they safe?"

"Lord Alfred had many demons under his command," Whitehall said. "And some of them were never successfully bound by anyone else. Those books are going to be targets for every thief in the world as word spreads—and you know it will spread."

"The demons will make sure of it," Emily said.

"Take them into the future," Whitehall said. "Go *now*. Keep them out of reach. And once you're there, destroy them."

Emily sucked in her breath. The books were tempting, even though she'd felt the evil surrounding them every time she'd laid eyes on them. And yet, now she had a demon on her shoulder, it was all too easy to wonder if that was still true. Could she touch the books without being repulsed? Could she *use* the books without feeling as though she was touching something unbearably filthy?

You can get used to anything, even hanging, she recalled Lady Barb saying once, *as long as you do it long enough.*

"If I can, I will," Emily said.

"If you can't, make sure no one ever finds them," Whitehall warned. "They're too dangerous to be allowed into unsuspecting hands."

Emily nodded. "I'll see to it," she promised. "They're still in the library?"

"Yes," Whitehall said. He looked down at the ground for a long moment. "We never found Robin's Book of Pacts. And I have no idea what's happened to Chambers'."

"It'll show up again," Emily predicted. "I..."

She turned, sharply, as she sensed the world *changing* behind her. The corridor was swelling open, as if it had turned to liquid; a Manavore, large enough to pass for a bus, ran towards them, even though it shouldn't have been able to *fit* in the corridor. Emily cursed, then looked at Whitehall. It would take far too long to set up the spell.

"How long?"

"Ten minutes," Whitehall said. He sounded bitter, resigned. "I'm sorry."

"I'll distract it," Emily said. It wouldn't be easy. She doubted the creature could see her, against the blaze of power from the nexus point. "And...if I don't see you again, tell everyone I said goodbye. And live long and prosper."

She gave him a last look, trying to fix his features in her mind, then ran forward, summoning her magic and pushing it forward. Mistress Irene would have slapped her for extruding magic in such a manner, pointing out the danger of filling the air with raw unfocused *mana*, but there was no choice. The Manavore rolled to a halt as it tasted Emily's magic, then spun around until it faced her. She felt invisible eyes peering at her and did her best to look back evenly, despite the strain on her reserves. There was no sense of anger, hatred or malice, merely a cool dispassion that surprised her.

The Manavore scuttled forward, claws reaching out to strike. Emily turned and ran, leaving a trail of magic behind her. She was all too aware that it could move faster than her, but it seemed content to swallow the magic she was obligingly pumping out. Was it intelligent enough to realize the disadvantages of killing her, unlike the farmer who owned the goose that laid the golden eggs, or did it not *see* her? Her body wasn't saturated with sloppy magic.

Gritting her teeth, she hurled a fireball behind her as the Manavore kept moving, snapping at her heels. Perhaps it wasn't stupid after all, she thought, as she picked up speed. If she slowed down long enough to draw runes, it would consume her before she could even begin; if she kept moving, she'd eventually run out of reserves—and tire. And when she did, it would overrun and kill her.

Crap, she thought. She reduced her *mana* output, trying to distract it, but the minute her output grew too low the Manavore started to flow back towards the nexus point. *This is going to get me killed.*

She hit the creature with a fireball, cursing under her breath as it turned back to resume the chase. The choice before her was nightmarish. She could break contact at any moment, if she chose to allow the creature to start making its way back to Whitehall. And she had no idea just how much time he needed before the Manavores could be isolated and expelled from the castle. Hell, she had no idea if Bernard or Julianne were still *alive*. History said they would survive—it struck her, suddenly, that she had never had a chance to say a proper goodbye—but she had no idea if that would hold true indefinitely. Master Keldor had been credited with writing a book, she recalled; had he written that before his death, or had another magician taken the name?

An idea struck her as she fled down the stairs, the Manavore in hot pursuit. She ran past the library and straight into the statue chamber, feeling the last of her reserves dwindle to nothing. And the lower her reserves became...she stumbled as her legs threatened to give out, only the grim memory of Master Chambers' death keeping her on her feet. Gritting her teeth, she thrust her awareness ahead of her and linked into the spells she'd intended to use to freeze herself in time. As soon as the Manavore ran into the chamber, she drew on the spells and lashed out at the creature, trying to drain its magic and shove it back to its own realm.

The Manavore *screamed*, a sound that echoed in her head even as she fell to the ground and covered her ears, desperately. She turned, just in time to see the stone walls warping and twisting around it; a second later, the world spun madly as it died. Emily retched as the floor heaved, as if she was on a boat in the middle of a dreadful storm; she felt desperately seasick for a long moment before the sensation vanished, leaving her lying on the stone floor. Even in death, the Manavore cast a long shadow.

And I sensed something when I explored this section for the first time, she thought, pulling herself upright. *All that remained of the Manavore...*

She found herself struggling to breathe as she felt Whitehall's will working its way through the castle. Her body *hurt*. Her reserves were almost gone. It wasn't easy to keep going, not when she wanted to just collapse to the floor and sleep, but there were other Manavores in the castle. Perhaps they'd all be flocking to the nexus chamber, ready to consume the source of magic itself. Or perhaps Whitehall had already isolated them and the battle was about to end.

The demon is gone, she realized, dully. *What happened to it?*

There was no time to worry about it, not now. Gritting her teeth, she stumbled back to the library and unpicked the wards. The two books were sitting on a table, surrounded by a pair of wards that should have taken her hours to unravel. But they broke the second she touched them. She puzzled over it for a long moment, then realized that Whitehall must have been planning to ask her to take the books for a long time. He'd keyed the wards to allow her to take the books at will. Picking them up—they still felt unpleasant to the touch—she carried them out of the room and back to the statue chamber. She'd just have to make sure they were isolated and then destroyed as soon as she got back to her own time.

She dumped the books on the floor, as soon as she entered the chamber and started to test the spells. But all her work—all her careful work—lay in ruins. The Manavore's remains—the impression it left on the air—had changed everything. She couldn't use the chamber as she'd planned, yet she *had* to use the chamber. Her recollections *told* her she had used the chamber.

Gritting her teeth, she started to work to rebuild the spells, one by one. But everything had changed. She wondered, grimly, if she could alter the interior dimensions of the school to shift the Manavore's remains away from her spells, but Master Wolfe hadn't even *begun* to craft the interior before his death. There was no help for it. She'd have to adjust her spells to compensate for its presence and hope for the best.

I could go back up and ask for help, she thought. *But...*

She shook her head. She'd already interfered too much. There was no way to know how much was too much, and how much would cause her to blink out of existence. She had to go back to the nexus point...

As soon as the spells were in place, she picked up the books and walked to the center of the room. The spells glimmered around her, ready and waiting. She took a long breath, mouthing a prayer to a God she'd never really believed in...

...And knew, a second later, that she'd made a terrible mistake.

Chapter Thirty-Seven

FOR A LONG MOMENT, PANIC GRIPPED HER MIND.

She couldn't move. She couldn't even feel her body. Her heartbeat seemed to have stilled; she couldn't even *breathe*. She was trapped in stone, yet awake and aware; she was trapped, held in place by her own magic. Panic battered at her defenses, trying desperately to push her magic away from her body, but her own spells held it firmly in place. She couldn't move, she couldn't break the spell. She'd keyed the spells to be broken—slowly—by her own touch, yet she couldn't even *begin* to touch herself. She was trapped.

It felt like hours before she managed to gather enough of her mind to focus and take stock of her situation, but it was pointless. Her spell had failed. No, it had worked, but only in part: her body would be preserved until her past self touched it, but her mind was still active, all too aware that it was trapped in stone. Horror ran through her as she realized she'd be completely mad by the time her past self touched her stone body. There was no hope of keeping herself sane without magic. Hell, she had no idea how long she'd been trapped in stone. She hoped—prayed— that it had already been a year, but cold logic suggested otherwise. Not knowing just how fast time was progressing probably wouldn't help either...

Absolute despair washed through her mind as she realized she'd effectively killed herself, yet she could never die. The Emily that would escape the spell, centuries in the future, would be utterly insane, armed with all the knowledge and power she'd gathered and hoarded over the last five years. She doubted her future self would be sane enough to make sure the time loop was completed, hurling her past self back in time...hell, she might just think it would be *better* to break the time loop.

But I did it once, she thought. *Didn't I?*

"Well," a quiet voice said. The amused condescension running through its tone would have made her flinch, if she could have moved. "This is a mess, isn't it?"

Emily cursed, mentally, as the demon stepped into view. It was familiar, all too familiar: it was the same demon she'd met under Mountaintop, hundreds of years in the future. Or was it? The demon she'd met had assumed that form—massive bulging eyes, a grinning mouth of unkempt teeth, a dark outfit glittering with chains and metal skulls, a shock of uncombed hair—to prove a point. Perhaps this demon had merely copied the same form. Or perhaps, from the demon's point of view, their first meeting had already taken place.

They exist outside time and space, she thought, as the demon reached forward and stroked her stone chin. *All times are now to them.*

"Of course it's a mess," the demon added, answering its own question. "You're trapped in stone by your own power. Quite a mess for anyone, particularly now. No one is going to find you for nine hundred and seventy-two years."

It smirked, unpleasantly. "And you've already been trapped for--" it made a show of consulting a pocket watch hanging from a chain "--around five minutes, forty-seven seconds."

Emily felt numb horror running through her mind. It had felt like hours. She would have liked to believe the demon was lying, but...demons couldn't lie, not directly. And no matter how she thought about it, she couldn't see any attempt to mislead her. There had been no weasel words, just a blunt statement that allowed no room for misunderstandings. Five minutes...she didn't know how she'd stand another hour of being trapped in stone, completely alone.

And having the demon for company won't be much of an improvement, she thought. *It could drive me insane by talking.*

"Well, quite," the demon said. It drew back so its huge yellow eyes could peer into Emily's unblinking gaze. "But it's not much fun if you can't talk back, is it?"

Emily had only a moment to realize that the demon must have read her mind before the world blurred around her. Her body...*changed*. The demon, she realized numbly, had yanked her into the mental plane, the place where she'd confronted the demon that had invaded Whitehall before Grandmaster Hasdrubal's death. She shivered as the mists rose up around her, forcing her to remain focused on the demon. It drifted in front of her, its mere presence holding her spellbound. She knew better than to take her eyes off a demon.

Think, she told herself, sharply. *It wouldn't have done this unless it wanted something.*

"We can talk normally," the demon said. The mocking tone hadn't faded. "But not, I'm afraid, for very long. Time is not quite on our side."

"I thought you had nothing but time," Emily said, tartly.

"Time is...a confused structure," the demon said. "And you know that you have to get back to the future—and you have to arrive relatively sane."

"Relatively sane," Emily repeated.

The demon shrugged. "If you are not sane, as you have already realized," it said, "the loop in time will not be closed. History itself will shift. And everything will change."

Emily shivered. She knew it was telling the truth.

"But you *will* arrive, relatively sane," the demon added. There was nothing, but amused confidence in its voice. "You will be there because you will make a bargain with us."

Emily stared. "I'd rather die."

The demon cocked an eyebrow. "You'd rather screw up the timeline so completely that it would never recover?"

It went on before Emily could say a word. "Whitehall and his commune will all die, rather than managing to gain control of the nexus point. The remainder of the magicians will be hunted down, one by one, by the Manavores. And then the Faerie will attack the mundanes and turn them into puppets, twisting their bodies and souls for their sick enjoyment. And that will be the end.

"You'll never come to the Nameless World. Your stepfather will rape you when you turn seventeen. He'll be arrested, of course, but the damage will be done. You'll slit your wrists by the end of the year."

It paused. "And that's the *good* option," it said. "You don't want to know what *else* could happen."

"You know what *will* happen," Emily charged.

"Of course," the demon said. "I know you'll make the bargain with us."

Emily swallowed, hard. Bargaining with demons was dangerous. She hadn't needed Whitehall—or Aurelius—to tell her that the demons always rigged the bargains in their favor. And yet, she knew that demons couldn't lie directly. It was the one true restriction on their powers. They could tell the truth in a manner calculated to mislead, they could deliberately omit pieces of information, they certainly never *volunteered* information...but they couldn't actually lie.

And she had to go back to her own time. *To Caleb*, she thought. And the demon knew it too.

No ambiguity, Emily thought. *No room whatsoever for misinterpretations.*

She cursed under her breath, forcing herself to *think*. The demon had her over a barrel—and it knew it. If she turned down the bargain, she could simply be returned to the statue and left there for a few hours—or days. Trapped in that living hell, unable even to scream, she knew she would break eventually. And yet, something kept nagging at the back of her mind, something that didn't quite add up. The demon couldn't lie...

...But it can mislead, she thought. *And if it's trying to mislead me now...*

She met the immense yellow eyes as evenly as she could. "How are you even here?" she asked. "Robin summoned you, didn't he? You should have gone back to the Darkness when he died?"

The demon snorted. "Robin should really have been more careful when he made that deal with us," it said. "But he was so desperate to have you that he never bothered to consider the fine print."

Emily contemplated the puzzle for a long moment. "You trade blood—energy—in exchange for spells," she said, finally. "Your deal allowed you to claim the remainder of his energy when he died, which allowed you to remain close to me."

"Correct," the demon said. It gave her the kind of look a particularly irate teacher would give a moron who'd stumbled on the correct answer. "And you couldn't banish me because it wasn't you who *summoned me*."

"Robin was going mad," Emily said, slowly. "No *wonder* he didn't look at the deal very closely."

"He tried hard to be quite specific," the demon informed her. Its voice dripped with malicious amusement. "It was really quite elegant, the way he worded the bargain. If you hadn't had a few extra protections, my dear girl, you would be his devoted slave right now."

"And you goaded him into it," Emily said.

"Humans are really quite simple," the demon said. It made a show of shrugging its shoulders dramatically. "None of you are actually *imaginative*. It's always power, long life, or women...or men, sometimes. Watching how you screw yourselves up is always amusing."

"And you kept giving them spells that damaged their minds," Emily said. "Why?"

The demon leered, again. "Why not?"

It hung in the air, mocking her. "Have you never taken pleasure in someone else's pain?"

"No," Emily said.

"Liar," the demon said. "Did you not enjoy watching Melissa suffer because of the pranks you played on her?"

Emily felt a stab of guilt. Alassa had dragged her into the pranking war throughout first and second year, although they'd slowed during third year and stopped altogether after fourth year. And yes, there had been times when she'd enjoyed it.

"Melissa could strike back," she said. "She *did* strike back."

"You still enjoyed it," the demon said. It paced around the mental plane, then slipped up behind her to whisper in her ear. "And that opened the path to greater malice, did it not?"

"I didn't," Emily said.

"But others did," the demon countered. It put its lips next to her ear. She felt nothing, not even a hint of breath. "And once you start crossing lines, my dear, it's easy to cross the next one. And the next. And the next. And then you lose all sense of right and wrong."

"Damn you," Emily said.

"Quite," the demon agreed.

Emily looked into the mists, but saw nothing. "Why do you do this?"

The demon stepped in front of her, recapturing her attention. "It's funny."

Robin was insane, Emily thought, again. Something kept nagging at the back of her mind, something important. *Robin was insane, and that meant...*

She looked up at the demon. "You said I'd make the bargain," she challenged. "What sort of bargain will I make?"

"I can't answer that question," the demon said.

Emily held its inhuman gaze. "Can't, or won't?"

She smiled as everything suddenly fell into place. Robin had been insane; he'd made an incredibly bad bargain because he'd been too far gone to notice the loophole. And the demon *could* have waited until *she* was insane too, if it had wanted *her* to make an equally bad bargain. The demon had her over a barrel, true...but she had it over a barrel too. If she didn't go back to her own time, all the demonic prophecies would be completely invalid...

...And if *that* happened, she had a feeling that it *would* cause the demons more problems than they could handle.

They depend on everything falling into place, she thought. *And they have very little wiggle room.*

"You need me to get back relatively sane," she said. "And you're in a poor position to bargain."

The demon snorted. "So are you," it pointed out. "I could put you back in the stone for the next five hours, you know."

"But you won't," Emily said, with a confidence she didn't entirely feel. "You need me to complete the time loop. And I won't do that if I go mad."

"How true," the demon said. "But tell me. Are you *sure* you *really* understand what's going on?"

"Yes," Emily said.

She pushed on before the demon could say a word. "This is what I want," she said. "I want to be petrified, my body and thoughts frozen in time, until ten minutes after my past self touches me. To me, it is to seem like an instant between now and the moment I wake up. A blink of an eye. Nothing more."

"Of course," the demon said. "We wouldn't want you messing up the timeline because you've gone insane."

Emily took a breath. She could ask to be healed, but she doubted the demon could be trusted to do it properly.

"And this room is to remain hidden until Cabiria and I come along," she added, carefully. Cabiria had entered the statue room first, after all. She might just have avoided a major hiccup by the skin of her teeth. "No one else is to enter until the time-loop closes."

The demon smiled. "Close shave there, eh? You wouldn't want to miss anything important."

Emily looked it in the eye, ignoring the jibe. "Why me?"

"Destiny is tangled around you," the demon said. It rubbed its hands together with amused glee. "And the choices you make will reshape the world."

Its smile twisted into a bitter grimace. "For better or worse."

Emily frowned. What did it mean?

The demon gave her no time to think about it. "And how much are you prepared to pay for it?"

"You *have* to send me back," Emily said. She fought down the urge to match it, smirk for smirk. "I don't have to pay at all."

"You do," the demon said. "There's always a *balance*, human. Everything must be paid for."

It leaned forward. "I will honor my side of the bargain," it said. "But in exchange I want two things from you. First, I want your word that you will not destroy either of the two books Lord Whitehall asked you to take into the future. And second, I want some of your blood."

Emily shuddered. She'd had more than enough experience with blood magic to know that giving a demon some of her blood would be disastrous. There were spells to cut the ties between her blood and herself—she used them religiously—but she had no idea how effective they'd be against a demon. Blood magic had always been a danger to her, if only because she had no close relatives in the Nameless World. There was no risk of the magic becoming confused, unsure who to target.

And I can't destroy the books, she thought. Whitehall had asked her to destroy the books, yet he hadn't made her swear an oath. And yet, she didn't want to disappoint him. *There's nothing stopping me from handing them over to someone else to destroy—or merely throwing them into a pocket dimension and forgetting the coordinates...*

She forced herself to think. If she was right, if the demon *had* to help her, she had more bargaining power than it wanted her to think. But if she was wrong...

I have to be right, she thought. *They have to give people what they ask for, even when it isn't precisely what they want. And if all those visions of the future are suddenly rendered invalid...what happens to the deals they made with the DemonMasters?*

"I can swear not to destroy the books," she said, wondering if the demon would insist on closing the loopholes. Demons were supposedly subtle, but it had left her a loophole big enough to drive a car through. Or did it *want* her to cheat in some way? "But you can't have any of my blood."

"I *need* your blood, freely given," the demon stated. "There *has* to be some trade."

Emily swallowed. Just for a second, the demon had looked disconcertingly like a drug addict.

But it might be telling the truth, she thought. *If the demons draw on power—on life—it might explain why they don't already rule the world.*

"Very well," she said. "And the blood..."

She glared at the demon as it looked up, eagerly. Blood...for all she knew, the demon planned to lay claim to a gallon or two of her blood. She wouldn't survive that, any more than she would survive a demand for a pound of flesh. And the demon wouldn't be amused by an argument that it should *only* take a *pound*, no more. It had the power to make sure it kept the letter of the agreement if it wished.

"I give you a droplet or two of blood," Emily said, carefully. If she didn't set the terms with no wiggle room, the demon would take advantage of her. "No more than two or three milliliters. And I get to separate the blood from me first."

"Well," the demon said. "Of *course.*"

Emily paused. "And the blood cannot be used for anything else."

"I will use it to complete the bargain," the demon said. "And nothing else. But you must not destroy the books."

Emily closed her eyes for a long moment. She had a feeling that she wasn't going to get anything else, not when she was in such a poor bargaining position. And yet, the loophole was still open, taunting her. She might not be able to destroy the books, but she could render them useless. The demons would never be able to use them to cause havoc in the future...

"Very well," she said, again. "Do it."

"Cut your palm," the demon ordered.

Emily frowned, inwardly, as she reached into her belt and found the knife she'd borrowed from Julianne. They were on the mental plain. She could cut her palm all she wished and no blood would flow. Or was the mere act of cutting her palm symbolic, granting the demon permission to take what it wished? She was tempted to ask, but she suspected the demon wouldn't give her a straight answer. It might not even have one.

She made a cut in her palm, wincing at the pain. Blood—or the impression of blood—welled up onto her skin. She muttered the spell to separate the blood from herself, hoping that it would work properly. The demon might have given its word, but she knew better than to trust it. There might be a loophole she'd missed.

"Two droplets," she said. The pain was real—or was it? "Where do you...?"

The demon sprang forward, grabbing hold of her wrist in an unbreakable grip. She yelped and tried to pull back, but it was impossible. It bent over, a long leathery tongue—impossibly long—emerging from its mouth and licking at her palm. She shuddered in horror at the sensation, struggling against the disgust that threatened to make her throw up. And then the demon let her go, blood dripping from its teeth. Its tongue caught the last droplets before they could fall into the mists.

"Very tasty," it said.

"Fuck you," Emily managed. She felt dirty, horribly violated. Her palm felt as though it would never be clean again. She rubbed it against her dress, but the sensation refused to disappear. "You..."

"I'm afraid we lack the equipment for such...matters," the demon said. It was laughing at her! She felt a hot spike of anger mixed with embarrassment and forced herself to calm down before she did something stupid. "Although a few of the DemonMasters believe otherwise."

It lowered its voice, as if it was confiding a secret. "You won't believe what some of those guys are up to."

"I don't want to know," Emily said.

The demon shrugged. "Time is pressing," it said. "Are you ready?"

Emily nodded, curtly. "Do it."

The demon raised its fingers, snapping them in the air...

...And the world blinked.

Chapter Thirty-Eight

D UST. DUST EVERYWHERE.
  Emily cursed her own mistake as she swallowed hard, then hastily cast a spell—using her dwindling reserves—to filter the air. She'd forgotten the dusty air. Her past self had left the chamber with Cabiria and the spell, as she'd planned and the demon had promised, had worn off shortly afterwards, returning her body to normal. She'd felt stiff, the last time she'd been turned into stone, but this time she felt almost normal, save for the tiredness plaguing her bones. Maybe she was just too tired to feel stiff.

She stumbled forward, carefully picking her way down the corridor and out of the chamber before her past self—her contemporary self—returned. The statue of her couldn't be there, as she recalled. Professor Locke had to dismiss the statue as nothing more than an illusion, just as she remembered. The wards felt normal, pulsing against her mind; this time, she sensed a faint acceptance within them that marked her as one of the founders. No, the *last* of the founders. Whitehall and the others were long since dust.

They didn't recognize me before now, she thought, numbly. *Or perhaps they did—they let me twist aspects of themselves against Shadye...*

She forced herself to remember the twists and turns of the underground passageways as she heard the sound of her past self heading back down the corridor. There should be a door...there. She slipped through the door, then sent a mental command into the wards; the door slid closed, then vanished. No one could find it, let alone break in, without access to the control systems. And that level of access had long since gone.

Until now, she thought. *I can manipulate the school at will.*

She sagged against the wall, then sat down and took a long moment to gather herself. How long had it been since she'd eaten, since she'd had a chance to rest? The wards pulsed around her as she drew on them for strength, even though she knew she'd pay for it later; she'd have to sneak up to the surface long enough to find a cache of food before the school started its long collapse into rubble. She scanned the underground tunnels, watching through the wards as Professor Locke led her past self into one of the power control rooms, then closed her eyes as the entire school rearranged itself. Professor Locke had inadvertently triggered a defense system.

The wards have grown, Emily thought.

She shook her head in awe. It was a shame that Master Wolfe had not lived long enough to see what his work had become. He'd *definitely* been a genius. His network of spells had adapted to changing circumstances until they'd developed a form of intelligence in their own right. She wondered, absently, just what had happened between her disappearance and the tunnels being sealed, then dismissed the thought. The remains of the Manavore—the twists in the pocket dimensions under the school—would have discouraged anyone from exploring long before Bernard had closed and hidden the gates.

He probably thought it would be better if no one had access to the control room, she decided, as she stumbled to her feet. Her body felt tired and worn, but she couldn't rest just yet. *And as long as he kept the link to the wards, he was probably right.*

She checked the wards to make sure the path was clear, then placed the books in the sealed chamber before she started to make her way to the upper levels. No one would come to steal either of the Books of Pacts, ensuring she would have time to hide them within a pocket dimension and throw away the key. She *would* keep her word to the demon, she told herself; she wouldn't *destroy* the books. But they'd be rendered completely unusable. No one could hope to find them, even if they had her under their control. The coordinates of the dimension would be completely scrambled.

And if I hurl them into the future, she thought, *they'll be lost forever.*

Her fingers traced the covers of the books as she frowned. They felt...dead, as if something was gone. Even the aura of evil seemed much diminished. Perhaps she was now blind to their evil—she'd carried a demon on her shoulder for nearly a week—or perhaps it was gone altogether. The demons bound within the book might be gone too. And that meant...what?

She contemplated the problem as she made her way to the gates. The demon must have known she'd intended to cheat it, yet it had left a gaping loophole that allowed her to honor her word to Lord Whitehall as well as keep the letter of her bargain. *That* seemed odd. It had had her in a blind. Surely it could have driven a harder bargain, *knowing* that she would take the bargain. Had there been a way to jump forward in time without its help after all? Or had its *real* goal been to render the books useless?

Or perhaps it wanted some of my blood, she thought. *But I made sure to render the blood useless first.*

She shook her head. If she'd made a mistake, if she'd been pushed into doing something terribly stupid, she'd find out sooner or later. But she'd seen no alternative.

Whitehall was in chaos, students stumbling around trying to find their classrooms and bedrooms; she passed unnoticed through the throng as she made her way into the kitchen pantry. Sneaking into the pantry was an old tradition at the school, she reminded herself as she hastily located a box of preserved ration bars, but using the wards to ensure she could neither be detected nor caught was probably cheating. She made a mental note to make sure she paid for the supplies as she found a trunk and stuffed it with paper and pencils as well as food and drink, then levitated it back down to the gates. It wouldn't be too long before Grandmaster Gordian started trying to interrogate the wards, pinning down precisely what had happened.

They won't tell him I'm in two places at once, she reassured himself. She had to smile darkly at the thought of just what he'd say, when—if—he discovered that she had more access rights to the ward network than he did. But perhaps it would be better to keep it to herself. *They won't tell him I'm here until too late.*

There were no guards on the gates as she walked into the lower levels, then down into the underground complex. The wards were already going to work, cleaning the dust and filtering the air, although it would be days before she could walk through the complex without using wards to keep the dust out of her mouth. She hurried down to the second level, bypassing the trap that had snarled her and Cabiria last time and paused outside the control room. It would be so much easier to take the books now, wouldn't it? But her recollections insisted that she'd seen the books *before* they'd vanished.

I did take them, she thought, morbidly. Professor Locke had been right, after all, when he'd accused Emily of stealing the books. *But I hadn't taken them when they forced an oath from me.*

She checked the control complex, then walked through a hidden door into Master Wolfe's chamber. It looked as if no one had set foot in the room since his death—she felt a sudden stab of burning rage at how casually Keldor had murdered such a man—and the bedding was nothing more than dust, but it would make a safe place to hide while she waited. She dumped the trunk of food on the floor, opened a bottle of water and drank it gratefully, then tucked into a ration bar. Sergeant Miles had been right when he'd complained that they tasted like cardboard—it seemed to be a universal rule—but they would keep her alive. With a little work, she shouldn't need to leave the chamber until the time came to take the books.

I'll have to go steal some bedding too, she thought, as she finished her meal. *I won't be able to sleep on the stone floor.*

She checked the wards again, making sure her past self was safe, then sat down at Master Wolfe's desk, placing a large sheet of paper in front of her. Using a memory charm to jog her thoughts, she slowly worked her way through everything that would have to happen; the theft of the books, the slow collapse of the pocket dimension, Frieda's disappearance...she'd have to force herself to do nothing, when that happened. Her recollections insisted that Frieda had been trapped and there was nothing she could do to change it. All she could do was make sure that Frieda survived.

And I'll have to master blood magic, she reminded herself. *I'm going to need it.*

The thought made her shudder. To reach into someone's mind, to alter their perceptions until they were biddable...it was unthinkable. And to do it to *herself*...she'd heard enough horror stories about students who'd cast compulsion charms on themselves to know it wasn't something to do lightly. She and her past self—her other self—were essentially the same person, after all. They might blur together into one mentality if she screwed up the spell.

And there's no time to practice, she added, as she rose to her feet. It was nearly night; the lights would be going out all over the castle. She was tempted to try her luck sneaking around without the wards, just to see if she could avoid being caught, but she pushed the thought out of her mind before it could tempt her *too* much. *And who could I practice on?*

She slipped back upstairs, then headed to the Armory to steal some bedding. Having access to the wards made it far too easy to avoid the handful of wards Sergeant Miles had placed around the section and remove a bedroll, a chamberpot and some additional supplies. There was no shower within the chamber, nothing she could use to take a bath or wash herself thoroughly; she silently promised herself that she'd sneak into the upper levels long enough to take a shower, once her past self was safely out of the way. Unless that ran the risk of someone seeing her twice and wondering why she was in two places at once...

...Or why she had a scar covering her cheek.

I just have to be careful, she reminded herself. She could have the scar healed, after her past self was dispatched into the nexus point. *Very careful.*

She closed her eyes and slept as soon as she returned to the chamber, after setting the wards to alert her if someone passed through the gates and entered the underground complex. Her dreams were odd, half-remembered flickers of memory that faded almost as soon as she opened her eyes. She couldn't help wondering, as she forced herself awake the following morning, if the demon had given her a little parting gift, although she knew it could easily be caused by close proximity to her past self. She tested and retested her mental defenses, then ate breakfast before settling down to work. She'd only get one shot at sending her past self back in time...

History says I will succeed, she told herself, firmly. *But it could be wrong.*

It was the waiting that got to her, she discovered, over the next few weeks. She'd never deliberately sought out someone else's company since she'd been taken from Earth, but she couldn't help feeling trapped and isolated in the ancient chamber. It would be easy, she kept thinking, to walk up to the other levels and spend some time with Frieda, Caleb or the Gorgon, yet it would run the risk of shattering the timeline. She raided the library, read countless books and worked hard to catch up with her schoolwork while waiting, but she still felt alone.

I should rewrite the history books, she thought, one evening. She'd reread all the history books she'd read in first year and noted just how many inaccuracies were classed as gospel truth. *Professor Locke would appreciate it.*

She shook her head at the thought. Whitehall—Lord and Master Whitehall—hadn't quite lived up to his reputation, while others were distorted or simply erased from the history books. There was no mention of Master Chambers or Master Gila, as far as she could tell; Master Keldor was barely mentioned, his writings long-since lost to time. But there was no suggestion that he'd betrayed Whitehall. Perhaps the *real* Whitehall had chosen to suppress that part of history, knowing that no one would reveal the truth. It wouldn't do to have anyone think he could make a mistake.

The thought caused her a stab of pain. To her, Bernard and Julianne were living, breathing individuals; to history, they were dust and less than dust. She would never see them again, unless they'd found a way to fall forward into the future. Their children—somehow, she was sure Bernard and Julianne would have had children—were dust. If there were any descendants left, it was unlikely they knew anything about their ancestors. The Grandmasters would hardly have welcomed anyone who had a claim on their school.

And now, I have a claim on the school, she thought. *Gordian is really not going to like that.*

She tossed the problem around and around in her mind as the days passed, one by one, until Professor Locke and his unwilling assistants stumbled across the library and the control room. Emily watched from a safe distance as Professor Locke, already consumed with the burning urge to uncover the secrets of the ancients before he died, touched the console and triggered another series of defenses. As soon as they were on their way back upstairs, she slipped into the library, carefully dismantled the protective wards and placed the books and scrolls within her trunk. One of the books was clearly a long-dead Book of Pacts—she wondered, absently, if it had been Robin's—but the others were utterly irreplaceable.

I'm sorry, she thought, thinking of her past self. Professor Locke was going to accuse her of stealing the books, even though she was innocent. *But I suppose I got told off before I actually did the crime.*

She took the books back to her chamber and started to go through them, using the wards to keep the fragile parchment intact. Most of Master Wolfe's notes were there—she couldn't help noticing that several other people had added their own impressions afterwards—enough to let her complete the work her past self had begun. Or would begin, several weeks in the future...she scribbled a series of notes to herself, working out the sequence of events, then finished hunting through the pile of books and scrolls. The final scroll practically leapt into her hand the moment she touched it, magic flickering around it. She cursed her own carelessness as she checked the spell, realizing that the scroll was tied to her magic. It was a more subtle spell than she would have expected from the past.

The spell seemed safe enough, so she carefully unrolled the parchment and began to read. It wasn't easy; Bernard—his sigil was at the top of the sheet—had written in a language she didn't know, using an alphabet she didn't recognize. She cast several different spells to help her translate the words, but none of them seemed to work perfectly. Far too many words were hazy, suggesting that the spell couldn't decipher them completely.

Emily, she read. *If you are reading this...*

She felt the tears well up, again, as she worked her way through the scroll. Bernard and Julianne *had* had children, one of them named after Emily herself. She shook her head—Emily was an uncommon name, suggesting that history had forgotten the other Emily—and then read onwards. Bernard admitted, gently, that the stories surrounding her had already gotten out of hand, even after his father-in-law had started trying to suppress them. It hadn't been until later, much later, that Whitehall had told Bernard the truth.

We argued, Bernard wrote. *I accused him of trying to hide your involvement, of trying to hide everyone's involvement. We were arguing so badly that I didn't quite believe it when he told me that you were from the future. We nearly fought a duel over it.*

Emily stared. Whitehall and Bernard had nearly fought a duel? Bernard hadn't believed his old master? But he would have found the truth unbelievable...

And then he stopped telling everyone about me, Emily thought. The Dark Lady would become a half-remembered myth, a woman who might well not have existed at all. Her stories would grow and change until they were completely unrecognizable. *And that ensured that history remained on course.*

The last section noted that the tunnels would be sealed, ensuring that no one could gain access to the control spellware. Reading between the lines, Emily suspected that someone *had* tried to do just that...Bernard referred to a handful of events without actually going into details. It was frustrating—he'd probably assumed she could just look up the details in a history book—but there was nothing she could do about it. Her friends had long since passed away, leaving a legacy that had changed the world.

She read the final line, then closed her eyes in pain. To her, Bernard, Julianne and Lord Whitehall were living, but they had lived and died nearly a thousand years in the past. She would never see them again; no one would. And so much had been forgotten that the full story would never be known. It would be buried in the depths of history...

I'm sorry, she thought. *I wish...*

She blinked away tears, then rolled up the scroll and went back to work. Master Wolfe's notes, books "borrowed" from the Black Vault, her own observations...she had everything she needed to plan her next move. And when her past self came to fix the damage Professor Locke had inadvertently inflicted on the school, she'd be ready.

And then I can step back into the school, she thought. She couldn't wait to see everyone again. She'd seen a few of her friends through the wards, before she'd forced herself not to do it again. Looking at Caleb had only made her heart ache. *And perhaps the rest of the term will pass uneventfully.*

The thought made her smile, sardonically. She knew she wouldn't get her wish.

Chapter Thirty-Nine

*H*ERE WE GO, EMILY THOUGHT, WATCHING AS HER PAST SELF RAN INTO THE CONTROL ROOM and blasted Professor Lombardi. Professor Jayne had barely any time to react before she was hexed too, although she shrugged off the hex within seconds. *Here we go...*

Her past self touched the column and thrust her mind into the network. Emily altered the wards just a little, enough to ensure that neither of the professors could intervene, then touched the control systems herself. The repair work was already well underway, but it was inadequate. She cringed at the thought of just how close they'd come to complete disaster as she started to complete the job, fixing mistakes in the programming as soon as her past self made them. It wasn't an easy task, but she had the advantage of knowing precisely what she'd done in the seemingly recent weeks of hard work to identify and devise solutions to each of the problems.

And some of my additions held even after the entire structure started to collapse, she thought, morbidly. She checked on the tutors as her past self finished the job. They didn't seem inclined to interfere, thankfully. Emily didn't want to hurt either of them. *The rest of the programming could be smoothed out too.*

She shook her head, hastily. Master Wolfe's core programming was still in existence, even though it had grown until it was almost unrecognizable, but she doubted that smoothing it out would be a good idea. Unpicking every last spell component would take decades; it made her think, suddenly, of some of the stories she'd heard about *really* old computers. They'd had programs that ran, automatically, at preset times...and no one, at least no one still working for the owners, had known what they did, or why they'd been written.

And they were afraid of what would happen if they took them out of the system, she recalled, wryly. *They just didn't want to rock the boat.*

Her past self tried to scan the school for the books. Emily *pushed*, hard; she thrust her past self right out of the network. She watched through the wards, grimly, as Professor Lombardi put her past self to sleep, then levitated her up and out of the chamber. He was going to bear a grudge, she suspected, even though he had forsaken—or would forsake—the right of vengeance. She, a mere student, had blasted an experienced professor into the wall.

My grades are going to suffer, she thought. Professor Lombardi would probably be justified in demanding higher standards from her now, although his standards were already terrifyingly high. *And Professor Jayne won't be much better.*

She watched and listened, through the wards, as Professor Lombardi told Grandmaster Gordian what had happened. Emily couldn't help wondering—not for the first time—just how strong the temptation had been, for Gordian, to slit her throat while she slept. But he merely listened to the explanation, without saying a word. Perhaps he was a better man than she'd thought.

And it's time to make the final set of preparations, she told herself. *And if I mess this up, history is screwed.*

Gordian, thankfully, had banned all further visits to the control room, using the wards to seal the chamber. He hadn't realized—yet—that *Emily* would always be able to go in and out of the chamber, unless she removed her own access permissions from the spellware. Hell, Professor Locke would never have *discovered* the chamber in the first place, if Emily hadn't been with him. She checked to make sure he *was* taken out of the castle, as Gordian had told her, then started to work. Blood magic was complex and dangerous even when used on a different person.

And all my defenses will be useless against myself, she thought. *And her thoughts might slip into my mind.*

The nexus point, she discovered as she went to work, existed at all points of time simultaneously. She couldn't help wondering if it was linked to the demons in some manner—they too existed outside normal space and time—although it didn't *seem* to have a will of its own. And yet, setting up the equations to send her past self back in time proved a daunting challenge, particularly as she had to pop out at a specific point. She had a feeling that it might be easier to jump to another nexus point—she'd heard stories of people walking into one nexus point and coming out of another—but she worked on the problem until she thought she had a solution. If she appeared a handful of seconds before her magic started to weave itself into the spells taming the nexus point, it should work.

She rubbed her forehead as she hurried back to the chamber to get some sleep. Just how far *could* history be bent before unleashing havoc? She had no idea...she swore, under her breath, as she realized the demon might have been bluffing. Demonic predictions *had* to come true, didn't they? And all but one of the predictions involving her had yet to take place...she might just have been able to force the demon to help anyway or risk setting off a cascade of failure. And who knew what would have happened then?

I suppose I will never know, she thought.

The wards alerted her the moment her past self awoke and spoke to the Grandmaster, before asking Caleb to share a bed with her. Emily watched, feeling oddly annoyed at her own conduct; Caleb had his flaws, but he was no Robin. Or Bernard, for that matter. His mother would never have let him get away with treating women like *objects*, as if their thoughts and feelings were of no concern. And he was a good man. She made a quiet resolution in the privacy of her own mind, then walked into the nexus chamber and cast a series of wards into the air. It was vitally important, she knew, that her past self never laid eyes on her.

She checked the wards, carefully, as soon as she walked into the nexus chamber. Her past self was lying in Caleb's arms, looking surprisingly content. Emily flushed at the thought, then cut her palm and used the blood to draw out a trio of runes on the stone floor. Her awareness of her other self grew stronger, so strong that it nearly dragged her into sleep. She'd never heard of *that* being a problem, not when blood magic had been used elsewhere, but how often did people cast blood magics on themselves? It didn't happen.

Gritting her teeth, fighting against a whirlpool that threatened to drag her into a maelstrom, she reached out through the connection and jerked her past self awake. The surge of emotion surprised her, even though she'd prepared for it as best as she could. She hadn't quite realized what it *meant*, not when they were the same person. There was no difference between their thoughts.

Get up, she thought, as the link grew stronger. She sent a whole series of calming impressions, trying to make sure there was no flash of anger or fear that would break the spell. *Get out of bed.*

She pushed the call forward as strongly as she dared, battling hard to keep her past self calm and composed. The flurry of emotions told her, as if she hadn't already known, that her past self knew that *something* was wrong; she held the spell in place, tugging at her mind to make it harder for her past self to form a coherent thought. If anything, she thought, she'd underestimated the power of blood magic. A more ruthless practitioner could use blood magics to bind someone to him permanently.

The world seemed to blur around her. Gritting her teeth, she split her attention; one half keeping her past self under control, the other half opening doors and making sure that there was no one in a position to intercept the sleepwalker before it was too late. A pair of girls were blocking her past self's way; she cast a strong compulsion charm, holding them both in place until her past self had made her way past them. Gordian would know that *something* was up—she hadn't been able to find a way to lock him out again without setting off all kinds of alarms—but he wouldn't be able to do anything. Or so she hoped.

He didn't, she told herself, firmly. *No one got in my way.*

Her past self moved slowly, too slowly. But there was no way to force her to move faster, not without risking everything. She didn't dare lose control, not now. If she did, her past self might be able to put up defenses or scream for help. Either one would be disastrous. She pushed more and more calming impressions into her target's mind, trying to block the growing awareness that she was being compelled by an outside force. She couldn't afford to let go, not yet.

A flash of magic impinged on her attention. Gordian was awake and, unfortunately, aware that something was wrong. She hastily uploaded new orders into the wards, locking Gordian out completely. She'd probably be made to pay for it afterwards, but she found it hard to care. It was too difficult keeping her grip on her past self while, at the same time, fending off Gordian's increasingly desperate attempts to regain control of the wards. He'd uploaded some commands of his own, it seemed, after the command network was repaired.

He's got a short memory, she thought, nastily. *Didn't he realize that meddling with the system was what damaged it in the first place?*

She sucked in her breath as Gordian blasted his bedroom door with a hex she didn't recognize, blowing it off its hinges and sending the wood crashing to the stone floor. He ran out of the room, hurrying down towards the gates. Emily split her attention—again—and barred his path, altering the corridor so it led right to the top of the castle. Gordian ran into the old barracks and stopped, dead. She hastily repaired the damage she'd done to the corridor, leaving him with ten flights of stairs to run down before he could get to the nexus point.

Her past self stopped, struggling to break free. Emily felt sweat running down her face as she reasserted control, forcing her past self to keep moving. It would have been easier, she thought, to use a direct compulsion spell—the one Robin had thrown at her hovered at the back of her mind—but her past self might well have fought it off. And besides, she needed Void's protections one last time.

Or Robin would have had me, Emily thought. *And any hope of maintaining the timeline would be lost forever.*

She concentrated on her past self and pushed her into the corridor leading to the nexus chamber, carefully freezing or deactivating a wide range of hexes intended to keep curious students and intruders out of the area. They hadn't bitten her before, she recalled, but there was no point in taking chances. Shadye had walked through the defenses, seemingly untouched; she was fairly sure Shadye wasn't a founder. Unless he was related to one of them...she dismissed the thought with a flicker of irritation. If Shadye *had* been related to Whitehall or Wolfe or any of the others, it hadn't helped him. He'd been such a poor magician that he'd turned to necromancy and lost his mind.

Maybe he was related to Master Chambers, she thought, darkly. *He took a whole string of shortcuts too.*

Emily glanced back at Gordian and swore, savagely, as she realized he was literally *flying* down the stairs. She hastily quashed the impulse to interfere with his spell, knowing it would send him slamming into a stone wall; instead, she twisted the dimensions around him, trying to send him back upstairs. But it didn't work as well as she'd hoped. Gordian had reached out and infiltrated the local command system, making it harder for her to trap him. He was a better magician than she'd realized...

Is that a honest judgement, her own thoughts mocked, *or did you feel he was inferior because you didn't like him?*

She slammed two doors in his path, then reactivated the defenses. Neither would slow him for long—she had no idea if the defenses would target the Grandmaster at all and there was no time to rewrite their spellware—but it should buy her some time. She reached out to the spellware she'd pushed into the nexus point, bringing it online, commanding it to draw power from the nexus itself. The gateway to the past opened up in front of her past self, beckoning her forward. But she stopped.

Emily bit her tongue to keep from swearing as her past self stood in front of the nexus point, swaying on her feet. The blood had turned black, like the sigils in the Book of Pacts; it was no longer usable for magic. And her past self was free.

Move forward, Emily urged, silently. Gordian was running down the corridor at terrifying speed, magic spinning around him as he readied himself for battle. *Move, you stupid...*

Her past self started to turn. Emily ran forward in desperate frustration, slamming into her contemporary self's back and shoving her into the nexus point. Her contemporary self fell, her entire body twisting in directions Emily's mind couldn't quite grasp. It was all she could do, as she hastily cancelled the spells, not to fall into the gateway herself. If she did...

...Would she have been forced to repeat everything, again and again?

She stumbled and collapsed to her knees, suddenly very tired. The nexus point was glimmering in front of her, calling her on. She wondered, vaguely, what would happen if she walked into it, now the spells were gone. Would she *really* be trapped inside? Or would she emerge warped and twisted, if she emerged at all? Somehow, she pulled herself to her feet and cast a cleaning spell on the floor, destroying all the evidence of her blood ritual. Gordian probably had plenty of grounds to expel her, if he wished, but there was no point in giving him extra ammunition.

The Grandmaster burst through the door, wearing a long nightshirt that looked like a tattered old robe. He stared at Emily in shock, one hand raised in a casting pose; she braced herself, unsure what would happen if he tried to curse her. She'd rebuilt her defenses as best as she could, while she waited under the school, but Gordian was a formidable magician and she was so—so—tired. She wasn't even sure what had woken him in the first place.

"Emily," Gordian said, finally. "What *have* you been doing?"

He looked her up and down, his eyes disbelieving. Emily didn't really blame him. Her clothes were dusty and threatening to fall apart, her hair was practically grey from dust and her face and hands felt dry, too dry. And she stank. She'd been able to steal a few sponges to wash herself, but she hadn't dared go for a shower. There had been too much danger of accidentally being seen.

And he doesn't know how I took control of the wards, she thought. *She* still didn't know what had alerted him, if anything. Perhaps he'd just had a bad feeling and snapped awake. It wasn't as if he didn't have the right to cast monitoring spells, ones not connected to the wards or the nexus point. *He has to be worried...*

"It's a long story," she managed, finally. She *still* didn't like Gordian, but he had a right to know the truth. Besides, the kink in the timeline was now past. It wasn't as if she needed to dissemble any longer. Or hide what she could do. "Might I suggest that we go to your office and discuss it—alone?"

Gordian lifted his eyebrows. "After your last discussion in my office?"

Emily winced. To her, the last meeting had been months ago; to him, it had taken place only a few *hours* ago. She rubbed her forehead as she tried to think. From her point of view, she hadn't seen Caleb for months, but from his point of view she hadn't been gone at all. She had the feeling she was going to be suffering from something very much like jet lag for months to come.

"Yes, sir," she said. She took a long breath. She'd had jet lag before, after using portals to step across the entire continent in an instant, but this was going to be different. She was several months older, yet no one would ever know it. If nothing else, calculating her birthday would be a major headache. "We have to talk."

Gordian nodded and led her back upstairs. She wondered why he was being so trusting—*she* would have been deeply concerned about a student breaking into the nexus chamber—and then decided he probably already knew that things had changed. She'd twisted the school around him, after all. Perhaps she should be surprised he hadn't tried to stun her on sight. It wasn't as if he didn't have the power, particularly when she was so tired...

And he must be wondering just what the hell is going on, she thought. *His world has turned upside down.*

"Please, be seated," Gordian said, as they entered his office. He must have sent a message through the wards, because a servant entered a moment later, carrying two steaming mugs of Kava. She took a grateful sip, and smiled. She'd missed Kava, desperately. "Now...what were you doing in the nexus chamber?"

Emily took a deep breath. "I fell back in time," she said, finally. His eyes went wide with shock. "And I was there when the school was founded."

Chapter Forty

GORDIAN WAS A GOOD LISTENER, EMILY HAD TO ADMIT. HE DIDN'T INTERRUPT, HE DIDN'T ask useless questions; he just sat and listened to her with every appearance of attentiveness. She was careful to make it clear that there were few true secrets from the past, few spells that were genuinely superior to anything from their era; she was *very* careful not to discuss the mimic-spell in any real detail. It would make a hell of a weapon against the necromancers, she was sure, but in the wrong hands it would turn into a nightmare.

Or more of a nightmare, she thought, as she finished her story. *Master Wolfe thought he could use the spell to become immortal. Someone else is bound to have the same idea...*

She sighed, inwardly, sipping her Kava as he contemplated her. Professor Locke *would* be disappointed; hell, he'd be shocked if he ever worked out the truth. Whitehall was unique because later spellcrafters had accidentally streamlined the spellwork that went into tapping the nexus point and using the power to create the school. They'd actually done a better job of keeping the power under control, but it had precluded any realistic chance of developing an adaptive system, let alone a form of intelligence. It would be simple enough, now, to tap a new nexus point and turn it into a second Whitehall, yet it would take decades before the project came to fruition.

"I see," he said, finally. "And how much of that story is true?"

"All of it," Emily said. She scowled at him. She'd left out the details about the demon—and the bargain she'd made with it—but she hadn't told him any lies. "Would you like an oath?"

A conflicting flurry of emotions flickered across his face, then vanished. "That will not be necessary," he said, stiffly. "Your ability to influence the wards is quite enough."

Emily felt a sudden stab of pity. She *outranked* him, literally. The only people who could have removed her access rights to the wards were dead and gone, nearly a thousand years ago. She could shut him out, she could take the school for herself, she could...she shook her head, tiredly. She shouldn't even consider the possibilities unless there was no other choice.

"I don't intend to abuse it," she assured him.

"Good," Gordian said. She rather suspected that he needed time to think about everything that had happened, including the possible consequences. "I think you'll have to write out a true account of everything that happened, back in the past."

"I already have, sir," Emily said. She closed her eyes, remembering Whitehall and Chambers, Bernard and Robin; the Manavores, the Gathering, the Book of Pacts... she'd decided to leave some of the details out, although she had no intention of telling anyone that. The complete truth would only cause problems in the future. "It's just a short account, as factual as possible."

"I suggest you let me read it first," Gordian said.

Emily nodded, frowning as something fell into place. The demon might just have intended to manipulate her into allowing *knowledge* of demons to become common once again. Perhaps the *real* endgame lay there, with magicians starting to summon demons back into the Nameless World. And they would, she knew; Shadye and his ilk had driven themselves mad just to boost their power. Were the books, in the end, completely irrelevant? Or was she just jumping at shadows?

I'll be second-guessing myself a lot, in the future, she thought, bitterly. *And I may never know the truth.*

"And that leads neatly to another point," Gordian added. "What *did* happen to the books?"

"I took them, after I returned from the past," Emily confessed. "Leaving them in place would have upset the timeline."

"Oh," Gordian said. "I think they should be returned, don't you?"

"They should be kept in the Black Vault," Emily said, reluctantly. Giving up the books went against the grain, but she had to admit he had a point. Besides, *she* knew enough to recreate Master Wolfe's work...perhaps she could sell the knowledge to Mountaintop, if they'd managed to lay claim to a nexus point. "Some of them are quite dangerous."

She sighed, inwardly. The third Book of Pacts would be added to the others and then tossed into a pocket dimension. She *thought* it had expired long ago, but there was no way to be sure.

"Very well," Gordian said.

He sighed. "But everyone will try to travel in time now, won't they?"

"They can't," Emily said. "I used my own magics as a guide—anyone else will just be jumping blind."

"Really," Gordian said. "And if you succeeded...why not someone else?"

"I succeeded because I *had* succeeded," Emily explained. "What came first—the chicken or the egg?"

Gordian shook his head slowly. "I shall meditate on that," he said. "For the moment, perhaps the whole story should be kept secret."

Emily nodded. There *was* a loophole in what she'd told him. No one could jump back in time now, not without a navigational beacon, but Gordian *could* create a beacon for himself in the present and then jump backwards in time from the future. If, of course, the spellwork surrounding the nexus point was disposed to allow him. Emily hoped—prayed—that her tampering had made any future time jumping impossible.

It's too dangerous to mess with, she thought.

"I will keep it a secret," she said. "Perhaps some of the truth can be told another way."

"Perhaps," Gordian agreed. "Do you have anything else you want to tell me?"

"I want to become a teacher," Emily said. She'd taught Frieda and Julianne and quite a few others in the past. And she'd enjoyed it. "*That's* what I want to do with my life."

Gordian's face froze, just for a second. "You'll need experience," he said, finally. "But I dare say you have the"—his face twisted—"*clout* to win a post at Whitehall."

"Yes, sir," Emily said.

"We shall see," Gordian told her.

He rose. "You're excused from classes for the next two days, in any case," he added. "I believe Sergeant Miles wishes to...discuss...certain matters with you."

The theft of supplies from the Armory, Emily thought, numbly. Sergeant Miles would have noticed the supplies were missing. He had more of an eye for detail than just about every other magician she had met. *And he's not going to be pleased about it.*

"For what it's worth," Gordian told her, "you have my full approval if you wish to take him up on his offer."

Emily blinked. "His offer?"

"His offer," Gordian said. He looked her up and down, then sighed. "And I suggest you have a shower, perhaps more than one, before you go to bed."

"Yes, sir," Emily said. "I'll find and return the books tomorrow."

She'd expected worse, she thought, as she left his office. Gordian had every reason to be angry with her, even though she'd had very good reasons for preventing him from entering the nexus chamber ahead of time. But she *did* have access to the wards. Trying to expel her might have been difficult, particularly as she'd made it clear she wanted to stay. Maintaining the *status quo* might have been the best of a set of bad options.

She climbed the stairs slowly, feeling the school welcoming her. She'd grown to like the old castle, but the new one was her home. She wondered, as she turned into the dorms, if she could draw memories from the wards. It would be nice to watch her friends live the rest of their lives, building the school and taking the war to the Manavores...

...But she wouldn't be able to help them, not any longer.

They succeeded, she told herself, as she slipped into the bedroom. *They succeeded in founding a whole new era, and that's all that matters.*

Caleb was still asleep, one hand reaching out to where she'd been, two hours and three months ago. She watched him for a long moment, then turned and hurried into the shower, tearing her dusty clothes off and dropping them on the floor. They'd practically turned into dust themselves; she summoned a dressing gown from her closet as she closed the door and turned on the running water. Stepping under the warm water felt like heaven; she closed her eyes and luxuriated, feeling the dust falling off her body and vanishing into the drain. She reached for the bottle of soap, without opening her eyes, and scrubbed herself thoroughly. It felt as if she was removing layers upon layers of dirt, grime and dust.

And how often, she asked herself, *did I think I would never be clean again?*

It felt like hours before she turned off the water, rubbed herself down with a towel and looked in the mirror. She'd expected to see bruises all over her body, but they were long gone; instead, she looked fit and healthy and reassuringly normal.

She no longer looked out of place. Even the scar on her cheek had faded after she'd returned to the future.

She touched the scar lightly, then pulled the dressing gown on as she heard someone stirring outside. Cabiria wouldn't be coming back to the room, not until morning; she checked the wards and discovered that Cabiria was using another bedroom, granting Caleb and Emily some privacy. She felt a rush of affection as she stepped out of the shower and smiled as she saw Caleb sitting upright, looking at her.

"Caleb," she said. She darted across the room and hugged him tightly, pressing her lips against his. He seemed taken by surprise, but kissed her back. "I...I love you."

The admission surprised her. She'd missed him, more than she cared to admit; she sat on the bed and kissed him again and again, as if she didn't want to let go. She could tell he was surprised, but she didn't blame him. *He* thought it had only been a few hours since they'd gone to bed.

"Emily," he breathed. His hand touched her cheek, his eyes going wide. "What happened?"

"It's a long story," Emily said. She'd have to discuss it with him, then work some of what she'd learned into their joint project. "I can tell you..."

She stopped as she came to a decision. It scared her—perhaps it would always scare her—but perhaps it was also time to take the bull by the horns. She loved him and she liked him and she cared for him...

...And perhaps it was time to face some of her demons.

"Caleb," she said. She found herself suddenly grasping for words, feeling his body pressing against hers. Her heart was beating so loudly she thought he could hear it. "Caleb...take me to bed."

Epilogue

"B ITCH," TAMA MUTTERED. "FILTHY BITCH."

His body *hurt*. It felt as though he was nothing more than a walking bruise. His face hurt, his chest hurt and there was a dull throbbing pain between his legs that suggested that having children was now impossible. It was hard, so hard, to comprehend that he'd been beaten by a girl, a girl who had literally had her hands tied behind her back. She'd bested him with magic and she'd bested him without magic... cold savage hatred flared through him as he staggered to his feet. He was going to find her and he was going to do unspeakable things to her...

He stopped, dead, as he realized the implications. The bitch had escaped; he was *sure* she'd escaped. She'd escaped the punishment she should have faced for murdering Master Gila, she'd escaped Master Chambers' revenge after brutally slaughtering his apprentice...she just kept twisting until she got out of trouble. He didn't understand how she did it...no, he did; he understood all too well. She was spreading for Whitehall, offering him her body in exchange for illicit lessons and protection from other men. There could be no other explanation. A woman could manipulate a man in ways that no other man could match, convincing him that he was the master when, in truth, he was being ruled by his gonads, his mind blinded by lust and desire.

"Bitch," he snarled, again. "Unnatural bitch!"

Master Wolfe's body lay on the ground, very definitely dead. Tama searched it anyway, hoping to find something useful; there was nothing, save for a silver wand and a tiny stone knife, barely larger than his index finger. The latter felt odd in his hand, as if it had once touched great power, but no amount of poking unlocked its secrets. He turned to look at the control column and sighed. The magic surrounding it was far beyond his comprehension. He didn't have a hope of taking control for himself.

"Bastard," he swore. He checked Master Keldor's remains, but anything useful he might have carried had been burned to a crisp. Her spells, no doubt. *She* had been involved in creating the spells, hadn't she? Perhaps she was spreading for Master Wolfe too. How like a woman to urge a man to keep something precious for himself, when it should be shared with all. "Bastard."

He turned and kicked Master Wolfe's body, hard. It twitched.

Tama stared. Just for a moment, he recalled all the stories about corpses that rose from the grave and returned to extract a horrific revenge on the living. Master Keldor had studied death magics extensively. Perhaps he'd done something to his former friend. But the twitch didn't reoccur. Tama told himself, firmly, that he'd imagined it. He drew back his foot to administer another kick, striking Master Wolfe in the arm...

...And the corpse dissolved into eerie multicolored light, rising into the air.

Tama stared, unable to move. What *was* it? The pulsing cloud of magic felt almost like a living creature, but he'd never seen or heard of anything like it. A cold malevolent hunger assailed his mind, keeping him rooted to the spot even as he started to panic; he was convinced, all of a sudden, that he was being studied even though he couldn't see any *eyes.*

And then the cloud started to move forward.

His trance snapped. Tama turned to run...

But it was already far too late.

End of Book Ten

Emily Will Return In

The Sergeant's Apprentice

Afterword

Something that has always amused me, when I read certain fantasy (and even sci-fi) books is the endless quest to dig up and rediscover the knowledge of the past.

In some cases, this is justified. Magic largely slipped out of the world years before the events of *Jonathon Strange and Mr. Norrell*, so both of the titular characters have good reason to dig up old books and study them to see how old spells can be used in the modern world. In the world of *Mistborn*, the Lord Ruler buried so many secrets that digging them up forms a major part of the series. (This is averted in the *Wax and Wayne* sequel books, although it also is quite important in *Elantris*.) But in many other books—*The Black Magician* series, the *Foundation* series (yes, really)—this makes little sense.

Humans are incredibly inventive creatures. When we know something is possible, we can and we do duplicate it; when we have so much to build on, we can and do develop something more. Our modern society rests on the shoulders of giants— Galileo, Newton, Einstein—and future society will rest on the work of Stephen Hawking and his peers. In a world of magic, particularly one with a strong tradition of pushing the limits, I simply do not see why a past society should be radically more advanced than present-day society.

Certainly, there are things we don't understand about the past. The secrets of Roman bridge-building, for example, were lost somewhere in the decline and fall of the Roman Empire. But there is no way the Romans could match our society, when it comes to building bridges. The limits of their technology were just too far behind ours. One might get a very efficient steam engine, if one tried. But could it really outdo a modern car?

One of the core ideas of the *Schooled in Magic* series, as I see it, is that there are no secrets that will remain forever unknown and unknowable. Magical knowledge marches on—and while the Sorcerer's Rule may play a role akin to patent protection in our world, the knowledge that something is possible will spur other wizards to attempt to duplicate it. I didn't want—and I still don't—artifacts from a bygone age that are not only far superior to anything from the present day, but beyond understanding and duplication. (Mind you, I did have an idea for such artifacts being duplicated—eventually—but that will have to go in a whole different book.) This is a universe based on magic, rather than science, yet it is still functionally *rational*.

So why should Lord Whitehall and his comrades be vastly more capable than Grandmaster Hasdrubal and his?

They shouldn't.

It's actually interesting to study just how little we truly *know* about ancient history. Quite a bit of our understanding of the Roman Civil War and the rise (and assassination) of Julius Caesar comes from Cicero. But this has its limits—Cicero was hardly the mover and shaker he liked to think of himself as being. He had *some* influence, but—as Pompey noted—no actual power base. Or, if you want an example closer to our time, there was the strange affair of Edward IV and Eleanor Butler.

It was strongly suggested that Edward secretly married Eleanor Butler prior to his actual (and also secret, at first) marriage to Elizabeth Woodville, rendering his children with Elizabeth illegitimate.

Naturally, this was *very* convenient for Richard III. If Edward V (the older of the famed Princes in the Tower) was illegitimate, *Richard* was the legitimate king. But was this actually true? On one hand, it *does* fit Edward IV's known patterns—he married Elizabeth in secrecy, even to the point of seriously damaging England's international standing—but on the other hand, it only came out when Edward was dead and there was a strong party in the wings ready to take advantage of it.

Richard III—usurper or rightful king? We don't know.

The Nameless World doesn't know anything like as much about its past as it likes to think, something I have endeavoured to make clear. Nor did our own ancestors. The "truth" in many situations was often buried, forgotten or lost between a morass of claims and counter-claims. Trying to establish what really happened can be a nightmare, academic reputations resting on handfuls of documents that may have been mistranslated, forged or simply lacking in data. (Most early accounts of WW II made no mention of the Ultra Secret, for obvious reasons.) And that's not including headaches like politically-driven revisionist history or feminist retellings of the past where women were far more important (and equal) than they ever were in real life.

Our ancestors were *human*. Not one of them was wholly good or wholly bad. They were creatures of their era, born and raised in societies that were often quite different from ours in all sorts of ways. By our standards, Richard III was a figurative bastard who stole his nephew's birthright; by theirs, Richard was recovering the throne from a *literal* bastard who had no right to it. And far too much of what we "know" about the past simply isn't so.

I trust you enjoyed Emily's voyage to the past. If you did, please leave a review—every little bit helps.

Christopher Nuttall
Edinburgh, 2016

Appendix: Magic and the Magical Community Pre-Whitehall

The original human settlers of the Nameless World, although rather mystified by their arrival, did not realize at first that they were on a *mana*-rich world. Indeed, some of them never realized that they'd moved from world to world at all. However, it was not long before the *mana* started to take its toll on the human population. A small number of human children were warped by the *mana*, becoming the first magicians. Their powers materialized shortly afterwards, usually during puberty.

This was often disastrous. The magicians had very little understanding of how their powers worked or how to handle them. Random surges of magic tended to produce disastrous results, ranging from accidentally harming or killing their families to emotional storms and outright madness. Local communities rapidly started to kill the magicians out of hand, fearing that it was the only way to keep them from becoming a major threat. Only a handful of the early magicians remained sane long enough to escape their communities before it was too late.

Unknown to the magicians, their fits of madness were caused by attempts to channel more power through their minds than they could handle. (Later, similar problems would account for the madness brought on by necromancy.) Unaware of the dangers of pushing their powers too far, too quickly, they would often obtain great power at the cost of their rationality. Even if a magician was lucky enough to escape madness after one power surge, like Emily in *Trial by Fire/Wedding Hells*, repeated attempts to boost their power eventually tipped them over the edge. Magicians who survived so long rapidly acquired a reputation for being mad, bad, and dangerous to know.

That was not the only problem. Surges of power caused damage to their bodies: in men, it reduced sperm count; in women, it damaged or destroyed their eggs. Female magicians, assuming they survived long enough to have children, rarely managed to carry a child to term; male magicians rarely had more than one or two children. The "curse," as it came to be known, would later serve as justification for denying women magical training.

Matters were complicated by demons. A handful of magicians discovered that it was possible to summon demons and bargain with them, trading blood (life) for knowledge and services. These services often came with a sting in the tail; the demons might teach the magicians how to cast newer and better spells, but the spells would be impossible to edit and tended to have nasty side-effects. Quite a few spells were far more *mana*-intensive than they should be, ensuring further damage to the caster's mind and body. A number of magicians *did* realize the danger, but very few were willing to abandon demons entirely.

Despite these problems, the magical community was starting to take shape. An experienced magician—a master—would often take a younger magician as an apprentice, teaching him magic in exchange for loyalty and support. Two or three masters, in fact, would band together for mutual support, forming the very first communes. Small villages would tend to form around these magicians, often trading their services for protection; magician-dominated villages tended to be safer in uneasy times, despite the risks of working too close to magicians who might explode with rage as they sank into insanity.

It was Myrddin the Sane who laid the groundwork for the second great age of magic, although later historians barely recall his name. Myrddin was the last student of one of the first DemonMasters, a man whose collapse into madness was brought to an end by his student stabbing him in the chest. Myrddin—correctly—blamed his master's decline and fall on the hordes of demons he had summoned and bound to his service and resolved, privately, never to have anything further to do with demons. Although he assumed he would be doomed to remain a hedge wizard, Myrddin discovered that slowly testing and expanding his powers brought far better results, without the madness. Myrddin moved from commune to commune, teaching his spells to magicians who might otherwise have sold themselves to demons.

Myrddin's teachings spread rapidly, although many DemonMasters saw little value in them—and, later, saw them as a threat to their positions. Unlike nearly every other master, Myrddin actually spread his teachings openly; he encouraged—demanded—that everyone he taught spread the word as far as possible. He also took apprentices who, as part of their oaths, swore to forsake demons as much as possible. Lord Whitehall was the last and greatest of his apprentices (and also the only one history remembers, at least as far as it knows).

Unknown to Myrddin, his work helped trigger a different school of magic that would later be just as significant as anything else. Potions was regarded as the only activity suitable for girls—perversely, this was because it wasn't considered magic—and the daughters of magicians were encouraged to study brewing and take students of their own. Their brews, however, wouldn't work without magic; surprisingly, potions-brewing taught the precise control required, by magicians, to keep from falling into madness (and to avoid the curse.) The fits of madness brought on by magic were absent in brewers because their magic had already emerged and was helping them to brew. As this was largely unrecognized by the other magicians, brewing became regarded as a female activity.

Having reached this point—and having developed a few traditions of its own—the magical community stagnated. It had always had an uneasy coexistence with mundane communities (both communities preferred to avoid the other as much as possible) and it wasn't uncommon for a secret to be discovered, lost, and then rediscovered several times in a row. (Myrddin was about the only senior magician willing to share most of his secrets.) It was not until Lord and Master Whitehall led the Whitehall Commune to the long-lost castle—and the last of the DemonMasters were killed—that the magical community entered the third era of magic...

Demons are both immensely powerful and surprisingly limited, although very few humans have any understanding of their true nature. Even the most knowledgeable DemonMaster, holding a dozen or so demons in thrall, knows very little about them. But even they would acknowledge that demons are, at best, jerkass genies. They have to obey the letter of the law, if summoned, but they will happily take advantage of any loopholes in their orders to screw over their would-be "master."

What little *is* known can be outlined fairly quickly.

Demons fall into four orders, First to Fourth. First Order demons are the most powerful, capable of granting almost anything in exchange for a price; Second and Third Order demons perform smaller feats for their masters. Those feats tend to have limits—a demon can kill, if the price is right, provided the rules are honored—and not all magicians are willing to call on them. Fourth Order demons offer knowledge to their masters—again, if the price is right.

A summoning can be done as a once-off ritual or a deliberate attempt to bind the demon into the DemonMaster's Book of Pacts. In the case of the former, the demon will trade blood—either from the DemonMaster or blood willingly given by a volunteer—for whatever the magician requests; in the case of the latter, the demon will serve the DemonMaster until the DemonMaster runs out of credit or dies (or the book is destroyed).

About the author

Christopher G. Nuttall was born in Edinburgh, studied in Manchester, married in Malaysia and currently living in Scotland, United Kingdom with his wife and baby son. He is the author of twenty novels from various publishers and fifty self-published novels.

Current and forthcoming titles published by Twilight Times Books:

Schooled in Magic YA fantasy series

Schooled in Magic — book 1
Lessons in Etiquette — book 2
A Study in Slaughter — book 3
Work Experience — book 4
The School of Hard Knocks — book 5
Love's Labor's Won — book 6
Trial By Fire — book 7
Wedding Hells — book 8
Infinite Regress — book 9
Past Tense — book 10

The Decline and Fall of the Galactic Empire military SF series

Barbarians at the Gates — book 1
The Shadow of Cincinnatus — book 2
The Barbarian Bride — book 3

CPSIA information can be obtained
at www.ICGtesting.com
Printed in the USA
LVHW030241311018
595214LV00006B/638/P

9 781606 193167